Praise for Catherine C.

'The narrative brilliantly describes the physical imperative they have to be together – not just the snatched times alone, but the magnetic pull they have towards one another when other people are around, their almost uncontrollable urge to touch one another and the risks that brings.'
– *Hilary Ely, Vulpes Libris*

'It's hard to pigeonhole this book to a specific genre. It's a love story, yet sometimes defies the label. It's contemporary, yet dwells quite a bit in the past. As to its audience – I think this would appeal to readers who don't need to be led by the hand and who enjoy challenging relationships. Wholeheartedly recommended.'
– *Gilly Fraser, the Indie eBook Review*

'Heart-warming, realistic and page-turning.'
– *Lorraine Kelly*

'Czerkawska tells her tale in a restrained, elegant prose that only adds to its poignancy.'
– *The Sunday Times*

'Uplifting ... The reader finds themself deeply immersed... superbly researched.'
– *Undiscovered Scotland*

'A compelling read, with a satisfying blend of history, nature and romance.'
– *Amanda Booth, The Scots Magazine*

'Blisteringly eloquent.'
– *The Scotsman*

Ice
Dancing

Catherine Czerkawska

Published by Dyrock Publishing

Copyright © 2021 Catherine Czerkawska

Cover Photograph © 2024 Michal Piasecki
Cover design by Lumphanan Press
www.lumphananpress.co.uk

ISBN: 978-0-9557364-2-1

– Chapter One –

YOU DON'T NEED a partner for line dancing. You do it with other people but you don't touch anybody. I think that was one of the reasons why I liked it. You get out of the habit of touching after a while. Not like dancing on ice, where you have to trust your partner not to let you fall. My friend Annie and I had begun line dancing the year before. Classes were just starting up again for the autumn when Joe Napier came to the village and everything changed.

Sometimes I try to pin down exactly how it happened, and although I pretend that it was a gradual thing, that it crept up on me, I know it isn't true. It was swift and unexpected. I used to think betrayal began in the mind and your body followed after. Now I'm not so sure. Now, I think it can be something quite simple and sudden. There's some configuration of features, something about the walk, about the look and maybe even the scent of the other person. Something that seems to engage all your senses at once. It isn't comfortable. But there you are, with your mind full of him. And you can barely speak. Dear God, you can barely breathe. And soon you find yourself going to bed early so that you can think about him or her in the space between waking and sleeping. But do men think like that? I don't know. I still don't know for sure. Maybe they do.

There was more to it than that though. There was something else about him, some painful vulnerability. I noticed it even then. Is that the real female failing I wonder? Not the desire to change a man, so much as the compulsion to heal him. And is it ever possible? You see Joe was damaged. Not that you would have known it. Not that you would ever have guessed from the look of him, from the magnetism of him. The dangerous charisma. Not at first, anyway. All that came later.

I have to admit, I found the line dancing difficult. I wasn't what you'd call a natural. I knew what the dances were called – things like Slappin' Leather and Walk the Line and The Electric Slide, but I never remembered which was which. Our village hall was big and chilly with a high vaulted ceiling, and the country music wailed and echoed round it, so that Sharon had to shout out loud above it. Even so, we sometimes misheard her and moved in the wrong direction. Well, some of us did.

Annie got the hang of it quite quickly, although it took me a bit longer. She's got a natural sense of rhythm and she seemed to remember the movements of the dances from week to week. She can dance well with a partner too, and maybe that helps. As soon as she heard the music she knew just what to do, but it took me a bit longer. I've always been a day-dreamer. I'd suddenly stop concentrating and forget what came next and bump into the person next to me. Nobody minded though. It was a good laugh.

Afterwards a group of us usually went to the pub. There was Annie and myself, Sharon the dance teacher and three younger women, Verena, Hazel and Cheryl, as well as a few other people who only came occasionally for one reason or another, people we knew, but not well. They were working mums, part time work mostly. I probably worked longer hours up at the farm, a lot of it office work. There's plenty of boring paperwork on a farm these days, a lot of it done online. They were younger than Annie and me, but we identified with them. We used to break out in small ways, but really, we were all afraid of too much change, afraid of rocking the boat. Having toddlers, as they all did, doesn't help. I can remember Annie getting so fed up with hers when they were very young that she shut herself in her wardrobe to stop herself from going mad. You think it'll never end, but it does. Now they drive us crazy in different ways.

That autumn when Joe came to the village, my husband Sandy still thought I ought to be going to the Women's Rural with the other farmers' wives, instead of doing outlandish things like line dancing and t'ai chi. His cousin Mary went to the Rural every week. There were cookery demonstrations, talks about all kinds of things, classes on handicrafts from time to time: embroidery, card making, scrap-booking, decoupage. Every year the village branch would walk away with half the prizes at the local flower show for things like a Knitted Bed Jacket and a Soft Toy or a Selection of Items for a Finger Buffet. Some of the handicrafts were wonderful, especially the embroidery, but I couldn't do it. I'm making myself sound pathetic but I was never very good at practical things and I didn't enjoy them. Not really. I live inside my head too much, if that makes sense.

Annie and I went to one of the Rural meetings when we were trying things out to see what might suit us, and it was quite enjoyable. But the competition on that occasion was for a Pair of Gent's Shoes, Well Polished. That was some years ago, mind you, and I expect they've moved with the times. Hope so, anyway. We started giggling and couldn't stop. We both wondered why the gent in question couldn't polish his own damn shoes. Except that damn wasn't what Annie said. We didn't even polish our own shoes very often. In fact Sandy sometimes polished mine, and his were generally covered in mud. The ladies of the Rural were a friendly and talented crowd and we liked them very much. It just wasn't for us, that was all. Maybe that should have told me something, but it didn't. Not then.

The pub that night was nearly empty, the short tourist season almost over. Around eleven o'clock, I thought I ought to be going home, and Annie came too. I always had to make the choice between drinking and driving, unless somebody offered me a lift, and drinking generally won out until the nights got too wet or too cold. Some of the older kids were gathered around the old phone box in the centre of the village. It's a tradition, even though it has no phone now. They lurk in groups, messaging each other instead of talking. I've seen them doing it. I asked my daughter about it once. 'It's easier if you're shy,' she said. I suppose there's some sense in that. Sometimes some of them go up the road through the woods where they can deal in various illicit substances without being disturbed. I was relieved to see that Fiona was not among the kids around the phone box, but that made me wonder where else she might be. I hoped she was safe at home. As usual, Annie walked part of the way with me and I left her at the junction between the main road through the village and the street where she lived.

Annie and Tim have an old cottage that started out by being quite small: a long, low, weaver's cottage. But then Tim got to work on it and added an extension, a fitted kitchen and a conservatory. Then he built a summer house in the garden. Annie liked the results of it all, but Tim never knew when to stop. He seemed to need to be project planning all the time. Now he was talking about moving and starting all over again. She said she would divorce him first. Annie worked in the gift shop at a nearby stately home. She was ostensibly their buyer, which meant that she got to go to all the trade shows, and sometimes she would take me as well, but more often than not she found herself behind the counter during the busy tourist season, dealing with demanding visitors.

I often used to wish that Sandy would get to work on the farmhouse but he wasn't very handy, for a farmer. I used to do the decorating myself, but the place needed much more than cosmetic touches. Drumbrethan was a cold, draughty old house. Ancient in parts. Some of the outbuildings looked positively mediaeval. And there was a cellar with a peculiar vaulted ceiling beneath one of them that went right down to bedrock. Maybe it had been a hill fort in a previous life. We were high up on a hillside and never a day went by without a wind blowing around the place, sometimes a strong breeze and sometimes a shrieking gale. One spring, the wind lifted the corrugated iron roof right off the barn and set it down in a field, half a mile away, narrowly missing a herd of cows that had just been put out to grass lower down the hill. The whole place needed rewiring and replumbing. A few of the sockets still took round pin plugs and some of the pipes were old-fashioned lead. I sometimes worried that the lead in the water might have affected Fiona's brain. Was that why she kept behaving the way she did?

'No,' said Annie. 'That's just teenagers, Helen. Nothing to do with pollution.'

That night, I left Annie at the end of her street and carried on by myself, turning off the main road a few hundred yards out of the village. It wasn't really cold yet, though there was a chill in the air. There ought to have been a moon but it was much too cloudy, so that all you could see was a pale glow in the sky where it should have been, like a lamp seen through an opaque window. I was glad of the torch although I'm never afraid on this road. Much too familiar. No cars passed me but I could see occasional headlights down on the road through the village.

I went past Turner's Wood and then I was on the long stretch of road that leads across open fields towards the farmhouse. Just as I was passing my friend Louise's cottage – it had been lying empty ever since the funeral, back in the spring – I noticed a light in the downstairs window and wished that I had brought Jess, our collie, with me. She would have been happy to wait outside the village hall for me. I had left the upstairs hall light on myself, because that was the one Louise had always kept burning, even through the night. For all the years she had lived in the countryside, she had never quite got used to the absolute dark. We live in a very dark place. Which is fine when you can see the moon and the Milky Way, but not when clouds dim the skies. The upstairs light was switched off now and instead there were lights on downstairs in the kitchen, to the right of the stone-floored hallway.

I felt the hairs prickling on the back of my neck. I knew that I ought to go home and get Sandy to come back down with me, but whoever was in there might be gone by the time we got back. In any case, what had Louise left behind that was worth stealing? Rural crime was a problem, even here, but it usually involved expensive machinery. The curtains had been drawn, so I could see nothing of what was going on inside. I stood very still by the wooden gate, my hand on the low stone pillar, and then I became aware of movement and saw that the front door was open. The hall was in darkness but I could make out a head, faintly outlined by a glow of light filtering into the hallway from the kitchen.

A voice called out sharply 'Who's there? Is anybody out there?'

A man. He sounded American. And wary.

'I live up the road. At the farm. I was just wondering ...'

The tall figure in the doorway laughed. He sounded relieved.

'Jeez, you scared the shit out of me.'

'Who are you?'

'I'm Louise's cousin.'

'Her *cousin*?'

'Is that a problem?'

'No. I just didn't know about you. She never mentioned you.'

There was something very silly about holding a conversation in the dark, so I switched on my torch and shone it in the direction of the figure in the doorway. Dazzled, he raised his hand to his eyes.

'For Christ's sake, don't do that!'

'Sorry.'

I switched it off, but not before I had run the beam over the front of the house and seen the car parked on the short stretch of overgrown driveway leading to the ramshackle shed. It couldn't really be called a garage. Louise had used it as a glory hole. As far as I knew, it was still full of her junk. Floor to ceiling. We had always planned to clear it out. I had offered to help her, curious about the contents. But we had never quite managed it.

'I'll be away home then. Leave you to it.'

'Excuse me but do you have milk at your farm?'

'Plenty of it, but I can't sell you any.'

'Why not?'

'It's against the rules.'

'Oh.'

There was a pause.

'I can give you a drop of milk,' I ventured. 'We always have plenty in the fridge.'

'That's OK. I can manage for tonight. I've got some beers.'

'You can get everything you need in the shop. Down in the village. It opens at eight.'

'Right.'

'It's just down the road there. On the right hand side as you come into the village.'

'Sure.'

He moved backwards.

'Goodnight, Mrs ...'

'Breckenridge.'

'Breckenridge?' He seemed to find the name funny.

'Helen.'

'See you around then, Helen.'

'Yes.'

The door slammed shut. I walked home. I hadn't even asked his name.

Annie and I used to go to some evening class or other every winter, but we never seemed to stick with anything for longer than a year or two at the most. We began with t'ai chi, although neither of us could do it. We forgot the moves all the time. Then there was yoga, which we started the autumn after my Fiona was born and David, Annie's youngest. I loved yoga, would prefer it to the line dancing if I'm honest, but the teacher got pregnant and gave up. I enjoyed lying down on my mat and relaxing at the end. The instructor used to ask us to imagine that we were somewhere we had been happy.

'Take yourselves to that place in your mind,' she would tell us.

I always used to close my eyes and go to Poldarrach. It's only about ten miles from the village but hardly anybody local knows about it or if they do know, they neither care nor go there. I knew about it because I used to go on my bike when I was a girl. I used to lie on my back among the stones and watch the clouds sailing by and dream about all the things I was going to do in the future. I had it all sorted out in my mind: a four year honours degree in History at Edinburgh or Glasgow University and then maybe a job in a museum or even some research. Maybe I would go abroad to Italy, Spain or America. Anything seemed possible then. All I knew was that I didn't plan on coming back to the village for more than the occasional holiday.

But I knew that I would always want to come back to Poldarrach.

The scent of that place on a warm day was like nothing else, like nowhere else. It used to be a village, hundreds of years ago, but I didn't know that then. Annie and I went to a talk about it, although that was much later. It was the year we decided we were stagnating, so we signed up for a series of local history lectures, but it meant driving into town, and we only went to a couple of them. After that, winter set in, the nights were dark and the roads were icy and we couldn't be bothered.

One of the first lectures was all about Poldarrach. I thought it was my secret place, but it turned out that a few other people knew about it as well, historians I mean. The lecturer told us that the path through Poldarrach used to be an ancient pilgrimage route. He was big and blonde with a shaggy beard. Annie fancied him, but not enough to keep going to his lectures through the winter weather. He told us that Poldarrach was a 'classic example of a Galloway village before the improvements and clearances of the seventeenth and eighteenth centuries.'

Poldarrach must have been an important village once upon a time; there had been an inn and streets of houses and a watermill with its own millpond. All the farmers from the smallholdings round about came there, bringing their corn to be dried and ground. You could see heaps of stones all over the place. I had never known what they were until the lecturer told us they were kilns, and explained how the corn was parched to stop it sprouting before it was ground up into flour. The plants that grew at Poldarrach were interesting as well. There was bog myrtle, good for keeping away the midges in summer, and there was yarrow and meadowsweet in season and blueberry bushes and something that smelled like caraway.

I had always noticed these plants. I had been vaguely interested in them, rubbing them between my fingers to smell the sweet, aromatic scents of them, but I think it only struck me when we were listening to the lecture that maybe they were the kind of plants people used to grow for a purpose, not just ordinary wild flowers but things for cookery or for medicine. My mother and father had lived in the town for most of their lives and they didn't know one wild plant from another. I had to find it all out for myself. But that was when I was young enough to be full of a kind of hungry curiosity about everything. What became of that desire for knowledge, I wonder? Is it still there somewhere? Buried beneath the demands of my everyday life?

Well perhaps it is.

Many years later, the summer before Joe came to the village, in fact, I had said to Sandy, 'Why don't you come up to Poldarrach with me again?' and he had said 'Why?' so it was plain to me that he didn't remember much about it. He'd been there with me once before. I should never have taken him but I did, when we were first going out together. It was my place. It was special. You keep wanting to share things, wanting the men in your life to understand, don't you? But he didn't like it at all. He didn't see the point.

He said, 'Is this all there is then? Just these funny wee piles of stones?'

And then the first time I went back in years, I was with Joe. And that was different too. But everything was different with Joe. Or I thought so. Afterwards, I thought about his silences and wondered if I had misinterpreted them. One thing's sure, though. He came gliding into my life and changed everything. He didn't intend for it to happen any more than I did. I think it took us both by surprise. Like a bolt of lightning. Like a puck to the head, as Joe would say.

I didn't mean to hurt anyone. But that's what we always say, isn't it? I expect that's what somebody else said about Joe all those years ago, rationalising the damage. 'I didn't mean to hurt you.' Sometimes I still catch myself thinking, isn't line dancing better? Safer? Isn't it? Where you rely on yourself and you don't touch anyone else at all?

– Chapter Two –

MY DEAR FRIEND Louise had died the previous spring while the weather was still cold. She was eighty seven, quite old really. A good innings, as people said. Foul play not suspected. But she didn't look it, not until she became very ill, anyway. At first, she found it harder to walk up to the farm for her mid morning cup of coffee. Pains in her legs, she said, vaguely. 'Must be rheumatism.' Sometimes I would go and pick her up in the car. More often I would just go down and have my coffee with her instead. Louise always had good coffee. She used to buy the beans in one of the Italian cafes in town and grind them herself. Then I took to getting more and more of her groceries for her, whereas before it had just been the heavier things. She had always prided herself on being able to walk to and from the village stores for her newspaper and the few things she needed each day, but it began to be harder for her to get back up the hill.

I can remember driving home from town one morning in autumn and seeing Louise sitting on a boulder by the side of the road, her grey head in its red woolly hat bent low over her knees. She looked like a small gnome, wizened and shrivelled. Shocked, I pulled up, got out and took her in my arms.

'What's the matter, Louise? Are you not well?'

She focused on me with difficulty and tried to smile but when she spoke, her voice was husky. 'Oh Helen! I just felt exhausted all of a sudden. I don't know why. The legs just went from under me.'

I got her into the car, took her home to her cottage and called the doctor, in spite of her protests that she would be 'just fine'. The house smelled stuffy and a bit sour and that wasn't like Louise either. She may have liked clutter. I liked it myself, but it was always clean clutter. Then there were hospital appointments, and soon blood tests and X rays gave place to CT Scans. I felt scared and panicky, the way you do in the face of serious illness, grasping at straws of hope. First they said there was no tumour. They were sure there was no tumour. Then maybe there was a tumour. Or perhaps there was more than one. And suddenly the disease seemed to take wing and fly through her body. The hospital wasn't a good place for her to be. Too used to patching people up and sending them home, the young staff seemed phased by incurable illness and almost impatient with the intractable nature of her suffering.

Just before Christmas, we managed to get her into the local hospice. She kept saying, 'This is like a five star hotel, Helen,' which was true enough. It was sweet smelling and comfortable. They would even co-ordinate the colour of her crocheted bedspread with her nightie. They kept her free from pain, free from fear and indignity, but by the end of February she was dead. I was with her at the end. You think it'll be terrifying but it wasn't, not in the hospice. It was like a prolonged departure, infinitely sad but in no way frightening. By the time she died, we had said all our goodbyes.

I missed her though. Desperately. Still do. But back then, I felt bereft. Does that sound foolish? My own parents are both dead and I was an only child, like Fiona. I've got one elderly unmarried uncle living in a flat in Glasgow and that's about it in terms of relatives. We used to have big family gatherings up at the farm, but they were all Sandy's family, not mine. Half the people in the parish seemed to be related to Sandy in one way or another. Cut one, they all bleed. That's what they say in the village.

'It's all right for you,' I kept telling him, 'But I'm an orphan' and he used to laugh but I was only half joking. When I lost Louise, I was orphaned all over again.

Louise Marshall was my friend, an even closer friend than Annie, and I could tell her anything. I would go to her when I was feeling depressed, when the farm was getting me down, and she would always cheer me up.

'You're a fine young woman, Helen Breckenridge,' she would tell me in that forthright way she had. When I protested that I wasn't really young, she would say, 'Well you are to me!' and she was convincing, even if I didn't always believe her. 'And you're so bright. Just look at yourself.

Don't you let anybody put you down. One of these days you'll show them all. You've a lot of living to do yet, lass!'

She had been in that cottage below the farm for as long as I could remember. When I had married Sandy and moved up to Drumbrethan, eighteen years earlier, she was there to welcome me with a bunch of flowers and cuttings and plants from her garden to get mine established: pieris, buddleia, old scented roses, geraniums, peppery phlox, foxgloves and lots more. She was already sixty nine then, but she still seemed very youthful and energetic. She had a dog at the time, a wiry terrier called Teddy, and I would see her striding through the fields with the dog at her heels. Sandy's mother had only ever grown rigid rows of leeks and cabbages, but it was Louise who gave me my flowers.

Now, whenever I walked or drove past her cottage I would get a lump in my throat. I wanted her back all the time. Once or twice I'd even lifted the phone and dialled her number, only to hear the bell ringing and ringing in the silent house, just a few hundred yards down the road. Daft or what? I mean God knows what I would have done if anyone had answered. Sandy kept wondering aloud what would happen to the cottage and if it was going to be sold. He kept saying that we could do with the accommodation for Bruce, who helped out on the farm and travelled in by bike every day from a rented place in the next village. He kept nagging at me to try to find out, but it wasn't that easy. There was nobody to ask.

'You have the key to the house!' he would say. 'Go and look. There might be an address book or something. I don't know why you didn't say anything about it while she was alive.'

The truth was that I had often thought about it when Louise was in the hospice. I had wondered if I should ask her if she had made a will. I thought she might be worrying about it. Did she want me to contact anybody? But I couldn't bring myself to do it, in case she thought I was fishing for something for myself. It didn't seem right somehow. And then the morphine would kick in, and Louise would float in and out of lucidity, and the moment would be past. So I never asked.

After she died, we found that she had made all her funeral arrangements in advance. There was nothing for us to do except order a spray of flowers and attend the service in the village kirk. It's an old church and what I chiefly remember about that service is the timelessness of it all, with the farmers in their dark suits and the minister standing up to give the eulogy in front of a stained glass window depicting the Sermon on the Mount, the organist playing rather badly and the small choir singing very sweetly. Louise had even specified exactly who she wanted to hold the eight cords which, according to the old Scottish custom, lowered her coffin into the grave. It was a sunny day, the day of her funeral, for all that the winter had been a wet one, and the church was pretty full because although Louise had few relatives, she had made a lot of friends in the village over the years. The farming community was out in force as well as a trio of elderly ladies: Maisie Murtagh, Betty McGowan and Ella Dunlop.

The Co-op undertaker gave out the 'coffin cards' so that the people who had been asked to hold the cords would know which one they were to take. On one side there was the president of the bowling club, the butcher who came round in his van every week and the fish man who came all the way from Pittenweem in Fife, although I think Louise's cat ate most of what she bought from him. On the other side was the local publican, Fergus, standing next to another farmer and elder of the kirk, a man called Malcolm Moody who had always had the reputation of being 'sweet on' Louise and who got quite emotional and stumbled on the planking that lay around the grave. Next to him came Jimmy Fraser who does all the pensioners' gardens. Much to our surprise, Annie and I were placed at the head and foot of the coffin. Sandy was scandalised. For one thing, it's still a bit unusual for women to take a cord even now. It's not so long ago that women didn't go to the cemetery at all. For another, he thought that he should have been asked instead. But Louise was always my friend rather than Sandy's. He hardly knew her. She was just the 'auld yin doon the road' to him.

There were plenty of refreshments, alcoholic and otherwise, in the pub afterwards. Louise had arranged for all that and even paid for it in advance although she had told me nothing about it. It was a good wake and if you can ever be said to enjoy a funeral, we managed to enjoy that one.

A few days after the funeral, I had a phone call from Louise's solicitor, wondering if I would be prepared to keep an eye on the property.

'Is the cottage to be sold?' I asked, cautiously. It still seemed like an intrusion on Louise's privacy.

'I'm afraid I can't say.'

'I'm sorry. I shouldn't have asked.'

'No, no.' He cleared his throat. 'There's no reason why you shouldn't ask. I didn't mean that at all. It had already crossed my mind that the farm might be interested in buying the cottage. Since it used to belong to Drumbrethan once upon a time as it were ...'

'I think it did, years ago. And we might be interested. If ever it comes on the market.'

'But in fact, I really don't know if it's to be sold or not. Not yet.'

'I see.'

'If Mrs Marshall's heir does decide to sell, I'll keep you informed.'

'So there is an heir then?' I was very surprised. 'She never told me she had any living relatives.'

'Oh yes. There is an heir. But I'm not sure what his plans are. So if you could ...'

'We'll keep an eye on the place. We've been doing it for months anyway.'

'That would be kind of you, Mrs Breckenridge. Thank-you very much indeed. You'll be recompensed of course. And if there are any out-of-pocket expenses, just send the bills to us.'

Later on I relayed this conversation to Sandy.

'You'd think,' he said, wolfing down shepherd's pie and baked beans, 'You'd think that she might have left the cottage to you.'

'Why on earth should she do that?'

'You were the best friend she had in this place. You were like a daughter to her.'

'No I wasn't.' The conventional expression irritated me. 'We were the best of friends, it's true. I loved her very much. But there's no reason for her to leave me anything. Least of all a house.'

In fact Louise had left me a thousand pounds, 'for Helen to spend on herself,' the will had said, which surprised me since I knew how little she had in the bank. There couldn't have been much left after the funeral bill had been paid. The other thing I had inherited, not surprisingly, was Louise's cat, Siggy. He was a white Persian with a pale grey haze over his fur as though he had brushed up against something grubby, and his eyes in his owlish face were large and green. He was a distressingly high maintenance cat. You had to brush him every day, otherwise his fur got all matted. Jess, the collie, was afraid of him. He was not like the rest of the farm cats, used to outdoor living but nervous of dogs. Siggy had no fear of dogs at all. He was a pet, and Jess felt that he was in danger of usurping her privileged place in the kitchen. Siggy missed Louise almost as much as I did. Most nights he would leap up onto my lap and pad himself a bed there, purring like a small engine, demanding comfort.

'So who is getting the cottage?' asked Sandy when he had finished his shepherd's pie.

'I don't really know. The solicitor was very cagey. He just talked about the heir but he didn't say who the heir was.'

'And I don't suppose you asked.'

'No. I didn't really feel I could ask.'

'You and your conscience, Helen! Didn't Louise ever mention this person to you?'

'No. Never. She never really talked about any relatives. Well, hardly ever.'

Louise had been widowed a long time ago. I knew that much. She had told me that she had been born and brought up on the outskirts of Glasgow. I knew there had been a sister, Lottie, because she had once shown me a photograph of the two of them taken when they were children. They were wearing identical shapeless velvet dresses with lacy collars, although Lottie was a couple of years older than Louise. But Lottie had died while she was still a young woman and Louise hadn't been very forthcoming about the rest of her family.

Louise possessed an old photograph album and once or twice we had looked at it together. I remember two photographs in particular, lying loose in the front of the album. One was a heavily posed studio portrait of a man wearing an old fashioned suit and a shirt with a high white collar. He had a small moustache and he was conventionally handsome. The other was a tiny snapshot of a young man who, even at this distance in time, looked ... beautiful is the word that comes into my mind. He was not so much handsome as beautiful. Men can be beautiful, the young and the very old, in quite different ways. He was standing in a garden, smoking a cigarette and smiling at the camera. Or whoever was behind it. He was quite small but almost indecently good looking, with dark hair and a long straight nose, high cheekbones and a wide mouth. He seemed very exotic and foreign and I wondered who he could be. I looked at the back of the snap but there was nothing written there.

Louise had pointed at the first picture, the studio portrait, and started laughing. 'Ah now – that was my Uncle Fred. Frederick Napier. My mother's younger brother. Much younger. But he liked to be called Freddy. He eloped you know! It was all very romantic. He eloped with an Italian girl called Francesca.'

I had been going to ask her why they had eloped and where to, but before I could do it, she had already set Freddy aside and was gazing at the other photograph. The softened expression on her face silenced me.

'Never settle for second best, Helen,' she told me. Just for a moment, she looked sad, as though remembering something that pained her. Then she tucked the picture back into the album and gave a little shake of her head. Something intervened. I don't remember what. The phone rang or the doorbell, and Louise put the album away. So I never found out who the beautiful young man was. I meant to ask her, but I always forgot.

It was, I suppose, something more that we had in common, this lack of relatives in a village where everybody seemed to be related to everybody else and could count on a dozen or more cousins. She had married young, I knew that. One Christmas Eve, when we had both been at the sherry, she told me that her husband, Malachi Marshall, had been much older than she was. He had been a mining manager somewhere in Ayrshire. She had done a course at some kind of secretarial college in Glasgow and had been working in the mine office, unusual for a woman back then. I reckon she must have been very clever.

She and Malachi married in the early forties but no children came along and it had not been a particularly happy marriage. Malachi was, as Louise put it, 'Not a nice man when he had a drink or two in him.' He had died some time in the fifties – I got the impression that Louise's chief emotion had been one of relief – and since the house went with the job, she had to leave her home quite quickly. Malachi had left her just enough insurance money to buy herself a small place, a cottage or a flat. Louise had no ties and had always fancied proper country living, not the compromise of a small mining town.

'I always wanted a country cottage, like on a chocolate box. Roses round the door, you know? That was what I had in my mind. And me a Glasgow girl, eh? I came to the countryside by degrees!'

And so she had moved south to this village that lies midway between the green pastures of Ayrshire and the hills and forests of Galloway. The cottage had just come on the market. It was called Drumbrethan Cottage, after our farm. It was handsome rather than chocolate box pretty: a sturdy stone building with two dormers at the front. But it had a rambling rose clambering up the front wall, an untidy garden where hedge sparrows and blackbirds nested, and a fine view from the back windows across a patchwork of fields and woods to the distant sea. Louise always said she had bought it mainly for the potential she had seen in the garden.

Louise's solicitor was right. It had once belonged to our farm, a superior labourer's cottage, but it had been sold many years before by Sandy's grandfather who had probably been short of cash at the time. He was often short of cash, being far less careful with his money than his grandson, my husband. When the elderly widower who had first bought it and lived in it for most of his retirement died, Louise had seen it advertised. It had been as simple as that. As easy as sticking a pin in a map. Over the years, she had gradually managed to have it renovated, a bit at a time, scrimping and saving in order to do so. It was in pretty good condition now, much better than the farmhouse. She had made the garden beautiful. But she had never mentioned children to me, or indeed any relatives other than her sister and her husband Malachi and the slightly dubious Uncle Freddy. She had certainly never mentioned an heir, still less an American heir.

The morning after I'd first seen Louise's cousin, I drove down to the village shop with the egg delivery. It always gave me a little pang to see someone else behind the till in that shop. I found myself, subconsciously at least, looking for my parents, remembering the way it used to be. The new owners, Alastair and Diana Devine, had turned it into a sort of mini-market, but there was always a long queue at the till because people liked to linger and talk. I suppose the shop was the grown-up equivalent of the telephone box; the place where all the news got chewed over until the next juicy bit came along.

Alastair and Diana had moved to the village from Glasgow, but Alastair in particular could gossip with the best of them. People either started living at the pace of the place or moved away altogether. There were no half measures. Mind you, they had upset some factions in the village by making changes to the shop. Oddly enough, it wasn't that they stocked fewer items. In fact they stocked far more than my parents: lots of fresh fruit and vegetables, wholemeal and other flours for baking, interesting jams and pickles and local honey, as well as all the usual convenience items. Now, there were people in the village who wouldn't set foot in the place. The word on the street was that it was too middle class. The honey had been a particularly contentious item. I spread it on my toast most mornings.

Annie said, 'If folk think bread flour and vegetables are middle class, God help them.' But there were people in the village who would drive five miles to town and back for a couple of items rather than use the village shop.

'I hear there's somebody staying in Louise Marshall's cottage,' Alastair said to me, as soon as I opened the shop door.

'How did you know that?'

'Bush telegraph, Helen.' He grinned at me. 'Well, the postman saw him this morning.'

'He's Louise's cousin.'

'Have you met him then?' he asked me, sorting out Sandy's Daily Record and my Radio Times from a pile on the counter.

'I spoke to him on my way home from the line dancing last night, but it was too dark to see much. I thought he was a burglar at first.'

I got my basket and began collecting the few things I needed from the shelves: bleach, a box of tissues and a bag of plain flour.

Sandy always said that he saw me first in the village shop. We moved there when I was fifteen. Before that, my parents had a convenience store in the nearby town, opening early and closing late, selling everything from sweets and tobacco to newspapers and groceries, but they had wanted something a bit easier. That was the plan, but I can't say it worked out like that. The hours were supposed to be shorter, but when you keep a village shop and live on the premises as well, people think they can bang on the door for milk or cigarettes at any time of day or night, and they frequently do.

After we moved, I carried on going to school in the town, but when I came home in the afternoons, I usually helped out in the shop, and that's where Sandy says he first saw me. Our eyes met over the bacon slicer. There was a bacon slicer in those days. It was an old fashioned shop and the bacon slicer was a bit of a relic, even then. He came in most days for his cigarettes and his newspaper, always the Daily Record, and trampled mud and cow shit all over my mother's clean floor. If I was in the shop he would tease me and make me giggle. His dad Stewart was alive then, and Sandy was helping him to run the farm. But by the time we were married, some years later, Stewart Breckenridge had had his first heart attack, and Sandy was already doing the lion's share of the work up at Drumbrethan.

If you had told me when I was still at school and helping out in the shop that a few years later, Sandy and I would be married, I wouldn't have believed you. That wasn't the plan at all. I was destined for much more exciting things or so I thought. We'd been in the village a couple of years when I went off to university. I'd worked hard and got my place at Edinburgh. I was only seventeen and three universities had offered me unconditional places to study history. Dad was incandescent with pride and kept telling everyone who set foot in the shop all about it, much to my open embarrassment and secret satisfaction. Mum said she was pleased as well, but I could tell that she was worried. She had never been adventurous. She didn't begrudge me my freedom, but I think it frightened her a little.

'Are you sure?' she kept asking me. 'Are you sure you want to go?'

After a while, she said, 'Why don't you go to Glasgow University? Then you could travel every day. You needn't leave home for a while. It's what everyone else at the school is doing, isn't it?'

She was right. Most of the people in my class – well the handful who were going on to university – were taking up places at Glasgow or Strathclyde or Paisley. But I had my sights firmly set on the capital and I wasn't about to change my mind. I can remember those feelings of intense expectation and nervousness, all mixed up together. I can remember mum and dad driving me over to Edinburgh for Freshers' Week, with all my stuff heaped into their old car in suitcases and boxes. I can remember my first sight of the castle, and the sphinx-like shape of Arthur's Seat, giants eyeing each other across the city.

I had got a place in a hall of residence. My room was small and warm with a view of Salisbury Crags. My parents hugged me and mum looked as if she might be going to cry. I was trying hard to keep my tears inside but after much prevarication they left, and I made for the kitchen, feeling a bit desolate. We made coffee and then later, somebody opened a bottle of wine. The air was alive with our shared sense of anticipation. And I remember thinking, 'This is it. This is where it all starts for me.' Anything seemed possible.

It was in the autumn term of my second year, not long before my nineteenth birthday, that the phone call came. Dad was in hospital. He had had a massive stroke, dropping down suddenly and without warning in the middle of the shop. I caught the next train home and went straight to the hospital, but he never fully regained consciousness. Mum and I sat beside his bed and I held his hand. After a while, he squeezed it, just one little squeeze, and I never knew whether it meant sorry or I love you or just goodbye or all of those things wrapped into one. And then he died. I wondered why his eyes wouldn't close properly. I didn't realise he was dead until the nurses came and took me away.

For a long time I felt as though somebody had kicked me, a hard blow right in the middle of my body, a punch that sent me reeling, gasping for air. But alongside my own grief came the growing realisation that mum couldn't manage. She had never lived alone. She had married young, and dad had seldom travelled anywhere without her, so her own company alarmed her, threw her into a panic. After Christmas, that first dreadful Christmas without dad, I knew I should be thinking about going back to university. My friends kept phoning me up to tell me so, and so did my Director of Studies. Eventually, I travelled to Edinburgh to see him, and when he suggested that I take a year out, I agreed. We both thought it would be best. Mum would adjust and I could make a fresh start the following autumn. So I packed my bags again, and somebody else's dad gave me a lift home.

I helped out in the shop of course.

'That's nice for your mum,' said the people in the village. 'She needs you at a time like this. How is she doing?'

They would always ask that. Never, 'How are *you* doing?'

Even if they had asked me, I would probably have told them I was fine. But I wasn't really. I was struggling. Sometimes they would tell me, 'You're doing a great job there, Helen,' when I handed them their morning papers or weighed out their cheese.

'Are you going back?' they would ask, and I would always say, 'Oh yes. That's the plan.'

I could see that some of them wondered why I needed a university degree in a useless subject like history when here I was, nicely established in what I'm sure they called 'that little goldmine of a business'. After all, they were thinking, what good was history when it came to finding a job? A job was the main thing in the village. Money. Security. Settling down. Especially for women. This was twenty years ago, of course, and it's different now. Although sometimes when I look at the young mums in the pub after line dancing, I wonder how different it really is.

I read a lot. I read all my set texts and did a lot of work on my own. I meant to go back to Edinburgh and finish my degree. Except that during my year off and while my mother and I were missing my dad, I also started going out with Sandy Breckenridge. I was bored and sad and he was interested in me. It seemed exciting. He was seen as a bit of a catch within the very small world that was the village. He would have been twenty six then, a big, attractive lad and still unmarried.

'Time Sandy Breckenridge found himself a wife.'

That's what the old ones were saying, the ones who stayed in the shop for half an hour at a time, talking to my mother, commiserating with her, widows themselves. 'Time that lad found himself a wife.' The farmer wants a wife. Like the old skipping game.

In February, I went to the bowling club dance in the village hall and the music was very loud, to make up for the fact that the band couldn't play or sing all that well. Sandy was good looking in a thickset, sexy and old fashioned way, like a forties film star. He came over and asked me to dance and he kept treading on my toes but I didn't mind because I couldn't dance very well either. I could do the waltz and the Scottish dances we had learned at school: the Gay Gordons, Strip the Willow and the Drops of Brandy. Sandy seemed very grown up, mature and confident. But then I was only nineteen. What did I know? Of course he was confident. This was his time and place.

He asked me to the cinema a couple of times, and then we started going out regularly. I was bored out of my skull with working in the shop but I was also in mourning for my father and, now that I think about it, for my time in Edinburgh. Sandy made up for it somehow, gave me something else to think about, a space in my mind that could be filled with thoughts of this man who had the knack of making me laugh. We went to the cinema in town and we used to go to a Chinese restaurant afterwards, but Sandy would only ever have steak and chips. He said he didn't like foreign food, but he's never tried it yet, so far as I know.

Sometimes we went to the Young Farmers' dances and Sandy would stand up at the bar with the other men and talk shop, and I would sit at a table with the girls. From time to time they would bring drinks over to us to keep us happy – Bacardi and Coke, vodka and orange squash, or sometimes a Martini and lemonade – sweet, sticky drinks, deemed suitable for young women. And if I was lucky I would get a dance, a 'bit of a bop' he called it, and if I wasn't, well it was nice to have a gossip with the other girls, people I had gone to school with, and Sandy would always take me home afterwards. If we were walking he would kiss me in the porch round the back of the shop and if we were in his car we would do a bit more than kiss, but not much.

We didn't go the whole way before we were married which, in retrospect, seems odd. We went as far as makes no difference I suppose, but Sandy was quite straight-laced about stuff like that and besides, we had a short engagement. I wasn't a virgin when we got married though. I didn't tell him, but I had lost my virginity in Edinburgh to a strapping mechanical engineer from Yorkshire after a university disco and an inadvisable amount of strong cider. It had been a disappointing encounter and I almost felt as though it didn't count, so I said nothing to Sandy and he didn't ask. I don't think he ever realised. I don't know if it would have mattered to him. You never know with men, do you?

He asked me to marry him the Easter after my father died and he bought me a ring, a big diamond in a pretty setting. His mother thought he had spent too much on it. I could see that by the look on her face. I don't know why I agreed so quickly but I fancied him like mad. And I knew it wasn't going to be easy for me to go back to university. I knew mum would start to cry and say she couldn't manage. The year off had been a bad idea after all. She had simply got used to having me around all over again. I didn't think I could face her tears, but I wanted something to happen. I wanted something to change. And so I said 'yes' to Sandy.

Just once, I asked my mum if she thought I was doing the right thing.

'Of course you are!' she said. 'I'm certain he's right for you, Helen.'

But then she would say that, wouldn't she? My mother's inclination had always been to go for the safe option. The farm was a good one, even though dairy wasn't the most lucrative thing in the world, and besides, Sandy was a nice man.

'He'll see you right,' mum kept saying. 'You could do an awful lot worse than Sandy Breckenridge.' Which was nothing less than the truth.

– Chapter Three –

SANDY AND I were married that autumn, when I was just twenty. I had no idea what I was doing. The best way I can explain it is that it seemed like a good idea at the time. I loved Sandy for his kindness, his commonsense, his warmth, but I had few points of comparison. I had been in the habit of reading stories in the old fashioned women's magazines my mother sold in the shop and in those, people often married the boy next door and lived happily every after. I'm not saying they made me want to marry Sandy. That wouldn't be true at all. I wasn't that daft. But they influence you whether you realise it or not. They make an impression.

After the wedding, I carried on helping mum in the shop. I knew nothing about farming. I had to learn it all from scratch. Most farmers seem to marry farmer's daughters and that way they know what's involved. Sandy was very patient. I used to leave gates open like a townie and have to chase beasts about the fields. I used to forget to put the hens in at night. I could never wake up early enough. I did so many stupid things during those first few months, but he never lost his temper. He coped with my steep learning curve and managed to be good natured and loving about it as well, and after a year or two I just fell into the way of it.

I'd always imagined we would have a big family. I wanted to fill the farmhouse with kids. Things might have been different if that had happened. I'm prepared to admit that. But in the event there was only Fiona, and we had to wait a long while for her. People kept asking, 'Are you not thinking of starting a family yet?' As they do, thoughtlessly. Then Fiona came along, and that seemed to satisfy them. I suppose we could have seen the doctor, tried to do something about it, but I would never have got Sandy to go, not in a month of Sundays. He knew the doctor too well. They drank in the same pub and he would have been mortified.

I never quite got used to the farm though. Never loved it the way Sandy loved it, in his blood and bones. It's a cold, wet place. *Dreich* is the Scots word for the damp, grey days we so often have. The mud gets you down. You spend your life in mud and muck. Everything is filthy, all the time: boots, fingernails, clothes. Your soul. That's what it feels like anyway. Quite early on, I began to wonder what on earth I had done and why I had done it. But I just thought that I'd better get on with it. I could see no alternative. I respected Sandy and I cared about him. He was a good man, so there was no other course of action open to me.

For a few years – human nature being what it is – the shop that had once seemed like a prison became a kind of refuge for me. I would go down there first thing, after I'd given Sandy his breakfast, between jobs, and then I'd help out down there for half the day before coming back to help on the farm. Mum and I would drink coffee and eat biscuits and gossip about village things, between customers. I would do the books for her along with the farm paperwork, and all of that kept me busy. I carried on doing it right through my pregnancy. When Fiona was born, I took her down to the shop in her Moses basket and all the old ladies of the village made a great fuss of her. After a while I stopped hankering after other things and found what seemed very like contentment. I fitted in with the life of the place. I had friends, chiefly Louise and Annie. We had our occasional evening classes. When Fiona started at the village primary school, I joined the PTA and helped with fundraising. I even made tray bakes for various events, although I remember 'distressing' packets of supermarket mince pies to make them look home-made before one of the school Christmas Fairs. It was as though the village had found a place for me whether I liked it or not, growing around me, incorporating me willy nilly into the rhythm of its life, as a tree will grow to accommodate and finally encompass an obstacle.

It went on like that, each season blending into the next, until five years ago when mum was sixty and I was thirty five. Like Louise, a few years later, mum just started to go downhill. She was quite quickly diagnosed with cancer and she was dead within the year. Then the shop was sold to Alastair and Diana and I was back up at the farm, trying to persuade Sandy that I ought to be doing something else with my life, although he said that being a farmer's wife was a full time job. And so it was. It was a full time job. It was just that I had never intended for it to be *my* full time job. More years passed and there was nobody to blame for my dissatisfaction except myself.

Until Joe Napier arrived in the village.

I know that sounds odd, a romantic and retrospective exaggeration, but it's the truth, and if nothing else, I want to tell the truth. Five minutes after Alastair and I had been talking about him, the shop door opened, and he walked in. At least I assumed it was Louise's cousin, because I hadn't seen him properly the night before. He looked very foreign in this small village where most people tend to be either friends and neighbours, or visiting builders and other workmen, dressed in the uniform of overalls, high visibility jackets, tackety boots. I've always thought that those television soaps where a character needs to hide and runs away to a village have got it completely wrong. You can't hide in a village. Everybody notices a stranger. Everybody is curious. This particular stranger was tall, dark and handsome too, with wide-set brown eyes. It was a striking face and you couldn't help but admire it. I would have put him at about thirty at the most, eight or nine years younger than me, but then I'm not much good at guessing ages. He was wearing faded jeans with tears in them that could have been a fashion statement but were probably just tears, a white tee-shirt and a shabby leather jacket. He walked with a bit of a swagger. Annie would have said he fancied himself. In fact she did say it, when she saw him.

'Fancies himself that one. Nice bum.'

He didn't always look you straight in the eye, and there was something about the way he stood, even though everyone assumed he was so confident. There was something almost wooden about him, something about the way he would occasionally wrap his long arms around his body or the way his eyes just sometimes slid away from yours. But I don't know if I noticed any of that back then. Probably not.

'Hi there.' He grinned at me.

'I'm surprised you recognised me.'

'I recognised the voice.' He turned to Alastair. 'We spoke over the wall yesterday. In the dark. She thought I was robbing the place.' He shook hands with me. 'Joe Napier, ma'am.'

'Did you drive down?' I asked, a little bemused by this form of address. It reminded me of the way our old coalman used to call my mother 'Mistress'.

'I thought I'd walk. Fetch my stuff later.'

'Well, I've got the pick-up. Do you want a lift back? Once you've got your shopping.'

'If you don't mind waiting for me.'

Alastair raised his eyebrows at this but I ignored him.

Joe loaded a couple of boxes of groceries into the back of the pick-up: tins of beans and tuna, cornflakes, bread and butter, milk and chocolate biscuits, firelighters and matches and bananas, as well as half a dozen of the fresh eggs I had just brought in.

'You could have got your eggs direct from me,' I told him, once we were out of the shop and out of earshot of Alastair Devine. 'More cheaply, as well.'

'Is that where these came from?'

'That's right. My chickens. Free range and well fed.'

'How come I can buy eggs but not milk from you?'

'It's just the way it is. Regulations.'

'I'll bear it in mind, ma'am.'

We turned off the main road and bumped our way up towards the farm.

'You can call me Helen.'

'OK. Sure.'

'You'll be staying for a while then?' I asked.

'That's the plan.'

'We've all been wondering what was going to happen to the cottage.'

He shot me a sideways glance, showing the whites of his eyes, the way Jess looks when something takes her by surprise.

'Have you?' he asked.

'Well, you know what it's like in a village.'

'But I don't. I've never lived in one before.'

I wondered why he was living in one now, but said nothing, waiting for him to explain.

'She left the house to me,' he offered, after a while.

'I see.'

'I'm glad you see, because I'm not at all sure I do.'

'Well, she must have been very fond of you.'

'She didn't know me.'

'Did she not?'

'How long was Louise Marshall here then, Helen?'

'Oh – fifty odd years. Twice as long as me. We moved here when I was a girl.'

'Well, the fact is, I never met her.'

'Really?'

'No. Louise's uncle was my grandfather. Does that make us cousins of some sort? But I never met her, never spoke to her on the phone, never so much as had a letter or a Christmas card from her. Then all of a sudden I get this letter from a lawyer telling me she's left me this place. Do you know why? Did she say anything? I can't imagine why I was even on her radar!'

We had pulled up in front of Louise's house.

'I don't know why,' I told him truthfully. 'But maybe there was no-one else.'

'I was going to sell it without even seeing it. Then I changed my mind.'

'I didn't know Louise had American relatives.'

'She didn't. I'm from Canada.'

'I'm sorry.'

I knew Canadians didn't like you assuming they were American. It was like foreigners thinking the Scots were English. Afterwards I realised that the accent is very different but at the time I didn't hear it.

'Louise's Uncle Fred went to Canada. Didn't she ever tell you?'

'No. Well ...' I hesitated.

'What?'

'She once said he eloped. But I had no idea where to.'

Joe let out a hoot of laughter. 'Eloped? What else did she say?'

'That was all. There's a photo of him somewhere in the cottage. In an old album. You'll probably find it if you're sorting her things out. She said he eloped. But we never talked about it again, though I kept meaning to ask her.'

'I suppose she was right. He did elope. With my grandmother. I'll tell you all about it some day.'

He opened the door of the pick-up and got out, went round to lift out his groceries and came back to my window. 'Thanks for the lift, Helen. I'll know where to come for my eggs in future.'

'You know where we are if you need anything.'

'I'll remember that, when I do need anything.'

I thought he was good looking but cagey. Interlopers. That's what they call them in the village except that they pronounce it 'interlowper'. Even after I got married to Sandy, whose family was built in with the stones, even after I had been living here for years, I was still an interloper. Joe Napier would never be anything else.

I didn't see him for a week or so after that, although sometimes I could hear hammering when I passed the cottage so I thought he must be doing some repairs. Then one day I saw that the hire car had disappeared and in its place there was an old four wheel drive. It looked as though it had seen better days.

Fiona was very taken with Joe. She came into the kitchen one evening when I was making pastry and perched on the table to talk to me.

'Isn't he gorgeous?' she said, with a sigh. 'I wish I could go out with him!'

I was baking apple and blackberry pies for Charlie McGowan's fiftieth birthday party. It was going to be held in the village hall and we had all been asked to bring a contribution. But I might have to do these again. The pastry wasn't coming together right. It was more like cement than pastry. Maybe my hands were too warm.

'He's much too old for you, Fiona.'

'Everyone thinks he's just ...' She paused and shook her head, lost for words.

'Is he?'

'Oh come on, mum!'

'Well. I wouldn't know if he was sexy or not, would I?'

'Yes you would. Why wouldn't you? You're not that old.'

Fiona was always telling me that I should wear more make-up, buy myself some new clothes and generally make something of myself. She had seen too many makeover programmes on TV. Sometimes she would infect me with her enthusiasm and I would make a half-hearted attempt to do something about myself, but there were few occasions for me to look glamorous in the village.

'What does he do?' she asked.

'I don't know.'

'Where is he from?'

'Canada.'

'No, I mean where in Canada.'

'Fiona, I really *don't know* anything about him.'

The pastry was all wrong. I was trying to roll it out and it kept breaking into little bits. I hated people watching me while I was cooking. I wanted to tell Fiona to go away and let me work in peace but I couldn't. It was so seldom that she wanted to talk to me about anything these days.

'That pastry's like cement!' she said suddenly.

'I know. I'm going to have to bin it and do it again.'

'I wonder what he does?'

'Ask him when you see him.'

'I never get to talk to him.'

'Maybe he'll pass the phone box on the way down to the pub.'

It just slipped out before I could stop myself. The village phone box had no phone, these days, now that everyone had mobiles, even the kids. But the village had adopted it. There was a little second hand book exchange, and notices about this or that function, and a few plants during the summer months. People even trimmed it up for Christmas. The kids often congregated around it at night until someone chased them away for making too much noise. Fiona gave me one of those looks. She knew I didn't approve of all this loitering about the village. She had taken my ruined pastry and was rolling it into a fat sausage between her palms. 'Will I put this out for the birds?'

'If you like.'

It always surprised me that Fiona should have kept her childhood love of birds and beasts. She still liked to keep the bird table well stocked. She couldn't bear cruelty to animals. Pity she didn't feel the same about her own species.

I got out the plain flour again.

'I'm off.' Fiona was at the door. 'I'll put this on the bird table on the way out.'

'Where are you going?'

'Just to the village.'

'Well don't be late. I want you back in before eleven.'

'OK.'

'If you don't come back in time, I'll send your dad down there for you.'

The threat was all in the shame of it, not in Sandy's anger. He could never really be cross with her. I was always the bad cop in our house.

She didn't dignify the empty threat with a response. She was gone, slamming the door behind her. I began spooning flour into my bowl. Maybe this time it would all come together right.

The clock on the mantelpiece had struck eleven and there was no sign of Fiona. I had tried phoning her but her phone was switched off. Sandy had been watching an old Bond movie and – uncharacteristically – had drunk a couple of very large drams during the course of the evening. He had been complaining of rheumatism so perhaps the whisky was medicinal. By half past ten, he had fallen asleep in the chair and had only woken up to stagger to the lavatory, from where he had struggled up to bed. I had heard the creak of wood and groan of springs as he flung himself onto the mattress and not long after, his snores came reverberating through the ceiling.

I couldn't send him down to the village in search of Fiona, could I? Ten minutes passed. I turned on the television and flicked between channels: plump men and women were indulging in naked ball games somewhere in deepest Europe. In America, mothers were putting their tiny, tarty daughters through pageant hell. Savage pets. A large snake had eaten three rabbits and a Yorkshire terrier and now seemed to have its beady eye on its owner as well.

Siggy came and padded a bed on my knee. The autumn evening was chilly and Sandy had lit the fire but now it was burning very low and I hadn't bothered to stoke it up. Siggy was feeling the cold and I was the warmest thing in the room. He wasn't really savage, but if he came onto your knee and you didn't scratch his jowls, he would bite you, gently but with the hint of violence to come, until you did.

Another ten minutes passed. I had visions of Fiona lying drunk, drugged, raped, murdered. Abducted. This is the village, Helen, I told myself sternly. Safe as houses. No crime to speak of. Knocked down in the street then, I thought. Carted off to hospital. I tipped Siggy off my lap and phoned Annie. Her entire household kept late hours and I knew she would still be up.

'Have any of your lot seen Fiona?'

'Hang on a minute.'

I heard her running up the stairs. There was a pause. Then, 'No. Nobody has. But they've hardly left the house all night. Dean took the dog for a walk an hour ago. His girlfriend's here now. Why? Should she be home?'

'Oh you know what she's like, Annie. Eleven o'clock I told her.'

'It's only half past. She's probably at somebody's house watching a film. Do you want Tim to go out and have a look for her? He's still up.'

'No. She'd be mortified.'

'Give her another half hour and phone me back if she's still not home.'

'Are you sure I'm not disturbing you?'

'Have you seen what's on the telly? And our broadband's on the blink again.'

'Nothing worth watching.'

'Have a drink, Helen. Calm down. She'll be back in a minute.'

Another half hour passed. I paced up and down the kitchen, then made a mug of tea and drank it too quickly, scalding my tongue. I thought I might drive down into the village and go looking for her myself. I was on the point of phoning Annie again when I heard the rattle of a vehicle in the yard. Jess began to bark, frantically. I rushed to the kitchen door in time to see Joe Napier with his arm around a very drunken Fiona. He had half dragged her out of the front seat, but she was being uncooperative and he was having a hard time. He was holding her upright with one hand, although she's a big girl, her father's daughter all right, and she was giggling. Her skirt had ridden up and she was practically showing her knickers. Not that they covered much either.

'For God's sake!' I was so angry that I thought I was going to hit him. Or her. 'What have you done to her?'

'Not guilty, ma'am,' he said, mildly, reverting to his polite form of address. 'Don't you think we ought to get her inside?'

If he had let go of her, she would have fallen down.

I held the door open and he half carried my sixteen year old daughter into the kitchen and balanced her precariously on a chair. He looked as if he found it funny but was trying not to laugh. She had stopped giggling and started groaning, her head in her hands.

'Ooh, Mum. I do feel ...'

My reactions, honed by years of experience, were pretty quick. When she was a little girl, Fiona had always turned to me saying, 'Mum, I do feel ...' and promptly vomited all over whatever I happened to be wearing at the time. Trainers were the worst. You could never get the bits of carrot out of the lace holes. So I was in there with the bucket just in time, and she was heaving and barfing into it. Not a pretty sight. Automatically I smoothed her head and glared at Joe Napier.

'Yeah,' he observed, laconically, leaning in the doorway. 'She did that in my car as well.'

'She was sick in your car? What happened to her?'

He shook his head. 'I don't know. Honest. You'll have to ask her that when she's sober. I just fell over her.'

'Fell over her?'

'When I went into the pub she was hanging about the phone box with the other groupies. Somebody in the pub told me who she was.'

'Groupies?'

'The phone box groupies. It seems to hold some major attraction for them. Don't you have cell phones over here?'

I must have looked at him blankly, too worried about Fiona to take in what he was saying.

'I wasn't drinking because I had the car,' he said, by way of explanation. 'Just fancied a bit of company which was why I went to the pub. When I came out, she was sitting on the pavement and I almost tripped over her. She couldn't stand up straight. I didn't think it was wise to leave her there, so I managed to get her into the car. I thought you might be worried about her. Then she was sick.'

'I'm so sorry. Do you want me to clean it up for you?'

He spread his hands.

'Don't worry. What's a bit of vomit between neighbours?'

'But I was so worried about her.'

'How old is she?'

'Sixteen. Oh God, what has she been taking?'

He was heading for the door. Not his problem. He still looked amused and faintly embarrassed.

'Oh I reckon it's just liquor,' he said. 'But she looks as if she's had some god-awful mixture.'

'I can see that.'

'I'd better be getting home. Hope she's OK. Night, Mrs Breckenridge.'

It was only after I had cleaned Fiona up and got her into bed that I realised I had never really thanked him. All I had done was shout at him.

The next morning, Fiona had a blinding headache. She didn't remember much of the night before at all. 'What did I do? What did I do?' she kept saying. She could hardly lift her head off the pillow and every time she tried to stand up she had to rush off and be sick again. I gave her painkillers and a lot of water but no sympathy at all. She said 'Sorry, mum,' and a bit later, 'I've made a fool of myself,' and then, 'What will he think of me? Oh my God, mum, what will he think?'

'I expect he thinks you're a daft wee lassie,' I said nastily. 'He can't have found it very attractive – watching you throwing up your guts into a black plastic bucket.'

'Oh God,' she said again, and made another dash for the bathroom.

Later on that morning, Annie rang me. 'Did the wanderer return?'

I told her all about it.

'Christ, I bet she's embarrassed.'

'She is.'

'Well she's going to feel even worse. Have you seen the paper?'

'No. I haven't been down to the village yet. Why?'

'The paper' meant the local weekly newspaper that was usually full of group pictures of coffee mornings or retirement parties, with the occasional burglary or brawl or lost dog thrown in for good measure.

'Your new neighbour's in it' said Annie.

'What? What has he done?'

'Nothing. It's what he *is* that they're interested in.'

'So what is he then? Come on, Annie. Don't keep me in suspense!'

'He plays ice hockey. He's come to join the Kestrels for the season. The coach says with his excellent record he'll strengthen their defensive line-up and be an asset to them and they're lucky to have a player of his calibre. Or words to that effect.'

The Kestrels were a professional ice hockey team that played out of an arena some miles away in the next town. Some of their players were Canadian or American, some European, some Scots. It wasn't the most popular sport in Scotland. When people talked about 'the game' here they generally meant football. Fiona had been to the hockey once or twice with her school friends but it had never appealed to me or Sandy. I knew nothing about it, though Fiona told me that all kinds of people went. 'Old people as well,' she said, pointedly, looking at me and her father.

'I think we'll have to go and see them play,' said Annie.

'Maybe we should.'

Later on, I took a bowl of eggs down to the cottage: big, brown, free range eggs. I had wiped them over with extra care so that they looked good.

Joe came to the door with a mug of coffee in his hand. He seemed surprised to see me and ever so slightly offhand. Or it may have been that he was just tired. He didn't invite me in and he didn't offer me a coffee. In fact he didn't say much at all. It felt strange to be standing on Louise's doorstep and not to be invited in. She had seldom locked her door in the daytime.

'I came to apologise. And to say thanks. I felt I was rude to you last night.'

'No you weren't. Don't worry about it. I'm just glad I found her. How's the patient?'

'Fine. Hung-over. Ashamed of herself.'

'Happens to the best of us.'

'I've brought you some eggs.'

'You didn't need to do that.'

'Well. Just to say thanks.'

I handed them over. He smiled and took them.

'I'll put them in the fridge and give you your bowl back.'

'Oh there's no hurry. I'm not short of bowls.'

There was a little pause. He still didn't invite me in, just stood there awkwardly with the eggs in one hand and his coffee in the other. So I went back home and tended to my hung-over daughter.

Sandy had slept through the whole thing. In the morning, he had been up and about early and when he came in for his lunch I told him that Fiona had a tummy bug. I don't know if he believed me or not, but he didn't argue. Later I took her more painkillers and weak tea and toast and warned her not to say anything to her dad. I assumed I could rely on Joe to keep his mouth shut.

'Thanks, mum,' she said.

'What did you drink?'

'Chloe brought a bottle.'

'But what was in it?'

'She'd gone round some of the stuff in her dad's drinks cabinet and taken a bit of each. She said it was a sort of cocktail.'

'What kind?' I asked. 'Molotov?' But it was wasted on her. She just shook her head.

'Chloe tasted it and she didn't like it, and the others didn't like it either, but I thought it was all right. So I finished it.'

'Why?'

'They bet me I wouldn't.'

'And if they told you to go play in traffic, would you do that as well?'

'It was OK. It tasted OK.'

'Oh, Fiona .'

'Then it started raining and I said I was going home. They went home too. I don't remember much after that. Well I remember being in Joe's car and him telling me to hold on while he got me home. And the next thing I knew, I was barfing in the bucket. But – oh mum – what will he think of me now?'

'And me,' I thought. 'What will he think of me?'

– Chapter Four –

IT WAS CHARLIE McGowan's fiftieth birthday and we had been invited to his party in the village hall. I didn't really want to go. I wasn't much good at parties, even parties like this one where I knew just about everybody. Besides, I was heading for forty myself and I didn't want to be reminded of my own advancing middle age. Charlie was living down in the village at that time. He was newly divorced and he had moved back in with his mother, temporarily he said, though she didn't seem to be so sure about that part of the arrangement.

Betty McGowan had been preparing for this party for weeks. She said she was doing it to cheer Charlie up, but he didn't seem to be too distressed by his divorce from Margaret. Their kids were grown up, and I don't think they had been getting on well for years. Then Margaret did a course in Business Studies at the local FE college and got a new admin job with the council and before too long there was a new man as well – somebody she was working with.

'A suit,' said Annie. 'A grey suit.'

She had seen them around the town together. The new man wore very fancy ties, allegedly. Annie swears you can judge a man by his ties, though what they're supposed to tell you, I'm not sure.

The divorce had come through, the house was sold and Charlie had been living with his mother for the past six months. His dad had been dead for five or six years and poor Betty said it was nice having a man about the house again, but you could see that it sometimes got her down that she was hopelessly lumbered with his washing and ironing and cooking. I think Betty hoped the party would be a kind of send-off for him, that it would encourage him to find his own place again, but everyone could see that she made him too comfortable. Sandy always said the only thing that would get Charlie away from the village would be some other woman who might be prepared to take him on and give him, on a regular basis, the one thing his mother couldn't supply. Which turned out to be true in the end. But he seemed to be in no hurry at that time. According to Tim, who was quite friendly with him, he went into town pubbing and clubbing at the weekends, went to all the 'grab a granny' nights, but he hardly ever saw anyone for more than a couple of dates afterwards. Once bitten, twice shy, I suppose.

The party invitation said 'Eight till Late' so we went down to the village hall at about half past eight. Sandy had put on the dark suit he always wore for funerals. I had used some of Louise's legacy to buy myself a new dress. For once I had paid the full price and not bought it in a sale or a charity shop. It was blue-green, soft, silky and clingy and I loved it. I had been growing my hair longer and, earlier in the year, Jessie McClure, the local hairdresser, had persuaded me to let her lighten my mousy brown to dark blonde and hide the few wisps of grey. Since then I had just about kept up to it, but it meant a visit to 'It's a Snip' every five weeks or so, and Sandy grumbled about the cost. But it made me feel a bit less middle aged, so I kept on going.

I thought I might try to put my hair up for the party but it kept falling down round my ears. I wasn't much good with my hair, and I wasn't much good with make-up either. Most days I just didn't bother. There was nobody to see me; only the cows and they had better eye-lashes anyway. While I was struggling with my hair, Fiona came into the bedroom wielding her own make-up bag.

'Here,' she said, brusquely. 'Let me do that for you, mum. You're so hopeless!'

She made me sit back in the chair and close my eyes while she worked on me, tucking a towel round my neck to protect the dress.

'Don't look until I tell you!'

'What's brought this on?' I asked her, ungraciously.

'I owe you, mum. You never told dad about … you know?'

'Well I hope you're making a good job of me. Don't overdo it, will you?'

'Don't worry.'

Using a variety of brushes and sponges, sticking her tongue out in concentration, she applied foundation, blusher, eyeshadow, mascara and lipstick. She seems to learn all this stuff on YouTube. Then she twisted my hair up tight at the back and teased a few curls out, spraying them gently into position. She stood back to look at her handiwork and I heard her sigh with satisfaction. Finally, she removed the towel, sprayed me with scent and said, 'Now you can look.'

I opened my eyes. The make-up had certainly done something for me. My skin looked smooth and pale, a slight blush on each cheek. She had somehow made my lips look fuller and my eyelashes longer and she had smoothed out my eyebrows.

'You look great, mum,' said Fiona, peering at herself over the top of my head.

'Are you sure?'

'Yes. I've made a great job of you. Now, off you go!'

Charlie's family had made a big effort for his party. There were tables set out with pink carnations in vases, scented candles and little sweets in dishes, and there was a bar at one end of the room. Fergus was running this with the help of his wife and one of his plump daughters. He had three of them, all big, blonde and buxom, always dressed voluptuously in contrasting pastel shades, like cakes on a plate. Contrary to the *fashionista* notion that you could never be too thin, practically every man in the village fancied them like mad. No wonder the pub did well. The food had been laid out on a couple of trestle tables in the downstairs kitchen. Everyone in the family, all of Charlie's aunties and cousins and second cousins twice removed, had contributed something: a big ham, plates of chicken and beef, rice and pasta salads, coleslaw and egg mayonnaise and a whole cooked salmon. Probably poached in more ways than one, observed Sandy. You could smell it all as you passed the door.

The hall was only half full when we arrived and the music echoed around the high ceiling. Charlie was looking very rosy and cheerful and his breath already smelled of whisky. We gave him the card that said, 'Oh No Five-O' and a bottle of single malt. Then we sat down at a table with Annie and Tim and the men went up to the bar to fetch us some drinks.

I had known Annie for years. It had been such a relief when she first moved to the village. She wasn't like my old school friends, or the farmer's wives I had mixed with until that point. Born and brought up in Dundee, she was bolder and brasher and she swore quite a lot, although when you got to know her better, you found out that this was mostly a front, because she was very kind and generous underneath it all. But she certainly couldn't talk about farming and although she obviously loved her kids they weren't the be-all and end-all of her existence. Sandy didn't really approve at first, but he got used to her eventually and he liked Tim well enough. Tim was much quieter. I don't suppose he could get a word in edgeways most of the time.

Annie's son David was about the same age as Fiona, so we had gone to the Toddler Group together and that was a relief too because when we first joined, it was a fairly po-faced organisation with rotas for everything from making the tea to putting out the toys. Annie surprised them all by bringing in a bottle of wine to celebrate my birthday, but most of the other mums joined in readily enough, and after that the whole atmosphere eased up a bit. We had been good mates ever since, and it was natural that we should sit together at Charlie's party.

The music was provided by a duo who looked as though they had started out when Adam – or Charlie – was a boy. They were called Two's a Crowd which I always thought was rather an odd name for a twosome. There was a smooth singer in a dinner suit, his hair slicked back with too much gel, and a smaller, balder musician who never really came out from behind one of those big keyboards that can reproduce any musical instrument known to man. It was so loud that you could hardly tell what they were playing. It practically knocked you back against the wall.

'Why do they do it?' asked Sandy, when he and Tim came back from the bar with our gins and a couple of beers for themselves. 'Can't hear a word anybody's saying.'

Every time the music started up again, we were deafened. You could feel the rhythm hammering through your body and it put a real dampener on conversation. There seemed no point in trying to talk over the din; all you could do was mouth at each other. So we drank quite a lot, instead. It gave us something to do and the drinks were cheap. Maybe that was why they did it. Maybe they got a cut of the bar. Then we sat and swivelled our heads round to watch the rest of the guests.

Betty seemed to have been very indiscriminate in issuing invitations to the party and half the village was there. But this is a small community and Charlie was on nodding terms with most of them. There was Ella Dunlop, eighty if she was a day, wearing a pretty floral two piece with white daisies on a blue and green background, large golden earrings and a green and gold necklace to match. She was dancing every dance with Johnnie Fraser who had lived by himself in the sheltered houses down by the park, ever since his wife died ten years before. They made a touching and dapper couple and they danced well together, never putting a foot wrong.

At the other end of the age range, there was a group of girls, cousins of the family, Annie told me. They were like a flock of exotic birds with their long legs and their constant twittering. They were dressed in tiny shorts and fluttery skirts. Everyone watched them dance, because they looked so pretty, so full of energy that you couldn't take your eyes off them. They knew it and even when they left the hall, just to go to the loo, they flew off together and then they all came back and swooped down to sit at the same table and drank fluorescent sticky drinks with enthusiasm.

'You look really nice tonight,' said Annie, eyeing me critically. 'Love the dress. But what else have you done to yourself?'

'Fiona did my make-up.'

'Well you should tell her to show you how she does it. It suits you.'

'Maybe I will. Sandy didn't notice though.'

'Oh well. Husbands don't, do they?'

'I suppose not.'

I sometimes thought I could have gone out wearing a feed sack and Sandy wouldn't have noticed. Or perhaps he would have approved.

Half an hour later, we were joined at our table by a couple called Les and Mandy who lived in the new houses that had been built in a field at the back of Annie and Tim's place. Mandy had the most beautiful hair I have ever seen, long and corn coloured. It seemed to have a life of its own, and you could see why she couldn't bring herself to have it cut. Les, on the other hand, was completely bald. They had a little girl, Lindsay, and her hair was exactly the same colour as her mother's, so you could tell it was natural. We were quite surprised to see them at the party, and I think they were amazed to be asked. They had only lived in the village for a year or two, but Betty – with last minute pangs of guilt about leaving people out – had gone around issuing extra invitations.

'We thought we'd better show face,' said Mandy. 'It was so nice of her to ask us. And unexpected.'

The duo struck up again and Tim asked me to dance. He's a terrible dancer but very enthusiastic, and just as we were lurching round the floor, I noticed Joe Napier standing by the bar, holding a bottle of beer. My first thought was that Fiona would be disappointed. If she had known he was going to be here, she might have come too, but she had refused her invitation and was spending the night with a school friend. Joe was wearing tight black jeans and a dark blue cotton shirt, open at the neck. He fitted in well with the other cowboys at the bar.

'There's your new neighbour!' Tim bellowed in my ear.

'So I see. I wonder what he's doing here.'

'Betty got talking to him in the shop and asked him. I think she's taken quite a fancy to him.'

'Betty has?'

'And Maisie Murtagh. She can't see beyond him.'

Maisie was Betty's best friend, a little square woman who, summer and winter alike, wore woolly tights, a belted coat with a stripy, furry collar that matched her hair, that was also stripy grey and blonde like the pelt of some strange animal, and furry brown zip-up boots on her fat little feet. She usually wore a striped woolly hat too. She had worn the same hat, to my certain knowledge, for the past twenty years. She was sitting at what passed for a top table with Betty and the family. They had started school together, the old one-roomed village school that had been turned into a private house some years ago. For once, she seemed to have abandoned the coat and boots in favour of a green dress and a pair of green satin dancing shoes with a diamante clasp on each toe. Her whole outfit could fairly be described as 'vintage'. The clothes made her look like a character from a TV costume drama. All Creatures Great and Small perhaps. She must have had the hat surgically removed, specially for the occasion.

'She made him a cake,' Tim yelled in my ear.

'Who did? Betty?'

'No. Maisie. And a tin of shortbread.'

'Where did you hear all this?'

'In the pub.'

'You don't go to the pub.'

'I was in there the other day. With a mate from work.'

'Ah.'

'Your new neighbour was in there too. There was a piece in the paper about him. He was embarrassed about it.'

'Was he?'

I felt disproportionately pleased to see Joe. That should have told me something as well, shouldn't it? But when something unexpected happens, we don't always recognise it for what it is. Especially when it seems impossible. He was standing at the bar with his bottle of beer, talking to Charlie and his pals, and he never even glanced in my direction. When the dance finished, the duo went off for a little break, so that meant we could hold a decent conversation again. With the usual sinking feeling, I saw Mary Black coming over to our table. Mary was married to Morris, and was one of Sandy's great multitude of distant cousins. She was younger than Sandy, and he had known her all her life.

She was tall and quite pretty, but absolutely everything about her irritated me, even her face and the way she talked. This was probably my fault rather than hers, but I couldn't help it. Her father was a pillar of the kirk in the old fashioned way, and Mary disapproved of all kinds of things: gambling, drinking, smoking, kids kissing in the street, make-up. You name it, Mary was ready to get up a campaign against it. The trouble was that when you spoke to her for more than two minutes, you realised that her morality barely disguised the fact that she was as thick as two short planks. She came out with these stupid statements and you thought, 'Where did that come from?' Or as Annie said, 'Lights on, nobody home, Helen.' But Sandy was very fond of her. So I had to put up with her.

Mary sat down opposite me with her ginger beer and lime. I offered to get her something stronger, but she shook her head.

'No, no. I'm driving. But in any case you know me. I never drink much,' she said.

Why did that infuriate me so much when if anyone else had said it, it would have seemed like a perfectly reasonable statement? It was clear that she just wanted to interrogate me about our new neighbour.

'Have you met him?'

'We've passed the time of day, Mary.'

'Looks a bit of a scruff to me.'

'I don't know much about him.'

'Is he staying long?'

'He hasn't said. But I think he's going to be working here.'

'Are you sure he isn't a squatter? How do you know he's who he says he is?'

'Mary, take my word for it, he's Louise's cousin. The solicitor knew all about him. And as far as I know he's here for the whole winter.'

'Oh well, if you say so.'

'He's Canadian. He wouldn't have come all the way from Canada just to squat in Louise's cottage. Would he?'

'Well that's no indication of anything, is it? I'd phone the solicitor if I were you.'

Sometimes Mary's stupidity made me want to scream out loud and assault her with anything to hand. My fingers itched to close around a nearby vase of pink carnations and beat her over the head with it. I sat on my hands.

'Mary, he's got the key. Take my word for it. He isn't a squatter. He's working here. Didn't you see the article?'

'Morris said there was something in the paper. But I don't hold with ice hockey.'

'Why not?'

'Dreadful foreign sport. Morris says they fight each other you know,' she sniffed disparagingly. 'Not like football.'

There were so many potential replies to that one that I just shrugged, overcome by a feeling of irritation so profound that it rendered me speechless.

'Not sure I'd like him living down the road from me, anyway. Where does he come from?'

'Ontario, I think. Somewhere near a lake.' It struck me that I was sounding as stupid as Mary. 'But we haven't talked very much. Honestly.'

'Do you think he's just gate crashed? Do you think I ought to get Charlie to throw him out?'

'Don't be daft, Mary. Betty asked him.' Annie had finally come to my rescue.

'Betty?'

'Yes. She and Maisie think he's a nice boy.'

'I don't believe it.'

'It's true,' I agreed. 'And he hasn't misbehaved himself yet. All he's done is stand there peacefully with a bottle of beer and laugh at Charlie's terrible jokes.'

They were terrible as well. They were the most boring jokes in the history of the world, but he fancied himself as a comedian and he would bombard you with one awful, unfunny story after another, until your eyes glazed over and all you wanted to do was curl up in a corner and die. Why is it only men of a certain age who can do that and think you might be remotely entertained by it? Don't they ever notice all those mouths stretched in thinly disguised yawns?

We were spared further irritation by the band who struck up again. At least the noise would shut Mary up.

Eventually she threaded her way back to her own table on the opposite side of the hall. Annie was purple in the face. 'God, Helen, you are priceless. Somewhere near a lake? There's an awful lot of them over there!'

'Who is she?' asked Mandy. She was new to the village and still putting names to faces.

'My husband's cousin, Mary. She and Morris have a farm a few miles outside the village.'

'Does she always go on like that?'

'Nearly always.'

'How do you put up with her?'

'You get used to it after a while.'

'I think I'd be plotting her death if I were you,' said Annie.

'Don't think I haven't thought about it.'

I danced a bit more after that. Les asked me up, and Tim asked Mandy and then me, but Sandy didn't dance again. When the band had another break, Betty announced that supper was ready and we were just to go and help ourselves. Sandy piled his plate high with salmon, chicken legs, roast beef and sausage rolls, but I wasn't feeling all that hungry. I think I had probably been drinking more than was good for me and I'm not really used to it.

Joe didn't dance much and he didn't join the smokers clustered outside. He spent a lot of time at the bar, drinking beer I think, not whisky. Later on, after we'd had our supper, and after Charlie had made his big thank-you speech and kissed his mum, and after his mum had burst into tears and had to be comforted with port and lemon – after all that, Joe *did* dance with one or two people. He asked up one or two of the younger, unattached girls, the glossy ones, the enviable ones. He danced with one of Fergus's voluptuous daughters, and I noticed that she giggled a lot. He must have been saying things to make her laugh. But he never asked any of the girls up more than once. He was just working his way around the room at random. Eventually, he came over to our table but he asked Mandy with the bonnie hair. I watched as he swung her round and made her laugh too. Then he brought her back to our table, smiled down at me and said, 'Hello, Mrs Breckenridge.' But somebody at the bar attracted his attention, and I thought, 'So that's that,' with a certain amount of regret. It would have been nice to dance with him. I wondered what was wrong with me. Instant ugly, that's how you feel when somebody so beautiful ignores you.

The guests had all had quite a bit to drink by that time. You know how it is? People start to laugh too much and say things they regret later. Sometimes they start crying or they get into stupid quarrels. Folk know each other much too well here. That's what makes drinking so perilous. If they were strangers it might be all right, but there are secrets buried deep within the community, and drunks are horribly inclined to want to dig them up. It's as if their tongues are suddenly too big for their mouths and words come spilling out. They spill drinks too and fall against tables, and sometimes when they're dancing they fall over. I usually try to go away before they get to that stage. Only this time I couldn't, because Sandy was enjoying himself, and I couldn't just walk away and go home all by myself. Not at this time of night. Not when I was a bit drunk myself.

After a while, Sandy went to the loo. He didn't come back for ages. I was just thinking of seeing if Annie might want to get up and dance with me – lots of the women were dancing with each other because the men were so pathetic – when Tim asked her instead. Mandy and Les were already up, so that left me sitting alone at the table, all by myself with an empty glass, and then I felt a little tap on my shoulder. I looked round and there he was. Joe Napier. Holding out his hand. Smiling at me.

So I got up and danced with him just as the music changed from fast to slow.

Hungry Eyes. They were playing Hungry Eyes. There was something old fashioned about the way he danced too. I mean he held me in his arms for a start, although not too close. He was big and tall and solid. We talked a bit but not much. Talking meant bellowing in each other's ears and I was afraid of spitting at him. Eventually he started laughing and shook his head, so we just danced. We danced, and I swear to God I never wanted it to stop. I found myself wishing that the man up there with his fancy suit and his sleek hair would just sing for ever. And I hadn't felt like that for so long. For so very long. If ever.

In the middle of dancing with him, I had two thoughts, one immediately after the other. One was – how warm he is – because he was. He was warm in every way, like a good fire, like the sun. And the other was – I hate my life. But that was a frightening thought, and I tried to shove it to the back of my mind and just concentrate on dancing instead. All the same I didn't really want to dance at all. I wanted to rest my head against his shoulder and stay there in a kind of blissful limbo. I remember thinking it was as well he couldn't read my mind, because he would have been out of there like a bat out of hell. It was that crazy. I hardly knew him, but I wanted to stop everything and just be in that one place, with this one man, holding me.

'Will you let me buy you a drink?' he said, casually, when the music drew to a halt.

Sandy still hadn't come back into the room. He must have been waylaid by the herd of young farmers who had been hanging about close to the food so that they could graze on the leftovers. He would be talking about wet weather and falling prices. They would all be complaining. With some justification, I might add.

'I'm sure I owe you a drink,' he said again.

'Why do you owe me a drink?'

'Well, for the eggs.'

'Oh no. They were just a wee thank-you.'

'You didn't have to thank me.'

'Maybe not, but I didn't need to bite your head off either. You were doing us all a favour. And she was sick in your car. I'm so sorry.'

'You were worried about her. It's natural.'

'I worry about her all the time.'

'She'll get over it.'

'Just so long as she gets over it before ...'

'Before what?'

'Before something awful happens to her. Before somebody takes advantage. Before she does something really daft.'

I don't know why I found myself confiding in him so quickly. Perhaps he gave me the impression of being refreshingly non-judgemental. Everyone around here had an instant opinion on everything.

He bought me a gin and tonic and I had taken a gulp of it before I realised that it was a double. We didn't go back to our table immediately, but sat by the bar, perching on a couple of stools there. I was aware that Annie and Tim would be watching and so would Fergus and his gossipy daughter.

He reached out and patted my arm.

'She's very young. We all experiment a bit at that age. Push the boundaries.'

When he touched me, I felt a little tingle go through my arm. I took another big gulp of my drink. My stomach was doing somersaults but I managed to pull myself together and make myself talk normally to him.

'I hear you've been getting on very well with our Maisie,' I said.

'Oh sure. Maisie thinks I'm the bee's knees. The best thing since sliced bread. She thinks I'm brilliant. Spot on.' He grinned. 'See how good I'm getting at the language?'

'How did you get to know Maisie then?'

'I offered to help her carry her groceries home and then I fixed her gate for her because it was off its hinges. And that did it. She was stuck on me. Do you think my halo looks OK?' He patted his head.

'She's a bit lonely.' Me too, I thought. Me too.

'Oh yeah. I know. But now she keeps giving me stuff. It's embarrassing.'

'What kind of stuff?'

'Berries from her freezer.'

'What sort of berries?'

'How would I know? All kinds of berries. Some are black and some are red.'

'Well that's all right isn't it?'

'The freezer's full of them already.'

'Louise used to pick them. But then she got too frail. She could hardly eat.'

I could feel the tears prickling behind my eyes. Bloody gin. I hoped he hadn't noticed. I took a deep breath.

'You miss her very much, don't you?' he said gently.

'Of course I do. She was my good friend.'

'And I suppose I'm no substitute.'

There seemed to be no appropriate answer to this, so I just smiled at him, fatuously.

'Anyway,' he said, 'Berries isn't all Maisie gives me. There was this little house made up of a washcloth and a couple of sponges, all pinned together.'

'They were for sale at the summer fair at the school. She must have bought in a supply back then. The kids in the Sunday School made them in aid of funds.'

'Oh and there was a packet of note things – they had dogs on them. I made the huge error of telling her I like dogs. I have to be very careful what I say to her now. If I tell her I like bacon and black pudding sandwiches she'll probably fill my fridge with pounds of the stuff.'

'Do you like bacon and black pudding sandwiches?'

'Yeah I do. They're a novelty to me. But even I can only eat so much pig.' He pulled a face. 'But I can't complain. Everyone's very kind here.'

'So you're enjoying the village?'

There was a pause. 'I suppose so. I suppose I am.'

'You're going to stay here then?'

'I'm under contract for the season,' he said.

I wanted to ask all kinds of questions. How long was the season? What had brought him here? What had he left behind? But I didn't ask any of those things. Not then. It seemed intrusive and I was trying to make a good impression.

'So,' he said. 'What do you do with yourself, Mrs Breckenridge?'

'Helen. I've told you. My name's Helen.'

'I kind of like Mrs Breckenridge. But Helen then. What do you do when you're not wading through mud and tending to your cows?'

'I don't tend to the cows much. Hens yes. Cows infrequently.'

'You must do something in your spare time.'

'I don't have much spare time. But I go to the line dancing. Does that count?'

'Line dancing? You mean ... long lines of people ... country music. All that shit. You mean they do it here?'

'It's OK really.' I could feel myself blushing scarlet.

'Does Sandy go?'

'No. Just me and my friend Annie.'

'Couldn't see Sandy doing it somehow.'

'It's an all female affair. The men don't come. Not in this village.'

The thought came to me again 'I hate my life' and I saw myself as he must see me: a bored, middle aged farmer's wife who goes to the line dancing once a week and dances all alone. I put down my glass and got up. It took a real effort but I got up.

'Thanks for the drink.'

'That's all right. Been a real pleasure, ma'am.' He looked into my eyes, smiling.

'Helen.'

'Oh yes. Helen. It's been a real pleasure, Helen.'

He was so open and easy. That's what I thought then, before I knew what else there was to him, before I took off the rosy specs and really looked at him, before I stopped being blinded by his apparent self-possession, and my own need for excitement. And yet all those things were true as well. Just that there was more.

'I'd better get back to my friends. Why don't you come over to our table?'

He shook his head. 'I'll have another beer with the boys and then I'll be off home. I'm walking.'

'All right. Thanks again, Joe. See you soon.'

'I'm sure you will, Helen.'

'What's he like then?' said Annie, when I got back to the table. 'The interlowper?'

'He's all right.'

'You'll be hoping you see a bit more of him!'

She nudged me and then she started laughing. She thought it was a hoot. Sandy came back to the table. He had been at somebody's hip flask. You could tell. His face had got very red and he was stumbling over his words. He stank of whisky.

'What's so funny?' he said, beaming round at us. 'Never mind. Never know what you girls are laughing at. Good party, eh? Hell of a good party!'

– Chapter Five –

I DIDN'T SEE JOE for a few days after the party. I thought I might have made a fool of myself, and Annie didn't help either. She kept saying 'Nice to see you and your neighbour getting on so well, oh look at you, you're going all pink, Helen,' and as soon as she said it, of course, I did go pink. I went more than pink. I could feel a big scarlet blush spreading over my face and down my neck. The more I denied it, the more she went on about it. So I kept myself busy in the untidy little farm office, and it seemed that Joe was busy in his house as well, because I didn't see anything of him at all that week.

On Sunday morning, Sandy and I went to church. Fiona stayed in bed. She wouldn't set foot in the kirk these days, although she had been christened there, and when she was a wee girl she had come with us every week and her name was on the wall, beautifully inscribed on the old cradle roll. Sandy and I never actually talked about religion and it sometimes struck me that he had the same unthinking loyalty to his faith as Mary. They were two of a kind. I was more sceptical about it all and yet I had moments of real conviction when everything seemed to make sense. But all those moments had more to do with my awareness of the history of the place than of any firm belief. I believed in something. I just couldn't be as precise about it as Sandy seemed to be.

There has been a church on the same site in our village for hundreds of years. Not the same church, but a building, a place of worship, and it's not hard to see how this might once have been a sacred place, a sun-filled clearing beside a burn. These days Sunday attendance is partly a social occasion. I used to think about the continuity of it all when I was listening to the minister intoning long prayers. He's a master of the art of adding one subordinate clause after another and another, *ad infinitum*, so that the 'amen', when it comes, always takes you by surprise.

Sometimes this intrigued me but at other times it just irritated me and I wanted to rush out and do something amazing and different. This feeling often came to me in autumn. I think it had something to do with the swallows and house martins getting ready to fly away. One of the smaller stained glass windows in the church shows a couple of blue swallows, swooping through a grey sky. I gaze at it a lot, especially in winter, when the kirk is cold and the sermon gets me down and the old pew – just too narrow for comfort – hurts my back.

House martins nested at the farm every year: rows of nests, like little beehives. Dozens of them. I once counted seventy nests in one of the sheds. At this time of the year, I would watch them assembling on the rooftops and phone wires, and I would think about all their sunny destinations. I was sorry to see them go. Sorry to see the empty nests, so carefully tended in May and June. I half wanted to fly as well, but the trouble was my instincts were all at sea. I didn't know where I wanted to go or what I wanted to do when I got there. Maybe Sandy and I were more like the jackdaws who huddled on our chimney stacks in morose twosomes all winter long.

Inside, the church was painted white with an upstairs gallery, which was where the local gentry always sat: Lord Darrach, who was very frail these days, and his wife Lidia, Lady Darrach, who bossed him about and had more of a plum in her mouth than he did. Whenever they heard her speak, people in the village would remind each other that she was just a miner's daughter who had made a good marriage. That wasn't strictly true. Mine owner's daughter would be more accurate. Lord Darrach was scrupulously polite and everyone liked him, even if they didn't like his wife very much.

Such people seemed to exist at one remove from many of us. They often lived behind high hedges, in large crumbling houses, with little disposable income. They socialised in exalted circles and they sometimes kept what the old men of the village scathingly called 'gentry horses' meaning horses that didn't work for a living, but I suppose most horses are gentry horses these days. Many of the big estates had hunting and shooting rights over the farms round about. Way back when the hunt still came through the village, the hunting fraternity used to say that it brought jobs to the countryside, but I couldn't say I ever noticed it. People never found much work helping out with horses and hounds in this part of the world. They worked on farms or as electricians and builders, gardeners and decorators. They cleaned holiday homes or cooked lunches for visitors in the pubs and restaurants or travelled to the nearby town, or even to Glasgow every day. The hunt used to come in and clog up the village street with their horseboxes. They clip clopped about on their gentry horses looking very pleased with themselves. Sandy wouldn't have them on our land, even back when it was legal, and I admired him for that. Not that he had any great love for foxes mind you. He'd lie in wait and take a pot shot at one now and again and his aim was usually good. But he couldn't bear the hunt at any price. He said he liked a clean shot better than watching one pack of animals tear another animal to pieces. There was a strong streak of good Scots radicalism in Sandy, particularly for a farmer. I mean they're not noted for it are they? In fact, in many ways, the farming community is as separate as the nabbery, which was that the village called the gentry. Like all villages, I suppose, we have factions: the county set, the farmers, and the village proper, but even the villagers are divided into incomers and locals. And there's a subset of English incomers who are occasionally the butt of supposedly harmless jibes which would, if they were directed at any other minority, be deemed inappropriate. We come together for the various community events, large and small, and it's a friendly place. But the fault lines – which run deep – sometimes appear on the surface and then people realise that the rural idyll is a myth.

I remember when the hunt came riding up our road one day and Sandy sent them packing.

'It's tradition, Mr Breckenridge,' said Lady Darrach from her high horse, and he said, 'Aye and so was slavery,' and they turned round and went away again.

Sandy was very quiet, but he was his own man and I loved him for that. He had always been a churchgoer, and when the new minister came, a young man who didn't mind Sandy being bolshie with the nabbery, he was asked if he wanted to be an elder and he agreed. Apart from attending meetings and helping to run the church, this also meant that on special occasions, like communion services, he got to sit with the other elders on posh carved chairs, and hand around triangles of sliced white loaf. Sandy was flattered to be asked. He said his prayers, he was a good man and a kind man. There was nothing at all about him to dislike.

The Sunday after the party, we went down to the village hall after church, as we so often did. I stood there, clutching my mug of weak instant coffee, while Maisie Murtagh talked to me in an undertone. She had been speaking to me for some time and I hadn't really been listening. I think she had been talking about her garden, and how she needed some help with the autumn pruning. It was a shame, wasn't it, she said, to see Louise's lovely garden going to rack and ruin. I nodded vigorously. Did I think Joe might tidy it up a bit? I told her I wasn't sure. I didn't think there was a hope in hell of Joe doing any gardening but I didn't have the heart to tell her. It occurred to me that I might volunteer my services. I liked gardening and I had helped Louise. Maisie must have noticed my lack of attention and drifted off to speak to Betty McGowan. Sandy was standing among a huddle of elders. They were eating chocolate biscuits and talking about church matters. The manse had recently been found to be riddled with dry rot and was becoming a worry to them. That word 'riddled' was peculiarly apt where dry rot was concerned. We had had it up at the farm on more than one occasion and there was a sinister, alien quality to it. It could make its way through stone. Turn two hundred year old oak beams to the consistency of cheddar cheese. At the manse, the bath had fallen through the ceiling. Fortunately the minister hadn't been in it at the time.

I saw cousin Mary heading in my direction and stared out of the window, hoping that she would be diverted by somebody else. Morris, as an elder, was in Sandy's little group and Mary had accosted a number of other people with her complaint of the week. I was pretty far down her list of desirable friends, but I was the only one in her line of vision, and she came swooping down on me. This week's grievance was the head-teacher at the primary school who had invited a reasonably well-known children's writer to talk to the kids and read them some of her stories. I had seen the usual photograph afterwards in the local paper.

The writer, a middle aged and motherly woman, specialised in books about witches and wizards with lots of lovely pictures that she had painted herself. Great fun. The kids must have enjoyed the talk but Mary didn't approve at all. She thought that witches and wizards were the work of the devil, even when they did silly things in kiddies' picture books, like falling off their broomsticks into haystacks or turning toy cats into real tigers with disastrous results. All of that went right over Mary's head. All she could see was her own horror of anything that smacked of 'the occult'. She had complained to the headteacher who she blamed for the whole thing and she told me all about how she had insisted on withdrawing Alice and Lindsay from the school that afternoon, so that they shouldn't be 'contaminated by evil'. She used those very words. I kept looking around, trying to find a way of escaping from her, but everyone else was deliberately intent on their coffee and their own conversation. Nobody was going to rescue me.

'I phoned the education authority to complain,' she said, with a smugness that made me want to shake her.

'And what did they say?' I asked. Actually I was quite interested by this time. I was curious to see just how far Mary would go in pursuit of righteousness.

'They were very sympathetic and they asked me to write in about it, but they said they hadn't had any other complaints.'

'Well, no. I don't suppose they had.'

'People are very feeble.'

'Maybe other folk don't think the same way as you do, Mary.'

'Why not?'

'Well I've read those stories – Fiona used to like them – and I honestly don't see any harm in them. It's just made up stuff for kids. It isn't going to turn them all into mini-Satanists.'

She pursed her lips. 'Ah, but who knows. It might trigger something in them. Who knows what the long term effects might be?'

God only knows what she might have gone on to say; probably something supremely tactless about Fiona and the phone box groupies being the work of the devil, but Sandy came over and rescued me.

'Time we were going, Helen. The roast will be overcooked.' He smiled at his cousin and put his arm round her shoulders. 'Hello, Mary. How's tricks?'

She relaxed, leaning over to peck him on the cheek. At least she approved of Sandy, I thought. At least he wouldn't contaminate her with evil.

There was no point in thanking Sandy for his intervention. He liked Mary. He would let her talk and just nod away without really hearing anything she said. It was his stomach that had been bothering him. There was the usual chunk of red meat cooking slowly in the oven. Fiona was in the house, but she could never be relied upon to smell burning or even respond to it when she did, so we went home.

After we had eaten roast beef, followed by apple crumble and custard, Sandy took his Sunday papers into the sitting room, switched on the television and put his feet up on the battered brown leather object that his mum had always called 'the pouffe' and that had become even more distressed since Siggy had taken to sharpening his claws on it. There were holes in Sandy's socks at toe and heel. His mother would have been horrified. Come to think of it, Mary would have been horrified. But I don't do darning and, to give him his due, he never complained. He would have worn them till they disintegrated. Time for new socks, I thought. He was planning his customary extended nap. Fiona had picked at her meal and then headed up to her room. Suddenly restless, I changed into jeans and a fleece and went for a walk, taking the dog with me. I followed the road down from the farm, but instead of going to the village or even passing the cottage, I went along one of the network of narrow lanes that lead out towards the high hill country, inland from the village. The fields on either side had a gilded brilliancy about them that you only see on autumn afternoons and the hedgerows smelled of mushrooms and late, sweet honeysuckle. There were never many cars on this road, and Jess ran here and there, sniffing, peeing intermittently, and running back to herd me along. Then she suddenly pricked up her ears and rushed off over the brow of the hill with her tongue lolling out like a piece of boiled ham.

I shouted, 'Jess, here Jess!'

I whistled and clapped my hands, but there was no sign of her, so I laboured on up the slope. Over the hill, the road flattened out and there was Joe Napier, resting his elbows on a gate, with Jess leaning against his legs, grinning happily. She didn't move but thumped her tail on the ground and waited for me.

I hadn't been wrong. The gin at the party hadn't clouded my senses that much. There aren't many genuinely good looking people in the world when you think about it. Not many at all. But Joe was so tall and athletic that the sight of him – as much as the hill – took my breath away.

'You look very rural,' I said when I got up to him. He bent down and scratched the dog's ears.

'Me and my faithful hound.'

'Jess likes you.'

'Jess seems to like everyone.'

'That's true.'

'Are you just out for a walk?' he asked. 'Or are you tending to the cows or something.'

Did I look as if I was tending to the cows, I thought, irritably. 'No. I'm not tending to any cows,' I told him. 'You're always asking me that!'

'I'm scared of sounding ignorant.'

'Well there are cows, but they're fine. I don't have much to do with them, to be honest. Unless they get out. Which they do sometimes. And I just felt like a walk.'

'Where's Sandy?'

'Asleep in front of the telly.'

'I suppose he works hard.'

'He does. He works with the cows. And a lot of other things besides. I look after the hens and do a mountain of paperwork. It's kind of boring. Record keeping, spreadsheets. Computer stuff.'

'Can I walk with you?'

'Of course. There's a turn-off further along. We can double back to the farm that way.'

'Come on then. You can show me.'

He set off, walking briskly, and I followed him. Jess rushed back and forth, herding both of us together.

I didn't know what to say to him. I had been talking to him about all kinds of things, but just in my head. Now that I was with him, I could hear my voice shaking as I tried to make conversation. It wasn't like me. Well, it wasn't like my middle-aged self. More like the tongue-tied teenager I used to be. I thought I had got beyond such stupidity but perhaps you never do. Eventually, he was striding along at such a pace that he pulled ahead of me and Jess lengthened her run to include both of us, anxious to keep up with him, anxious not to leave me behind. Then Joe stopped, looked round and waited for me.

'I can't keep up with your long legs.'

'Sorry.'

All unexpectedly, he took my arm and pulled it through his own. My heart lurched at his proximity, but there was nothing remotely sexual in the gesture. Not on his part, anyway. Some people have a very definite physical presence and Joe was one of them. He smelled of toothpaste and some spicy cologne or aftershave.

'How's that?' he asked.

'Fine.' It was too. Familiar in a good way.

A big oak tree marked the turnoff and Jess crouched down and watered its roots enthusiastically.

'This is where we turn back.'

'Shame. Do we have to?'

'Well it's about a mile back to the farm by this road, so it'll take us a little while to get there.'

'Good. I was enjoying walking. It's great out here. So where does that road go?' He gestured back the way we had come. 'I mean if we carried on walking instead of turning down here, where would we finish up?'

In the distance, a horizon of ragged pines, black against the blue, showed where the hill country began.

'Nowhere much. There are farms along there. Sheep farms mostly. Forestry Roads. Eventually it joins one of the roads south.'

It was the road to Poldarrach, but I didn't tell him that. Not then, anyway.

'So what have you been doing with yourself, Joe?' I asked.

'I've started clearing out Louise's shed.'

'That'll be a job and a half.'

'You're not kidding.'

'Do you want any help?'

'I reckon you've got enough on your plate.'

'With tending to my cows? I'm sure I could find the time to give you a hand. And I could do a bit of gardening for you if you like. I looked after Louise's garden for her when she was ill. She was very proud of her garden and I expect it wants putting to bed for the winter.'

'Well that might be good. I'd have no idea.'

'I could do a bit for you.'

'You could tell me what needs doing. I'd need a supervisor, in case I destroyed something precious.'

A crow waddled along the edge of the ditch like a wee fat minister in a long black coat. Jess ran at it, and it flapped into the air at the last possible moment, protesting noisily. Undeterred, it flew over the fence and landed a couple of yards away, eyeing her. Jess put her front paws flat on the grass and yelped at it, but it ignored her, plodding along, listening to the ground, eavesdropping on lunch. Joe seemed fascinated by it.

'So have you found anything interesting? In the shed, I mean?'

'Most of it was complete junk. But then right at the back I found ...'

He hesitated.

'What?'

'I think I've found Vezio's Gallopers. Or what's left of them.'

I stopped and looked at him blankly. 'Whose what? What are you talking about?'

'Didn't Louise ever tell you about the Gallopers?'

'No. What are they?'

His smile made him look unexpectedly boyish. We walked on.

'I have to tell you a bit of my family history to explain.'

'Go on then.'

'You can come in and see them if you like. Mind you, there's not much to see at the moment. I need to get them out properly.'

'So what are they?'

'Well, you know that my grandmother ran off with Louise's Uncle Fred?'

'Yes. Louise showed me Freddy's picture one day and said he'd eloped with an Italian girl called Francesca. That was the word she used. Eloped. I had this vision of windows and ladders in the night. But I don't think it can have been quite like that, can it? They ran away together. So they went to Canada. Is that right?'

'Yeah, that's right. Their son was my dad, Alex. He was their only son as it turned out. After him they had girls. I have a lot of aunts.'

'So who was Vezio?'

'Ah well, that's kind of complicated but Vezio was Francesca's father. My great grandfather. Vezio Ciccarello, that was his name.'

He said the name properly, I noticed, relishing it. Making it sound Italian, not Canadian.

'I see.'

'And he, Vezio I mean, used to take a little travelling carousel round Scotland.'

'A carousel?'

I must have sounded sceptical because he stopped again and turned to face me.

'No, I don't mean a big thing. This was small. Three little fairground horses on a wheeled platform, and you could hitch it up to a real horse and take it from place to place. Kids would pay for rides on it.'

'Really?'

'He was supposed to have made it himself. He was born in Northern Italy some time in the late 1880s I think and he married my great grandmother, Anna, not sure exactly when, but they were as poor as church mice. That's the way the story goes in our family. He was apprenticed to a woodcarver. But for some reason they came over to Scotland, looking for a better way of life maybe.'

'A lot of Italians did.'

'Anyway, about 1920, my grandmother Francesca was born. She was born here in Scotland. And there was a brother called Mario. A younger brother. But their mother died while she was still quite a young woman, and poor Vezio was left with the two kids to look after. He used to take them round with him, the kids and the carousel together. It must have been a strange kind of life for them.'

Jess had been fossicking around in the ditch. She came pounding up and thrust her nose into his hand. He patted her absent mindedly.

We walked on, and again he threaded my arm through his. Jess trotted behind him, for all the world like his dog.

'I guess they were part of a travelling circus for a while. But finally he settled down and opened a kind of toy workshop some place near Glasgow. I think he made rocking horses, Noah's Ark toys, things like that. That's what dad thought. But he must have stored his carousel away when he finally stopped travelling.'

'And that was when Francesca met handsome Freddy?'

'Yes. She was about seventeen. He was twenty seven. A decade older. A dangerous older man.'

'Like me and Sandy.'

'What?'

'I only mean there's a gap between us. Sandy isn't dangerous.'

'I kind of wondered. You look younger than him.'

'I'm not that young. Go on then. I'm enjoying this.'

I was. There was something strangely exotic about it all and I wondered why Louise hadn't told me. But maybe she hadn't known the whole story.

'Well, Francesca used to go dancing. She wasn't supposed to – too young and too Italian – but she would go anyway. And she met Freddy at a dance hall. This was back in the 1930s, before the war. He was a good dancer they say. He had a real bad reputation but he fell for Francesca in a big way. I remember my dad telling me how Francesca had on some kind of fuzzy sweater. He danced with her and got white hairs all over his good dark suit. That was the story Francesca told my dad when he was just a kid.'

'You're supposed to put it in the fridge.'

'What?'

'Angora. To stop it shedding.'

He looked down at me and started laughing. 'You know that, do you?'

'I do. But not everybody had a fridge in those days.'

'Yeah well, they told Vezio they wanted to get married but he wouldn't hear of it. He thought Fred was too old for her. And definitely not good enough for her. He was a salesman of some kind. Brushes and brooms. Nothing romantic. So they ran off. Eloped as Louise said.'

'That was brave of her.'

'She was crazy about him. They managed to get to Canada, managed to stay there. This was only a few years before the war. Maybe Freddy thought they would be safer away from Britain. And where Vezio couldn't get at them.'

'Were they happy together?'

'You know, I think they were. My dad used to say Freddy never looked at another woman again. But we never knew what had happened to Vezio's Gallopers. We thought they were long gone. Firewood.'

'And you've found them? These horses? This carousel?'

'That's what it looks like. But you're right – why would it be here? I can't figure it at all. I've found the three horses. One of them's almost in bits, two in pretty good condition. They're like miniature fairground horses. It would be a ride for a small child. And there's a kind of turntable affair. All stored away carefully at the back of the shed.'

'But why would your great grandfather's roundabout be stored in *Louise's* shed?' I asked him, puzzled. 'She was only Freddy's niece, wasn't she? She wouldn't have had anything to do with this Vezio.'

'That's what I've been trying to figure. The two sides of the family barely even met. Vezio blamed all the Scottish relatives for the fact that Freddy had lured Francesca away. He was very ...' He hesitated.

'Italian?'

'Well, yeah. And unforgiving. But maybe he got friendly with Louise before he died. I can't understand it any other way.'

'When did he die?'

'I don't know that either. Francesca wrote to him from Canada. At least that's what my dad used to say. She wanted to keep in touch. And apparently her brother Mario wrote the odd letter back, but her dad never got in touch at all. Except once, when he added a note to a letter from Mario. But then, just when my grandmother thought she might have been forgiven, there was nothing. Silence. A lifetime's silence. But it was wartime, of course. They always wondered if something had happened during the war.'

'I suppose so. The Clydebank blitz, maybe? Something like that. Glasgow had a hard time of it.'

'And now the Gallopers turn up. Here. In this place. Strange, isn't it?'

'And now that Louise has gone we can't even ask her.'

'I thought she might have said something to you.'

'No. She told me nothing at all about them. I never even knew they were there.'

We had been walking arm in arm all the way down the hill, but when we got back to the farm road I casually pulled my arm out of his and moved away from him on the pretext of hooking up Jess's lead. People from the village walked up here sometimes on a Sunday afternoon: couples, old men with dogs. It would never do for anyone to see me walking alone and arm in arm with my new neighbour. Word would get about. They would put two and two together and make ten.

'Do you want to come in and see the carousel?' he asked, innocently.

'I'd love to, but I have to get home. Sandy'll be looking for his cup of tea. He'll already be wondering where I've been.'

'Will he mind?'

I wondered what Sandy might mind. Me being out all afternoon with our new neighbour? Me walking arm in arm with a good looking young man?

'No. Of course he won't mind. But I'd better get home now. I'll come down and see it later in the week if you like.'

'Sure. But I'm out training in the mornings. And I've got a match on Wednesday. Come down some afternoon.'

I realised that I hadn't even asked him about the hockey. But then he had been too full of the story of his miniature carousel.

'What are you going to do with it?'

'I'm not sure. Maybe I'll try and renovate it. If I can find the time.'

'How's your woodwork?'

'Oh pretty good. I'm good at stuff like that.'

He stood there for a moment, staring at me, his hands in his pockets.

'Are you sure you don't want a coffee, Helen?'

'I do want a coffee, but I have to go home.'

'OK.' He turned away. 'See you soon then.'

'Yes. See you soon.'

I headed up the hill to the farm with Jess in tow. It wasn't easy being sensible. It wasn't going to get any better, either.

– Chapter Six –

THE WEATHER BROKE that week. One evening, after it had rained and hailed by turns just about all day and the yard was a vast mud bath, Charlie McGowan came up to the farm to sit in the kitchen and have a beer with Sandy. I pottered about, filling the dishwasher, listening to them and occasionally joining in. The conversation progressed from Charlie's mother to her friend Maisie, and then to Joe. Betty and Maisie never stopped talking about him and Charlie was jealous of all this, as he saw it, unnecessary adulation. As a football fanatic, he was scathing about ice hockey as well.

'Have you ever seen it?' he asked. 'They don't stay on the ice for very long! Half of them are foreigners. Bunch of fannies if you ask me!' This was rich, coming from Charlie, whose beer belly made him look eight months pregnant, but I said nothing.

'I just want Helen to keep well in with him,' said Sandy, opening another can.

'Oh ? Why am I to keep well in with him?'

'Well – you know – if he does decide to sell the place eventually, we might get a look in before it goes on the market.'

'I suppose we might.'

'Why do you want the cottage?' asked Charlie.

'Extra accommodation. Bruce could do with somewhere closer to live for a start.'

'I could do with somewhere to live myself,' said Charlie. 'I could rent it off you if Bruce doesn't want it. I think my mammy's getting a bit sick of having me hanging about the place.'

'Surely not,' I said.

'Are you taking the piss?' he asked, good humouredly.

'Just a bit.'

'Well, you never know,' said Sandy. 'Depends how long he stays.' He gestured in the general direction of Louise's cottage. 'Helen talks to him, don't you, Helen?'

'When I see him, I do. But that isn't very often. I think he'll be here for the whole season at least. He'll be on a contract.'

'When does it finish?'

'April or May, I think. '

I hadn't known, but Fiona had told me. Some of her friends were regular hockey fans.

'He's very polite,' I ventured, since they seemed to expect more from me.

'That's what Canadians are supposed to be,' said Charlie. 'It's a running joke in the States, the politeness of their Canadian neighbours.'

'He is polite. He even called me ma'am a couple of times.'

'She'll start getting delusions of royalty,' said Sandy, with a little snigger.

'Hey, Helen,' said Charlie, remembering that he hadn't told a joke for at least five minutes. 'Did you hear the one about this guy who walks into a pub with a cat and an ostrich?'

Later on, when Charlie had left, when the dishwasher was whooshing away in the kitchen, and Sandy was settled in front of the telly, watching a quiz show of some kind, I said casually, 'I think I'll go and see if Joe wants some help with Louise's stuff. He's been turning out the garage. Found all kinds of things.'

'Well it was a bit of a glory hole!'

'I offered to give him a hand to sort it out.'

'That's right, hen. You go and butter him up.'

Sandy was eating a big bar of fruit and nut chocolate and didn't want to share it. Jess was sitting very upright beside him. For once she didn't want to come with me. I think the chocolate had something to do with it. She had her eyes fixed on Sandy and she was drooling but she wouldn't get any. Siggy was curled up in my chair, eyeing both of them contemptuously. He didn't like chocolate.

'Off you go, hen. And while you're at it, mention the cottage. Introduce the subject. Tactfully. Ask him what his plans are.'

'Very tactful.'

'Well. You know what I mean.'

'I'll see what I can do.'

I shut the sitting room door and ran upstairs, put on a pretty top and brushed my hair. There was a bottle of scent on my dressing table. Annie had given it to me last Christmas. Sandy never noticed perfume. Years of muck-spreading had blitzed his sense of smell. This one was called l'Heure Bleu and Annie had told me that it was a vintage scent, and hideously expensive, which was why she had only been able to afford to give me a tiny bottle of eau de toilette. It was richly, almost bitterly, spicy and sensuous, and I adored it. I felt different when I was wearing it. I sprayed it between my breasts and on my wrists, and then I wondered if I had overdone it, flapping my top to dissipate the smell. I went downstairs, got a bottle of white wine out of the fridge and wrapped it in a plastic carrier bag, slipping on my jacket. The rain had stopped but a chilly wind had sprung up.

I walked down the hill in a hurry. Otherwise nerves might have got the better of me. The clouds had lifted a little and over in the west the sun had emerged very low in the sky, all crimson and golden over the sea. I knocked on the front door and there was a pause. Then Joe opened it. He was looking harassed and he was brandishing a fish slice. But when he saw me, he smiled, sheepishly.

'Hi, Helen. Good to see you. Come in.'

'Are you cooking?' I headed automatically for the kitchen.

'Cooking? No ... oh!' He looked at the fish slice. 'This? No.'

'What are you doing then?'

'I was chasing a mouse.'

'With a fish slice?'

'It was in my kitchen bin. I lifted the lid and it came rushing out at me.'

'It came rushing out, did it?'

He started to laugh, self consciously. 'I don't like mice.'

Six foot three and built like a brick cludgie and scared of a mouse.

'They're not even house mice.'

'What are they then?'

'Just wee field mice. There's no harm in them. We always get one or two coming in at this time of year. Autumn and spring. Autumn when it gets cold, spring when they run out of food.'

'Are you sure?'

'Yes.'

'So how do I get rid of them?'

'I could lend you some traps.'

'Traps?' He looked appalled.

'Yes. Mousetraps. You know? You melt the cheese onto them, or better still a nice lump of chocolate. They love chocolate.'

I resisted the temptation to say that so did my husband.

'And then what?'

'Well, then they get beheaded.'

He winced.

'It's very quick. They don't know anything about it.'

'How do you know?'

'They're only mice, Joe. Plenty more where that one came from.'

'Jesus, I couldn't do that.'

'Well you'll just have to put up with the beasties then. You're in good company. Our local poet quite liked mice too.'

'Who's that?'

'Robert Burns. And it's no good trying to hit them with that!' I nodded at the fish-slice. 'That isn't very kind is it? You might stun it but that's all.'

'I guess so.'

'You can get humane traps if you want. Catch them and set them free in the morning.'

'Does that work?'

'No. They just come right back in again. Although I suppose you could set them free a long way away if you really wanted. Take them for a car trip first. But that's just as cruel, because they die of starvation anyway. Wait till you see the spiders we get here. They're more or less the same size as the mice.'

We were both laughing now. I said, 'I thought you'd be into all this hunting stuff, being Canadian and all.'

'No. I've never been into all that bullshit. Don't like guns either.'

'Softy.'

He was suddenly serious. 'I wouldn't say that.'

'Just where mice are concerned? '

'Yeah.'

'I could lend you Siggy. He was Louise's cat. Louise was never troubled with mice. I think they can smell when there's a cat about the place.'

'Maybe.' He had opened the fridge door. 'Want a beer?' The fridge seemed to be full of Molson and not much else. Maybe it was time Betty and Maisie came up with more packets of bacon and tins of cake.

'I brought you some wine.'

He raised his eyebrows in surprise. 'That was good of you.'

'I told Sandy I was coming to help you sort out Louise's stuff.'

He pulled a face. 'I wasn't planning on doing that tonight. Do you mind?'

'Not at all. Maybe I should go then.'

'No,' he said. 'Don't go. Stay. Stay and talk to me, now you're here. I could use some company.'

He picked up a couple of glasses and nodded at the bottle. 'Come through. Bring that with you.'

The sitting room, with windows at front and back, was flooded with evening light. It was as though someone had poured it in, and now it was trapped in there, turning all of Louise's shabby possessions into treasures. Joe put the glasses down on the coffee table, went over and pulled the curtains at the front of the house where the window looked towards the road. But he left the curtains at the back open, and the light continued to pour in, growing in intensity, filling the room. There was a fire burning in the grate and the whole space seemed warm and golden.

'Sit down, Helen.' He picked up the bottle and opened it. He had given up calling me ma'am.

I saw then that there really was something magical in the room. It was an old fairground horse, smaller than usual, with a fierce face, carved with rosettes and ribbons, and with the remains of flaky paint and gilding still visible here and there.

'Is this one of the Gallopers? Is this what you meant?'

'For sure. Isn't it great?'

'It's wonderful. God, Joe, I had no idea!'

'This is the best. The second one's not too bad. The third is more or less in bits.'

'Do you think you can restore them?'

'I can do something with them. Maybe even get the whole thing working again.'

'So you're into woodwork?'

'I like working with my hands. I like physical stuff. My dad restored an old American rocking horse when I was a little kid and I helped him. He always said the secret was not to do too much.'

He poured out a couple of glasses of wine and we sat down opposite each other with the angry horse between us. It was a strange creature, quite out of place in this familiar cottage.

'Have you had any more ideas as to why Vezio should have given it to Louise?'

'None at all. When did Louise and her husband marry?'

'Just after the war, I think. Malachi Marshall was older than she was. Have you found the photograph album?'

'Not yet. Do you know where it is?'

There was a set of bookshelves tucked into one corner of the room, and I went over to them. The books were all higgledy piggledy, just as Louise had left them, detective novels mostly: Agatha Christie, Ngaio Marsh, PD James and a couple of Ian Rankins and Val McDermids I had bought for her when she was growing more frail and couldn't get into town. 'I like a good murder mystery,' she had said. There was an atlas and a heap of old Reader's Digests, and a row of book club Dickens, bound in mock green leather with gold tooling on the covers. There was the usual jumble of catalogues and leaflets, recipes and out-of-date timetables, just the kind of things that make you sad when somebody dies and you come across them afterwards. I had never managed to bring myself to clear them all out. Now I leafed through them.

'Here we are.'

Tucked in at the bottom of the heap was a slender photograph album made of some kind of crinkly brown paper. I brought it over and Joe came and sat on the couch beside me so that we could look at it together.

Inside were snapshots neatly arranged in little 'corners'. But there was a whole heap of miscellaneous photographs, unidentified groups and single studio portraits. They were undated and undatable except perhaps by the style of people's clothes. There was a wedding picture of Louise and her husband, both of them wearing badly fitting suits. Malachi looked very grim and worried, though Louise's prettiness shone through the ugly wartime 'costume'. She had been like a small flower at that time. And very young. It brought a lump to my throat. There were pictures of anonymous babies, tiny snapshots of pleasure boats and seaside excursions, fishing trips and men on bicycles. There was one I had never seen before, of Louise and Lottie as little girls, perched on a couple of beach donkeys, and they were wearing droopy sailor suits with bloomers.

'They must have been hell to wear,' I remarked.

'Yeah. Can you imagine if you ever got them wet?' Joe reached over and sifted through the photos until at last he seized on the picture of Fred. 'Here he is. My grandfather, Freddy. There's a copy of this at home. Mom keeps all the photos in a big wooden box. We get them out when the family's all together.'

'Is your dad still alive, Joe?'

'No. Dad died very young. I was only thirteen. But my mom's still going strong.'

'Do you have brothers and sisters?'

'One sister. Frankie. She's two years younger than me.'

'Was she named after your grandmother?'

'Sure.'

He was sifting through the pictures again, absorbed in them. 'Wow!' he said, suddenly, and pulled a photograph out of the pile. 'Look at this!'

I recognised it immediately. It was the young man with curly black hair. He was standing in a garden. Grinning at the camera. Smoking a cigarette.

'Isn't he beautiful? I've often wondered who he was.'

'I've seen that one before and I know who he is,' said Joe. 'That's my grandmother's brother. That's my great uncle Mario. Good looking guy, wasn't he?'

He looked angelic; like something from an old Italian painting, not soft angelic but hard and a bit dangerous. I stared at the picture. He had a look of Joe, though Joe was much taller and altogether broader and his hair wasn't curly. It was straight and thick, like the dark pelt of some animal. Mario had been slighter and more fragile with black curls. But they had the same Roman nose, the same regular features. The same smile.

'Vezio's son?'

'That's right.'

'So what became of him?'

'I told you. We don't know. He wrote to Francesca from Scotland for a while, and we have this picture, or something very like it, at home. So he must have sent it. And then everything went quiet. Dad kept meaning to try to trace them for her but he never got round to it. Didn't Louise say anything about this picture?'

'No. Not really.'

She had said something. She had said, 'Never settle for second best.'

But I didn't tell him that. It didn't seem particularly relevant.

'Maybe I should do something about that as well. While I'm here,' said Joe. 'Try to find out more about our family history. My sister's very interested. Does some stuff online. But it's mostly mom's side she's looked at so far.'

'What are your plans?' I asked, casually. 'For next year, I mean.'

He took a long drink of wine. 'I'll be here for the whole season. Till April at least. After that I don't know.'

He never seemed to want to talk about 'back home' very much. Or when he did, he talked about the past, his mother and sister, his early childhood. And his hockey, but only in the most general terms. Snippets of information. But you would have had to be blind and deaf not to see that there was something he was avoiding. I don't mean he was being particularly secretive. It was just that you felt he was avoiding something in his own mind and consequently in his conversation. There was something he skirted round all the time, pausing, thinking before he spoke. I found myself wondering whether he was married, whether there was a girlfriend (and looking at him I wondered how there could not be a girlfriend somewhere in the background, maybe more than one, waiting anxiously for letters or phonecalls) and why he had decided to come to Scotland and stay for so long. Maybe he needed the work. I wondered what professional hockey players got paid. I didn't know whether it was lucrative or not but I realised that at the higher levels is must be.

He gathered the photos up and slipped them back into the album. 'I'll take these home with me when I go. My mom might recognise some of them. Where would I go to try to find out more about my family, Helen?'

'There's the record office in Edinburgh, I suppose. I think you can go there and look things up and get copies of certificates. But you could probably do it all online, even from Canada. We have a computer up at the farm. You can come and use that if you like. There's a site called Scotland's People. It can get a bit expensive though.'

'I think I'd rather go to Edinburgh. Hey, maybe you could come with me. Show me the city.'

'Maybe I could.'

'Would Sandy be able to spare you?'

'From seeing to all those cows? I expect so.'

It was a casual invitation. He clearly liked my company, but that was all. I could see that. And maybe he was a little lonely here. Or would be until he made more friends. But the thought of going to Edinburgh with him gave me a kick of excitement. I hadn't been to the city for years. Truth to tell I had avoided it. It was too painful to go back to the place that had seemed like a promised land to me. I had been only once, with Annie and the kids on a village trip, and it had been extraordinarily bitter for me. To my surprise, all kinds of buried sensations of disappointment and resentment had come bubbling to the surface. I could hardly bear it. Now, if I wanted to go Christmas shopping or to visit a theatre or a museum, I went to Glasgow. The shopping was better there anyway. But I had an inkling that it might be different if I went with Joe.

'And meanwhile, I'll do some work on Vezio's Gallopers. When I have any spare time.'

The sun had set and a bank of clouds was rolling in from the sea. Soon it would be dark. Joe got up and switched on the lamps, pulling the curtains across, shutting out the night. Then he bent down and hauled a big bag out from where it had been stashed behind the couch.

'Sorry about this,' he said. 'It stinks. I should have moved it earlier.'

I had wondered about the faint smell of stale sweat that hung about the room. 'What is it?'

'Hockey kit.' He shoved it in a cupboard. 'I don't even smell it any more but it's never very fresh. You can only wash so much of it. The rest of it just simmers away, stinking. The gloves are the worst. You'd know about it if I opened the bag!'

'Why is there so much of it?' I asked, curiously. The bag seemed enormous.

'Padding. We wear a lot of padding. Shoulder, shin, elbow pads. Shorts. Other kinds of protection too.' His smile was full of mischief, suddenly. 'I'll show you some day, if you like!'

'We'll have to come and see you play. It's nice having a famous neighbour.'

'I'm not exactly that.'

'The local paper seems to think you are.'

'That's because I'm an ex NHL fish in a very small pond.'

'What's NHL?'

He looked amazed at the depths of my ignorance. 'National Hockey League.'

'Oh.'

'You don't know very much about the game, do you?'

'Almost nothing.'

'I'll get you some tickets.'

'I don't mind paying.'

'No, but Sandy might.'

'I don't know the first thing about hockey. Do women go?'

'Honey, everyone goes. Little kids, babies, grannies. Even here everyone goes – out of those that do go, I mean.'

'I expect Fiona would enjoy it.'

'She would. You too. It's fast,' he said. 'There's nothing else like it. Playing ... watching ... Even at this level, it's the best game in the world. Best thing in my life really, wherever I play. I love it. You'll enjoy it too, Helen.'

I finished my wine. 'I think I'll have to get back to the farm,' I said, reluctantly.

'Do you have to?'

'I think I should.'

The wine had gone to my head. Our eyes met and then we both looked away, faintly embarrassed all of a sudden.

'Sandy'll be coming to see where I am.'

'You'd better go then.'

I was so out of practice with this. Was I fooling myself? Was his apparent interest in me genuine? Or was he just being polite and a little flirtatious? Bored, maybe. Seeing just how far he could go. How far I might go.

'Do you want me to walk you back up the road?' he asked, courteous as ever.

'No. I'll be fine. It's only a few hundred yards.'

'But it's dark.'

'I know it like the back of my hand, Joe.'

Still, he saw me to the gate. At the bend in the road I turned back and saw him standing there, silhouetted against the light from the open door. He raised his hand and I waved back.

Sandy was still watching television with Jess asleep at his feet and Siggy curled up beside him.

'Hello, hen,' he said, eyes fixed on the screen. 'Did you mention the cottage to him?'

'Only in a roundabout way.'

'Oh well. It's a start.'

– Chapter Seven –

I FOUND MYSELF AT the ice rink the following Saturday afternoon. I was on taxi duty for Fiona and a couple of her friends; they had been planning this outing all week. There were three of them: Fiona, Lizzie who lived in a converted farmhouse on the other side of the village and was mad about horses and a girl from the new houses called Shona. Lizzie was very slender and pretty with long hair. She was always combing it out like a mermaid. Clever too. Shona was one of the phone box crowd, a big, bony girl who wore very short skirts that showed off her knobbly knees. She looked, as my mother would have said, as if someone had cut her hair with a knife and fork. She was, I thought with a great deal of sympathy, the plain friend; the one who would make Fiona look good. Lizzie didn't need any help to look good. I liked Shona. She was always chatty, unlike some of the other kids who would just hang their heads and hunch their shoulders and say as little as possible. She had personality. I hoped that, like the ugly duckling, she would soon turn into a swan. Perhaps better than that, she would become a sleek and grown-up duck.

They piled into the car, all three of them in the back so that they could discuss the relative merits of passing males. I felt even more like a taxi driver than usual. Shona had swapped her usual short skirts for a pair of shorts and tights and yes, her bum did look big in them, but she was clearly hoping for the best and the benefits of Lycra. I was wearing my biggest, warmest sweater. It was always chilly in the rink.

Sometimes Annie would come but none of her kids liked skating, so I was usually on my own. I would take a book or a magazine and make frequent visits to the coffee machine or the loo to get warm. I didn't skate these days. I had never been very good at it, even as a kid. When Fiona was little I had tried it again, because Sandy wouldn't take her and she wanted to learn. But I had struggled around and fallen on my backside several times and hadn't been able to get up, which was embarrassing. The stewards, who all looked about fourteen, had had to skate over and help me. Eventually we had paid for a course of lessons for Fiona, and she was a competent skater now, better than I had ever been.

The new rink was a cheerful place with a big ice pad. All the little girls wanted to do figure skating, so there were lots of classes. The teachers were always desperate for boys to join but there was only ever one boy for every dozen girls. The boys would learn to skate to the point where the teacher wanted them to do the elegant one-legged bit, and then they would turn all macho and go and play junior ice hockey.

The figure skaters were just finishing a practice session as we arrived, and a swarm of little girls rushed off, wearing pretty white skates, tan tights and bright bunchy skirts. Fiona and her friends took their skates into the changing room, struggling to find space among the twittering infants, and I went out and bought myself a polystyrene cup of coffee and found myself a seat. I took out my book and prepared to read. But there were some skaters already on the ice and I watched them while I sipped at the bitter brown liquid.

Whoever was choosing the music was fond of Cher and the Suga-babes and Paloma Faith and that was fine by me. The ice pad wasn't busy yet, though more people were arriving all the time. There were a few beginners, staggering round, clutching the barriers like survivors from a shipwreck, and there were tiny kids in bright ice hockey shirts, New York Rangers, Toronto Maple Leafs, Chicago Blackhawks, and a number of Kestrels shirts too. They went zipping from end to end, swinging their arms from side to side in imitation of their hockey heroes. Fiona and her friends came out onto the ice just as Cher began to sing Heart of Stone and I noticed the man who was skating expertly in time to the music in the middle of the rink.

It was Joe Napier.

He wasn't dancing. You couldn't really call it dancing. It was much more casual than that. He was wearing a white fleece and narrow blue jeans and he had his hands tucked into his pockets which in itself was impressive, because if I try to do that I immediately fall over. He was just moving about, quickly and smoothly in time to the music and he was

– I'm trying to remember how it impressed me at the time – he was using the edges of the blades with great skill. He would stop suddenly, turn and go backwards, and then just as suddenly go forwards again. When he stopped like that you could hear the swish as the blades dug in and see a little spray of snow. It was obvious that he was just doing it for the hell of it; that he was relaxed, fluid, like a fish in water. He looked completely right. This was where he was supposed to be. It was the very sexiest thing I have ever seen in my life.

The girls had seen him too. Fiona skated up to the barrier. Her cheeks were pink and not just from the cold.

'Mum. Mum!' she hissed. 'Look who's over there!'

'I can see him.'

'Do you think we should go and speak to him?'

'Well, you could say hello.'

At that moment, Joe skated up behind her and put one hand on her shoulder and then saluted me over her head. 'Hi Fiona. Hello there, Helen.'

The three girls clustered round him, congratulating him on his skating, basking in the reflected glory of knowing such a hero. Other people had been watching him with admiration or envy, whispering his name. He talked to them for a few minutes, joking with them, making them laugh. I was just going to return to my cooling coffee when the girls set off round the rink, giggling as they went. But Joe came off the ice and sat down beside me. Which meant that people started looking at me too and that made me uncomfortable. I could feel the flush rising from my chest to my cheeks. He bent down and began to retie his skates, tugging energetically at the laces.

'They get loose,' he said.

'Don't you have a game this weekend?'

'Tomorrow. Home game.'

'You skate like an angel.'

'Didn't know they did.'

'What?'

'Skate.'

'Well, if they do, that's the way they're going to do it.'

'Thanks.' He sat upright but didn't stand up. He wasn't looking at me. He was staring into the distance, jiggling his knee up and down, his thoughts elsewhere.

'How long have you been playing hockey?' I asked.

He focused on me with a jolt. 'Since I could skate. Since I could walk. The stick was bigger than I was and even then it was cut down from my cousin's. But I started playing properly when I was five.'

'No wonder you're so good then.'

'And I worked my way up. I was going right to the top. Believe me. Nothing was going to stop me.'

I was puzzled. Ignorant as I was, even I could see that the really big hockey money, huge money sometimes, was to be made on the other side of the Atlantic. Not here in Britain. Not in this league. True, Canadian and American players came here to make a bit of cash and maybe to see Europe at the end of their careers. And yet Joe was telling me he had been successful back home.

'Oh I've made a fair bit of money out of it,' he said. 'For a limited time. But things didn't work out. The same week I heard I'd got the cottage, I was talking to the Kestrels' coach. He wanted me. He thought he couldn't afford me. But I wanted to come.'

'How long can you do it for? I mean what age do people usually stop?'

'Few more years maybe. You kind of run out of steam. Or your body does. That's the problem. The knees go. Coaching's always an option.'

'You don't look as if your knees have gone.'

'No. Maybe not. But I can feel them. I can feel them most of the time and that's not a good sign.'

'You're still young, Joe, aren't you?'

'Maybe I'm not young enough. I'm thirty one.'

'You're a lot younger than me, anyway.'

Nine years, I thought. Not an impossible gap, but a gap all the same. And then I thought, what was I thinking of? What did it matter? I gave myself a little shake.

He stood up, looming over me, even taller in his skates. 'Why aren't you skating, Helen?'

'Me? Oh I don't skate.'

'Well, you should.'

'I used to, a bit. But I've forgotten how.'

'Nobody forgets how. It's like riding a bike.'

'Well I did. Besides, Fiona wouldn't like it.'

'What do you mean, Fiona wouldn't like it?'

'It would embarrass her.'

'Who cares?'

'I do. I care.'

'Well I don't. Come on,' he said briskly. 'Skate with me.'

'How can I? I don't have skates.'

'Hire them.'

'No. I can't.'

'What size shoes do you take?'

'Six. But I can't.'

He ignored me. Instead he clamped on his skate guards and headed out towards the Skate Hire. He came back some time later, carrying a pair of slightly battered blue skates.

'These will do. They're not great, but I had them sharpen them for you.' He ran his finger over the blades. 'Not too much, though,' he said. 'These should be just right.'

'Joe, I can't.'

'Of course you can. Just do it.'

I could see Fiona on the other side of the ice, casting anxious glances in my direction. I could read her mind. 'Don't do it, mum,' she was thinking. 'Please don't do it.'

He knelt down and started to undo the laces on my old trainers. This was too intimate. My heart wouldn't stand the strain. I looked dizzily at the top of his head as he bent over my foot, the soft, almost furry hair, the white scalp beneath. I swear I almost reached out to touch it. The impulse was so strong. So foolish. I caught my breath.

As though suddenly aware of my feelings – perhaps I had communicated them – he looked up at me, with a grave, open stare.

'I think you should let me do that,' I whispered.

'All right.' He sat back on his heels, spread his hands, let me take off my trainers and put the skates on myself.

'I don't want to skate,' I said, even while I was fumbling with the long laces.

'Here. Let me.' He bent down again and began to do them up. 'People here never tie them tight enough. You see all these little kids wobbling around with shaky ankles. No wonder they can't skate.'

'I think you've cut off all circulation to my feet.'

'They'll be fine. They'll loosen up as soon as you get on the ice.'

'I'll fall over as soon as I get on the ice.'

'No you won't. I won't let you.'

I had forgotten how difficult it was, like setting foot in an alien environment. And it was worse because Fiona was staring at me. No, more than that, she was glaring at me from the other end of the rink. I could feel it all the way down the ice. And then I stopped caring about Fiona because the feet slid from under me and I fell flat on my backside. And it was sore.

Joe bent down and pulled me into a sitting and then into a wobbly standing position.

'Oh, Helen!' He tucked my arm under his and I could feel him laughing all the way down his arm. 'I'm sorry. Are you OK?'

'Fine. Bruised my bum and my dignity, but I'm fine.'

My cheeks were flaming but he didn't seem to care.

'You just have to get your confidence back.'

'It's easy for you to say. You don't fall down.'

'But I do fall down. Hockey players fall all the time. It's what we do. I'm a D-man Helen. Sometimes it's the only way to stop the puck. Falling doesn't matter as long as you get back up again.'

'What's a D-man?'

'I play in defence.' He grinned. 'Hockey 101,' he said. 'It's my job to stop the other team from scoring.'

'I thought the goalie did that.'

'Yeah, well he does. But we're supposed to stop the puck before it gets to him. We don't always manage it though.'

'Yes, but you're well padded when you do it. You wear all that kit don't you?'

'Well, that's true.'

'Doesn't it take forever to get dressed?'

'You get used to it. It goes on in layers. Come on. Try again.'

He was so sure of himself on the ice. That was what was good about him. It was his space, and he could work magic in it. I staggered about with him for a bit, and he said, 'Look, you're trying to slide your feet forward, but that's not the way to do it. You have to push the ice away from you instead. Watch.'

He left me clutching at the barrier and skated away from me in a straight line, exaggerating the push and then came back to me, doing crossovers in an elegant semi-circle.

'If you were a kid, I'd give you a chair to push. That's what we do back home. One of those chairs with metal runners.'

'That would be good.'

'I'll have to do instead. Take my arm again.'

I took his arm, clutching it like a drowning woman.

'Now, don't do anything for the moment. Just relax and try to keep your skates reasonably straight and let me do all the work.'

He skated off gently and took me with him. My knees locked and I almost fell over again, my other arm flailing. But he held me up easily. He was a full head taller than me. 'Relax. I can feel you all tensed up through your arm. No wonder you keep falling over.'

'I can't help it.'

'You can. You have to learn to trust me. Drop your shoulders. No, *drop* them.'

I relaxed slightly.

'Let me do it,' he said. 'I can do it for you.'

'I know.'

'Don't grit your teeth like that.' He patted my hand, the one that was clutching convulsively at his arm. And then he said, in a low voice, 'For God's sake, Helen. You're not gonna get hurt. Let yourself go, why don't you? Just let go.'

And I did it. I let go, not of him, but of myself. I relaxed and trusted him to do the work for me. I let him take me where he wanted. They were playing Cher again. This time it was Jesse James. He skated quite slowly and he took me with him. I began to breathe properly. My knees relaxed. We went round like that several times. Fiona and her pals were leaning against the barrier, watching. Fiona was looking daggers but Shona was laughing, in a good way. She waved as we passed and Fiona grabbed at her arm, shaking her head. But I didn't care.

'We're embarrassing your daughter,' said Joe.

'I know.'

'She'll survive.'

'I know.'

On the third or fourth circuit, I don't know which because I'd lost count by then, he said, 'Now, you have a try. Move your legs. Push. Push the ice away.'

'I don't know if I can.'

'Don't worry. I won't let go of you. I won't let you fall again. Just push the ice away.'

And I did. And it was easy. By the time we were going round again, I had begun to get the hang of it. I was skating. It felt magical. I should have let go of him and tried it by myself. I should have done that. It would have been the sensible thing to do, but I didn't. And he didn't seem in any hurry to let me go either. Instead he put his hand over mine where it was linked through his arm. We just skated around together and we didn't even say very much. Eventually, because I felt I had to, I said, 'Don't you want to go and practise or something?'

'No.' He squeezed my hand. 'No. I'm fine. I don't need to practise. This is just for fun. You quit worrying about me and worry about yourself for a change, Helen.'

'I just thought ...'

'Don't think. Just do it. Are you enjoying this?'

'Yes. It's fantastic. I don't know when I've enjoyed anything so much.'

'Well then. Fiona will get over it.'

And we skated.

Later, we came off and drank hot chocolate and watched the other skaters go by. Fiona and Lizzie were trying to show off. Shona couldn't skate well enough to show off, but she was up for anything and didn't seem to mind if she fell over.

A couple of boys came sliding over, carrying hockey magazines.

'Joe! Will you sign these, Joe?' they asked, nudging each other, giggling. He didn't have a pen, but I found one in my bag. That started something and a whole group of kids beset him. Patiently he signed his name on everything from paper napkins to the back of a young girl's hand.

'What happens when you want to wash it off?' he asked her.

'I won't wash it!' She went back on the ice, looking over her shoulder at him. And at me.

'Do you want to come back on?' he said, at last.

'I do but I don't think my legs will carry me.'

'You're not used to it. Maybe you should sit this one out. Otherwise you won't be able to move in the morning.'

'I think you might be right.'

'We can come back again another time.'

'Can we?'

'Sure,' he said. 'Sure we can.'

'Why don't you go back on?' I said.

'Do you want me to?'

'I'd like to see you skate again.'

There was a pause. He squashed his empty cup flat. Then he got up and went back onto the ice, tossing the cup into the bin as he left.

In the control box, someone had put on Too Lost In You, and lowered the lights just a little. It was strange. Other people were still skating, but he made them look clumsy. He skated gently and deftly around them and among them, not bothering them at all, making patterns on the ice in time to the music. He skated like a dream. He was showing off now. I knew fine he was showing off for me and everyone else, unable to resist the temptation of that music and those sexy words. After a while, people went to the side, just so they could watch him. The stewards stood with their arms folded, defensive and a bit jealous. Players didn't usually do this. They normally kept themselves to themselves. But here was Joe, putting on a display for free. It wasn't done.

And what Joe was doing, it wasn't exactly dancing, but it was rhythmic and fluid and sometimes it was acrobatic. A man sitting behind me tapped me on the shoulder and said, 'Now you know why they call him Sky Napier. Good, isn't he?' And I nodded but he was more than good. He was utterly and completely beautiful out there on the ice. The music was part of the magic, sensual and insistent. He seemed like nothing but movement. I could have watched him all day. A creature of ice and fire. Bright and enticing.

When the song finished he came off to scattered applause which he acknowledged with a little grin and a bow and a handclap of his own. He said he had to be getting back to the village. The girls were ready to leave as well. I had promised them fried chicken on the way home.

'Why didn't you ask him to come for something to eat?' asked Shona, who was completely smitten.

'I think he had things to do.'

I tried to visualise myself sitting with Joe around a family sized bucket of chicken pieces, but my imagination failed me. Besides, I wouldn't have been able to eat anything at all.

'Mu-u-um' said Fiona, stretching the word out so that it had lots of exasperated syllables. 'How could you?'

'It was very nice of him,' I said. 'Nice of him to give me a lesson.'

'I think you did great,' said Shona. 'I think it was very brave of you.'

'Wicked,' echoed Lizzie.

'But skating with him like that, and everyone watching. I thought I was going to die.' Still, Fiona had modified her disapproval slightly. Now she was looking at me with a sort of grudging admiration. 'Mind you. You did it. I can't believe you really did it.' She grinned at me suddenly.

'I don't think anyone even noticed me. Except you lot of course. They were probably too busy watching Joe.'

'My mum would never do anything like that,' said Shona, wistfully.

'You're lucky,' said Fiona, her small white teeth tearing into her third piece of chicken. But she was still smiling, shaking her head at me across the plastic table top. 'Just don't do it again, mum. Please? Promise me you'll never embarrass me like that ever again!'

– Chapter Eight –

Ididn't see much of Annie until we went to our line dancing class the following week. When we stopped for a water break, we sat down together on the floor and leaned against the wall.

'I've been hearing all sorts of things about you,' said Annie, nudging me in the ribs.

'What have you been hearing?' I could feel myself blushing again.

'Just that you've been seen skating with a certain sexy hockey player.'

'Word certainly gets about.'

'Of course word gets about. You know what this place is like.'

'Who told you?'

'I think Lizzie must have told Dean. She said he was giving you skating lessons. And she said Fiona was absolutely mortified.'

'She was a bit. And it was only one lesson. Hardly even that.'

'I expect she was jealous. And maybe surprised at you.'

'She was that all right.' Surprised and also proud of me in a strange way, though she didn't want to admit it. 'She fancies him like mad. The attraction of the older man.'

'Yes. Or the younger man.'

'Oh shut up, Annie. It was just a bit of fun.' I drank my water and mopped my sweaty forehead with a crumpled tissue. I suddenly felt exhausted. I could have crawled home and got straight into bed.

'Was it?'

'Don't look at me like that. You know what I mean. He's a nice guy and a good teacher.'

'I'll bet he is. He certainly looks fit.'

'He is fit.'

'He's got a lovely bum.'

'I haven't looked at his bum!'

'Of course you have. Nice well developed thighs too. Skater's thighs. You should ask him to come to the line dancing.'

'Oh God, Annie. Can you see him prancing about with us?'

'Not really, no. But he'd be a nice addition. We could do with some men,' she said wistfully. 'Especially men like that.'

Sharon was preparing to start the class again. The music blared out.

'Pub afterwards?' asked Annie, putting her water bottle back into her bag.

I stood up and pulled down my baggy tee-shirt to cover my own bum. I didn't feel it was quite as lovely as Joe's. 'Yes. Why not?'

We danced.

There were so many of us in the pub, all of us claiming to be replacing lost fluids, although line dancing wasn't quite the same as aerobics, that we took up a couple of tables and, inevitably, we started talking about the Harvest Fair. It was held about this time each year and it was a major fundraising event for the village school and the church. They always split the proceeds between them. Sandy, as a church elder, had been involved in planning it for weeks, and one of our spare rooms was full of the junk that people had donated to the bric-à-brac stall. I was always given the task of collecting it with Annie and with Mary, who liked to get involved as well. It was one of those events where people recycled all their unwanted possessions and not just junk either. There were undesirable raffle prizes: table mats with hideously cute kittens on them or boxes of crumbling bath cubes and bottles of sinister and unknown origin that had been doing the rounds for years. You could still see the marks from previous tickets that had been taped to them. They all came back to the Harvest Fair every year like homing pigeons.

'You should ask your friend Joe to give you some stuff for the bric-à-brac,' said Mandy, going up to buy more drinks. We had a kitty in the middle of the table. When it was finished we would go home. 'I'll bet there's a fair amount of junk up in that cottage.'

Annie nudged me. I trod on her foot, heavily. She said 'Ouch' and sniggered. I wished she wouldn't do it. It was beginning to get on my nerves.

'There's a load of stuff in the shed,' I said. 'I'll see if he wants to give us anything. But I think he's going to have to hire a skip if he really wants to clear it out.'

'That bad?'

'The house is fine. But the shed's full of junk. Louise was a bit of a hoarder on the quiet.'

For some reason, I didn't tell them about Vezio's Gallopers. In fact I didn't really want to tell them anything about Joe. On the other hand there was a part of me that wanted them to go on talking about him so that I could listen. It was inadvisable, but I couldn't help it.

'Want me to come?' asked Annie, nudging me again.

'No thanks. I can manage. I'll bring it down with the other stuff in the pick-up.'

'And I expect he'll help you.'

'Well I think he's hot and I don't care who knows it!' said Mandy, plonking my glass of Pinot Grigio in front of me.

'Helen thinks he's lovely too, don't you?' said Annie.

The only thing that made it all right was that everyone thought it was a big joke, even Annie.

'Who's this?' asked Sharon. She lived a few miles outside the village and shopped in the nearby town. She hadn't met Joe yet.

'Helen's new neighbour,' said Mandy. 'Louise Marshall's ... what? Nephew?'

'Cousin of some sort.'

'Oh yes, I've heard about him,' said Sharon. 'He's the Canadian hockey player who's living in the cottage near your farm, isn't he? The kids all think he's cool as well.' She was a PE teacher at the local secondary school. She was very popular and I think the kids told her more than they ever told their parents.

'He is,' said Mandy 'without a doubt, the most attractive man I have ever seen. And that includes Les.'

'Don't let Les hear you say that!' said Annie.

'He wouldn't mind. He knows. I've told him.'

'So what is it about this hunk that's so wonderful?' asked Sharon.

'He danced with me at Charlie's party and I thought I was going to pass out,' said Mandy. 'It's something to do with how fit he is. That and the accent. The accent's so sexy. And he's friendly. Not full of himself, you know? In fact I think he's quite shy.'

'And Helen lives next door to this paragon. Lucky Helen.' Annie winked at me.

'But I don't see him all that often. I can't watch him from my windows or anything.'

'What a thought!' Mandy's eyes were gleaming.

'No, but she went skating with him!' said Annie.

Everyone was looking at me now. 'I didn't go skating with him. I was at the rink with Fiona and her pals.'

'And he skated with you?'

'He persuaded me to come onto the ice. I didn't really want to, but he insisted.'

Mandy pursed her lips and blew out a long sighing breath. 'Lucky old you.'

'Well, it was very nice. He's a really nice guy. But I was only on the ice for a little while.'

'What does Sandy think to all this?'

I had no idea what he thought about it, because we hadn't really talked about it. Fiona had moaned about it, and Sandy had said, 'Why shouldn't your mum go skating if she wants to? I don't see the problem,' and that had been that.

'So what is this hunk really like?' asked Sharon.

'Well?' Annie looked at me. 'What is he like Helen? You know him better than any of us.'

'I hardly know the first thing about him. I think Mandy's right. He is quite shy. He doesn't say much about himself, you know. Well, not to me anyway.'

'Which you deeply regret!'

'I think he gets fed up all by himself in that cottage. Maisie and Betty keep bringing him food parcels.'

'Don't think he'll be on his own long,' said Annie.

'Helen's giving you the wrong impression,' said Mandy. 'He's tall. Solid. Dark hair. Nice face. White teeth. When he smiles. Which isn't often.'

'They might not be his own teeth,' I observed. 'He plays ice hockey, remember. He might have lost them years ago. They might be dentures for all you know.'

Actually I found out later that he had indeed lost one front tooth, but they weren't dentures; just some expensive bridgework that he took care to protect with a gum shield afterwards.

Still, that made them all laugh, spluttering into their wine.

'I don't care about his teeth,' said Mandy. 'I still think he's lovely.'

'I know what we'll do,' said Annie who had been organising publicity for the fair, putting up posters, drumming up business.

'What?'

'We'll ask him to open the fair. Inspirational or what?'

It was usually the minister's wife or Lady Darrach who performed this important function. They took turns. Nobody had been asked yet but they had probably made assumptions.

'I'd rather see a hockey hunk than Lady D any day,' said Mandy.

'We'll get a photographer out. Get some press coverage. That ought to bring in a few folk.' Annie nudged me. 'Do you think he'd do it?'

'I don't see why not. I'll ask him if you like.'

'That's all right, ' said Annie, thoughtfully. 'I'll give him a ring later on. Don't see why you should have all the fun.'

'Brilliant,' said Sharon. 'Just brilliant.' She was running the raffle. 'Point him in my direction, and I'll tell you what I think.'

On Friday afternoon I went down and helped Joe to pile a load of white elephants (the expression amused him) into the pick-up: old gardening tools, Pyrex bowls, kitchen utensils that had seen better days, wobbly fire tongs and a heap of jigsaw puzzles that had kept Louise occupied during her final illness. I didn't suppose Joe would care to spend his winter evenings doing jigsaws.

'How were you after the skating?' he asked, cheerfully.

'I got a lot of flak from my daughter. And my friends.'

'They're just jealous.'

'Yes, well they all fancy you.'

He actually blushed. 'I didn't mean that!'

'Didn't you?'

'No. I meant it was very brave of you to give it a try. Come on. Let's get this stuff down to the village.'

A bunch of dads and grandads had been working at the hall the night before, moving furniture and putting up trestle tables. On Saturday morning, Annie and Mary and I rushed about unpacking and pricing. We always got antique dealers coming out from the town to pounce on bargains, so we had to have our wits about us. Anything that looked as if it might be worth something had to be priced up. Annie agreed with me about this, but Mary always worked to her own peculiar system. Perversely, she had priced a crappy little ashtray with a picture of a winsome Scottie dog at three pounds, while she was planning to sell a lovely old landscape in oils for a pound.

'Mary, you can't do that,' said Annie, eyeing the man in smart jeans and an expensive jacket, who was lurking beside the painting, waiting for Joe to declare the fair open. 'It's worth an awful lot more than that'

'Why?' asked Mary indignantly. 'It's very dirty. My mother in law left it. I thought I'd have a good clear-out. It almost went in the skip.'

'Annie's right,' I said. 'It should be a tenner at least and it's much too cheap at that.' I nodded surreptitiously in the dealer's direction.

'I'll have it myself.' Annie got out her purse.

'You can't do that,' said Mary. 'You're not supposed to do that.'

'Why ever not? So long as the school and the church get the money, what does it matter? I'll put in fifteen pounds. OK?'

Mary put the notes in her money belt, grumbling. Annie took the painting and stowed it under the table with her bag and coat. The dealer muttered under his breath and transferred his attention to a plate with a picture of Vesuvius on it. I had priced it at five pounds. It just looked like the kind of thing someone might collect. The dealer obviously thought so too because later on he bought it, even at a fiver, which made me wonder if it wasn't worth more. Mary went around with a frown and pursed lips for the rest of the afternoon. I thought she would hold a grudge about it for months if not years.

The fair was due to open at one o'clock. Most years, Lady Darrach did the honours with an all purpose speech that she enunciated very loudly and clearly, as though talking to a group of slightly deaf foreigners. For the duration of the opening speech, people would hover beside the bric-à-brac and the home baking with their hands resting on the things they coveted, all ready for the off, like competitors in a race. Joe was quieter and more diffident than Lady D. He said he was glad to be in the village and happy to be asked to the Harvest Fair. He said it was all thanks to Louise who he knew was much missed in the village, and he got a round of applause for that. He asked everyone to support their local hockey team, well their only hockey team really, and that got a round of applause too, though most of them neither knew nor cared about ice hockey. Then he declared the fair well and truly open and the scrimmage began.

The first half hour or so was always hectic. All you could see were hands stretching towards you and people with avaricious faces elbowing each other out of the way. Two large ladies, strangers to the village, almost came to blows over a brass coal box with a broken hinge. I had to placate the loser by finding her a cafetiere at a bargain price. Mary dropped a whole box full of old glasses and cups and broke most of them.

After the first rush had subsided we gave each other a break now and again to go and look at the rest of the stalls. There was a plant stall with cuttings, where I managed to grab a couple of rose geraniums and put them behind our own table. I loved the scent of them and if I kept them indoors they would survive the winter. The home baking stall looked as though a cloud of particularly voracious locusts had descended on it, leaving only a few dry looking scones in plastic bags. They were the kind that people make with too little liquid and cut out with tiny cutters, and bake to within an inch of their lives so that they look very neat but taste like sand. I've often thought that you can tell a lot about people by the scones they make. They're all different and their size and consistency bear a strong resemblance to the baker. My scones are always soft and a bit untidy – blousy if you could ever describe a scone in that way – but I comfort myself that they taste very nice. Sadly, Mary makes perfect scones, neat and tasty too.

Annie and Mary went off to have tea, and I manned the bric-à-brac stall by myself for a bit. Fiona came in with her friends and they spent a lot of money on the bottle stall in hopes of alcohol but, to their bitter disappointment, all they managed to win was a tin of beans and a dusty bottle of non-alcoholic ginger cordial, one of the annual returnees. The bottle stall wasn't allowed to be photographed this year. It had to remain unofficial because the kirk authorities, in their wisdom, had decided that such stalls were the devil's business. Our kids were up the woods indulging in underage sex and illicit substances and the kirk was busy banning bottle stalls. It seemed symptomatic of some malaise at the heart of rural Scotland, but I wasn't sure what.

I could see Joe progressing from stall to stall. At the face painting table he was mobbed by kids demanding autographs. Next to the face painter, there was a second-hand toy stall, and that was where a whole other kind of recycling went on: games and other things that children had outgrown or found unplayable. Sad and sticky soft toys. Mutilated and sinister dolls.

After a while, Annie came back. 'Mary's got tied up talking to someone,' she said. 'Go and get some tea, Helen. Things have calmed down a bit. I can manage by myself now.'

I went to the kitchen where they were serving teas and joined Maisie and Betty at the only vacant table with my shortbread finger, my buttered pancake – except that it wasn't butter and I could definitely believe it wasn't – and my cup of stewed tea.

'How's that young lad?' asked Betty. 'Do you think he's looking after himself? The last time we went up to see him, his fridge was full of beer.'

'I'm sure he'll manage, Betty'

'You should keep an eye on him,' she told me, accusingly.

'I do try.'

Maybe I try a bit too hard, I thought. Maybe I try a bit more than I really should.

When I finished my tea and went back into the main hall, Joe was standing at our stall, talking to Annie and poking about among the remaining junk. The sight of him did my heart good.

'Don't buy any more crap for God's sake,' I said, coming up behind him.

'Helen. I wondered where you were. I'd better buy something though, hadn't I?'

'Go and get some raffle tickets then. At least most of the prizes are edible or drinkable.'

He grinned and shambled off.

'Spoilsport,' said Annie. 'I was enjoying myself.'

'I could see that.'

'You're just jealous.'

'Annie, trust me, he needs more junk up there like he needs a hole in the head.'

The afternoon wore on. Joe bought his raffle tickets. Across the hall, Sharon caught my eye and gave me a big thumbs up, nodding vigorously. I hoped Joe hadn't noticed. But he was the undoubted star of the show. He had a go at 'Beat the Goalie' out in the garden and he won every time. He seemed to have this uncanny ability to judge the available space and place the ball just where the goalie wasn't. Then he had a spell as goalie and stopped everything that came his way. I suppose it was easy compared to hockey. The photographer from the local paper came and took lots of pictures of him doing it. He signed autographs for all the kids and a number of teenage girls and a few middle aged women too. Courtesy of all the local publicity, he seemed to have slipped easily, and with considerable grace, into the role of big fish in our very small pond. He ate some short-bread and he was nice and mildly flirtatious with Betty and Maisie, who pursued him, trying to make him buy miscellaneous pieces of junk they thought might be useful to him. He resisted all of them and eventually came back to our stall and said he was heading home.

'What about your raffle tickets?'

'Here.' He gave me the counterfoils. 'You hang onto them. If I win anything you can bring it up for me. I'm never very lucky at these things'

But when the minister drew the raffle at the end of the fair, Joe had won the bottle of whisky. (Apparently the church's disapproval of alcohol hadn't extended to raffle prizes yet.) I went up and got it for him.

'Mandy's right,' said Sharon, when I came back. 'He's gorgeous.'

'I know. But he's very young.'

'How old is he? Early thirties?'

'Very early. Thirty one, I think.'

'Good toyboy material.'

'Don't be daft.'

'Well, we can dream can't we? Just because we've no credit, doesn't mean we can't do a bit of window shopping.'

When the fair was over there was a huge amount of clearing up to do, although the tables could be left for the young farmers to dismantle the next day. Most of the men, including Sandy, had headed off to the pub anyway and would be in no condition for the task tonight. I would go home when we had finished, and then there would be Sandy and Fiona to be fed. Of course I could have stopped the car and dropped the whisky off at the cottage on the way up the hill. That's what Sandy would have suggested. But Sandy knew nothing about it. He was down in the pub with his cronies. So I slipped it into my bag, intending to take it down to Joe later on.

– Chapter Nine –

WHEN I GOT home, I met Fiona on her way out. She had decided to spend the night at Lizzie's house, which suited me just fine. At least Lizzie's parents were very protective and didn't like their daughter hanging about the phone box any more than I did. Then Sandy phoned to say that he had gone home with Morris for another drink and now he was holed up at Glencarse, Mary and Morris's farm, over the other side of the village. He was going to have steak and kidney pudding with them because Mary had made one specially. Did I want to drive over and join them?

I didn't want to join them.

Mary's puddings were very good, like all her cooking, but I wasn't very hungry. I told him I was too tired to move and in any case, I lied, I had drunk a couple of glasses of wine and shouldn't really be driving. Sandy didn't seem to mind. He hoped I hadn't already cooked anything. No, I said. I hadn't started yet and it was only going to be pasta anyway. I was sure he would prefer Mary's steak and kidney.

'What about getting back?' I asked. 'Are you going to stay the night?'

'Well, I thought I might do that, unless you want to come and pick me up later.'

'Not really. I thought I might have another glass of wine. And I'm tired. Been on my feet all day.'

'Bruce will be there first thing in the morning. If you're all right on your own.'

'I don't mind. I'll be fine. I've got Jess to keep me company.'

I hoped I wasn't sounding too enthusiastic. I was aware of a flutter of foolish anticipation in my stomach.

I made myself a chicken sandwich and sat at the kitchen table, watching Saturday night television with people making fools of themselves in one way and another. Sometimes the programmes embarrassed me so much that I could barely watch them. Annie was always telling me I was too inhibited and repressed and needed to let myself go a bit more. Maybe she was right. I had a glass of wine and then, to convince myself that I really couldn't have driven over to Mary and Morris's place, I poured out another glass. But I wasn't hungry. I fed half the sandwich to Jess and drank the wine much too quickly. Siggy watched balefully from his favourite place on the warm enamel top of the kitchen range. Eventually he deigned to come down and eat a scrap of chicken, much to the dog's indignation. They eyed each other, Jess with her hackles raised and poor Siggy's fur bristling with frightened rage. He looked like a big grubby snowball. But eventually they seemed to agree a truce. Jess went to her bed and Siggy settled down, well out of harm's way.

I went upstairs to get changed. I was planning to take the whisky down to Joe. But what I actually did was take out half the things in my wardrobe and try them on, one after another. Some were too tight and some were too big and some were all wrong. I began to wonder if I wasn't body dysmorphic. Did my size really change so much or was it just that my perception of it fluctuated from day to day? Did I, in fact, know who I really was, never mind what size I was? There were things I had bought at the sales and regretted later. And some of them were charity shop or eBay clothes, designer labels bought for a few pounds, but they never seemed to fit in with my other things. I really needed to clear out my whole wardrobe and start again.

I got very hot and bothered and my head ached. I took two paracetamol tablets and crept under the bedcovers. Sadness settled around my heart, soft and heavy, a bit like when Siggy came and slept on my chest in the night. I closed my eyes and tears trailed down the sides of my face onto the pillow.

'Stupid,' I thought. 'Don't be so stupid.' But I wasn't quite sure what I was crying about. I might be depressed, but at least I hadn't made a complete fool of myself.

I fell asleep – the unwise combination of wine and paracetamol probably – and I woke up only when Jess started barking, whining and scratching at the door. Someone was ringing the doorbell. I pulled on the nearest thing to hand: a pair of ancient jeans and a baggy sweater that had somehow finished up on top of the pile of clothes. Then I went down, barefoot, to open the door, cursing my unexpected visitors. It was probably Annie and Tim, come to drag me off to the pub. Jess was rushing about now, wagging her tail.

When I opened the house door, there was Joe, just on the point of going away again.

'Helen.' He was holding a bulky plastic carrier. 'I thought you were out.'

'No. Sandy's out.'

'Is he?'

'I fell asleep.'

I hoped my eyes weren't still red. He paused on the doorstep as though he didn't quite know what to say or do.

'Tiring day?' he asked.

'A bit. It always is when it's a village thing. Come in. I've got something for you.'

'I know. My raffle prize.'

'How did you know?'

'Maisie phoned me to see if I'd got it yet.'

'God, didn't she trust me to give it to you?'

'I don't know. Anyway, I thought it was a good excuse to come and see you. I've brought Sandy some beers.' He followed me through the hall.

'You shouldn't need an excuse to come and see us. I was going to bring your whisky down for you just now. Well, I was if I hadn't fallen asleep. It's a malt. Laphroaig.'

'Say that again.'

'Laphroaig. I don't drink much whisky but Sandy tells me this is a good one.'

'Great.'

The sitting room was cold but the fire was ready laid in there, and I knelt down and put a match to the newspaper twists. It all began to blaze up nicely.

'Sit down. Make yourself comfortable, Joe.'

He sat down on the couch and stretched out his long legs. He was wearing his habitual jeans, tee-shirt, blue fleece.

'This is nice,' he said, looking round.

'It needs redecorating. One of these days I'll get round to it. I do most of the decorating round here. But it really needs more than that. I suppose it needs a complete renovation.'

'No. I meant your stuff. Your pictures, and things.'

'Oh they aren't really mine. They belonged to Sandy's family.'

I hardly looked at them any more. I had lived with all these things for so long that they just didn't register with me. But it was true that some of the furniture was very good, particularly the big chest of drawers where I kept embroidered table covers trimmed with crochet lace. Sandy's grandmother had made them and they were tricky to wash and iron but very beautiful. I didn't use them very often though. We didn't lead that kind of life. The piece of furniture was called a Kilmarnock Chest and it had little twisty bits of wood like barley sugar at the sides of the drawers. I liked polishing them with solid beeswax polish, the kind that smells of honey.

'Get a life.' That's what Fiona would have said. That's what Annie did say, quite often. 'There's more to life than polishing the furniture, Helen.'

I took out the bottle of whisky. 'Here you are.'

'Shall we open it?' he asked.

'Not for me. I've got some wine open though. Or would you prefer a beer?'

'Beer would be good. We'll keep the whisky for another time.'

I fetched him a beer and poured myself a glass of wine.

'Did you enjoy the Harvest Fair?'

He pulled a face, groaned. 'Oh sure. It was great. Does it happen every year then?'

'It comes round with monotonous regularity. That and the Gala Day and the Beetle Drive and the Daffodil Tea.'

They punctuated the year, these events, each following a set pattern. Eventually, they all seemed to blend into one.

He smiled. 'I get the picture.'

'You get used to it. I have.'

There was another of those embarrassed pauses between us.

'So your family have deserted you, have they?' he asked at last.

I nodded.

'Where's Sandy then?'

'He's gone over to see Morris and Mary.'

'Lucky old Sandy.'

'You've met Mary?'

'Sure. Is she a relative of yours?'

'She's Sandy's cousin. They have a farm. Mary and Morris. They're mostly farmers round here.'

'You don't include yourself?'

'Oh, I married in, but it'll be a few years yet before I stop being an interloper, an incomer. Like maybe another twenty.'

'There's no hope for *me* then!'

'Not a chance.'

'And Sandy actually likes Mary?'

He looked so puzzled that I started to laugh. 'Well, yes. He does. They grew up together. She drives me daft, but he likes her well enough. I think he's just comfortable with them. Mary and Morris both. They have a shared childhood. And Fiona's spending the night with her pal Lizzie.'

'Not down at the phone box?'

'No. Not down at the phone box, thank God.'

'So you're all alone up here.'

'I am. Me and the dog. And Siggy.'

'Do you mind?'

'Why should I?'

I topped up my glass and then I sat down on the couch beside him. I don't know what possessed me. He smelled lovely, of the spicy cologne or aftershave he always used. I regretted my shabby jeans and baggy sweater. But how could I possibly go upstairs and change now?

'The cat came down to see me,' he said, nodding at Siggy who had come stalking through from the kitchen to stretch by the fire. He clicked his fingers, but Siggy showed him a fluffy bum, and hunched his shoulders. He didn't like men. He was a lady's cat if ever there was one.

'I think he had hopes of finding Louise again so he was disappointed.'

'I'm sure he still misses her. I know I do.'

'I tried to entice him in,' Joe said. 'Bearing in mind what you said about the mice. I tried a tin of tuna.'

'And?'

'And he ignored me, didn't he? I don't think he likes me very much.

But then he found my kitbag and he sure liked that. He was trying to get inside it.'

'He tried to get inside it?'

'He obviously thought it smelled wonderful.'

'He's got depraved tastes!'

'He was very persistent. I had visions of arriving in the locker room, only to find a cat in my kitbag.'

'Oh, Joe, I'm sorry. Just kick him out if he does it again. He'll find his way back up here.'

But the shyness between us had eased. 'So have you had any more mice?' I asked.

'I haven't seen any more. But I've heard them at night. They stomp about the attic. Sounds like they're partying up there.'

'Just so long as they're not rats.'

'Jesus!' He looked absolutely horrified.

'This is a farm, Joe. There are bound to be rats. We have them in our barns. Every so often we have a blitz on them and kill as many as we can, but they always come back.'

I thought about the last time I had seen what the older people in the village called a 'rat flitting.' Many years ago now, Sandy had demolished one of the barns and there had been a mass exodus of rats in the face of the destruction of their home. Like Hamlyn before the Pied Piper, there had been rats everywhere and even the dogs had been scared of them, all except for a couple of fierce little terriers that we had borrowed from Fergus down in the village. They had had a gory field day, joyously flinging rodents about, breaking necks with gusto. In view of his reaction to a few mice, I thought I'd better not tell Joe about it. He'd probably pass out.

'As far as I know there are no rats down at the cottage. But you know what they say about rats, don't you?'

'What do they say?'

'That you're never more than six feet away from one. We could lend you the dog, if you want.'

'I don't think so, thanks. I'd get too attached to it and then I'd have to leave it behind when I go home.'

I didn't like the thought of him going home. It gave me a real pain, somewhere in the region of my heart. I was going to miss Joe when he finally went back to Canada. Even now, I could see that.

'Mind you, I do get a bit spooked sometimes. Being all alone in the cottage,' he said, surprisingly.

'Do you?'

'It's very dark. At night.'

'I thought you Canadians liked all this wilderness stuff.'

'Not me. I told you. I'm a townie born and bred.'

He fiddled with his glass.

'Have you been skating again?' he asked me, eventually.

'No.' I laughed. 'It wouldn't be the same without you there to hold me up.'

He looked sidelong at me. 'We'll have to make a date then.'

Change the subject. Quickly. Don't embarrass him. And yourself.

'What about the Gallopers? How are they coming on?'

'Fine. I've done a bit of work on them. Though I'm still no nearer to finding out why Vezio left them here with Louise. You'll have to come down and see them. Why haven't you been to see me, Helen? I've missed you.'

'Have you?'

'Sure. I like your company.'

I thought that was probably the simple truth. He was alone in the cottage and a stranger in the country and he enjoyed my company.

But there was no getting away from the fact that his proximity disturbed me. It took a real effort to move away from him, but I managed to slide a little way along the couch. He was like some great big shiny magnet.

'Joe? I asked him. 'Don't you have a girlfriend or a wife or something? Back home in Canada?'

It was the wrong question. It made him uncomfortable, but I didn't care. I needed to know. He folded his arms around himself and didn't answer me immediately.

'I'm sorry,' I said. 'I didn't mean to be nosy, but you just don't seem like the kind of man who would be alone in the world.'

'And why would that be?' He ran his finger around the top of his wine glass and jiggled his knee up and down.

'Well, look at you. You seem like such a ...' I hesitated. 'Such a nice guy.'

'Oh yeah, I'm a real nice guy, so somebody must have snapped me up.'

'I would have thought so.'

'Either that or I must be gay.'

'Which would be none of my business.'

'No,' he said, after a pause. 'No, it wouldn't.' His eyes were dark and opaque in the firelight. 'I'm not gay. But I am divorced, Helen.'

'I see.' Well I thought I did. 'I'm sorry.'

'Yeah well. So am I. So am I. But it was kind of inevitable. Hockey's pretty good at wrecking marriages you know.'

'Is it?'

'Well, the shaky ones. The ones that might come unstuck anyway. And ours was damn shaky.' He frowned. 'We travel about so much. Carrie used to come with me sometimes, but then we had a baby, a little girl, Alicia.'

'You've never mentioned any of this before, Joe.'

'I'm not very proud of it. Well, I'm proud of Alicia, but that's all.'

How long were you married?'

'About five years. We got married and then my career really started to take off. I was playing for a team I respected and making good money into the bargain.'

'So what went wrong?'

He didn't reply at once. He was looking at the floor, not at me.

'What ever does go wrong? Everything and nothing. We started to fight over just anything. Alicia wasn't a great sleeper.'

'I know all about that. Neither was Fiona. But it passes.'

'Yeah, well. It didn't help. There I was and I'd have a road trip or a flight and maybe a match the next day and I was getting no sleep. I'd get mad. And Carrie was getting no sleep either because I would be taking off and leaving her all alone with the baby. Which was hard on her. I know it was. Her family lived miles away. But we got through all that. We got through.'

'How old is your daughter now?'

'She's almost five.' He smiled at the thought of her, his face lighting up. 'She was born a couple of years after we were married and we've been divorced a year or so.'

'Do you see much of her?'

And why was he over here? How could he leave his little daughter and spend six months in another country? Who would ever want to do that?

'I see her sometimes. She's great. I love her to bits. But the divorce was kind of messy.'

'Was it?'

'Yeah. And that was all my fault, I reckon. Carrie would have been OK. But I hurt her too much.'

I waited, wondering if he would go on.

'You have to understand some things,' he said, after a moment or two.

'Like what?'

'Like the way hockey is.'

He leaned his head back against the couch.

'Tell me about it.'

'How long have you got?' He rubbed his hand over his eyes.

'Tell me about some of it then.'

'I reckon you'd be shocked.'

'No I wouldn't.' But I thought I might.

'Well ...' He hesitated, glanced at me, and then began again. 'Well, there are girls ... they get obsessed with a particular player. Like ... kind of like groupies I suppose. Puck bunnies.'

'Puck bunnies?' I laughed, but it wasn't very funny. Not really.

'That's what people call them. Puck bunnies. Rink bunnies. They follow the teams around and they get these crushes on the players.'

'I can see why.'

'Yeah well. It's a very physical game. It's fast and it's violent. Sometimes it's very violent and ...' He was having some difficulty continuing. It was as though he had set himself off on another train of thought, a different one altogether.

'But I do know what you mean,' I said. 'Lots of testosterone in motion. It can be very appealing.'

'Maybe.' He hesitated again, perhaps not sure how to continue without sounding conceited.

'So they fancy you,' I prompted him.

'Some of them are very young. Too young. And some of the guys take advantage. There's a lot of stuff goes on. Parties where ... well ... you know the kind of thing.'

'Not really, but I can imagine.'

He had rubbed his hair till it stood up in spikes. He spoke hesitantly, as though the words were being forced out of him, although I had done nothing more than sit quietly, listening.

'Not just sex but other stuff. A lot of drink. And maybe two or three guys will make it with one girl. It happens.'

'I see.' I couldn't pretend I wasn't shaken. This was worse than I had imagined. I mean I knew these things went on. In other sports too. Overpaid, overindulged young men and the even younger girls who hero-worshipped them. Of course I did. I read the papers. Watched the television. But it all seems so far removed from your own experience, doesn't it?

'Not all the time, and not every player. Just some of them. Some of the guys like to hunt in pairs. That's the way they get their kicks.'

'How do the girls feel about it?'

'Sometimes the girls go along with it, but I don't suppose they like it much. No, I don't think they ever like it much. How could they?' His voice had gone hard. I felt a wave of revulsion. He had been right. I didn't like this. It wasn't part of my world. I didn't like what he was saying at all.

'And what about you?' I asked carefully, not looking at him. 'How did you feel about it?'

'Me? No, I wasn't one of them. I tried not to get involved. Not in that kind of stuff anyway. It was never my scene. But it's kind of hard, you know? With some of the girls? I mean they'd send me birthday cards and things. One of them once sent me a pair of her panties.'

'You mean panties she'd *worn*?'

He nodded.

'How revolting.'

'Oh, Helen you're so ...' He stopped, shaking his head ruefully.

'What? What am I?'

He was still sitting alongside me but he turned to look at me. Then he just reached out and touched my arm, briefly.

'Nice. You're a nice Scottish lady. You don't mind me telling you all this?' he asked.

'No, Joe. I don't mind.'

'It's kinda nice to have someone to talk to.'

'Then tell me.'

'You see them watching you, waiting for you after games. They have this hungry look. Choose me. That's what they're saying. I'm not talking about the kids. You can spot the kids a mile off. But there you are in all this kit, the body armour, the gloves and helmets and skates. It makes you look even bigger than you are. We must look like ...' he hesitated again.

'Like warriors. Like gladiators I suppose.'

'It's a gladiatorial sport for sure. But it's all image. Fantasy. You strip off all that and ...'

'You're still fit young men underneath.'

'But we're fit, ordinary guys. Some of us aren't even that fit. Some of us have no teeth to speak of. Some of us have no brains to speak of. Some of us can't string two sensible words together. Most of us have been injured in one way and another. We have injuries. We have scars. A lot of scars. We're not what they think. It's more Slap Shot than Youngblood.'

'What's Slap Shot?'

'They're just old hockey movies. And besides a few of us are ...' he stopped.

'Are what?'

'Damaged. Car crash on ice.'

'How do you mean?'

There was a long pause. He stared into the fire but said nothing.

There are all kinds of damage. There are all kinds of scars: physical and the other kind. Or as Joe would have put it, as he did put it later on, it isn't just the puck to the head that fucks up your brain.

Poor Joe.

At last he pointed to his eyebrows where a couple of jagged lines criss-crossed there, and his nose that was slightly uneven. When you looked closely at his face, you could see that it was crazed with faint scars, like old stone, like a handsome but slightly distressed statue.

'Why don't you protect your faces in some way?'

'The younger ones do. But you can't see properly. It feels wrong somehow. The net minders do it of course, but they have to. They're face to face with the puck most of the time. We just have to take the risk.'

'Battle scars,' I said. 'And I suppose the girls like the scars as well. I suppose that makes you even more desirable.'

I remembered reading a book about ancient Rome and how the patrician ladies used to like to make out with the gladiators. Sometimes they would pay them. The thought just popped into my head, but I didn't tell Joe.

'That's about it. They collect things. They want to own your shirt maybe and they want you to sign it for them. That's a real big thing. And if it's a nice sweaty game-worn shirt so much the better. I figure in a way some of them collect scalps. They collect players. It isn't just the players who collect the girls, it's the girls who collect the players as well. I'm not talking about the kids here. I'm talking about grown-up women. Old enough to know what they want. You know what I mean?'

'I think so.'

'And it isn't just in Canada either. It's the same in the States. And here as well. It's started for me already.'

'Has it?'

'They get dressed up for the hockey. They do the make-up and the hair and everything. You get to know the faces. They lie in wait for you. They wait for you in the bar afterwards when you're having a beer. They send you get well cards if you're injured. They don't like it if you've got a partner: a wife or a girlfriend. They don't like that. And you should see what they write on Twitter and Facebook and all the other sites.'

'I don't do Twitter.'

'Just as well.'

I did Facebook though, on the quiet.

'But surely you can ...' I struggled to find the right words. 'Surely you can keep them at arm's length, can't you, if you really want to?'

Here I was, I thought, lecturing Joe about keeping the puck bunnies at arm's length. Here I was, with my head full of him.

'Sure you can,' he said. 'If you really want to. But do we always want to? Well, yeah. That's what I did, mostly. Most of us have them tagging along after us, and most of the time it's harmless. They get a kick out of it and we get a kick out of it as well, if we're honest about it. But that's as far as it goes.'

Could he see that I had a huge crush on him? Did he get a kick out of that too? Or had he simply not noticed?

'You wouldn't be human if you didn't enjoy it.'

'Only sometimes it gets out of hand.'

'Does it? Did it?'

'You see, there was this girl ...' He took a big gulp of his beer. 'She was just crazy about me and she was beautiful. Blonde hair, long legs. She used to wear a replica shirt with my name and number on it.'

'Most guys would be flattered by that kind of attention.'

'I was. But I should have been careful as well. I was a married man with a kid by that time and I wasn't careful at all.'

'Ah.'

'Carrie was at home with Alicia. We won. That was part of it. I can't tell you what it feels like when you win and win well. Jesus, Helen it's like sex. It's better than sex.'

'Only in this case it wasn't.'

I couldn't resist saying it.

'Wasn't what?'

'Better than sex.' Suddenly I felt more than ten years older than Joe. I felt positively ancient.

He had the grace to look sheepish. 'I met her in the bar afterwards. I was kinda drunk and she was all over me, and me and Carrie, we'd had a big fight. Poor Alicia had a bug and she had been grizzling all night long, and there I was ... it felt as if I was free for once and there was this sweet girl telling me how great I was.'

He had ground to a halt again.

What was he looking for, I wondered. Reassurance? Forgiveness? How could I possibly forgive him? Because really, what did any of this have to do with me?

'And I just thought, what the hell? She was willing. Eager, even. And the next thing I knew, there we were in the ...' He paused. 'You know. In the john.'

'Oh Joe!'

He started to laugh and I joined in, but it didn't sound very funny to me. It wasn't funny at all. I realised that he was just desperate to talk about it. Embarrassed and ashamed and desperate, all at the same time.

He wanted to tell someone all about it. Make a confession. But who could absolve him? Not me, that was for sure.

'What a fool I was! It was the disabled cubicle. There was plenty of room. And it was hot in there. Jesus it was so hot in there. It smelled of piss and worse. And there were people looking for me, trying to find me, calling my name, because the place was closing. The assistant coach found me. Found us. He was OK. He sent the girl home. I don't know what he said to her, but I remember he got her coat and her bag. He was polite to her. I think she was just embarrassed. He sent her off home in a taxi and then he sobered me up with coffee and took me home as well, but the guys knew. They would have been talking about it. I mean we always knew who'd been doing it and who hadn't.'

'So you made a habit of it?'

'No. No, Helen!' To my surprise, he caught hold of my hand. 'That was the point. It was kind of weird for me. Wrong for me. They knew that. I mean there were some of the guys who would have a different girl every game and sometimes more.'

I don't know what I said then. Maybe I just sighed. Still holding my hand, he turned and looked directly at me. It was as though he had been talking into empty air for a while, as though he had forgotten I was there. But now he focused on me, realising just how far he had confided in me. And perhaps my dismay and revulsion showed on my face, in spite of anything I could do to disguise it.

'I'm sorry,' he said. 'Ah God, Helen. I know. It was not good. I was to blame. I mean, she wasn't underage or anything, and she came on to me, but I still felt I was to blame. It wasn't the ...' he paused, hunting for the right word. 'Jeez, my old man would have said it wasn't the honourable thing to do. He died when I was thirteen and I can still remember him saying that. You have to act with honour, to act like a man, Joey.'

'But why are you telling me all this, Joe?'

'Christ, I don't know. Because I have to tell someone. And you're ...'

'I'm just here.' The thought depressed me.

He looked at me again and his eyes were faintly bloodshot where he had been rubbing them. 'No. Not just that,' he said. 'Maybe it's because I feel I can trust you.'

'So what happened then? Finish the story, Joe.'

'Oh the kid wouldn't let me alone. She was crazy about me. I'd given her exactly what she wanted, and now she wanted more. She started sending letters, emailing the club, lying in wait for me. All kinds of stuff. The guys would laugh about it. They all knew. They had been there. Got the tee-shirt. There's a rule. You don't talk outside the locker room. You say what you like in there, but you don't talk outside. Only I figure one or two of them must have told their wives or girlfriends. And ... and then ...'

'Your wife found out.'

'Carrie found out. I told her it meant nothing. It was just a one off. I had been drunk. All the usual fucking bullshit. Even then it might have been all right, but Carrie came to a game. Brought Alicia to watch her dad play. And the girl was there, waiting for me. I nearly had a heart attack when I saw her and I was off my game all night. The coach was pissed off with me. Then she got my home address from somebody and started writing to Carrie. Telling her what had happened and a few things that hadn't happened. A few things she made up. She was only eighteen, nineteen. I was lucky she wasn't younger.'

'Was it all worth it?'

'For a quick screw? No, no way it was worth it. It was crazy and it meant nothing. And it finally destroyed what we had. It hurt Carrie too much. But I thought afterwards, it wasn't the kid's fault. It was mine. I deserved everything I got. There was no going back after that.'

He had trailed to a halt. I didn't know what to say to him. I think for a moment he was alarmed by his own honesty. Once he had started, he had found it hard to stop talking.

'I don't know that our marriage was all that strong anyway,' he said at last. He let go of my hand and moved away from me, suddenly self conscious. 'I don't think we were that committed. Not like some people. Not like you and Sandy for instance.'

'Me and Sandy?'

He had taken me by surprise.

'Well you are, aren't you? You're such a solid couple.'

'Me and Sandy?' I repeated. 'Well I suppose we are. We've stayed together for years. But nothing's ever happened. I mean nothing to test us. He was my first real boyfriend.'

'Was he?'

'More or less. There was the odd relationship before we got together but nothing long term. And nothing like that has ever happened to me. I haven't been tempted. And I don't think it's ever happened to Sandy either. So how can I really say? How can I tell?'

I tried to picture Sandy with an eighteen year old fan in the disabled loos at the ice rink, or more likely at the cattle market or the agricultural show, but even my vivid imagination wouldn't stretch that far. Would he keep his cap and wellies on? I started to giggle. 'Oh God, Joe, I'm not laughing at you. Just at the thought of Sandy. But how would I know? Even if he was doing something like that, how would I ever know?'

'I think you'd know,' he said, quietly.

And yet, why should the thought of Sandy be any worse than the thought of Joe in that situation? Joe was looking at me with a strange expression on his face. Doubt? Shame? I wasn't sure.

'So that was it, really. We split up and Carrie took Alicia with her because how could I look after her? And then we divorced.'

'What about your friend from the rink.'

'She found someone else. A younger player. It was the image she was into. She found somebody more accessible, more available than me. We were kind of interchangeable for her, you know. Another one would do just as well. And when she heard my wife and I had split ... maybe she came to her senses then. Maybe she realised she didn't want me. Not really. I reckon she was sorry.'

'I think there's an age and stage you go through when you're old enough to be up for anything but still not old enough to see or even care about the damage you might be doing,' I said, thinking about it, trying to remember what it had been like to be eighteen or nineteen, buzzing with hormones, footloose and fancy free.

'Maybe. It was the buzz she wanted. The glamour. It wasn't like she was a real stalker or anything. She was a puck bunny, not a bunny boiler. Just young and pretty and besotted with the game and her hockey heroes. And I sure as hell didn't want her. Or only in one way, anyway. My bad. All mine.'

I shook my head. 'Poor Joe.'

'Poor nothing. It was my own fault. I don't deserve any sympathy. I brought it all on myself. A few months down the line, Carrie moved closer to her parents, so I don't see much of Alicia, and when I do, she gets upset, she cries when she leaves me, and then Carrie blames me. She says it's my fault.'

'As you would.'

'I can't complain, can I? It is my fault. Helen, I'm a mess. I'm such a fucking mess.'

'So you came over here? To get away from it all?'

'Eventually.' Again that opaque quality about the eyes. So perhaps there was more. But I was disturbed by how much he had already told me.

'Don't you miss your daughter?'

'It's what Carrie wants.'

'Is it what Alicia wants?'

'It's what Carrie says Alicia wants.'

'Ah.'

'What can I do? I am so *completely* in the wrong, Helen. You don't know. You just don't know.'

He was leaning forward, his head in his hands. I started patting his back, the way you do with a distressed child.

'Poor Joe,' I said again.

He turned towards me and because it seemed the right thing to do and because he seemed so needy, I put my arms around him and hugged him. Trying to make it better. But how could I possibly make it better? I could feel him trembling.

He said, 'Helen!' and then he kissed me.

Unfortunately I kissed him back.

I hadn't been kissed like that for years and I responded in spite of myself. It went on and on. I could feel his heart pounding against my breasts and his fingers biting into my arms and he kept saying, 'Oh Helen,' between kisses and our tongues touched.

Then an indignant Siggy leapt onto my knee and hissed at him. Siggy didn't like this at all. Maybe he thought Joe was hurting me. Claws dug in.

We parted, and stared at each other, breathlessly. Joe leapt up and said, 'Helen, I am so sorry! I am so sorry for this!' and ran out of the house, letting the door slam behind him.

I didn't sleep well that night. I dreamed a lot though: vivid dreams, that looped along the edges of my sleep and all of them featured Joe Napier. I was glad that my husband was away. I fell asleep just as a faint light began to show in the eastern sky. I slept on, while Bruce drove into the yard and let himself into the kitchen to make his own tea. It was only a returning Sandy who woke me, coming into the bedroom to get changed before he went to see to the beasts.

– Chapter Ten –

JOE WAS AVOIDING me, but I didn't mind because I found the memory of that sudden and unexpected embrace embarrassing and suspected that he felt the same. Nevertheless I kept hugging the thought of the kiss to me. It struck me that nothing changes. As you get older, you don't feel any different. It's just that the opportunities grow fewer and you reconcile yourself to not getting what you want. Only in this case I had got what I wanted, after a fashion, and now I wasn't sure that I wanted it at all. Sandy tossed and turned in bed beside me, apparently beset by nightmares, and I lay awake thinking of Joe.

The truth was that I was frightened. He had needed physical contact. I was a handy body. But now I was frightened of what he had told me about himself. Maybe I saw something else, something buried deep inside him that scared me even more. I didn't know what it was. Didn't much want to know.

Then one night Sandy came in after a trip to the village pub and produced an envelope from his jacket pocket. 'Ice hockey tickets!' he said.

'What?'

'Free hockey tickets from the guy down the road. For the game on Sunday. He said we've been a big help to him, settling in and all that. Good of him, eh?'

'Very good of him. How many?'

'Five. He said there's three for us and a couple for Annie and Tim. He thought we might all like to go together. He said we should go early and then we'll see the warm-up as well.'

'What's the warm-up?'

Sandy pulled a face to show me how stupid I was being. 'Well, I take it they go onto the ice and, you know, warm up before the game. But if you don't want to go,' he added, 'I can always ask Charlie.'

'Oh no. No. I do want to go. Don't you dare give my ticket to Charlie.'

'All right. All right. Keep your hair on, hen.'

We all went together in Tim's car and as Joe had suggested, we arrived early. I was surprised at how full the car park was and how crowded the arena seemed to be. It was a long time to face-off but already lots of people, most of them dressed in big, bright, replica hockey shirts, were crowding the entrances and the passageways, though most of the seats were still empty. I noticed that one or two of them even had shirts with the name 'Napier' and his number, 39, on the back. That was my age, although not for much longer. I didn't point it out, even to Annie. Tim and Sandy took themselves off to the bar for a couple of pre-match pints while Annie, Fiona and I did what a lot of other people were doing and pressed our noses up against the reinforced glass to watch the teams out on the ice as they warmed up.

'Well it isn't like a football crowd anyway,' said Annie, who had been to the occasional football match with Tim.

'What do you mean?'

'They look more of a mix for one thing. Look at them. Mums, grand-parents ...'

'There's a baby over there,' said Fiona. 'Isn't he sweet?'

He was about six months old. He had on a little Kestrels cap and a shirt to match.

'Mind you,' added Annie, 'From what I've heard, the violence happens on the ice, not off it. The fans are fine, it's the players who stir it up. Your pal Joe included.'

'Really?'

'Well, he's a bit of an enforcer, isn't he?'

I realised then that Annie had been doing her homework. I had no idea what an enforcer was.

'It's a big defenceman who protects the forwards,' she told me. 'And the forwards are the wee nippy guys who score the goals. The enforcer doesn't mind getting into the odd fight if necessary. This is a contact sport, Helen. I thought you knew.'

'Well I did, sort of.'

It certainly explained some of Joe's injuries. 'Where did you find out all this?'

'I looked up the team's website on the net. And I mugged up on the rules a bit. You should have a look online. They've got a Facebook page as well.'

I wished I'd thought of that. I don't know why I hadn't. Trust Annie.

We watched the two teams warming up for the game at opposite ends of the rink, shooting into the net and stretching their legs, performing impossible contortions down on the ice. The music was loud and cheerful and the players looked twice their normal size in all that padding. It was hard to tell which was which. Not that I knew any of them anyway. Annie was quick to point out Joe to me, though he wasn't looking in our direction. We were standing at the Kestrels' end of the rink, and I had turned away for a moment, when the sharp snap of puck against plexi-glass, right beside my head, made me spin round. Joe skated away fast, grinning over his shoulder.

'He did that on purpose,' said Fiona, delightedly. Suddenly she was behaving like a kid again. The warm-up finished and the big Zamboni came driving out onto the ice to smooth the surface. Just before he came off, Joe took a pile of pucks and skated around, tossing them over the barrier to little groups of waiting children. To my amazement, Fiona waited with them and came back clutching a battered puck. Annie nudged me. 'Would you believe it?'

'Not if I hadn't seen it with my own eyes! Like a ten year old!'

The seats were good ones, comfortable and central with a view across the Kestrels' bench, where the players sat with their coach, to the ice beyond.

The start of the game involved lights and noise and fireworks: the kind of Transatlantic razzmatazz designed to fuel our excitement, which of course it did.

'What *is* that smell?' said Annie.

The locker room doors had opened to let the players onto the ice for the game and with them came the unique smell of hockey kit, the scent that Siggy had found so irresistible: a pungent aroma of sweat on leather, mixed with the minty, herbal scent of the muscle sprays and rubs the players used.

'Pheromones,' I told her. She grinned.

The players were poised for the face-off and pounced on the puck so quickly that they almost took the referee's fingers off when he dropped it. But then everything about the game was very fast and close and immediate. The coach, who walked up and down behind the players' bench, was dressed in a smart suit, shirt and tie, but the players seemed to me like nothing so much as big, bright birds, or knights in armour. It did your heart good, just looking at them: the way they scrambled over the barrier as though at some prearranged signal, and skated off, fast and hard and graceful, the way they swooped and circled, the way they could suddenly change direction with a swish and flurry of snow.

The music was hard and loud too.

And over it all came the slap of puck on stick and the beating of drums and the whistle of the despised referee in his liquorice allsort shirt.

I spent the first period trying to work out the rules, with Annie talking in my left ear.

'Look at the way they pass to each other. They change over every few minutes. See how they've stopped. That's called icing. Something to do with the lines on the ice and where the puck is. Couldn't quite figure that bit out. But it means another face-off. Here it comes. Isn't Joe fit?'

I was glad of her commentary but jealous of it. Annie liked to mug up on things, liked to know what she was letting herself in for. And then she would act as if she had been coming to games for years. Joe scrambled over the barrier, stick in hand, and sat down on the bench. He didn't look up at us, though he must have known where we were sitting. The coach patted him on the shoulder. He said something to his team-mate and sat forward in his seat, watching the course of play.

Some ten minutes into the game the Kestrels scored. And then scored again. The net seemed very small and the netminder so big that he almost filled it, so you wondered how they managed it, but they did, and it was the same player who scored twice, with a little flick of his wrist on the stick. He was small in comparison with Joe and looking much too young to be out without his mother. His name was Casey. Fast and agile, he put the puck between the opposing defenceman's skates, and then immediately slithered around him to pick it up and shoot it straight into the back of the net. The people around us rose to their feet, waving their arms above their heads, and yelling. We got up and yelled too, caught up in the enthusiasm.

At the end of the first period, Sandy and Tim went off and came back with cups of coffee for us and trays of chips for themselves.

'Are you enjoying it?' I asked Sandy, stealing a chip, although I had said I didn't want any.

'You always do that,' said Sandy, indignantly. 'Why didn't you ask for some? The game's all right. I wouldn't go mad over it though. Not like the footie.'

'Wouldn't you? Why not?'

'Lot of fuss about not very much,' he muttered grumpily. 'Not like the real thing.'

'I think it's wonderful!'

It had a lot to do with the bright lights, the gleaming white of the ice and the colourful kit of the players. It had a lot to do with the constant motion, the hiss and spark of blade on ice. It was combative and exciting. This is what jousting must have been like, I thought. Or at least it must have aroused the same emotions in the spectators. And perhaps it had something to do with Joe. All I knew was I had never seen anything that filled me with such wild and disproportionate delight.

The first period had been relatively peaceable but in the second, perhaps because the opposition had the sense that the game was running away from them, things got harder and dirtier.

One of the visiting players stuck out his stick and deliberately tripped up the forward who had scored both goals. He was a big man, bigger than Joe, with a broad pink face, like a ham, and he got two minutes in the 'sin bin' for his pains.

'That's us on the powerplay,' said Annie. 'You see, we've got a player advantage now. Joe's quite a playmaker, isn't he?'

'A playmaker?'

'Sets up goals for other people to score.'

But the Kestrels couldn't score. Nobody scored in that period, though once the powerplay was over, the other team had the best of it, with a couple of shots pinging loudly off the metal posts of the net. Once or twice it looked as though the netminder was practically standing on his head, agile in spite of all the padding, and he saved everything that came his way. The whole game had speeded up. You could see that the players' hair, where it curled out from beneath their helmets, was damp with perspiration. The ham faced player had another go at our little forward, but Joe was suddenly in there, grim faced, body checking at speed, hurling the man into the barrier with a crash.

'Wow!' said Annie. 'Would you look at that? Wouldn't like to get on the wrong side of that one!'

'Is that legal?' asked Tim.

'I think so. That's the point. I think it is!'

Early in the third period, the Kestrels scored again, and then things between Hamface and another of the Kestrels, not Joe this time but someone called Ojanen, got quite nasty and there was a real punch-up. Both players dropped gloves and helmets and went at it hammer and tongs. The crowd stood up and cheered. We got up and cheered as well, all of us except Sandy, who sat resolutely in his seat and said 'Girls! Girls!' but that didn't stop us. Besides, Tim was up and shouting too.

After a bit, Hamface fell down, not so much because he had been knocked down as because the skates had gone from under him – it must be quite hard to have a proper fight on skates – and it was then that the officials waded in and propelled Ojanen and Hamface towards their respective sin-bins.

'Roughing,' said Annie, succinctly.

'Is that what they call it?' asked Fiona, giggling. 'God that was good!'

I didn't like to admit as much, but I had found it good as well.

Then, quite late in the third period, there was a melee in front of our goalie and the opposition scored, which was a curiously muted affair, although the small group of visiting supporters cheered loudly. They were all seated together at one end of the ice, not so much for safety as for mutual reassurance. This was a friendly crowd; they even applauded good saves by the opposition netminder. That made the score three one and, as Annie said, things can turn around fast in hockey. When they scored again two minutes later, I began to wonder if we were going to lose after all, and hoping desperately that we weren't. Then the Kestrels' coach called a time-out ('to settle them down' said Annie, knowledgeably and irritatingly) and the opposition pulled their netminder with one minute to go. The big man in his beautifully painted helmet skated off, back to his own bench.

Because they had sacrificed their goalie, this gave the opposition an extra player down the Kestrels' end of the ice. During that last minute, they threw everything they had at our team's netminder in an attempt to even the score, which would have meant going to 'sudden death' over-time. But nothing got past him, and then suddenly, magically, there was Joe, who had been rock solid in defence so far, with the puck against his stick and nothing in front of him but the empty opposition net, a long way away. The crowd were on their feet again.

'Come on, Sky!' yelled a man just behind me. 'Bury that biscuit!'

Annie dug her elbow in my ribs and then Joe did what he had been doing at the end of the warm-up and pulled back his stick ever so slightly. The last seconds of the game were slipping away on the big clock suspended above the rink. It was like watching an archer, releasing an arrow from a bow, and with about the same power and accuracy. The puck fairly sizzled down the ice and straight into the back of the empty net, with seconds on the clock, and that was it. We'd won, four two, and I realised that I was on my feet again, waving my arms about and screaming.

'Like a dervish,' said Sandy later when he was telling Morris and Mary all about it. He had laughed but he hadn't really approved of what he saw as a loss of self control. And you could see that Mary agreed with him.

There were presentations for Man of the Match, and then the Kestrels skated around the rink and applauded the crowds, hand against raised stick, and there was Joe, looking up at us and giving us a wave as he left the ice.

'He said we should go to the bar for a drink,' said Tim. 'He'll be out when he's had a shower.'

'When did he say this?' I asked.

'Down in the pub. When he gave us the tickets.'

'You didn't tell me that,' I said to Sandy.

'Fiona's too young to go to the bar. Tim and Annie can go.'

'Oh Dad!' said Fiona, preparing to argue.

'No she isn't,' said Annie. 'She can't drink, but she can go in. I've checked. Sixteen and over. She can have a coke. Besides, you're not going to sit out in the car waiting for us, are you?'

Sandy would probably have argued with me – it was obvious that he didn't want to go – but he usually gave in to Annie, so we all went to the bar.

Tim bought us some drinks while we waited for Joe. Fifteen minutes later, he came in wearing a team tracksuit, his hair black and sleek after his shower. I remembered his kiss and buried my face in my drink, glad that everyone was looking at him, not me. He came over to our table and patted Annie's shoulder, shook hands with Tim and Sandy and ruffled Fiona's hair. Then he hesitated before he bent to kiss me briefly, casually, on the cheek.

'Hello, Helen,' he said. 'Glad you could come.'

The forward who had scored twice was with him, his blonde mop wet and shaggy. Joe introduced him as Lee Casey, a fellow Canadian, and Tim went off to buy them both a beer. Lee sat down next to Fiona who was staring at him with obvious adulation. He didn't look much older than she was, though he told her later that he was twenty one and, like Joe, a recent addition to the team.

Lee was sweet faced and soft spoken and he gave the impression of being quite shy. That night he seemed almost relieved to be absorbed into a family group like ours, sheltered from the precisely made-up girls who clustered around the bar and cast hungry glances in his direction. They cast predatory glances at Joe as well but he ignored them, although I could see that he was aware of them. He was elated, animated with post match euphoria, his eyes shining. We had a couple of drinks and talked and laughed a lot. Even Sandy relaxed and began to enjoy himself. Before too long, Lee and Fiona were deep in conversation and had made arrangements to meet up in town the following Saturday afternoon.

Annie was chatting to Joe, charming him, monopolising him, and I didn't do a thing about it, because he seemed content to let it happen and I found simply watching him enough to make me happy. He was sitting next to her, on the other side of the table, and she kept touching his arm when she spoke to him, questioning him closely about the game. Tim didn't seem to mind. Annie loved to flirt and he was used to it. Then Sandy went off to the loo and before he came back to our table, Joe lifted his glass to finish his drink, raised his eyes and looked straight at me.

'OK, Helen?'

'Yes. I'm fine.'

'Did *you* enjoy the game?'

'I loved it. It was wonderful. Can't remember when I last enjoyed anything so much.'

'Me neither,' said Fiona.

'It's fire dancing,' said Lee, with a smile.

'What?'

'Somebody once said hockey was like fire dancing on ice,' said Joe. ' I thought you'd enjoy it. Will you come again?'

'We both will,' said Annie. 'Won't we, Helen?'

I caught a flicker of amusement in Joe's eyes.

'Of course,' I said. 'I don't know if Sandy will though.'

'Then we'll just have to have a girls' night out.' Annie nudged Fiona. 'Won't we?'

'Sorry?' Fiona looked vaguely at her and then back at Lee Casey. They seemed lost in mutual admiration of each other. It was plain that Lee couldn't keep his eyes off my daughter.

'We'll come to the hockey again. You and me and your mum.'

'Oh yes,' said Fiona. 'Any time. As often as we possibly can.'

I looked across at Joe. I thought I knew exactly how she felt.

– Chapter Eleven –

S ANDY DIDN'T SAY much about the hockey. I don't think he enjoyed it but he could see that we loved it, and he didn't want to spoil our pleasure. The following Saturday, Fiona went into town on the bus and met up with Lee Casey. I don't know what they did. Walked around the shops and sat in a cafe, I suppose. After that, they messaged each other a lot and then he phoned the house and asked if he could take her to the cinema during the week. I was pleased to get her away from the village phone box, but worried too. The gap between twenty one and sixteen is wide and I knew, from what Joe had told me, that hockey players were in demand. What would he expect of her? Would he look after her?

'You should have a word with him,' I said to Sandy.

Sandy looked aghast at the thought. 'What kind of word?'

'You know. Ask him to be careful. Remind him how young she is. He needs to look out for her.'

The players that needed them were supplied with cars courtesy of a local garage, so when Lee came to pick her up and drive her into town, I cornered him in the kitchen, while she was still up in her bedroom, and had a serious chat with him. He didn't seem to mind. On the contrary he gave me the impression of being polite and sensible.

'She's still very young you know, Lee,' I said. 'I don't mind you seeing her, but she'll take her cue from you.'

'Joe's already talked to me,' he said, surprisingly.

'Has he?'

'Sure. She'll be fine. I'll take good care of her.'

I hadn't seen Joe since the game. There had been a couple of meetings with the farm accountant, followed by all the ensuing paperwork.

Sometimes you wondered if it was worth while. Everyone's hand seemed to be out for the cash and there was precious little left for us. From time to time, usually in the middle of winter when everything was frozen and the yard was a sea of icy mud, Sandy would talk half-heartedly about selling up and moving on, but I knew he didn't really mean it. He didn't know any other way of life. Farming was what he did.

Then, Morris persuaded Sandy to go to a big agricultural machinery show in Edinburgh.

'We don't need anything and we certainly can't afford anything,' said Sandy.

But Morris had managed to find a reasonably priced guest house and just booked it for the three of them for the night.

'We could come back the same day,' complained Sandy. 'It would be cheaper.'

'We might as well make a trip of it, Sandy,' said Morris. 'Mary wants to go shopping. Don't you want to come too, Helen? Bruce would hold the fort for you here.'

The thought of spending two days in chilly Edinburgh with Mary was more than I could bear.

'No. You go off and enjoy yourselves. Besides, I'm not leaving Fiona on her own. Not now she seems to have a boyfriend. I want to keep an eye on her. Well, as far as I can. I'll be fine, honestly. I've got plenty to get on with here.'

So Sandy dug out the heavy tweed suit that he had worn to all the agricultural shows for as long as we had known each other, and I kissed him on the cheek and sent him off with his cap and his brown leather brogues, looking like a throwback to the forties. Except that he would blend in perfectly.

'Go easy on the beer,' I called, as he left.

It was quite a fine day, a lingering memory of the summer that, in reality, was long past. Fiona was planning to go to Shona's house for a while after school. She said they were working on a project together, although I suspected that she would just be using up her mobile credit on Lee. Shona's dad had promised to run her home later in the evening. The hens were fed, and the beds were made. There were jobs to do about the farm, but nothing that couldn't wait, and Bruce would manage all the essentials. So I walked down to Louise's cottage to see Joe, waiting until I judged that he would be back from his morning training session. He was in the shed, working on one of Vezio's Gallopers, assembling one of the horses that he had found in pieces and patching it with slivers of wood here and there. There were drifts of wood shavings and sawdust on the floor and the reek of wood glue hung heavily in the air. When he saw me, he stood up, brushing himself down. He seemed genuinely pleased to see me.

'Hey, Helen,' he said. 'How are you?'

'I'm fine.' I caught myself blushing again, remembering the kiss. He was obviously remembering it too. This was the first time we had been alone together since that night. We didn't quite know what to say to each other.

'Come to admire my work of art?' he asked at last.

'This is fantastic.' I patted the horse's wooden rump.

'Well it will be when it's finished. But it's a very long job.'

I hesitated, wondering if he would invite me into the house but he seemed very diffident.

'So what are you up to today?' he asked.

'Nothing much. Sandy's gone off to a show and Fiona's at school. Oh there's plenty I should be doing. But it's such a fine day for a change that I can't be bothered. We won't get many more days like this between now and Christmas.'

'What about the farm?'

'I've done what needs to be done. Bruce will do the rest.'

He looked at his watch. 'I think we need to talk.'

'Do we?'

Please don't, I thought. Please don't tell me how stupid I've been. What a mistake all this is.

'Yes I think we do.'

What was he going to tell me? That he had been carried away by the wine and the moment? That he was ashamed of himself? That we should avoid each other in future? I felt suddenly vulnerable.

'Do you want a coffee?' he asked.

I nodded. I didn't know what else to say.

We went into the kitchen, and he poured strong coffee. The room was full of the scent of it. Then we sat outside on the cast iron bench with its flaking green paint and we looked across to where a patchwork of fields and golden woods blended with the remote grey-blue brush strokes of the sea.

Joe had on a grubby tee-shirt. His arms were strong and sinewy. I clutched at my coffee mug, wanting to touch him, wanting to reach out and stroke his warm forearm that lay alongside mine. I had no idea what he was feeling.

So talk to me, I thought, but said nothing. I was walking along some terrible parapet and I daren't look down. My voice wouldn't work properly.

There was a long silence, broken only by the harsh cries of the jackdaws on the roof. I sometimes found myself looking up at them and wondering what they thought of us, engrossed as they were in their own rooftop world.

'What about some lunch?' he said at last.

I cleared my throat. My mouth felt dry. 'What about it?'

'I thought maybe we could have it together.'

'Where?'

'Well, what about here? I think I've got some bread and cheese.'

Before I had time to think better of it, I said, 'We could go to Poldarrach. We could take a picnic.'

It was like jumping from some great height. I felt dizzy and breathless.

'I haven't had a picnic for years. Not since I was a kid. Where's Poldarrach?'

'Not far from here. But we'll need to drive.'

'What is it?'

'Wait and see. A good place for a picnic.'

What about Fiona?'

'It isn't far. Besides, she's going to her friend's house after school. She won't be back till later on.'

'What do you want me to bring?'

'Nothing. Just yourself.' I finished my coffee and stood up. 'I'll pick you up in about an hour. OK? We'll take the pick-up. It'll be easier. I know where I'm going.'

'So nobody's going to miss you?'

'No, Joe. Nobody's going to miss me at all today. Time out, that's what this is.'

I went back to the farmhouse and set out some lunch for Bruce and his nephew. I left chicken soup heating gently in a pan on the stove, bread, cold meat and tomatoes on the table, with a chunk of fruit cake for afterwards. Then I made sandwiches with the remains of the beef and some horseradish and cut more slices of fruit cake. I packed them with a bar of chocolate and a bottle of home made ginger beer. I put them all in a willow basket that Sandy sometimes used when he was going fishing, slipped out of the back door into the yard and stowed the basket away under the front seat of the pick-up. Bruce was just driving up in the tractor as I closed the door, and I called to him.

'There's soup on the hob. The rest is on the table. I'm going out to lunch.'

'Thanks, Helen.' He always made my name sound like 'Huln'. He clambered down and started yelling for his nephew, Billy, who was in one of the barns. 'Bully!' he called. 'Haw, Bully!'

A strangled bellow in reply meant that Billy had heard and would be coming in any minute. Billy was skinny and always hungry. He could eat for Scotland.

'Going anywhere nice?' asked Bruce, taking off his boots. Jess fussed around him. She loved him.

'Just off with the girls.' I knew that he wouldn't want to know what I was doing 'with the girls'.

'Oh aye. While the cat's away!'

I suppose I blushed at that, but he didn't notice. He never looked straight at you anyway. He was a shy man with a bulbous nose, like a habitual drinker, which was unfair because he hardly ever had more than a pint or two. I had never seen him the worse for drink. He would fix his eyes on a point just above your left ear when he spoke to you. The remark was thrown away. It was what he always said when I went off somewhere without Sandy.

'Will I pull the door behind me when we've finished?'

'Yes. You've got your key?'

He felt in his pocket. 'I have.'

'You can leave Jess in the house when you're done for the day. I'll be back to give Fiona her tea. She'll be late anyway. Just help yourself to lunch and switch the stove off, would you?'

'Will do. Thanks, Huln. See you tomorrow.'

'See you tomorrow, Bruce.'

I threw a warm waterproof jacket into the pick-up. You can never be sure about the weather, even on a fine day. Then I drove out of the yard, glancing around to make sure I didn't have any unexpected visitors. It was unlikely at this time of day, particularly while everyone was away at the show. I stopped outside Louise's cottage and hooted. Joe came out and slid into the seat beside me.

'The picnic's under the seat.'

'You should have let me bring something.'

'This is my treat.'

We drove inland between tall hedges where the last of the honeysuckle was rampant but already withering. Blackberries lurked among the leaves, shiny jewels, not yet frosted. A few wasps clung to the fat berries and sucked their juices in hungry despair.

'This is the road we walked down that Sunday, isn't it?' said Joe.

'That's right, only this time we just keep going.'

We were heading in towards the hills. Soon, rocky slopes rose steeply on either side of the road and a burn tumbled alongside us. This was forestry country now although years ago, when I had first moved here, it had all been empty moorland. At first the marching firs had seemed intrusive but now times had changed and there were broad leafed trees as well, particularly along the edges of the plantations. I liked the birches best with their silvery white bark and their leaves like dazzling coins of light. Tourists always bypassed this area in their single-minded pursuit of the Highlands so it was quite unspoiled. You could see wind turbines, distant robotic ghosts, but not here. Not yet. There were otters living alongside the burns and you would often see dragonflies hovering over the pools and lochs.

We climbed higher and higher until there was open heathland all around us, burnished with dead and dying heather, with the occasional distant small farmstead perched in the lee of a hill and more remote turbines. I had always found it surprising how much the landscape could change in a few short miles.

'What do they do up here?' asked Joe. 'The farmers I mean.'

'Sheep farming. And wind farming now. Sometimes if feels as though the whole place will be covered with turbines. But at least they compensate the farmers. Either way, it's a hard life. They get snowed in most winters.'

'I bet they do. I know all about that.'

'Of course you do.'

'We had so much snow back home last winter that the guys who clear the roads couldn't keep up with it. A lot of the side roads were blocked for weeks on end. It was hard just getting about. And ice storms. You've seen nothing like it.'

His legs were too long for the front of the pickup and he kept shifting about. I was so conscious of him there beside me that it was painful. The land had flattened out into expanses of scrubby moorland interspersed with ragged patches of evergreen. To the right of the road, a wooden signpost, invariably covered with mud, indicated the narrow track to Poldarrach. I slowed and turned and then we were climbing up through tall pines with the sunlight filtering down in hazy lines and green grass between them, soft, long, weirdly lush, even now, in late autumn.

About a mile along this track was a car park, just a peaty clearing among the trees, and it was here that we left the pick-up, all by itself.

'Not exactly a major tourist attraction,' said Joe.

'No. You get a few people coming out at the weekend, but not in the middle of the week like this. Not at this time of year anyway.'

We fished the picnic basket from under the seat and set off along a narrow path through the trees. There's something magical about the track to Poldarrach. It has a lot to do with the way you don't see the place until you're almost on top of it. You wind your way up and down a path, barely more than a sheep track, fringed with heather and blueberry, and quite suddenly there's a wooden bridge over a burn, a deep, noisy, peaty, frothy tumble of water at this time of year, and then you climb up again over a steep bank and there it is: a ruined village set in a sheltered saucer of land among the hills. The sun dazzled us as we looked down at the piles of stones. Even in bad weather it was reasonably calm here. Today it was warm for the time of year and very still.

My stomach was crawling with nerves. I think I was afraid that Joe might say something stupid. But he didn't say anything at first. He just looked down into the hollow, screwing up his eyes against the low sunlight. And then he scrambled down the hill a little way, turned back and reached up towards me. I took his hand and jumped down to stand beside him.

'Tell me about it,' he said.

'It's very old. They say Robert the Bruce came here. But in fact the village was probably here even before that.

'Robert the Bruce?'

He seemed overcome by the age of the place in that lovely ingenuous way some North Americans have, valuing what we have far more than we do ourselves.

'There would have been lots of plots of land. Folk just grew what they needed on small patches. Onions. Kale. Weird white carrots apparently. Grains of some kind. Oats, probably. If they had a bad year they would go very hungry.'

'I reckon they would.'

He stared down at the ruins. The stone walls were only a couple of feet high at the most, but the pattern of the houses was still visible. Right in the middle of the village, there had once been a double row of cottages with a narrow alleyway running between them. The rest were set individually upon patches of ground, edged by low stone walls. Here and there, an ancient, twisted hawthorn marked a boundary between plots. The trees were old, perhaps descendants of hawthorns that had been planted there time out of mind, sacred trees back then, protective. A couple of big buildings had once faced each other across a broad track that traverses the edge of the village, winding up and out of sight into pine woods. This was the old pilgrim's way our lecturer had once told us about.

'That was the inn and there would have been stables on the other side of the track.'

'This is so amazing, Helen.' Joe seemed genuinely taken with the place, not just trying to please me. 'When did you first find it?'

'When I was a girl. We moved out to the village from the town. My parents took over the shop. It took me a while to make friends. So I just used to take off on my bike. For hours and hours.'

'But how did you find your way out here?'

I remembered how it had been and the way I used to sit among the stones, a dreamy but rather lonely teenager, trying to conjure the ghosts of the past for company.

'I used to go to the library a lot. I think I must have read a bit about it in an old book. Then I found it on a map. I just followed the track and found it and it seemed even more mysterious. I tried to find out more about it. It wasn't easy. Nobody knew anything about it. There's a lot of stuff on the net now, of course. But it was quite tricky back then.'

He set off along the path again and I followed him.

'How come you know so much about things like this?' he asked, over his shoulder.

'I've always been interested in history. That was what I wanted to do, you know.'

'Do what?'

'History. At university.'

'And did you?'

'No. Well, I did for a year.' I told him briefly about my father's death.

'Why didn't you go back to college afterwards?' he asked as he scrambled down a particularly steep stretch of path.

'My mother was very vulnerable. And then I met Sandy. You know how it is?'

He said nothing, only took my hand, helped me down and let go again.

We left the picnic basket behind a boulder, close beside the old pilgrim way, and then threaded the pathway between the houses. The summer vegetation had mostly died back here. The ground was dry enough at the moment and the paths were well drained and springy, though very soon the winter rains would come in real earnest. It could rain for days on end here, gales pushing rain clouds in from the west, torrential rain, day after day. A curlew rose above us, its sad call a string of bubbles in the air. I wondered what Joe was thinking.

The village was roughly circular with the Poldarrach burn running along the edge of what had probably been a cultivated area to one side of the settlement. Right in the middle of the village, there was a shallow depression, a dried up mill pond. The mill stream, now a dry meander with a ruckle of stones along the bottom, had once fed this pond from the burn and returned to it again just before the modern bridge. Straddling the dry stream, there was the remains of a sluice gate that had controlled the flow of water. Below that, the mill itself was just another large heap of stones.

It didn't seem to matter that the houses were only knee high. There was something about the shape of the space, about the pattern of the buildings, something that held the spirit of the village as surely as if it were still standing. You could feel it all around you. It was what nobody had ever understood. Nobody but me. For me, this space held the idea of the village as it had once been. We were standing on a stretch of green turf at the back of one of the cottages when Joe, who had been turning around restlessly, looking here and there, said 'It's kind of ...'

I waited for him to speak. He hesitated and then started again.

'It's kind of as if ...' He stopped again and shook his head.

'As if what?' I was almost holding my breath.

'It sounds crazy, I know. I don't have the words. And maybe I'm stupid. But it feels as if it's all still here. Spooky.' He stopped. 'D'you know what I mean?'

He picked up a fragment of white quartz, threw it high into the air and caught it in his clenched fist as it came down.

'So now you think I'm crazy,' he said.

'No. I feel it too. But nobody else ever has. Not that I've brought many people here. Hardly any, really.'

We circled the village together and then went back and found the picnic basket. Still within the magic circle of Poldarrach, we climbed up the broad pilgrims' track and sat down beside it on a patch of flowering thyme.

'So where does this track go then?' asked Joe.

'There was a shrine to a saint called Ninian, down on the coast, and this would take you there eventually. You can still go there. There's a cave where he used to go and pray. But I think the road was used for transporting animals as well. An old drove road.'

'Is that why the inn is where it is?'

'I suppose so. It must have been a busy place. What with folk grinding their corn and travellers passing through. You'd never know now, would you?'

I took out the picnic and Joe ate beef sandwiches with enthusiasm. I drank a glass of ginger beer and nibbled at some chocolate. I wasn't hungry. Happiness always took my appetite away.

'So why is it deserted? What happened?' asked Joe.

'Enclosures happened. Improvements.'

'This is an *improvement*?' He gestured round at the ruins in disbelief.

'Landowners started enclosing their land and putting sheep on it instead of people.'

'I don't understand.'

'Well before that, everyone would have had his own wee bit of land. There were communal fields as well, and the cattle would graze the hills roundabout. They must have been scrawny beasts, but healthy enough I suppose. Then the landowners decided to improve things. It was supposed to help the farmers, but in reality it only helped the landowners.'

'Typical,' said Joe.

'Pretty much par for the course. The sheep took over and a lot of people were forced to leave.'

'So when would this be?'

'I don't really know. Late seventeen hundreds maybe. This would have been a big place, home to a lot of people, so they would hang on to the bitter end. I always wanted to research this kind of thing, back when I had plans for a career, but I never got that far. This place would have made a good study. I was always into history.'

'I can tell. Didn't people protest?'

'They would get together and try to knock down the new walls at night. The landowner would have them built up again. But I suppose eventually they just thought, to hell with it all. Why stay where you're so very much not wanted? And there were alternatives by that time. So they went abroad if they could. To Canada sometimes. Made a fresh start. Which is fine for the young and strong. Not so fine for the old or frail. They died. But it's what people have always done. Tried to escape awful conditions. I don't know why people complain about economic migrants as though it were something new.'

'Sure,' he said thoughtfully. 'Moving away for economic reasons. It's what my family did as well. It's where so many Canadians came from.'

There was a pause while he ate another few sandwiches. He had a healthy appetite. But then there was a lot of him to feed.

'I still don't understand,' said Joe, presently, 'Why couldn't you go back to college after you married Sandy?'

'I was a farmer's wife. I *am* a farmer's wife.'

'So? Do you always describe yourself in terms of your husband's job?'

I raised my eyebrows. I was so used to people who would say, 'I'm not a feminist but ...' Sometimes I thought it would be nice to be able to say 'I am a feminist and ...'

But I had never quite expected to hear Joe of all people saying something like this. He didn't seem the type. But then he was full of contradictions.

'Oh, I have a lot of aunts,' he reminded me, laughing. 'Some high powered women among them. Scary but admirable. I don't always practise what they preach, but I agree with it. Honest!'

'Most people here didn't see the need for me to do anything. They told me Sandy was a good provider. And he is. And farming's still a partnership, when all's said and done.'

'It may be, but it doesn't sound as if it's one you chose for yourself.'

'I chose it by marrying him, I suppose.'

'We all need something of our own, Helen? Why not history?'

'Everyone here thinks it's a nice hobby for me. Helen's wee obsession with the past. So I don't talk about it much.'

He must have caught some bitterness in my tone because he reached out and very gently touched my cheek. 'Don't get mad at me,' he said.

'I'm not mad at you.'

It's just everyone else, I thought. Sometimes I felt mad at absolutely everyone else. Sometimes I would stop in the middle of some all too familiar conversation about how lucky I was to live in such a beautiful place, and realise how bored I was. And then I would be furious with myself as much as the other person, whether it was Maisie or Mary or even my good friend Annie. How had I let myself become like this? Surely only dreary people were bored with life. That's what my dad would have said. And he would have been right.

We cleared the remains of the picnic into the basket. Joe stood up, stretched and began to wander up the old pack road, bending down occasionally to look more closely at stones or shrubs. He was whistling to himself and seemed completely self absorbed and happy. I assumed he was searching for somewhere to have a pee, so I stopped watching him and looked down towards the ruins instead. The sun was dipping down the sky, the days shortening relentlessly, but it was fine and quite warm even now. The bowl of land where the village lay was empty and very still. Nothing moved down there. Even the curlews were silent. I felt very sleepy so I lay back on the turf and closed my eyes. Late bumble bees were still busy in the fading thyme and every so often I could hear one of them droning over my head like a small plane.

I must have fallen asleep, because I dreamed, briefly, about Poldarrach and in my dream, the houses were intact. The mill pond was full and the mill stream was running, making little ripples on its stony bed. People were moving through the streets. I was surprised to see Louise, hanging out washing in her back garden.

She said, 'I have to get my sheets done, Helen. It looks like rain.'

I said to her, 'Oh, Louise! I thought you were dead,' and she looked scandalised.

'Of course not. Whatever gave you that idea?'

I had such a rush of happiness that I woke up with a start and opened my eyes. Joe was sitting beside me, looking down at me. He brushed my face with a wisp of grass.

'You were dreaming. Fidgeting and whimpering.'

'That's what Jess does in her sleep. I was dreaming about Louise of all people. I was dreaming that she was still alive.'

'I thought you might be dreaming about me.'

'No. You weren't there.'

'Pity.'

As I sat up, he leaned over and kissed me, a real, dangerously passionate kiss. His tongue was in my mouth and he was kissing me so hard that it bruised my lips. This time he didn't apologise or run away. This time he really meant it, and I responded. I reached up and put my arms round him, and his shoulders were warm and hard beneath his shirt. I hadn't been kissed like that for years. I had almost forgotten how. It felt new and unfamiliar. Sometimes I had caught myself thinking, 'Nobody will ever want to kiss me again.' And I had honestly believed it was true.

'Oh my God, Helen,' he said when we came up for air. 'I've been wanting to do that again. I wanted it so much. I've thought of nothing else.' He hugged me close and spoke with his lips against my hair. 'I've been so off my fucking game. You don't know the trouble I've been in over you! Fucking stupid cross ice passes. You just don't know ...'

They had been playing away from home. They had lost, narrowly. Trust a hockey player to think of his game, first and foremost.

'Why?' I asked suddenly, moving away from him so that I could see his face.

'What do you mean why?'

'Why me?'

'Why not you, Helen. I think you're ...'

'What am I?'

'Have you looked at yourself recently?'

'Not a lot. I don't like myself much.'

'I only know that I look at you and I want you all the time. You have the right face for me.'

'Don't be silly.' I found myself faintly alarmed by his intensity. 'Joe, you could take your pick.'

'Don't treat me like a kid. I've been there and done that. Got a few more tee-shirts than I'll ever want or need. Fuck's sake, Helen, I'm telling you the truth.'

He clammed up then and started pulling at the turf. A sullen look settled on his features. I took his hand.

'Don't be like that.'

He shrugged. 'Like what?'

'All hurt like that.'

'I don't know what else to say to you, Helen. I don't know what to do to make you believe.'

'Believe what?'

'That I'm serious. That I'm telling you the truth. That I'm crazy about you.'

There was a passion in his voice and a clarity in his eyes that almost convinced me, but it worried me too. Whatever I had expected, it hadn't been this. We kissed again, our bodies pressed together on the springy turf.

Behind us, something coughed. It coughed in the exact tones of someone politely clearing his throat. 'Jesus!' said Joe, sitting up in alarm.

'Don't worry. Look!'

An old ewe peered anxiously at us over a hillock. Then, deciding that we were harmless, she bent to crop at the turf again, her front teeth rasping against the ground.

Joe started to laugh. We disentangled ourselves. Then he bent down and kissed me again, very tenderly.

'I don't want to leave this place. You're right. It's time out,' he said.

There must have been a choice. That was what I thought afterwards. There had been a choice and we had both made it. But I don't remember making it. There was a kind of madness in both of us and that day at Poldarrach, I think we both realised that it had overridden everything else: loyalty, caution, common sense. All those habitual virtues had been stripped away. For myself, it seemed as though I had been presented with the most extraordinary gift. If I allowed myself to think about it coolly, I could see that there was no future in any of this, but I didn't care. The future didn't matter. The present moment was sufficient. And I adored him.

– Chapter Twelve –

WE DIDN'T GO back to the pick-up immediately. We sat for a long time watching the sun move slowly across the ruined village, and the sky deepen and clarify with approaching evening. It grew very cold. Poldarrach looked like a stage set. Another kind of arena. I wondered what Joe was thinking. But how could I possibly know? The gulf between us, even then, seemed impossibly wide.

Joe slipped his arm round me, and I leaned into his shoulder, and we stayed like that, not saying very much at all. I wanted for us to be able to walk into the green and blue and gold of Poldarrach, like some kind of Brigadoon, and disappear forever. And I knew, or at least the sensible part of me knew, how foolish that was. So I made the first move. I tried to extricate myself, tried to stand up.

'I have to go home.'

'Do you?' But he only pulled me closer. 'Not yet. There are things I have to tell you. Things you need to know. Before we go any further.'

'Are we going any further?'

'I hope so.'

A few kisses. I could rationalise them as moments of madness. But did I really want to venture in any further? For once I had embarked on such a betrayal, there could be no going back. And yet I didn't think there was any future for the two of us either. How could there be?

'What things do I have to know?'

'About me. Things you don't know about me.'

'It doesn't matter, Joe.'

'It does matter. It matters a lot. You don't know much about me because I haven't told you anything.'

'You've told me quite a lot.'

'But not everything. You have to know what you're getting into.'

But maybe I didn't want him to confide in me too closely. Maybe I didn't want the weight of his problems on my shoulders. Not at that time anyway. Perhaps I had enough troubles of my own, even if they were mostly self inflicted.

'I don't want Fiona to get home and find the house empty.'

'Doesn't she have a key?'

'She does, but she'll worry. She'll think I've had a car crash or something. You know how it is?'

'Phone her.'

'She'll want to know where I am. I don't want to lie to her.'

He got up, uncoiling himself from the ground with a sigh and pulling me with him. 'You're probably right. Come on then.' He took my hand.

We kissed on the bridge and again under the trees where it was already dark: long, deep kisses with a touch of apprehension in them, our bodies already moulded together as though they belonged. All the time there was some sane part of me that was saying, 'This is crazy. This is impossible. What are you thinking of?' but I was well past caring. I knew it was mad and bad and dangerous but there were two people in my head fighting it out, and the reckless individual was winning the argument. No contest.

I drove home slowly with his hand on my knee. We met few other cars and certainly nobody I knew. I let him out at Louise's cottage, and we kissed again, very quickly, hardly a kiss at all, just in case somebody came round the corner. But nobody did. The road stayed empty.

'When will I see you again?' he asked. 'When is Sandy coming back?'

'Later on tomorrow. But Fiona will be home tonight. '

'Come when you can then.'

'I will.'

'You're sure?'

'Sure I'm sure.'

The house was dark and chilly. Bruce and his nephew had cleared the table after themselves and put the dishes in the dishwasher and the cheese back in the fridge. Jess came to greet me. She jumped into her bed in the kitchen, turning round three times and lying down with a sigh but she was as restless as I was. Supper time. I filled the kettle, went through to the sitting room and switched on the TV to be greeted by the East-enders signature tune. Siggy was asleep in Sandy's chair, curled around to conserve his body heat in front of a non-existent fire. He stretched and opened his owlish eyes to stare at me but didn't get up. He was waiting for me to light the fire. I flicked channels but couldn't find anything I wanted to watch, so I went back through to the kitchen.

I had just brewed a pot of tea, when the phone rang, making me jump.

'Mum?' It was Fiona. 'Mum? I tried earlier but you weren't there.'

'I had Jess out for a walk. We went up the hills for an hour or two.'

'Good.' She didn't really want to know where I had been, just that I was back. 'Did dad phone?'

'Not yet.'

'He'll be well smashed by now.'

'He will not.' I said it automatically, though it could be true. Sandy wasn't in the habit of getting drunk, but these kind of shows always involved alcohol. They were time out as well, after a fashion.

'Anyway,' I said. 'Why are you phoning?'

'Can I stay down here tonight? At Shona's?'

'What does her mum say?'

'She suggested it. Don't think she can be bothered to run me home.'

'What about your school stuff?'

'I can manage. My school stuff's OK. I can borrow a tee-shirt to sleep in and wash my knickers.'

'What about your books?'

'I've got those too. Oh go on, mum! We're watching a film.'

'I thought you were working.'

'We've finished.'

'Has Lee phoned?'

She giggled. 'Only once.'

'How long for?'

'Only ten minutes. Then we messaged. A lot.'

'Let me speak to Shona's mum.'

'Don't you trust me?'

'Yes. But I need to check that it's all right with her.'

Shona's mother seemed happy for Fiona to stay. I had been presented with the unexpected and dangerous gift of an empty house.

I poured out a cup of tea and drank it. Jess looked at me and thumped her tail on the edge of her bed, her eyes shining. I thought about Joe, down in Louise's cottage. I imagined him going to the fridge and taking out a beer. I saw him running his hand over the smooth body of one of Vezio's wooden horses. I was alone up here. He was alone down there.

The phone rang again. It was Sandy. His voice was slurred but he was controlling it very well.

'Hello, Helen,' he said. 'Mary says I have to do an ET so that's what I'm doing.'

'How's it going?'

'Fine. How's it going at home?'

'Things are fine here as well.'

'Bruce and Billy managing?'

'Of course.'

'Don't forget to shut the hens up for the night.'

'No. I won't forget.'

But I had forgotten and it was almost dark. I had better do it now.

'Have you had a good day?' I asked.

'Great. I met old Willie Burnett.'

'I thought he was dead.'

'So did I. He's as fit as a fiddle. Son's taken over the farm now.'

I really didn't want to get into one of those endless conversations about who was dead and who was alive, who was farming what land and who begat who. I knew from bitter experience that they could go on for hours, like passages from Genesis.

'What are you doing tonight?'

'We're going out for steak and chips.'

'Nice.'

'What about you?'

'I think I'll have an early night. Take a book to bed.'

'Is Fiona there?'

'No. She's staying down with Shona.'

'OK.' He sounded disappointed. 'You're sure she is with Shona? Not with that Lee?'

'No, she's not with that Lee. I spoke to Shona's mum.'

'Well that's fine then.'

He had wanted to say goodnight to her. He wasn't used to being away from home. He always felt homesick, even if it was only for a night or so. I felt a pang of remorse.

'You could phone her there if you wanted to, you know.'

'No. She'd only be embarrassed.'

'I don't think she'd mind. In fact I think she'd be pleased.'

She would pretend to be embarrassed, but it would just be a pose, for Shona's benefit.

'Well, maybe I will then.'

I gave him the number. 'Have a nice time,' I said. 'See you tomorrow, Sandy.'

'We might be late. We're going back to the show for a few hours in the morning.'

'Don't worry about it. I'll manage fine.'

I hung up, put on my wellies, and went out to see to the hens.

A few years ago a fox had got in among my chickens and caused terrible devastation. There had been blood and feathers everywhere. They kill and carry on killing you see. They don't do it out of malice. But we put chickens in small spaces and clip their wings so that we can collect their eggs. The fox literally doesn't know when to stop. The chickens panic but don't fly away and he just goes on killing. It's what he's programmed to do. He can't help himself. Cormorants do the same thing when they find inland fishing lakes well stocked with trout. The instinct that ensures their survival in the wild is a disaster on a domestic scale.

I went down and shut the chickens in their coop. They were already in there for the night anyway, creatures of habit, and all I had to do was slide the door after them. I fed Jess and let her out for a pee. I still hadn't quite decided what I was going to do yet. The farm was quiet and when I closed the back door, I felt a bit like a chicken in a coop myself. Jess curled up in her bed again with a sigh of contentment. Siggy opened an eye but didn't move. He was cross with me because I hadn't lit the fire.

I went upstairs and took a shower but instead of getting into my pyjamas, I dried my hair and then I did my make-up, trying to reproduce the effect Fiona had achieved. I dressed carefully but casually with some vague idea of not giving the wrong impression. With nightfall and a full moon, a frost had come and the stubble on our fields was glistening. When

I was ready to go out, I clicked on the answering machine and switched off all but one of the lights. Then I went into the yard, locking the door behind me, leaving Jess and Siggy to their own devices. Siggy had a cat flap and Jess had been out all day with Bruce and would probably sleep till morning.

I walked towards the cottage in the chilly evening, with my breath steaming, but by the time I got halfway down the lane the doubts were already creeping in. No matter what Joe said about what he felt, I found it hard to believe him. I saw myself knocking on the door and Joe ignoring me or, worse, opening the door to stare at me in dismay. Part of me would be disappointed. But I was not yet past the point of no return and part of me would be relieved. I should turn around and go right back to the farm and do exactly what I had told Sandy I would be doing. I should go to my chilly bed all by myself with a good book and a nice cup of tea.

Fortunately – or perhaps unfortunately – when I turned the bend in the road, I saw Joe muffled up in a big fleece, slumped on the bench outside the cottage in the moonlight, a beer in his hand.

He looked up eagerly when he saw me and as I got closer, I could tell that I wasn't imagining it. He looked delighted at my unexpected appearance in his garden.

'Helen! How did you get away?'

'Fiona's sleeping in the village. She phoned.'

'And Sandy?'

'He's at the show till tomorrow.'

'Were you coming to see me?'

He looked as if he couldn't believe his good fortune.

'Do you want to see *me*?'

'What do you think?'

'I think we shouldn't be doing this.'

But he had already put the beer down and pulled me close. He started kissing me again, forehead, cheeks, lips, fingers laced in fingers.

'Come to bed with me, Helen,' he said, in my ear. He ran his hands up and under the sweater. His fingers were ice cold on my skin. 'Come to bed with me now.'

Oddly, I don't remember making that final decision. I think I was a little out of my mind. I remember an exciting unfamiliarity about it all, a frenzy of kissing and touching, and struggling out of clothes. Then came the sudden moment of caution, because I wasn't that stupid, neither of us were. There was the awful wait while he scrabbled around looking for protection. I know that when I finally found myself naked in bed with him, I was suddenly aware, with a shock, that this was the bed where Louise had once slept. It was her big indulgence, that bed. She had told me once that she was a restless sleeper and liked to have room to move.

'I can't be doing with these piddling single divans!'

So she had bought herself a big brass bedstead with a springy mattress. The bedroom was chilly, and we slid under the quilt, Louise's quilt, that still smelled of the dried garden lavender she always used, and between the sheets that smelled faintly of Joe. And then we lay still for a moment, our bodies touching, lips against lips, hardly breathing, relieved to be here at last, just taking pleasure from this proximity, from the knowledge that we needn't hurry. That we had all night.

All the same there came a moment where I wanted him to hurry, needed him deep inside me, called out to him.

We made love in ways I had never known before. Joe was adventurous and vigorous and I remember being embarrassed by his obvious experience and my lack of it and being surprised and intrigued all over again by the sheer, demanding messiness of good sex, the gloriously sticky sweaty sensuality of it. But the power of my own response to him took me by surprise, and then I didn't care, because he just swept me along with him and there was nothing but sensation which only bred more desire.

Later, we got up and made toast and coffee and sat huddled together on the couch in the sitting room, not because it was cold in there, but because we couldn't bear to be apart. At about half past ten, the telephone rang, startling us both. I had guilty visions of Fiona, leaping to conclusions, phoning her father, telling him. But it was only Betty McGowan, asking Joe if he would donate a prize to the Over Sixties Christmas Raffle. If he could donate a hockey stick or a signed shirt they would sell more tickets to the youngsters. Betty was a night owl and always lost track of the time.

'Yes, Betty. No, Betty. Yes, Betty, I'm sure I could. A shirt probably. I can sign it.' He was sitting beside me, one arm around me, the other holding the cordless phone. It was the one I had bought for Louise during her last illness so that she could keep it beside the bed.

There was a pause, though I could hear Betty clucking at the other end. Joe insinuated his free hand inside the robe, his robe, though I was wearing it, a blue towelling dressing gown that smelled of soap.

'No I'm fine, Betty. I know it's late but I've been doing some stuff about the house,' he said. He grinned at me. Then he took one of my nipples between his fingers, pinching it gently, almost absent-mindedly.

There was a long spell of nodding. 'Mhm. Mhm,' he kept saying. I reached up and touched the back of his neck where the hair grew longer, the dark hair that you could see just below his helmet when he was on the ice. Hockey hair. He sighed, then shook his head. 'No, Betty. I'm fine. Never felt better and that's the truth. I think this place suits me.'

At last he managed to finish the conversation. 'Sleep tight, Betty,' he said, gently. He put the phone down.

'She said I sounded tired.' He held me at arm's length and looked at me. 'You look tired too, honey.'

He had on shorts and a big tee-shirt with 'Hockey ain't just a matter of life and death – it's more serious than that,' written on the front.

His face was even more scarred than I had noticed. One elbow too, below the sleeve of the tee-shirt, was bumpy and misshapen.

'Look at you,' I said, touching the marks. 'Have you been injured often then?'

'Comes with the territory.'

'When you're an enforcer.'

He pulled a face. 'I don't like that word much. I just don't like being messed around, it's true. If you have to drop the gloves, you do.'

All hockey players took off their gloves before an on-ice fight. I had already learned that much.

'So what happened to your face?'

I ran my fingers over his right cheekbone.

'Puck to the head,' he said. 'Vulcanised rubber at high speed. Does a hell of a lot of damage. I have a metal plate in there.'

'Poor Joe.'

'I was out for quite a few weeks with that one. There's a song back home. It talks about love being like a puck to the head.'

'Does it?'

He slipped a hand inside the robe again, taking my nipple between thumb and forefinger. It grew hard to his touch. He edged the gown open and leaning forward took the nipple into his mouth, running his tongue up and down over it.

'Stop it.'

'Why? I like it. Don't you?'

I pulled his head closer. 'I love it ...' I couldn't help myself. Unwise as they might be, the words just tumbled out. 'And heaven help me, but I think I love you, Joe.'

'Do you?' he asked. 'Well that's just as well.' He pushed me down on the couch, nudging my legs gently apart with one knee. 'Because I surely love you.'

A little while later, I went through to the kitchen and made coffee for both of us. I think the sudden and mutual mention of the 'l' word had shocked us both. It had just slipped out, but how could either of us retract it now? And did it mean the same thing to both of us?

'So you enjoyed the hockey game?' he said at last. 'I couldn't get much out of you in the bar.'

'Annie was doing the talking.'

'So I noticed. She usually does, doesn't she?'

'I suppose so. I didn't know it could be so fast and furious, Joe. And I didn't know about the fighting. Well, not really.'

'What did you think about it?'

'It was so exciting. They call you Sky, don't they? That's what somebody was shouting. Come on Sky Napier. And that time when we were skating too.'

He had been ferreting about on the bookshelf and he came back with an old Canadian hockey magazine. He flicked through it and opened it at a picture. It was a photograph of himself, but much younger and very fresh faced. There was a sort of beauty about his face then, as there is now. But back then, it was thinner, unscarred, symmetrical, the hair longer and very dark. He was leaping up at speed to avoid a player who had fallen over, and the camera had caught him in mid air. I reckon there were a few feet between him and the ice.

'Sky Napier,' said the caption.

'It was always what they called me. Even when I was a kid. I could always jump if need be. And I was a great one for lobbing the puck over the plexi as well. I used to get into a lot of trouble for that. Endangering the spectators.'

'Sky. That's nice. I like it. God, but you were good looking then.'

'Was I? I was very young then.' He looked at the picture and frowned. 'You would never know would you?'

'What?'

'What a goddamn fucking mess I was.'

Were you?

'Oh sure. Sky fucking Napier. Shit for brains.' He shook his head, lost in the past suddenly.

'What kind of mess?'

'All kinds of mess. I was drinking too much for one thing. The only reason I ever got away with it was because I was so young and my recovery times were shorter. I would get up and look at myself and think, "Hell, I can't play." But I would sort myself out in time for the game. Usually.'

'Why?'

'Why what?'

'Why were you doing it.'

'Because I hated my life.'

His words curiously echoed my own, but that must have been before his marriage, before his troubles with his wife began. He had told me nothing to justify or explain such a statement.

'Why didn't you stop. Do something else?'

'No,' he said patiently. 'I didn't hate hockey. The hockey was what kept me sane. I wouldn't have survived without it. I loved the hockey, heart and soul. I just ...'

He sighed, looked at me, shook his head. 'Never mind. Let's not go there eh? Let's not spoil things. I'll tell you soon. But not tonight.'

'All right. But I don't mind listening if you want to talk.'

He shook himself and stood up. 'Not yet,' he said. 'Sometime I'll explain. I promise. But not yet.' He stretched out his hand to me. 'Let's go back to bed. Let's make the most of the time we have. C'mon. Come back to bed with me. Now.'

We made love without shame or inhibition. We used all Joe's meagre supply of contraceptives. As though he felt the need to reassure me, he said, 'This is all I've got. I had them at the bottom of my bag. I don't do this stuff nowadays. I really don't.'

'Oh no. Not much.' I laughed.

'You know what I mean. You're the first for a long time.'

I looked at his grave, dark face in the muted light of the bedroom and I believed him. Joe didn't lie. He just didn't tell me the whole truth. Not then, anyway.

We slept very badly. We were exhausted, but it's difficult to sleep with someone you hardly know. And after all, I had never attempted to sleep – really sleep – with anyone except Sandy. Not as an adult, anyway. The electrical engineer in Edinburgh didn't count. We hadn't even got as far as the bedroom. I had slept with Fiona when she was just a toddler and used to slide into the bed beside me whenever Sandy got out of it.

'Has he gone?' she would say, coming through when Sandy had got up for the early morning milking. 'Has he gone yet, mum?'

I missed that, lying with my arms around her, listening to her quiet breathing.

But it was very strange to be curled up there in Louise's unfamiliar bed with Joe's big, hard body beside me. He was a restless sleeper, continually jiggling about, tossing and turning, snoring a little when he slept, and he was warm, warmer than me. I reckon he was playing hockey in his dreams. When the light began to filter into the room at around four o'clock, we made love again, and then we both fell fast asleep, really, deeply asleep and when I woke up it was half past five. I tumbled out of bed in a panic, struggling to get into my clothes.

'What's wrong?' asked Joe. He looked puzzled and very sleepy, with his face unshaven and flushed, his hair ruffled.

'I have to get back to the farm. Bruce will be arriving any time now. Early milking.'

'So?'

'So he usually comes into the kitchen expecting his morning tea. I must go.' I leaned over and kissed him. 'Oh Jesus. I must go!'

'Jesus has nothing to do with it, honey.'

He was warm and sexy, and I would have given anything to be able to get back in beside him.

I rushed out of the cottage in the dark, slipped my smart shoes off and waded over the muddy fields, avoiding the road. I daren't risk being seen by Bruce. Then the fat really would be in the fire. Delivering eggs at this time in the morning didn't seem like a very credible excuse. I scrambled barefoot over tussocks and molehills. The grass was damp with another sprinkling of frost, starred with white mushrooms, and my feet were scarlet where they weren't muddy. I stood in a cowpat and said, 'Oh shit' and started to laugh.

I ran across the garden and made it through the front door of the house that was well hidden from the lane, just as Bruce was coming into the yard. I rushed down the hall, unlocked the kitchen door and then flung myself into the downstairs bathroom. It would never do for him to find me in this state. Even unobservant Bruce might notice something odd. I ran some water in the bath, and washed the mud and the bits of cowpat off, just as Bruce came into the kitchen and shouted, 'Hi Huln'.

'Morning, Bruce,' I called over the sound of running water. 'Put the kettle on. Won't be a minute.'

I dried my feet, splashed water on my face and went out to speak to him.

'You're dressed early,' he said in some surprise. He was used to seeing me in my dressing gown.

'Fiona's away in the village. I had an early night.'

'Nice and peaceful for you,' said Bruce, casually. He was spooning tea into a pot. 'When will the boss be back?'

'Tonight, probably. They're having a few more hours at the show today.'

'He'll have been on the beer last night then?'

'Oh I expect so.'

'You'll have been at a loose end ?'

'Not really. Nice to get the place to myself for a change.'

I took a gulp of tea and put bread in the toaster. I didn't feel guilty, only triumphant at the success of my deception.

'Best get to work, Huln' said Bruce.

When he had gone, I took a long hot shower. I was alarmed to find that my thighs were faintly bruised and that I was very tender with all the unaccustomed lovemaking. I rubbed skin cream into myself, dressed in jeans and a long sleeved shirt and tried not to think too obsessively about what I had been doing with Joe. Later, when I was cooking breakfast for Bruce, the phone rang.

'Did you make it?'

'Only just. I went through the fields. Barefoot. I'd have ruined my good shoes otherwise.'

'I went back to sleep.'

'Lucky you.'

'You tired me out. Are you OK?'

'Yes. I'm fine.'

'Are you sure?'

'Yes. I'm sure.'

'You don't regret it? '

'No. Of course I don't regret it, Joe. Not a minute of it.'

'When will I see you? I need to see you.'

'I don't know. Soon. I'll think of something.'

'Me too.'

What if Joe came up to the house when Sandy was home? Presented himself at the door. 'Do you know what your wife has been up to? Do you know what your wife has been doing with me?'

What had I got myself into?

'Joe ...' I said. This was a new dance, and I didn't know any of the right moves, nor which way I ought to face. This wasn't like line dancing at all. It was more like dancing on ice. Tricky and precarious and slippery and you were reliant on your partner to steady you.

'Now you're worried.'

He could read my mind.

'No. No, I'm not.'

'Listen. You don't have to worry, Helen. I won't make things hard for you. At home.'

'Of course you won't. I know that Joe.'

'Just as long as you do. You can trust me,' he said.' Honest. Besides ...' There was a long pause. The line crackled. Our phone lines rubbed against trees and crackled all the time.

'I love you, you know,' he said suddenly. 'I love you a lot. That's the problem.'

'It is a bit of a problem, isn't it? It would be much easier if ... if it was something casual.'

'For sure it would. But it isn't.'

I'll see you soon, Joe. As soon as I possibly can.'

I hung up. The bacon was overcooked, the sausages like sticks of charcoal. I could hear Bruce coming into the yard, whistling.

There it was again. The 'l' word. Love. There could be nothing casual about such an admission.

What had we done? And how was it all going to end?

– Chapter Thirteen –

AT ABOUT SEVEN o'clock that night, Mary and Morris dropped Sandy off at the door. He looked very relaxed and happy and it was obvious that he had had a good time. Jess was ecstatic as usual and even Siggy deigned to purr and rub up against his legs. He had brought a carrier bag full of leaflets showing monstrous pieces of red or green or yellow machinery like giant Tonka toys, none of which we could afford. He had also brought me a bottle of elderflower cordial, which was nice, except that I made it myself every year and had a store cupboard full of the stuff. Then he produced a big horsy headscarf with a blue and red border. It looked like something the queen might once have worn on her Balmoral holidays.

'Mary thought you might like it.'

'Did she? I must remember to thank her.'

'Do you like it?' asked Sandy. He seemed worried. Had it just possibly crossed his mind that he had never, in all the years of our marriage, seen me wearing a headscarf either on my head or even round my neck? Probably not.

'Yes, Sandy. It's lovely.' I gave him a kiss on the cheek. 'And it was nice of you to think of me.'

'I missed you. You should have come.'

'Maybe next year, eh?'

Soon after that, the weather deteriorated with a vengeance. There would be no more idyllic trips to Poldarrach for Joe and myself. The rains came teeming down, front after front racing in from the west and dropping grey sheets of water onto our fields. Sometimes it felt as though nothing had happened between Joe and me. How could anything possibly have happened? Maybe I had imagined the whole thing. As usual, I went to the library van in the village every week and got out more books, history mostly. I found myself studiously avoiding the love stories. There we were, Sandy and myself, sitting quietly in front of the television every evening, just as we had done for the past eighteen years. I was reminded of that scene at the end of Brief Encounter. One Saturday afternoon, I switched on the television to find Rachmaninov's heartrending melody filling the room, while Celia Johnson talked about her 'ordinary *men* in an ordinary *mec*' but it was too much for me and I switched it off. Fiona talked to Lee on the telephone or texted for hours on end. But Joe didn't phone me, and I deliberately didn't walk past the cottage. I even drove past with averted eyes. I felt terrified of what might happen next. I still felt as though my whole world was on a cliff edge. All of us might wash away with the rains. The destruction would be terrible. Chaos would ensue.

Inevitably though, I saw Joe down in the mini-market. Our eyes met over the baked beans and the tins of tuna, but there was nothing we could do about it. Our fingers couldn't even touch, though I thought I might faint with the terrible physical imperative of wanting him. I just stood there, dizzily, watching him. I think he must have felt the same because he paid for his things and then hung about by the door, but he was too big for the place and kept having to move to let people get past, and I could tell that Diana wondered why he was lingering there. Lust makes you so reckless. Maisie was in, buying her morning rolls, and she was chatting away to me and to Joe. We kept nodding and smiling and agreeing with her, and as we did, our eyes kept meeting and sliding away again. I had to plant my feet firmly on the ground and hold onto the wooden shelving to stop myself from being drawn towards him. The desire between us seemed so visible, so tangible, that I couldn't imagine why everyone else in the shop couldn't see it. Eventually he left, on his way to a training session, he said, and by the time I came out he had driven away.

Needing an escape from the farm, I went down to the line dancing that week. When I left, Fiona was doing her homework without any prompting from me. Sandy was in his office, wrestling with the computer, which he hated and seldom if ever worked on.

'I'm going to the pub afterwards.'

'Fine, but I'll probably be in bed when you get back.'

'Haven't seen you for ages,' said Annie as we changed into our trainers. 'How are things?'

'Fine. Sandy went to Edinburgh with Morris and Mary. I went to Poldarrach.'

I didn't say who with. I let her assume I had taken the dog. I had this terrible urge to talk round the subject, but always managed to avoid coming right out with it. It lurked there at the back of my mind though

'Why didn't you tell me? I'd have come with you. I could do with the exercise,'

'It was just a spur of the moment thing. I wanted to go back there. I needed to think.'

'Do you remember the lecturer … the one that told us all about it?'

'I do. You fancied him.'

'I did at the time. I wonder what our next craze will be?'

'Why? Are you thinking of giving up the line dancing?'

'No. But these things never seem to last very long with us, do they, Helen?'

'I think I might stick with this for the moment. It suits me.'

'Oh it suits me too. Just that sometimes …' She sighed. 'Don't you ever get bored, Helen? Don't you ever want something different? Something that has nothing to do with your family? And I don't mean some piddling little evening class. I mean don't you ever want to be just Helen, instead of Sandy's wife or Fiona's mum?'

Joe's lover, I thought. Just one more role.

'Sometimes I do.'

'Oh well!' She stood up. 'Maybe some day.'

I wanted to tell her. I needed to tell someone. To confess, perhaps. But I couldn't bring myself to do it. How could I? I trusted her as much as I could trust anybody, but she would be shocked. Annie was flirtatious but she was nothing if not faithful to Tim. I knew that, however supportive she might be, and in spite of all those jokes and digs about fancying Joe, she wouldn't approve. And she might let something slip to Sandy. Better not to talk about it at all.

We learned a new dance, or rather the rest of them learned a new dance and I fell over my feet and kept turning in the wrong direction.

'What's the matter with you?' asked Annie, when we had a break.

'You're worse than usual. You seem to be miles away. Are you feeling all right?'

I was miles away. In my mind, I was at Poldarrach or in Louise's bed, with Joe.

'I don't know. I can't seem to concentrate.'

'Not coming down with anything are you?'

'I don't think so.'

'Are you doing anything for your birthday?'

'I was hoping nobody would remember.' It was going to be our wedding anniversary the following week and my fortieth birthday on Saturday. I was at the stage where I preferred to forget about birthdays. They came marching round with a horrible inevitability and took you up and over a hill you didn't even want to climb.

'I have a birthday book. I look in it every week.'

'God, Annie, you're so efficient.'

'I know. Well I am where birthdays are concerned. So, is Sandy going to take you out anywhere nice? I mean it's special, isn't it? This one?'

'I don't think he's remembered.'

'I'll jog his memory, will I?'

'If you like. But I don't want a party. Do you hear me? Nothing like that. I mean it!'

'Are you sure you're all right, Helen?' She looked at me curiously.

'Yes of course.' I stood up. 'I'm fine. Really. Just feeling my age. Well, not so much feeling it as regretting it a bit. Forty years coming up and what do I have to show for it?'

'Fiona?'

'Well that's true. She's worth everything. But I won't have her much longer. Not really. She'll be off to university soon and then it'll just be me and Sandy most of the time.'

After the line dancing I went for a quick drink with the girls. I had half expected that Joe might be in the pub and then I would have been able to cadge a legitimate lift home, but there was no sign of him. I remembered that he had been away the night before, playing somewhere in England, but he would be back by now. I made my excuses – great big yawns and the plea of being very tired – and left early. It was pouring with rain again, and the road was dark and shiny. I had taken an umbrella but a sudden gust of wind turned it inside out and I resigned myself to being drenched by the time I got home. My feet skidded on mud and fallen leaves. Of course I couldn't pass the gate of the cottage without stopping, and once I had stopped, I found myself walking up the pathway and knocking on the door.

'Come in,' he called. 'It's open.'

I looked round to make sure that nobody was watching me, but the road was deserted, so I slipped inside.

'I thought you might come,' said Joe. 'Hoped you might. I remembered you had your line dancing tonight.' He still found it funny. He looked up at me. 'God you're so wet. Does it never stop raining in this Godforsaken place? Come over here.'

He was in the sitting room, cross legged on the floor, and he had been sorting out a great heap of papers: letters, family photographs, magazines and newspaper cuttings that Louise must have hoarded for years. He stretched out his hand. I knelt down beside him and he pulled me close and kissed my damp cheeks and my lips, stroking my wet hair. He made me sit by the fire, and then went off to make coffee for us. When he came back he had fetched a towel as well and he rubbed at my hair, clumsily but tenderly.

'You don't know how much I miss you when I don't see you,' he said.

'Me too.'

'I just want to be able to talk to you. I'm going stir crazy down here,' he said. 'I can't take much more of this. Especially not with this weather.'

'It's *dreich*. That's what they call it here.'

'What does that mean?'

'Damp, grey, depressing.'

'That's about right. But it would be OK if you were here.'

'I'm sorry.'

'It isn't your fault. There's nothing we can do about it, is there?'

'I don't think so.'

'I want you all the time, Helen. You're in my head. I'm stuck on you. I'm sorting out Louise's stuff, just to take my mind off you.'

'So I see.'

'Can you stay?' he asked.

'For a bit. We usually go to the pub after the class. But I left early. They won't expect me at home just yet. Have you found anything interesting?'

'I'm not sure. Maybe.' He held out a newspaper clipping to me. It had been slipped between the pages of one of Louise's gardening books. 'I almost missed it,' he said.

It was yellowing and musty and was dated some ten years previously, from a Lancashire paper, not one I knew. Perhaps Louise had made her own enquiries. It would have been good to have been able to ask her.

'What is it about?'

'Read it.'

It was headed '*The Anniversary of the Tragic Loss of the Arandora Star*' and was one of those pieces of local history that you sometimes get in smaller newspapers. '*Fifty years ago,*' it said, '*after Italy entered the war, more than 4000 men of Italian origin living in Britain were taken into custody as enemy aliens. The authorities commenced a hurried policy of deportation, and many innocent men were caught up in our rush to rid ourselves of what were seen as potential spies. In early July 1940 the SS Arandora Star set sail from Liverpool for Canada, with a complement of 1600 including crew members and a military escort. The internees included over seven hundred Italians, and almost five hundred German civilians. The ship sailed on Monday July 1st and, at 7 am on July 2nd, she was torpedoed by a German U-Boat. Lifeboat provision was poor and when she sank, some four hundred and eighty Italians and one hundred and seventy five Germans were lost at sea. The destroyer St Laurent picked up survivors and brought them to Greenock on the Clyde. It was only the following year that the full casualty list was released.*'

Joe watched me read the piece. 'Well?' he said.

'You mean, you think Vezio and Mario might have been aboard this ship?'

'Maybe. It would explain quite a lot wouldn't it?'

'And maybe they were drowned. It would explain some of it. But Vezio must have been well past military age. Fifty or more. Would they have deported him?'

'Would it have made any difference at that time? If they thought he was an enemy alien? Seems to me it's happening all over again in some places anyway, and not just with potential enemies. Alien is enough of an excuse.'

'You're probably right. We treated the Italians very badly during the war. Louise told me about it. Some cafes were even burned down in Glasgow. People who had been born or lived here for years and years. And Mario would have been quite young. People can be horrible.'

'They can. I think he was born in the early 1920s.'

'That would have made him roughly the same age as Louise.' I looked at the piece again. 'She got married towards the end of the war or just after. To Malachi. And that would have been after ...'

'After the Arandora Star went down.'

'Maybe with Vezio and Mario on it. I wonder how we could find out whether they were rescued or not?'

'What about the record office in Edinburgh?'

'We could probably look it up on the internet.'

'But it would be more fun to go to Edinburgh. Well, it would be fun if you could come with me.'

'People would talk.' I hesitated. 'It would look suspicious.'

'Only because you feel guilty.'

'Don't you? Feel guilty, Joe?'

'No I don't. Listen, Helen. If nothing had happened, you wouldn't be arguing now, would you? You'd come with me like a shot.'

'But something did happen. It's happening now.'

'All the same ...'

'When are you thinking of going?'

'Next Saturday maybe. We have a midweek away game and then a home game on Sunday.'

'I can't go on Saturday. I'm not sure the Record Office would even be open. And besides, it's my birthday.'

'Is it?'

'And don't ask me how old I am.'

'How old are you?'

Well, he had to know. All he had to do was ask somebody down in the village. 'A lot older than you. I'm thirty nine now.'

'That's my number. On the ice.'

'I know. And I'll be forty on Saturday.'

'Not that much older than me. And forty's not old!' He didn't seem surprised or discomfited.

'I feel pretty ancient.'

'Are you going out with Sandy then?'

'I don't know. I think Annie has something planned for lunchtime.'

'OK.' He looked disappointed. 'What about the week after? I'll have some time off. It's just a case of finding out when.'

'I suppose I could come.'

'We could spend the whole day together.'

'We could. Oh Joe, it would be such a luxury.'

He had filled a bin bag with Louise's rubbish. Now he took a green plastic storage box, piled all the remaining letters, photos and papers into it and shoved them onto one of the shelves.

I looked at my watch. 'I have to go home, Joe.'

'Right now? This minute?'

'Well. Soon.'

'It needn't take long.' He was already unfastening my shirt. I didn't object. 'You know,' he said, conversationally. 'I want to screw you senseless. And it needn't take long at all. Well, not if you don't want it to.'

Just because you're physically intimate with someone, just because you want to be near them, just because they're in your mind the whole time, you still don't know too much about them. Do you? You think you do, but you don't. You simply gloss over the questions. Love spawns a kind of joyful complacency. No problem is too great to be overcome. You think that desire breeds familiarity, but it's the illusion of familiarity. You may know the contours of a body, but that doesn't mean that you have any idea of what's really going on inside the other person's head, just as you may know the shape of a country without knowing what it's like to live there. Lust is no guarantee of knowledge. No. Lovemaking is just the beginning. As you peel away the layers, that's when you find out more. And it isn't always something you want to hear.

It must have been an hour later when I went back up to the farm. I could hardly bear to drag myself away from him, but I did. Somehow. Sandy had gone to bed early but Fiona was still up. She had been on the internet, as usual, talking to people online or looking at those vast fan fiction websites she sometimes frequented and contributed to. At least it was a change from messaging Lee, something which she seemed able to do for hours on end, back and forth, swift, flirty conversations.

'Hi, mum' she called. 'How was the line dancing?'

'Fine.'

'Did you go to the pub with the girls?' She always used the word 'girls' with a little ironic edge to it.

'Just for an hour or so.'

I went into the kitchen to make myself a hot drink.

Fiona called through from the office. 'Mum. Come and look at this.'

'What?'

'It's on the net. You have to come and look. You'll be interested, though.'

I went through and leaned on the back of her chair. I was weary and not just with the dancing, but I had no premonition of the bombshell that was about to hit me.

Fiona was staring at the screen, her face flushed and avid.

'Look at this,' she said.

I looked over her shoulder.

IS THIS THE VIOLENCE THAT IS KILLING OUR SPORT?

It was a newspaper headline in big, bold, exclamatory letters.

'What's this?'

'Joe!' she said. 'It's Joe!'

'What do you mean?'

'I typed his name into Google and just look what I came up with.'

'How did you find this?'

'Easy. I put in Joe Napier. I tried Lee first and I got stats mainly, but not many, because he's so young. So then I tried Joe because I knew he had been in the NHL. For a little while anyway. Not long though. They let him go. I think they had to let him go.'

She hit the back button and I saw a list of references: several thousand references to Joe Napier

'They aren't all him,' she said. 'There's a maths professor in Massachusetts with the same name. And someone selling firearms down in Texas. Then I put in Joe Napier and ice hockey and NHL to narrow it down.'

I had already found the Kestrels' website, had read about the team, had looked at Joe's statistics on there and his picture. I had read the rules of the game too, so that the next time we went, it would make sense without Annie's constant commentary. Joe had promised to get more tickets for us very soon, although we were planning to go anyway and pay for the privilege.

But I hadn't looked for Joe specifically like this. Why hadn't I thought to look for Joe? Maybe I hadn't wanted to read about his marriage. Maybe that was it. Maybe I hadn't wanted to come up with any smiling wedding photographs from the Canadian newspapers.

I suppose when you're Fiona's age it seems the natural thing to do, if you want to find out about somebody. I had already suggested that Joe might find out about Vezio and Mario online. Why hadn't I thought that it might be possible to find out about Joe himself? But then I hadn't needed to by then. I thought I knew him.

Fiona pressed the forward button, and the piece flashed up again. There was an illustration, obviously a fight of some kind, on the ice. It was blurred, the two central figures almost unrecognisable, but all the same there was a terrible violence about the picture and about the attitudes of the pair and the players standing around. It was different from the fight we had seen at the game, and more serious somehow. There was blood, a pool of it, scarlet against the white ice.

'What is this?' I asked.

'I told you. It's Joe!' Fiona turned to me triumphantly. 'No more Mr Nice Guy eh?'

'What on earth do you mean, Fiona?'

'This was only last year.' She scrolled up, then down again. 'Look at the date. He lost his temper big time and got himself a five game ban. But that's not all. He's been a really bad boy, mum. Look at this.'

She flicked back to the list of references. Some of them were quotes from articles and none of them were reassuring. In fact 'Is this the violence ...?' was the least of it. I scanned the other headlines. '*Sky Napier Grounded, Problems on ice and off, Coach's fury, What's with Sky? Keep your temper Joe, Sky's hit rock bottom.*' It went on and on. Terrible, glib headlines. I couldn't believe what I was seeing. Could they be talking about the same person as the man I thought I had begun to know and most certainly desired? The man that I had imagined I loved.

Just wait till I show my pals!' said Fiona. She hit the print button, and the printer sprang into life.

– Chapter Fourteen –

Fiona took the printout up to her room but I stayed in the office, clicking from article to article, reading about this other Joe Napier, the one I barely recognised.

'*Don't believe the myth that no-one gets hurt in hockey fights,*' said one of the pieces. '*Players, particularly so called enforcers, can get broken noses, cuts to the eyes and a great many other unpleasant injuries.*' I knew. I had seen them. I had run my fingers across the scars. '*Cross checking, high sticking and various other illegal checks, particularly from behind, can be even more dangerous. In this case big bad Joe – Sky – Napier tangled with Sharks defenceman Chris Wallis, and Wallis lost, big time.*'

Chris Wallis, whoever he was, had spent the night in hospital with suspected concussion and Joe had been suspended for several games. I clicked back and read more. It was a catalogue of misery, but always the same story. 'Sky' Napier, the bright young man with the world at his feet, success and prosperity assured, had – within a very short space of time – been drinking too much, training too little, and losing his temper too often, too violently. The wonder of it was that he had avoided prosecution. But he had changed teams often as well, eventually sliding down the leagues, and you could see the pattern. Even I, who knew so little about the game, could see the pattern. The coaches would look hungrily at his obvious skills in defence, or as a winger, or both, because he had always been an intelligent player. He had always been a wonderful skater too: strong, agile, skilful, and capable of scoring occasional goals when need be, but a big powerful presence on the ice as well. He was certainly a playmaker: someone who could set up goals for other people to score. His points for what were called 'assists' were high for a defenceman. So much I had learned over the past few weeks.

So they had looked at him and thought 'If we can sort him out, give him a little discipline, he'll be an asset to the team.' And they had started with high hopes. But they hadn't ever sorted him out. Each time there had been a honeymoon period when the reformed Joe could do no wrong, and then somewhere in the middle of the season he seemed to sabotage himself, things had always started to go downhill, and the old demon had emerged: the Joe who drank, who got into fights on the ice and off, who might lose his temper and throw a game away on a whim. Nobody could handle him for long. Nobody had wanted him for long it seemed. Not even his wife.

I felt sick. My head ached with it. My heart was pounding. Was this the reason Joe had wanted to get away from Canada in a hurry? Was this why he had come to Scotland? Was this why his ex-wife didn't want him to see too much of his daughter? This must have been what he had been keeping to himself, all those times when I had felt there was more to be said, but he wasn't saying it? This must have been what he was trying to tell me when he had said, 'there are things you ought to know. Things you have to know about me.'

Oddly enough, Sandy was more inclined to be forgiving than I was. Not that he would have been if he had known everything. But the next day he read the piece that Fiona had printed out.

'It's that kind of game,' he said. 'Like rugby. These things happen. Heat of the moment. That's the way it is.'

'How can you say that?'

'Just so long as he doesn't try any of it down in the pub, I don't care.'

But that was the problem of course. He had behaved badly not just on the ice, but off it as well. He had told me so himself, but I had made excuses for him. I had thought he was being hard on himself. But even he hadn't told me the whole story. And now that Fiona and her friends knew, word would soon get about. I wondered what the rest of the village would think about it all.

Actually, the rest of the village didn't say very much, or if they said it to each other, they kept quiet where Joe himself was concerned. Maybe his reputation made them nervous, but there's a good deal of tolerance in your average lowland Scots village, a sense of seen-it-all-before-live-and-let-live.

To my certain knowledge our village had played host to a retired bank robber who could never be persuaded to leave his house, even when the roof almost fell in after one winter gale, (this resulted in wild speculation about buried loot) and – but this was just a rumour – an ex spy, who took up winemaking in his retirement and supplied village parties with vats of elderflower champagne and a far more potent bramble wine. People would no doubt gossip about it all, but if Joe kept his head down they might be prepared to give him the benefit of the doubt. Even Betty and Maisie refused to believe most of the stories about him and told me that if he had behaved badly in the past, they thought he must be a reformed character now.

'I speak as I find,' said Maisie, 'And I've always found him to be a nice, polite young man, so I won't believe ill of him now.'

Mind you, Maisie would have found it hard to believe ill of the devil himself, so that was no recommendation. Still, it was true that Joe had behaved impeccably since his arrival on all counts except one, but that one concerned me very closely. I was shocked by what I had read but I found myself conjuring excuses for him. I didn't know what I was going to say to him when we met again.

Annie must have reminded Sandy to get a move on with planning something special for my birthday, or maybe Fiona did, because when I came down on Saturday morning, there were a couple of cards on the table: a very sentimental one from Sandy and a funny one from Fiona, as well as a big bouquet of flowers from both of them. I was touched.

'I thought we might go out for a meal tonight,' said Sandy. 'Celebrate our anniversary and your birthday at the same time. I've asked Mary and Morris. And I've booked a table.'

My heart sank. 'What about Annie? And Tim?'

'I didn't want to make it a big party. I thought you wouldn't want a big party. You know what you're like.'

What was I like, I wondered? I no longer knew. I kept surprising myself and not always for the better, either.

'Annie said she was coming up to take you out for lunch anyway. She wanted to treat you. Just the two of you.'

Annie and I went down to the pub, where we ate ham salad

sandwiches and drank wine. She gave me a card, and my present: a silver brooch with an intricate Celtic design.

'Mary and Morris,' she said. 'Wow. That'll be a really fantastic evening won't it?'

'I can't tell you how much I'm looking forward to it.' I crossed my eyes and poured more wine.

'You know,' she said. 'And this is definitely the wine speaking ...'

'What?'

'I sometimes wonder how you and Sandy ever got together.'

'It seemed like a good idea at the time. The wonder is that we've stayed together.'

'But you have.'

'True. Lack of opportunity maybe? He's a good man.'

'Yes he is. And good men are hard to find. Talking of *bad* men, have you heard all this stuff about Joe?' she asked. 'How he's had all kinds of problems in Canada? I wondered what he was doing over here. He must have taken a hell of a pay cut to come. Most of them come for the cash, but he could have earned much much more at home. If he'd behaved himself.'

'It was Fiona who found it. On the net.'

'Was it? I did wonder. Have you talked to him about it?'

I shook my head. 'No. I haven't seen him.'

'Will you say something when you do?'

'I suppose I'll have to. But God knows what.'

'Maybe he's finally turned over a new leaf.'

'Maybe he has.'

Annie wanted to talk about it but I tried to head her off. I needed time to think. But I found myself wondering not if he would do it again, but why he had done it in the first place. What imp of self destruction would get into this apparently polite and talented young man again and again? The break-up of his marriage had just been part of the pattern. As soon as I could, I changed the subject. We had a moan about advancing age and how we hated to be reminded of it.

'Birthdays eh? Life's a bitch and then you die,' said Annie. 'Drink up, girl. You need to be well tanked up if you're spending the evening with Morris and Mary.'

Tim gave me a lift back to the farm. Apart from the flowers, there had been no evidence of a birthday present that morning, but when I got home, it was obvious that Sandy had been up to something. He ushered me into the sitting room.

'Surprise!' he said and pointed into the corner of the room. Sitting there was something I can only describe as a small wooden mausoleum, an ornate but chunky cupboard, with double doors and strange turned pillars on either side. No wonder he hadn't attempted to wrap it up.

I didn't quite know what to say to it. I didn't even know what it was. So I stepped backwards, grinning foolishly.

'Gosh,' I said.

'Do you like it?' He sounded anxious.

'Yes, of course I do.'

This was a lie. It was truly hideous. But I must have sounded enthusiastic enough because he flung the doors open with a great flourish. Inside was the television set, and the Sky box, each neatly installed on its own shelf.

'Ah. Very clever.'

'But do you like it?'

'Yes.' I gave him a kiss. 'It's lovely, Sandy. Just what I've always wanted. Where on earth did you get it?'

'That big dip and strip place near Glasgow.'

'You mean this was once an antique?' I knew the place he meant. They bought in nice pieces of old furniture and dunked them in baths of acid. What on earth had this been when it was old?

'No. I don't think so. But they've started making things out of odds and ends.'

'Cannibalising things. I see what you mean.'

I wondered who had thought of it. Who, in the name of God, had looked at all these miscellaneous bits of junk and thought 'television cabinet'. The mind boggled. I thought about Vezio's Gallopers, down in the cottage, and Joe's long strong fingers, smoothing that beautiful wood.

Fiona came in. 'Well?' she said. 'Do you like your telly cupboard, mum?'

It was plain that she thought it was hideous too. But for once, she had managed to keep quiet. I could see that she was trying hard not to laugh.

I instantly felt defensive on Sandy's behalf. 'Yes. I do like it.'

'Really?'

'Yes really.'

'Random.'

For once, it seemed like exactly the right word. It was a deeply random piece of furniture.

We went to a restaurant in the next village, a place called The Weavers, because it was in a building that had once been an old weaver's cottage. It was a welcoming place and the food was good, so we should have had a lovely time. In fact I would rather have gone with Sandy and Fiona, just the three of us, and then I might have enjoyed myself, but we had to suffer Mary and Morris as well. Sandy always assumed that I liked Mary as much as he did. Maybe it was my fault. Maybe I had never told him that I didn't. Not in so many words.

The food provided a safe topic of conversation for a while, but when we were deep into our main courses, Mary said, 'Any more news on the cottage front, Sandy?'

She was always saying things like that 'On the cottage front. On the garden front. Weatherwise. Workwise. Schoolwise.'

'Not yet.' Sandy was eating a large piece of blue and bloody steak. He liked his meat rare. In fact he had once been known to say, 'Just wipe its arse and take its horns off and it'll dae for me' to a startled waiter, but that was when he was much younger. He was behaving himself tonight, in honour of my birthday.

'Can't you get him out?' she asked. 'That Canadian.'

I rose to Joe's defence in spite of myself. 'What on earth do you mean? It's his cottage, Mary. He owns it. You know? He inherited it.'

'Yes but by all accounts he's not a very desirable neighbour.'

Sandy looked across at me. 'Helen knows more about him than I do.'

'He's a nice enough young man.'

'So he's planning to stay the whole winter then?' asked Morris. He had big glasses, like Clark Kent. Come to think of it, you would have to be quiet and mild mannered, living with Mary.

'I think so. The ice hockey season finishes in April over here.'

'Do you think he might sell you the cottage after that?'

'He might. Depends if he decides to stay with the team for another year, or if he wants a holiday home in Scotland.'

'Waste of good living space,' said Sandy, suddenly. 'We could do with that cottage. Very useful.'

'So who exactly is he?' asked Mary, curiously. 'What's his exact relationship to Louise Marshall?'

'His grandmother went off to Canada with Louise's Uncle Freddy just before the war. Which makes him a cousin of some kind, I think.'

'So why did Louise leave him the cottage?'

'I have no idea. She certainly never mentioned him to me. I don't know too much about him, really. I don't know what problems he's had in the past but he seems to be OK now.'

'He's smashing' said Fiona. 'But not as fantastic as Lee Casey.'

'Who?' asked Mary.

'Fiona's been seeing another hockey player.'

Mary looked disapproving. 'Well I sincerely hope he's a nice young man. Not like this Joe.'

'Oh he is, Aunty Mary,' said Fiona. 'He's lovely, isn't he, mum?'

'Yes,' I said loyally. 'He's very sweet. '

'Sweet?' echoed Mary, as though she had never heard the word before. 'Is he another Canadian then?'

Fiona nodded.

'Why don't they have Scottish players? Seems daft to me. Taking jobs from our lads.'

'They have some but they need to train more of them up,' said Morris, unexpectedly. 'That way they wouldn't need to import so many of them.'

It wasn't a very nice word: 'import'. In some ways, it was as bad a word as 'alien'. It made me think of Vezio and Mario being deported on the *Arandora Star*, if that was what had happened to them.

Sandy finished his plate of steak and chips and belched discreetly. He never ever put his knife and fork together, but always left them sprawled across his plate. It was one of those things that could irritate you to the point where you wanted to commit murder. Mary looked across at him and smiled. She always tolerated behaviour from Sandy that she would never stand from Morris.

'Ah, that was good,' he said, leaning back in his chair. He had left his salad on the side of the plate, like a piece of decoration. So had Morris and Mary. All his family did that. Nothing green and uncooked ever passed their lips. It was a Scottish thing. My father's family had been the same, though my mother had been different. She had liked her greens and tried to persuade everyone else to eat salads too. It had always made me wonder whether there wasn't foreign blood in her. And in me. Though as far as I knew, I was Ayrshire to the bone.

Sandy raised his glass to me. 'Happy birthday, Helen. Many happy returns.'

The others raised their glasses as well, and echoed him. And I suddenly felt like a complete shit. I wanted to cry. Sandy was a good man. I hadn't intended any of this. I excused myself, went to the loo and, like all women, hovered over the seat. Nothing worse than sitting down on a splashed seat. Then I washed my hands and brushed my hair. The mirror distorted my face like a fairground mirror, giving it a bizarre quality. Once, years ago, when I was still at school, I had taken a summer job in a hotel in the Highlands. One of the guests, an elderly but still handsome photographer, confined to a wheelchair, had told me that he thought I was beautiful. He hadn't made a move on me or anything; he just complimented me with casual warmth and said that he would like to take my picture. But I had believed him. It had changed my perception of myself. We all need a little validation. And now, even though I no longer thought I was beautiful, I had begun to believe Joe when he told me he loved me. But still the habitual misgivings beset me. Why me? Was I safe, because I was married? I would make no demands on Joe. I would make things easy for him. I *had* made things easy for him until now. But I had a lot to lose. Everything, in fact. It was all madness, and I ought to put a stop to it right now.

I put on some lipstick and fluffed up my hair. Then I took a deep breath and – full of good intentions – went back out to join my family.

– Chapter Fifteen –

GOOD INTENTIONS OR no, I wanted Joe all the time. Images of us making love flitted across my inner eye. It was as well nobody knew what I was thinking. It was bad enough that I could do nothing to banish my craving for him, but alongside this was a vague sense of repulsion, fear, pity or some uncomfortable compound of all three. Reading the articles and extracts online, however dispassionately – and how could I ever call myself dispassionate when I was so possessed by desire? – I still couldn't help thinking that Joe had serious problems. There was something wrong somewhere. And yet nothing I had seen or heard from him, except perhaps for a slight secretiveness, would have lead me to suspect that he was anything but a successful and skilful athlete. Which was frightening. Deeply, horribly frightening. Perhaps it was the fracture in my perception of him that scared me more than anything else. Was I walking into danger with eyes wide open?

On Friday night, Fiona was doing another sleep-over with a friend, and Sandy had gone off with Morris to a Community Association meeting. I knew that they would go to the pub afterwards and he would be out for several hours; it would be at least midnight before he came in, so I took my chance and went down through the dark fields carrying a flashlight, with my breath steaming in the cold air.

There was a light on in the garage, a single inefficient bulb hanging from a wire. Joe had cleared a space for himself and was in there, working on the Gallopers in the gloom, so absorbed that he didn't see me at first, and I could stand quietly in the doorway, watching him, his long fingers moving precisely and competently over the wood. He had done quite a lot to them in a short time, even assembling the horse that had been in pieces into a recognisable whole. He had not repainted them, but had left the original flaking paint in place wherever he could, and where it was gone completely, he had oiled the wood. That's what he was working on now. The Danish oil smelled very fresh and pungent in the warmth of a fan heater.

At last he became aware of me. 'Hello, stranger,' he said. He glanced at me over his shoulder but didn't stand up or come over to me. He carried on polishing away at the last of the three horses. He looked very serious, surly almost.

'I'm sorry I couldn't come any sooner.'

'Couldn't you?' He carried on working. 'I wonder why?'

'I just couldn't get away. I had to wait for my family to go out. Besides, I think people might be talking about you.'

'They've been talking about me ever since I got here, honey, so what's new?'

'What's new is the way they're talking and what they're saying. Haven't you noticed anything?'

'Sure I've noticed. I don't get quite so many food parcels from Maisie these days. But it was bound to happen. Word was going to get about sooner or later. I'm no angel, Helen. Everyone on the team pretty much knew that before I came. I don't know why but I kind of figured nobody here would be very interested. They're not much into hockey, are they?'

'I'm so sorry.'

'Why? It isn't your fault if I've behaved like a shit.'

'I just wish you'd told me.'

'What should I have told you?'

'Well, stuff like this for a start.'

I had a print-out of the magazine article in my coat pocket. I had been carrying it about with me. '*Is this the violence* ...' I pulled it out and handed it to him. It was folded and creased and he spread it out on his knee so that he could read it. Then he swore, very softly, under his breath. 'Fuck!' he said. 'I didn't even know this was on the net. But why wouldn't it be, when you think about it?' He stood up and crumpled the sheet with a sudden, angry gesture. 'Who showed you this?'

He loomed over me in the shadows and I found myself inadvertently backing away from him. He stopped, taken aback by my alarm.

'You're scared of me!'

'I'm sorry, Joe.'

He wiped his hands on his jeans and shook his head, repeating, 'Why should you be sorry? You haven't done anything.' He was clutching his arms around himself in the familiar defensive gesture. 'And now you're afraid of me.'

'I'm sorry I saw it. It seems so ... intrusive, somehow. An invasion of your privacy.'

'What else have you seen?'

'There's a lot on the net about you, Joe.'

'I'm sure there is. What made you look me up?'

'I didn't. It was Fiona. The kids do, don't they? It's what they do. But once she had found it all ...'

'You were curious.'

'Can you blame me?'

'No. No, I can't. And I was going to tell you. I promise. I was going to tell you everything. It was just hard, you know?' He went back to crouch down by the horse, running his fingers over its wooden flanks.

Some of it's ... well it was hard for me to read. In fact I *didn't* read all of it.'

'Why not?'

'It made me sad.'

'Sad?' That pulled him up short. He looked almost tearful, his eyes glistening in the muted light.

'It didn't seem like you. That's all. But maybe I don't know you very well after all.'

'No. Maybe you don't. I don't need anyone to pity me. I'm not looking for pity.'

'I didn't say I pitied you. Just that I was sad for you.' The sympathetic tears prickled behind my own eyes. 'Is it true, Joe? Is any of it true?'

'Yes. Yes, it is. Well. A lot of it's true. I expect there's some exaggeration in there, but I have to hold up my hand to a lot of it.'

'Then why? Can't you tell me why?'

'Oh Jesus Christ, Helen.' He sat down suddenly on the floor and leaned back against the horse. 'I don't know. Maybe I need anger management, eh? Maybe it's the way the game is.'

His eyes slid away from me, even as he said it. He wouldn't look me in the face. He looked into the middle distance, frowning.

'It sounds more like gang warfare.'

'No. No, it isn't like that. I'm a big guy. I've got weight and strength on my side.'

'I know that.'

'And it's my job out there. If someone's going after our players, it's my job to step in.'

'And crack their skulls off the ice?'

'You still don't understand, do you? You go at speed, and you get angry. They do the same. You do what you're supposed to do, but sometimes it all goes too far. OK, there are times when I may have been out of order. But the Chris Wallis thing ... He'd been winding me up the whole game. He knew what was coming. Christ, Helen, anybody would have lost it with him. Wallis himself said it was an accident. We've spoken since. He doesn't bear any grudges. It was just that the press made a big thing of it.'

'But what about all the other stuff? There's been so much. So many other things. Off the ice as well as on it.'

He stood up again in one fluid movement. 'What is this, Helen? The fucking inquisition?'

The vitriol in his voice made me blink and I turned away. I would have walked out of the door but he was beside me. He caught at my arm. 'I'm so sorry. You didn't deserve that.'

'No. I didn't. And it scares me. It's true. You scare me when you're like this! I can't cope. I don't need this, Joe. I really don't need this.'

'Don't go.'

I hesitated and was lost. 'I don't want to go. But I don't know what to think.'

'Maybe I just have trouble with authority.'

He was trying to make some kind of joke of it, but I didn't feel like laughing.

'Listen. Listen. Please. I'll admit I've had some problems. But I can play the game. I can still do it. I've sorted myself out. I'm sure I have. I'll be fine. I've had plenty of offers for next season.'

'Have you?'

'Stuff happens. Clubs know it. It's no big deal. I've had a couple of calls since I've been here. One looks OK. Player coach. Place not a million miles from Carrie. And Alicia, which is more important. Carrie and I are never going to get back together, but I do want to see my daughter.'

He pulled me close to him, rubbing his hands up and down my arms, trying to reassure me, perhaps trying to reassure himself as well.

'I thought if I let the publicity die down a bit ... everything's a nine days wonder with hockey. You don't take all this bullshit seriously. I can still do it, you know. I can play the game.'

The garage was gloomy and his eyes were dark spaces in his face. There was something desperately sad about him. Something sad and forlorn about those words, 'play the game'. What game was Joe playing now?

I had meant to be very cool and calm, but I began to cry and once I had started I couldn't stop. He said 'Oh Jesus, Oh honey, don't cry,' and put his arms around me, kissing me gently, as though he still had to prove that he could be gentle when he wanted. 'Helen. Don't cry. Why are you crying?'

'Because I'm afraid.'

'You know that I would never hurt you! Don't you? Don't you? How could I hurt you? I don't hurt women. Never. Ever. Well, not physically, anyway. I swear to you. I've never done anything like that. Not once. Not even been close.'

'I'm just scared of my own feelings, scared that I don't know you properly, but I've let myself get so involved with you. And I shouldn't have done it. We shouldn't have done it, Joe. It's wrong. And I'm not used to feeling like this.'

'Do you really feel guilty?'

'No, I don't. That's the problem. Or one of them. But I worry about *not* feeling guilty. And maybe I'm scared of being found out!'

'Why don't you tell him?' he said, suddenly. 'Why don't you just tell Sandy?'

It was the last thing I would have expected him to say. It took my breath away.

'Tell Sandy?' I echoed, foolishly.

'Yes. Tell him and have done with it.'

'How can I tell him? What good would it do? Then I'd lose Sandy and my home as well.'

'As well as what?' he asked.

'As well as you.'

'Who says you're going to lose me?'

'Oh come on!' I moved away from him, clenching my fists.' Of course I will, Joe. Of course I'm going to lose you. Are you daft or what? Or do you think I am? You're ten years younger than me. Come spring you'll fly off like the wild geese, and you'll leave me here. I'll have nothing. I'll be left with nothing.'

'I'm not intending to leave just yet. I've still got a job to do.'

'But it's a short term job.'

'I've got a house here.'

'You'll sell it. You'll go home.'

The inevitability of it choked me.

To my utter astonishment he said, 'Well, maybe I will. But even if I do, you could always come with me.'

I was speechless for a moment.

'Joe, that's a crazy idea.'

'Why should it be crazy? I think it's a great idea. We could be together all the time. Come with me, Helen. I know the bureaucracy would be tricky, but I'm not short of cash.'

'How can I? I'm a married woman with a teenage daughter and a farm to run.'

'Sandy can run the farm.'

'Not without me.'

'Nobody's indispensable.' He paused. 'Except maybe you. To me.'

'He relies on our partnership. I made that commitment to him and to the farm, all those years ago, and I can't just let it go now.'

I had thought about it though. It had certainly crossed my mind, though it had always seemed like a wild and impossible fantasy. I had found myself sitting in my kitchen, looking around and thinking 'How in God's name can you begin to unpick all this, the fabric of half a lifetime?' and then a sort of gloomy inertia would settle upon me, and I knew I would never leave.

'And what about me?' Joe asked. 'Don't I count in all this?'

'Don't make me feel any worse than I already do. It hurts. It hurts all the time.'

'I don't give a damn. I hope it does hurt. I hope it bloody does. I hope it never stops hurting you!' His mouth twisted and I saw that he really was close to tears as well. He looked young and awkward. My heart ached for him, for both of us.

He went back to the horse and started rubbing at the oiled wood again, very vigorously. It grew shiny beneath his fingers. The fan heater hummed in the background. It was very warm in the shed now. I watched him in silence for a while, just loving the sight of him. You could see why he seemed so powerful on the ice. His thighs were layered with muscle and there was a real physical tension about him, as though he could explode into action at any moment. He would be a formidable part of any team. Never a pushover. But even as his body distracted me, I could sense great waves of misery coming from him. In the heat of the garage I went over to him, crouched down and slid my arms up and under his tee-shirt. I rested my head on his warm back for a while. He smelled of the oil he was using, but he paused in his work.

'Joe, you must know I'm crazy about you.'

'It's not fair, Helen. There's something remarkable going on between us and you know it, and still you tell me that there's nothing we can do about it.'

'How can we? There's my daughter. And there's your daughter too. How can we possibly do this.'

Suddenly he turned round, pulled me off balance and lay me down, gently but firmly. His face hovered above me, shuttered and inscrutable. I no longer knew what he was thinking.

'We shouldn't be doing this. Somebody may come.'

'I don't care. I don't care.'

We were panting with anticipation and heat. All my senses were aroused to him. Frantically he pulled at my clothes and his own and we were kissing, touching, murmuring words of love and longing. We made love out there on the threadbare Indian rug that Louise had stored at the back of her shed. The wool made itchy marks on my back and then it made us sneeze. When we sat up again, we were both sticky with sweat, dusty, dazed and sated.

'I'm sorry,' he said.

'Why? I wanted it as much as you.'

'I could have hurt you.'

'But you didn't.'

'No. I didn't. I'll never hurt you. I want you, Helen, but maybe you're right. Maybe I can't have you. So I have to find a way of coming to terms with that.'

'I don't know what to do.'

'You mean there's a chance you might change your mind?'

'I just don't know, Joe.'

It was true. Nothing was solved, nothing answered. There was still some well of darkness deep inside him that I couldn't fathom. Something was wrong with him. I had no idea what it was, but it was there when we made love and it was there whenever we talked, in spite of everything he could do or say to reassure me.

– Chapter Sixteen –

THE TEAM WAS doing well and Joe was doing well too, basking in the glory of a string of wins. The local newspaper, anxious not to upset one of its major advertisers, dutifully reported the successes and printed pictures of the team, with Joe looming large, probably because he was so photogenic. He was asked to open a new pub in the town and was photographed with a couple of other players, all of them wearing Kestrels hockey jerseys, smiling broadly, pints in hand. The village regarded all this with a kind of wry tolerance.

'Do you think he's trying to redeem himself in some way?' asked Annie, after the line dancing.

'What do you mean?'

'Well, all these good works, promoting the team. It's not the picture that you get from some sources.'

'Maybe that's not a true picture either.'

'Ah,' she said, solemnly. 'The truth is out there I suppose. But what do you think?'

'I think he's had some problems in the past but he's put them behind him now.' It sounded like trite nonsense, even as I trotted it out, dutifully supporting the party line.

'Have you talked to him about it?' she asked.

'Not really. No. Why should he confide in me?'

'Because he seems to like you.'

'Yes, well.' I shrugged.

'And you like him.'

'Of course I like him. He's a nice man.'

'We hope.'

'Leave him alone. He hasn't put a foot wrong so far. He doesn't even get into fights on the ice. Look at his penalty minutes.'

'No, but he checks like a ten ton truck.'

'Oh well, that's different.'

'Try and find out, Helen.'

'Why do you want to know?'

'Because I'm a nosy cow. That's why.'

December was fast approaching and I had my pre Christmas panic dream, the one where it's Christmas Day and I've done nothing, no presents bought or wrapped, no cake baked, no turkey in the oven, and I'm running around wondering what to do. I have it every year and wake up sweating.

And then Sandy took my breath away by coming in from the pub one evening and telling me that he thought I should go to Edinburgh for the day with Joe.

'Why?' I asked blankly, genuinely shocked.

'Well didn't you say you wanted to go to the Record Office with him to do some family history stuff?'

'Yes, I did, but I'd forgotten all about it. I thought he was going to do most of it online.'

'He was talking about it in the pub and he said he'd quite like to borrow you for the day. He was joking, I know, but I said you'd been going on about doing Christmas shopping as well, so why didn't you go together.'

'I can't do that.'

'Why not? You know the city and he doesn't And he seemed to think it was quite a good idea. So why don't you go over on the train?'

'Yes, but ... a whole day?' I gaped at him, speechless for once.

'Look, the guy more or less asked my permission. Very straight. Man to man. I said you could do what you liked, and I thought a wee trip to Edinburgh would do you good. After all, hen, that's what you said to me when I went over to the show with Mary and Morris.'

'I know.'

'And I can tell you want to go.'

So we went.

We chose a rare day when Joe had no game and no training either. We left the village early, driving into the station. I was still amazed by Joe's audacity.

'How could you do it?' I asked. 'How could you bring yourself to do it?'

'Sandy was asking me all about my family history so I thought, hell, just go for it. I told him you had mentioned coming to Edinburgh with me but you didn't think you could get away from the farm. So he more or less leapt on that and said of course you could, it was time you had a break. I couldn't turn him down could I? It would have looked very strange.' He grinned at me, wickedly. 'It would have looked as though we had something to hide, wouldn't it?'

Even now, the memory of that conversation gives me a little frisson of retrospective disbelief. Even after everything that followed, the extent to which I was capable of that betrayal still frightens me. Not the betrayal itself, but my capacity for it.

We took an early but overcrowded train to Glasgow and then changed stations for the Edinburgh train which was full of businessmen and women, most of them clutching their phones, eyeing them constantly for messages, terrified of being out of contact for even half an hour.

I may not have felt guilty but I certainly felt very shy. This wasn't like being in the cottage or even being at Poldarrach. It was public and therefore embarrassing. Joe's Canadian accent drew people's attention, even on the Edinburgh train that was always full of tourists, summer and winter alike.

'Have you finished the Gallopers yet?' I asked as the train swayed through wintry fields towards Edinburgh.

'They're coming on. But we've been busy at the arena. New training schedules. I doubt if I'll ever get the whole thing to work properly. But they'll look good. Which I figure is all that matters. Preserving them.'

'What will you do with them when they're finished?'

'I haven't really given it much thought.'

'Could you get them home to Canada?'

'I don't know. I suppose I could ship them but it would cost a fortune. Besides, they belong over here. I could always give them to you, Helen.'

'Well, they'd be nicer than my birthday present from my family.'

'Why? What was your birthday present?'

I told him about the mausoleum. 'I shouldn't be complaining. It's very ungrateful of me.' More treason, I thought.

'It's more than you got from me. I didn't get you anything for your birthday.'

'Why should you? '

'But I want to. Maybe I'll get you something today.'

An older woman, sitting opposite, looked up from her novel. It was a fat and rather tattered book with an entwined couple on the front. She was wearing gold rimmed glasses and she looked over the top of them curiously, first at Joe and then at me. She didn't look disapproving or surprised, just intensely interested. Maybe she was a hockey fan who recognised Joe. Maybe she just thought he was worth a second glance.

'I don't know if Sandy would like a carousel in his front room,' I said, trying to change the subject. 'You could give them to a museum maybe.'

'I suppose I could.'

'Or sell them.'

'No. I wouldn't sell them. Where's this?' he asked, looking down towards the picturesque palace ruins on the shores of the loch.

'Linlithgow. Not far to go now.'

We got out at Waverley Station and walked straight up the Mound to the Royal Mile. It was cold, with a bitter East Coast wind blowing up from the Forth.

'This feels like home,' said Joe.

'I sometimes wish it felt like home to me too.'

'How long were you here, Helen?'

'Oh just a year. A year and a couple of months. Then dad got ill and it all went pear shaped.'

'Did you like living here?'

'I loved it. There was such a buzz about the place. The university and the city both. I was looking forward to moving out of halls, getting a flat, keeping house for myself.'

'And instead you finished up keeping house for Sandy.'

'It seemed like a good idea at the time. But I do miss the city.'

'I thought you were a country mouse.'

'I'm torn in two, Joe, and that's the truth. I never seemed to find out what I was, but I've nobody to blame but myself.'

We went into a café, down one of the closes off the Royal Mile, seeking warmth. The tables were small and set close together, and our knees kept touching. Wherever he went, there was never ever going to be enough room for Joe's knees. Then we did a bit of sightseeing, but at a spanking pace because of the cold. The lazy wind blew through us, while Joe looked up at the castle and down to Princes Street and to the Forth beyond. We didn't have enough time to see very much.

He kept saying, 'This is so beautiful,' like a typical tourist.

'You ought to come back here, Joe. Have a good look round. There's so much to see and you can't possibly do it all in a day or even a week. You should come here by yourself.'

'I'd rather be with you.'

'But we've only got today.'

'Maybe we can come again. In spring.'

'Well. Maybe.'

A wintry sun fought its way out of the clouds as we headed back towards Princes Street. We sat down on a bench in the gardens that seemed to have been turned into a sea of mud, not at all the way I remembered them. We sat there gazing up at the castle, at one remove from the roar of city traffic. Even the foreshortened and spiny roses looked as though they would never flower again. He slid his arm around me and I leaned my head on his shoulder. It was very peaceful, sitting like this, even in the middle of Edinburgh on a cold and wintry day. We seemed to be carrying our own blissful atmosphere around with us, just for that short spell.

'What will you do, Joe? When the season's over?'

'I don't know. Do you think I should sell the cottage to you and Sandy?'

I was surprised. 'Has he asked you about it?'

'No. But it has been mentioned to me.'

'Who by?'

'People were talking about it down in the pub. They said that Sandy wouldn't mind buying the place off me. Charlie McGowan mentioned it, for one.'

'That's because Charlie wouldn't mind renting it. And Bruce is after a place to live. Houses are hard to come by in the village. Don't you pay attention to any of them, Joe. You keep the house if you want it. I was supposed to sound you out about it.'

'But you never have.'

'No. Well other things happened didn't they? And besides, it's none of my business what you choose to do with your own house.'

'That's one of the things I like about you, Helen.'

'What?'

'You're so moral.'

'Moral?' I started laughing. 'Not where you're concerned.'

'No. Not where I'm concerned. Thank God.'

He leaned over and kissed me, his tongue in my mouth. His lips were dry and warm. He tasted of peppermint. Edinburgh went spinning around us, a blur of picturesque verticals, bare branches and traffic.

'But I can't make up my mind what to do about the house,' he said, when the world had settled down.

'Listen, you don't owe anything to Sandy. Louise left the place to you. You don't have to sell it to anyone.'

'I know that. It's funny. I knew nothing about her when I first came over.'

'You'd have liked her. She could always make me laugh. We used to laugh till we ached. Often about nothing much at all.'

'Helen, Helen,' she had said. 'You have to laugh or you'd cry.'

'Living in the cottage with all her stuff, I feel as if I'm getting to know her.'

'So don't sell it. Don't feel that you have to.'

'I suppose I could keep it. I could use it for holidays, even if I have to go back home.'

'That would be nice.'

Would it be nice? I thought of all those prospective years of waiting for Joe to come back. Writing to him, perhaps. Trying not to say 'I love you' too often. Looking after the cottage in his absence. Looking forward to each spring or summer. Maintaining the deception. It would be a sad way of living. And what about when he brought the new girlfriend? For there most surely would be a new girlfriend. There might be a string of them. What about when he brought a new wife? And children? To see Scotland. How would I feel then?

I didn't think I could bear it. I couldn't say any of it.

He kissed me again, long, deep kisses. In the busy city, where everybody was minding their own business, nobody noticed.

'Why me?' I asked. 'Why us?'

'Why does anyone ever want anybody else? You're right for me. I don't know how else to describe it. I love being with you. You just make me feel good about myself.'

'Do I?'

'You assume that I'm a nice guy and that makes me behave like one. And I haven't felt this good about myself for, oh for years. You've no idea how long.'

'You're not that old, Joe.'

'You've no idea.' He shook his head. 'But then I wonder, am I taking advantage of you? And that worries me. I just seem to have come into your life and stirred everything up for you.'

'Maybe I wanted to be stirred up. Maybe I needed it too.'

Around lunch time we did what we had ostensibly come to do and went to the Public Records Office to look for information about Vezio and Mario. It took a little while, though the assistant was very helpful, perhaps because she found Joe's story interesting but more likely because she found him interesting. You could see women going down beneath the full blast of his charm like trees in a hurricane.

We had been right in our assumptions. Both Vezio and Mario had gone missing from the Arandora Star, presumed lost at sea. And now we had the death certificates to prove it. We could have done it all online, but Sandy wouldn't know that. Sandy was very ignorant about computers.

'Poor old Vezio,' said Joe, as we negotiated the Princes Street crowds.

'He might have finished up in Canada. That was where the ship was going. He must have hung onto that thought. That he would see his daughter again. I think he was ready to forgive her, if not her husband.'

'I wonder what Mario made of it all?'

'He was young enough to make a new life. But listen ... Vezio quarrelled with Freddy's family, right?' I had been thinking about all this, trying to piece it together.

'Yes. He always blamed Freddy for stealing his daughter and, by extension, he blamed Freddy's family as well. That was what my grandmother always said.'

'But Louise was part of Freddy's family. So maybe he didn't fall out with all of them.'

'How do you mean?'

'Well, think about it.' I had the Gallopers in my mind. 'The roundabout was something really special to Vezio.'

'Yeah. He made the horses himself while his wife was alive and he loved them. He would never have given them up lightly.'

I couldn't help thinking of that photograph of Mario, beautiful, darkeyed Mario, among all Louise's souvenirs.

'Louise and Mario must have been about the same age. So maybe they became friends. In fact maybe they were ...'

'More than friends? It's possible I suppose. But how could it have happened?'

'Well, maybe after Francesca left, after she eloped, perhaps Vezio and Mario stayed in touch with Louise and Lottie.'

'With Freddy's nieces?' He looked sceptical.

'OK, so they *were* Freddy's nieces and I suppose that made them the enemy. But they were very young. Perhaps Vezio thought that it might be one way – the only way – of maintaining some kind of connection with his daughter, with Francesca.'

'It's possible, I suppose.'

'How could he fall out with two young girls? Louise and Lottie probably reminded him of his daughter.'

'Go on.'

'So if they kept in touch, maybe Louise fell for Mario. He was very handsome.'

'We're making all this up, aren't we?' He grinned at me. 'Telling stories.'

'Oh yes, of course we are. That's the fun of it. But it could be true.'

'I suppose so.'

'Besides, there were things Louise said. Nothing specific, just vague regrets about what might have been. And the fact that she kept his picture all those years. He was very good looking. Even in that old photo there was something about him. There was just something about the way she looked at his picture.'

'And then the war intervened?'

I nodded. 'The war and internment. I imagine they could maybe see what was coming beforehand.'

'They must have known what would happen.'

'And when he realised what was going to happen, maybe Vezio left his precious carousel with somebody he knew he could trust.'

'With Louise.'

'For when he came back. Except that he never came back. Nor did Mario. They died. Do you think it could be true, Joe?'

'I have no idea. But it's a good story.'

It could have happened like that. We would never know for sure, but it seemed a likely enough explanation. Why else had Louise kept the carousel all those years, even during her marriage, even after she was widowed and had moved house? Had she kept it in memory of Mario? You could see what he might have been like, even in a faded photograph. He must have been a bright light coming into her life, because that was exactly what Joe was in mine. Mario would have come into her quiet suburban existence. For all that he had been brought up in Scotland, he must have possessed a certain foreign charm. You could see it, even in that faded photograph. Some intimation of sunshine. How could she help but love him?

And then, suddenly, he was gone, snatched away from her. She might have hoped for a happy ending for a while. Until the sun had gone out for Louise as well, so that when Malachi Marshall asked her to marry him, she just gave in and went along with whatever else life had in store for her. But she had kept the carousel. I wondered what Malachi Marshall had thought about that.

What had she said to me once? 'You should never settle for second best, Helen.'

Were we embroidering the facts in order to justify our own infatuation with each other? But she had kept Vezio's Gallopers and maybe she had kept them just in case, one fine day, Vezio or Mario might come back for them. Or maybe she had just kept them in memory of Mario and the affair, if affair it had been, was so short-lived that there had been no time for disillusionment.

This was the story we told each other, Joe and I. This was the tale we made up, spinning a blend of dry facts and wild speculation into pure gold, as we walked through the chilly Edinburgh Streets. Even now, I still think of it as the truth, although I have no idea if it had really happened. There were no letters, no confessions, no usefully preserved diaries. Nothing. There was the photograph of beautiful Mario, and the cutting about the Arandora Star. There were two death certificates. There was the carousel, tucked away in Louise's shed for all those years, and that single casual remark, 'Never settle for second best.'

'And,' I said to Joe, after a while, 'There's you of course. We're forgetting about you.'

'What do you mean there's me?'

'You're a kind a proof.'

'How am I?'

'She left you the cottage, didn't she? And Mario was your great uncle. You were a link. You are a link. You even look a bit like him.'

'I don't. He was very small.'

'You do.' I laughed at his indignation. 'In profile you do. Even though you are seven inches taller and about twice as broad! You're the new improved Canadian model!'

He drew my arm through his own.

'I've done no Christmas shopping yet,' I said.

'Do you want to do any?'

'Not much.'

'I had other ideas.'

'What other ideas?'

'You'll see.'

– Chapter Seventeen –

WE WENT TO a hotel. I don't know how he managed to arrange it. Perhaps he had asked his team mates. Perhaps some of them were used to finding comfortable and discreet hotels that would accommodate couples who wanted to indulge in illicit sex in the afternoon. I never asked him. We walked up the hill from Princes Street, crossed George Street and went down the other side where the waters of the Forth were polished silver and grey in the distance. The hotel was in the middle of an elegant Georgian terrace, a tall, quiet, well kept house. The reception area smelled of lavender polish and the expensive out-of-season lilies decorating the desk. I think he had paid in advance. For the whole night. For which we couldn't possibly stay. But it wouldn't matter when we left. We were directed up a broad flight of stairs to a room on the first floor with a view down into a long back garden, its wintry desolation relieved by the unexpected froth of pink blossom on a viburnum and a scarlet splash of holly berries right at the end. Beyond the garden wall were more terraces of houses, falling away to the river, with the hills of Fife beyond.

The room was small and warm with a big double bed, damask curtains and framed scenes of Old Edinburgh on the walls. It too smelled of lavender and roses and I found a bowl of pot pourri on the dressing table. There was an empty wardrobe with real wooden coat hangers, not the slot-in kind, and an en suite bathroom. If the receptionist had noticed that we carried no luggage, she had passed no comment. Not a hint of a knowing smile crossed her lips. Joe had registered us as Mr and Mrs Napier and given the cottage as our address. I had said nothing at all.

It was a curiously formal setting. We weren't used to making love in such surroundings, and it made us a bit wary of one another. I excused myself and went into the bathroom, finding there a dish of miniature packets and bottles: soap and shampoo, body lotion and cologne. I had a pee, washed my hands, rinsed my mouth. I wondered what I was doing here. It all felt very unreal. When I went back into the room, Joe was already in bed, his naked shoulders and arms showing over the quilt, his clothes piled neatly on a chair. The room had that effect. You wanted to keep it nice.

'Come on in,' he said, pulling back the covers.

There was a packet of contraceptives, strategically placed beside the bed. I had gone on the pill during my year at university but then Sandy and I had been trying for a baby and after Fiona was born, no more children had come along, and I had more or less accepted my subsequent inability to conceive. But there had been no tests, we had seen no doctors. It had crossed my mind over the years that it might be Sandy who had the problem. Better safe than sorry, I thought now. Besides, I knew enough of Joe's past to make me cautious. I think he realised it too and took responsibility for my protection.

I undressed, self consciously, and slid in beside him. The room was warm but the linen sheets were cold. I shivered and closed my eyes. There was something acutely arousing about being naked in bed in the afternoon, naked between lavender scented sheets, cool and smooth, with the distant low pitched drone of the city traffic and the wintry birds, sparrows mostly, in the garden below. We were snug, nestled together and safe. Nothing could touch us here. Nobody knew where we were, except the receptionist and the porter below, and they didn't care.

We made love slowly, savouring each moment. We made love in the afternoon, and slept briefly in each other's arms. When we woke, alarmingly, embarrassingly, he moved down the bed and parted my reluctant legs and sucked at me, savouring me like some exotic fruit. This was something quite new for me.

Joe said, 'You taste so good.'

'Can that be true?'

'It's an acquired taste.'

I started to laugh. 'Don't tell me. Don't go there, Joe.'

'But I like to go there. And here, and here as well. Oh, Helen, I love all of you, altogether and that's the truth.'

The room was a safe haven. The bed was a downy nest. He got up and brought a little bottle of body lotion out of the bathroom and rubbed it delicately over my breasts and between my legs until I was roused to him again and then he slid inside me and we came together, rolled in the sheets that were warm now with the heat of our bodies. I felt tender and sore and thought I would have to be careful. Thrush, honeymoon cystitis. Reality lurked, just beyond the cocoon of this room.

There was a tray with a kettle, teabags and sachets of coffee and biscuits. We made tea and drank it in bed, ate biscuits and joked about the crumbs. But time marched on and it wouldn't do to stay too late. There was a long journey back for both of us. We lay together, face to face, and talked about leaving.

'I wish,' he said, stroking back my hair, 'I wish that we were really together. I wish we could stay like this and go to sleep again.'

'And get up and go out to eat, somewhere nice, and sit there for long time, and then come back here to bed ...' I said, dreamily.

'And be together all night long. I wish to God we could stay like this forever,' he said.

To my surprise and distress, he gave a gasp and turned away from me, burying his face in the pillow.

At first I didn't understand what was happening. I thought I had said or done something to upset him.

'Joe?' I said.

'Oh God,' he said. 'Help me.'

I reached out and put my hand on his shoulder. I could feel it shaking beneath my fingers. To my alarm, I saw that he was weeping into the pillow, crying with a child's passionate letting go.

'Help me,' he said again.

'Joe, my dear Joe, what's wrong?' I asked, horrified, but he only shook his head and carried on weeping.

I felt as though my heart might break for him.

Desperate to comfort him, I managed to put my arms round him and then his face was against me. I rocked him gently, shushing him like a baby. I stroked his hair and patted his back and still he sobbed, the tears streaming from his eyes, making my breasts wet and salty. He wept until there were no more tears inside him and I rocked him back and forth.

I've cried like that too, after bereavement. You feel empty. Not better, because the grief hasn't gone, but just empty. You exhaust all your tears and then you have to stop, for a while at least. But you know there will be more.

There was a box of pink tissues beside the bed. It was that sort of hotel. I pulled a handful out, held him away from me and mopped at his face. His eyes were red; his face looked almost bruised with grief, the old scars standing out, vivid scarlet against his pale skin. Was this all about me? Surely not. How could I imagine anything of the sort? This was a grief more damaging than anything I could have inflicted on him. I didn't have it in me to cause such pain. This was the unfathomable grief of long buried injury, of scars that went far deeper than skin and bone. It was the grief of some terrible, unimaginable betrayal.

After a while, even the residual sobbing died away. He moved away from me as though ashamed of his loss of control and sat on the edge of the bed, naked and vulnerable, with his head in his hands. He looked utterly defeated.

'Do you want to tell me about this?' I asked at last. 'I mean, can you try to tell me what's wrong with you? Please. I want to help. But I can't help if you won't talk to me. No matter what it is, you need to tell me.'

He nodded but then remained silent for a long time, searching for the words perhaps. And when they came, it wasn't what I thought it would be: some account of a failed relationship or problems with alcohol or even with drugs.

It was much worse than that.

He got back into bed, pulling the sheets around him. When the words came they were jerky and disjointed. Sometimes in a rush. Sometimes on the back of a great sobbing breath.

'I was fourteen,' he said. 'Just fourteen. My dad had died the year before.' He frowned, blew his nose on a pink tissue, sought to control himself. 'They have an instinct, don't they? For that kind of thing. Vulnerability. They seem to know. Like fucking radar.'

He looked at me and his eyes were still full of tears. I didn't say anything. I didn't even dare to touch him. I just sat there, listening, hardly breathing.

'You get drafted, you know,' he said at last. 'Sent away.'

'Sent away?'

'Yeah. Traded. Bought and sold. You don't argue. If you want to make it in pro hockey, you don't argue. It's the big one, the big goal, the dream. If you're good … and I *was* fucking good even then. I could skate. I could always skate. You were right. I can skate. That's what they always say, you know. If you can really skate they can teach you to play hockey.'

'You mean you were sent away from home?'

He nodded. 'It's a big, big country. Canada. People here don't realise just how big. Unless they've been. My dad was dead and this chance, my big chance, came along. You don't have much say in the matter. That's the system. Or it was back then. There are some changes now. If you want to get on. If you want to get picked. Drafted. If you want to make it in the game.'

'I can see that, but still.'

'But still, you don't say why would I want to go hundreds of miles away from home to stay with people I know nothing about.'

'I don't think I would have been happy if it was Fiona. Not at fourteen.'

'No, well, this guy, the coach, he came to see my mom. He told her all this stuff about me. What a great kid I was, what a great future I had. How he figured it would do me good. It was my big chance. He picked me out. He picked me. And it would be OK, because he would be there. He would look after me. It wasn't her fault. She thought I needed a father figure and he was so fucking plausible.'

'*Did* you need a father figure?'

He hesitated. 'My dad was dead. It was like … no. I didn't want a new dad. You know? But I wanted … something.'

'Not a father.'

'No. But I wanted a friend. I thought I could do with a friend. Someone to help me out. I was confused. You have to understand. I'm not … This isn't …' He stopped again, trying to work out how best to explain it to me. 'I mean there are great coaches, hockey coaches. I've met them. Seen them in action. The good guys. The kind I want to be. I've watched some of these guys take a bunch of raw kids and make them proud of themselves and proud of the game and show them how to have fun at the same time. If I was ever going to coach hockey that's what I do.

I'd make sure the kids had a lot of fun. The good, bad and indifferent. No matter. I'd make sure there was something for all of them. And I'd make sure they looked out for each other. I'd be there for them in all the right ways.'

'But that didn't happen to you?'

'No. It didn't happen to me.'

'So what did?'

There was another pause. He shook his head.

'I didn't really want to leave home. But I didn't argue. If you want to make it, if you want to make it all the way to the NHL, you don't argue. You pack your kit and you go. Besides people said he was one of the good guys too. That coach. They said he brought out the best in his players. I thought I was lucky to be chosen. That's what everybody told me. And I agreed with them. I thought I was so fucking lucky.'

He started to laugh, but the laugh turned into a sob. I handed him more tissues, and he rubbed at his eyes. His tears were infectious and I could feel them starting in my own eyes, my voice wobbling when I tried to speak.

'I'm sorry,' he said. 'Now that I've started, I can't seem to stop.' He meant the weeping. 'It's crazy. I reckon you don't want to hear all this.'

'I think I need to hear it, Joe, don't you?'

'OK. But it isn't nice. It isn't a nice story.'

'How can it be? When you're so distressed. Oh my darling, how can it be?'

I wanted to take him in my arms, but that wasn't what he needed. He didn't need anybody to touch him at that moment. He just needed to speak. He just needed somebody to listen. He heaved a sigh that threatened to turn into a sob again, but he took a deep breath and carried on talking.

'You see, you get billeted with a family. It's all vetted. All very strict. They're supposed to look out for you. More often than not, they do look out for you. And they were nice enough. I had this great room at the top of the house. My own shower. Everything. They were kind and friendly and I had everything I could need.'

'So what went wrong?'

'They were friends of the coach, had been for years.'

'And?'

'And he was always round at their house. You know? Sometimes he would stay the night. And because there were two beds in my room, he would have the spare bed. In my room. The family thought it would be nice for me to have some company. All guys together.'

He paused at that, assembling his thoughts perhaps. I just sat there, waiting for him to go on. Feeling sick.

I had begun to understand.

'It didn't happen the first night,' he said. 'Or even the second. But all the same I couldn't sleep. I don't know why. I couldn't sleep with him in the room. I just lay awake listening to him breathe and I thought that he was doing the same thing. I kind of figured he was awake, there in the dark, listening to every move I made. It bothered me. Do you know, when I think about it, he never laid a finger on any of us. Out on the ice I mean. In public. And that was kind of weird in itself. Maybe he was being too careful. I mean most coaches will put an arm round you, or ... well they won't keep you at arm's length like that. Why should they? When it's innocent. Nice. They'll maybe ruffle your hair, or give you a push or a pat on the back. It's a contact sport. You need that kind of thing. It's natural. Only he never ever touched any of us. Like that. Out there. Normally. Never.'

I waited patiently for him to continue.

'And then one night I heard him get out of bed and he came over and d'you know, I wondered if I was dreaming? He sat down on the bed beside me. He said "Hi Joe." He sat beside me and I realised that he was trying to touch me and, like, playing with himself at the same time. I didn't know what the hell to do. I was young. I was quite naive. I pretended to be asleep. I rolled over, away from him, and just pretended to be asleep. I didn't know what else to do. I was so ... I don't know. I wasn't so much shocked as surprised. Can you understand that? I thought I was going crazy. I figured I was imagining it at first. But I could feel him, his hand on me, and he groaned and then he just got up and went back into his own bed. As if nothing had happened. And I figure he went to sleep. And that was the start of it.'

I wondered why I hadn't guessed it sooner. He was an attractive man. He had once been, I was sure, a beautiful boy. It wasn't only little girls who were in danger. And besides, you didn't have to be beautiful. Just vulnerable. I could hear him, the coach, that pathetic, inadequate bully. I could imagine the words he must have used to confuse and coerce the young boy, almost before Joe told me them. 'You like it, don't you? You enjoy it. A little give and take here, son. Work with me on this, son. You won't tell, will you? Besides, nobody will believe you. They'll say you wanted it, encouraged me, you do like it don't you ... you do as I say and see where it gets you, son.'

Such an extreme betrayal, such a terrible, unforgiveable abuse of power.

I sat up in bed in that safe, cosy nest and listened, full of pity and anger for the young boy Joe had once been, for the man he had become. He must have talked for an hour. Once begun, he couldn't stop. He had to tell it all. The story came tumbling out of him. Every last dreadful detail. The assaults had happened over a number of years: at the billeting house, in the locker room after the match, sometimes in the coach's hotel room during away games. They had stopped just short of rape.

'Only because I wouldn't let him,' said Joe, wiping his eyes again. 'He knew I meant it. So he just touched me, or he made me touch him.'

'Dear God, Joe! Was there nobody you could tell?'

'I used to try. I used to make my mind up that I would tell my mom. Or the physio. Or my billeting family. But I was too fucking scared when it came to it. Too much of a coward. I thought it was my fault. Something about me. All the time everyone is telling you what a great guy he is. And he's telling you this is your secret. Just between the two of you. You just work with me on this one, Joe, he used to say. Work with me! Jesus! I can still hear his fucking voice in my head and it makes me sick to my stomach. You know it makes sense, he would say. You just play along with me and I'll play along with you. He did too. That made it worse somehow. My career was going great. When I think about it now, I'm surprised I could play at all, but I did. I played well at that time. Maybe I got rid of all the aggression on the ice. He created it and then he controlled it. I was like his creation. And I felt so fucking guilty about it all the time. Maybe I had something to prove. Like the fact that I was a real man. Or that was the way my mind worked. That was how I rationalised it.'

He smiled, but it was more of a grimace. The hatred in his voice – not just of the man but of himself – alarmed me. It was as though my mind could barely encompass what he was telling me. And at the same time I had the stirrings of an anger on his behalf, a rage so powerful that I could hardly speak. It was the titanic anger of a mother and a lover combined. I patted his hand and it seemed like a useless and ineffectual gesture in the face of such evil.

'How often?' I whispered.

'Oh he must have done it to me sixty, seventy times. Maybe more. Over the years. Over those years. I lost count. Of course I should have told my mom. But she would have had me out of there like a shot and I didn't want that. I only wanted to play hockey. I thought, if I told, the sky would fall. He said, if you tell, you know it's all over, don't you? Christ I was a kid. I had this dream. I wanted to make it in hockey. I just wanted the other stuff to stop, you know? I couldn't tell the guys on the team, because they would think I was delusional or malicious, out to get the wonderful coach into trouble. I couldn't tell my billeting family because they were old friends – Jeez they practically worshipped the ice the guy skated on – and I thought they wouldn't believe me either. They wouldn't have believed me. Nobody would have wanted to believe me. Nobody would have dared to believe me. The team was doing so fucking well.'

'But he abused you Joe. Horribly. Criminally. And he betrayed your trust so profoundly!' The words just burst out of me in the dim room. Joe threw me a look that was part relief, part desperation, as though he needed some kind of reassurance or absolution from blame.

'Maybe you're more sure of that than I am,' he said. 'I felt guilty. Hell I still feel kind of guilty.'

'Why should you feel guilty?'

'Because I felt as though I had betrayed some ideal. The game is such a part of the community, back home. It's hard for you to understand over here where its influence is minimal. You have to think football to get even close to it. And then some, because it involves women as much as men, moms as well as dads. It's as though all your self respect and all the ideals of the community, of the families, of the folks who support the team, are sort of bound up together. When it's good, it can be very, very good. The best.'

'And when it goes wrong?'

'Oh sure.' He was shivering, though the room was warm. He pulled the sheets more closely around him. 'Then it's very, very bad.'

'Weren't there others? There must have been others.'

'Sure there were. Later on, I found that there were more of us. Plenty more. I only heard about a few, but I reckon there must have been dozens of us over the years. Christ, we were like a harem. He could take his pick. And you know what's the worst thing? The very worst thing?'

I shook my head.

'You have no control over your body. My body responded to him and I was disgusted with myself. I felt filthy. You know, there's a part of me that's still disgusted with myself, Helen. A lot of the time I just hate *me*. I hate what he did, but I hate myself for what I let him do to me. Do you know what it's like to hate yourself so much of the time?'

Again I shook my head. I had been ashamed of myself and sometimes I had hated my life. But I had never despised myself in that way, never felt such self destructive disgust.

'How could you help it? You were a boy. A child. He held all the cards, didn't he?'

'He made out I wanted it. He said it so often that I began to wonder if I did want it. If he saw something in me that ... something that he could exploit.'

'Well he sounds like a filthy, manipulative bastard to me.'

Joe looked up at me. He had been elsewhere for a while, deep in that terrible past. I could only begin to guess at what it must have done to him. It was beyond my comprehension.

'Yes,' he said, simply, and as though it had hardly occurred to him before, as though the fact had just dawned on him, as though my putting it into words had begun to make it believable for the adult Joe, at least, even if the child inside him still couldn't bring himself to accept it. 'That's what he was, wasn't he? A filthy, manipulative bastard.'

'How long did it go on for?'

'It went on for years. When I got older, I changed teams, but he managed to engineer it that he moved as well. I started drinking; it was the only thing that made me feel better. Took the edge off. When I was drunk I didn't care. And when I drank – which I sometimes did before a game as well as after – he would ground me. So then he had me to himself. I was always his favourite. People knew that. They kind of accepted it . I don't know why he had this thing about me. Maybe there was some weird kind of affection mixed in with his obsession. Maybe because I had never let him go the whole way. Maybe I was some kind of challenge to him. Some of them, on the outside, even assumed I was gay, assumed I was his boyfriend. That it was my choice! Which was an insult to gays everywhere, when you think about it. I know some great players who are gay and none of them, not a single one of them, would ever, ever … Jesus Christ, why would they?

So then I had something to prove to myself as well and I used to … well … that was when I treated some of the girls badly. I was never violent. Not off the ice, anyway. I just wanted to prove that I was one of the guys. But I treated myself worse. I think I wanted …' He hesitated. 'D'you know I think I wanted *not to be.*'

The stark simplicity of those three words tore at my heart.

'So what happened? How did it end? Did it end?'

'It ended because I got away. I played myself out of it. I made it all the way to the AHL and he couldn't follow me there. I had the NHL in my sights. He was a good coach but he wasn't good enough. Ironic really. I was better than he was. I outplayed him. And then a few years ago, somebody else blew the whistle. Oh not me. I didn't do it. Didn't have the guts. But it turned out there had been plenty of others. You think you're the only one but you never are. It's just that when everyone keeps quiet, when everyone keeps quiet because they think they're alone, and nobody will ever believe them – nobody finds out. And even if one or two kids did speak out, back then, they were right to be scared because – hell – nobody did believe them! He was nothing if not promiscuous.

But then, I suppose things began to change. People had realised just how fucking clever some of these guys can be. How manipulative. And one or two people spoke out. But even then, his friends stood by him. They say times have changed, but I don't think that part of it has changed at all. They claimed it was all lies. Claimed he was a fine servant of the game and a great role model for young Canadian boys! Somebody wrote that in a newspaper article. I remember every fucking word of it. He got arrested but they bailed him. He got bail!'

'What happened to him, Joe? Did it go to court?'

There was a long pause. Joe rubbed his face with his hands. His skin looked raw in the dim, wintry light.

'The bastard killed himself,' he said. 'He took an overdose. They found him dead in a cheap motel room, like in a crap movie.'

'So he was a coward. Right to the end.'

'I guess he was.'

'How did that make you feel?'

Incongruously, he started to laugh. 'I was fucking furious. D'you know, I thought he'd got away with it again. I still do. Finally got away with it. Nobody could do anything to him. There would be no retribution. No final reckoning, nothing. So after a while, I thought, put it all behind you, Joe. You have to forget all about it and get on with your life. I carried on playing. I met Carrie and we got married. I put on this face. This is me now, I thought. Make a fresh start. Forget it ever happened. I thought I'd be OK. Only these things have a habit of coming back at you.'

'I'm sure they do.'

'Carrie couldn't understand why I lost my temper all the time. She went for counselling you know. About me. And they said I should go on an anger management course. They told me I had to learn to manage my unreasonable anger. That's what everyone kept telling me. Joe you have to learn to manage that crazy temper! Fuck's sake why wouldn't I be angry?'

'You mean you've never told anyone? Joe?' I could scarcely believe it.

'No. I never told anyone. Not even Carrie.'

'Why not?'

'I couldn't tell her. She'd have been too shocked.'

'But she was your wife. You must have talked. She must have loved you.'

'She didn't love me enough.'

'How would you know? If you never gave her the chance? Oh Joe!'

'I was so ashamed. How could anyone ever love me enough for that?'

'My darling, how could they *not* love you?'

He seemed thrown by my outburst, almost puzzled by it.

'But you're shocked, aren't you?' he asked. 'You must be.'

'Of course I'm shocked. Who wouldn't be? But I don't blame you. I just can't bear to think about this happening to you.'

'Isn't there something in you that looks at me and says, he must have wanted it, asked for it?'

'No!' Again, I think my vehemence surprised him. 'Not even remotely. Are you mad?'

'I think I am, just a little.'

'I'm just angry *for* you. And I can't bear to think about you keeping it to yourself all this time.'

'There was one of the other guys. He wrote to me once. It was after I'd screwed everything up yet again. I burned the letter because I didn't want anyone to see it, but I remember it. He's younger than me. I thought he might have been involved because he was a mess for a while too. You could track it back. See which teams he'd been with on the way up. But he sorted himself out. I couldn't be sure till he wrote to me. He told me to deal with it. He said, if you don't deal with it, it'll destroy you. It stays inside you and it grows till it fills every corner of you with the pain of it, and because you can't get rid of it you try to destroy yourself instead.'

I just couldn't bear it any longer. I held him in my arms, rocked him, tried to soothe him. The tears began to course down his cheeks again.

'You've told me now, Joe. You've told me. It wasn't your fault. None of it was your fault. Didn't you know that?'

'I don't know.' He released his breath in a great shuddering sigh. 'No. Yes. But maybe I needed to hear someone else say it as well.'

'You should have spoken about it before. You should have told someone a long time ago. Got help. Professional help maybe.'

'I've never trusted anyone enough,' he said simply. 'I don't think I've ever loved anyone enough either.'

It was already growing dark when we left our sanctuary. Recklessly we held hands all the way home on the train and walking between stations in Glasgow, although we didn't say much to each other. He stared out of the train window at his own reflection, and I closed my eyes and leaned on his shoulder. We didn't care if we were seen. We hardly broke the contact between us at all.

When we stopped at the cottage, I kissed him gently. It was physically painful to be parted from him.

'I never got you a birthday present. I was going to do that in Edinburgh.'

I hugged him, held him close for a moment or two longer. But it struck me that he had given me something very precious anyway. He had given me his trust.

'Will you be all right?' I asked.

He seemed exhausted. His face was pale and his eyes were bloodshot, but he looked straight at me when he said, 'I'll be OK.'

'You're sure? I can't bear to leave you like this.'

'I'll be fine for now. Don't worry. I'm worn out. And I've got training tomorrow. So I'll go to bed. I think I could sleep for days.'

'Promise me at least you won't blame yourself any more.'

'I'll try.'

'And maybe think about getting some professional help?'

'Maybe. I'll think about it. When will I see you again?'

'Soon. I'll get away as soon as I can.'

There was soup on the hob, when I got in, and Sandy ladled it into a bowl for me: chicken, potatoes, leeks. I didn't deserve it.

'Did you make this all by yourself?' I asked him.

'Well actually Mary brought it over. She said you'd be needing something hot when you came in.'

'That was nice of her. Maybe I should go away for the day more often.'

'Maybe you should,' said Sandy. He paused. 'Let's us see what we're missing.'

If my face was flushed, it could have had something to do with the coals of fire heaped on my head. I felt bad enough already without them. Bad, but still not really guilty. Not guilty enough to stop, anyway. My love for Joe had finally overridden my loyalty to Sandy. The only thing that really shamed me was the ease with which I could lie about the day.

I sat at the kitchen table to finish my soup and ate some bread and cheese while Sandy made a pot of tea.

'How was Edinburgh then?'

'Very nice.'

'Did you do much shopping?'

'Just window shopping. We went up to the Royal Mile so that he could see the castle, and then we spent so long in the Record Office that we didn't really have time. I think Joe's going to spend a few days there in the spring. On his own. Have a good look round. Do the tourist bit.'

'Did he find what he wanted?'

'Yes, he did. We got death certificates for his great grandfather and his great uncle. They were Italians, living over here. Vezio and Mario. They were deported during the war, even though they had lived here for years and years.'

'Enemy aliens. That's what they called them. They were Scots Italians, not enemies.' Sandy sounded very fierce, all of a sudden.

'I know. Then the ship was torpedoed and sank. They never came back.'

'Poor sods,' said Sandy. 'Poor, poor sods.'

'I think Louise knew them. Ages ago, when she was very young, in Glasgow. We think that may have been why she left the house to Joe in the end. Even though the relationship is so distant. There had to be some reason and it's as good an explanation as any.'

And maybe, I thought, she had known something else. Maybe with some intuitive, prescient part of her head or her heart, Louise had known that one day Joe might need to seek sanctuary here.

– Chapter Eighteen –

SANDY WAS VERY busy about the farm and elsewhere over the next few weeks. We didn't have a lot to say to each other. He would come in, eat his dinner and then either go to the pub or put his feet up in front of the television. Either way, he didn't seem to want to talk to me. We didn't fall out over anything. We weren't in the habit of communicating much on any level these days, but what little conversation we had seemed to have ground to a halt.

Once or twice, I asked, 'What's wrong, Sandy?' but he would just shake his head and say, 'Nothing. Just tired, that's all. Aches and pains. The dark days don't suit me.'

They didn't suit me either. Sometimes I would go out and walk for miles, just to breathe fresh air – cold, damp air, for sure – and stop myself from thinking too much about Joe. He was often away during this pre-Christmas period; his schedule was punishing and in between times he was training at the arena. Nothing could alleviate my desperation to be close to him except physical exhaustion. So I worked on the farm or walked with the dog until my feet were sore and I tried not to think about anything much at all.

It didn't work. I worried about Joe all the time. I hoped that a healing process had begun for him, but how could I possibly know? I thought there would be no miracle cures. I might have been right when I said that he needed professional help. There he was, floundering in a sea of terrible memories, and I ought to be with him. But how could I be with him without hurting Sandy and Fiona, when they had done nothing to deserve it? And if I'm honest, maybe because thinking about Joe made me think about lost opportunities and dashed hopes, I worried about myself as well.

My stomach ached and I felt sick a lot of the time. I almost went to the doctor, but what could I tell her? And what on earth could she prescribe for such a deadly mixture of pity and love. It was the genuine article all right. I couldn't bear Joe's pain, and if his future happiness meant that he should go back to Canada and start to rebuild his life there without me, then so be it.

One night, Annie invited me round, ostensibly to talk about the summer holidays. She had been thinking that we might all go away to-gether. Sandy always said he couldn't get away from the farm, but she thought it would do us good to have a proper holiday. Bruce and his nephew could manage the farm for a week. She fancied Italy, but that might be pushing the boat out a bit. Tenerife was a real possibility, she said. We could fly cheaply from Glasgow and rent a villa together. Fiona would come and Annie's younger kids. They would all rub along together for a week. But not Dean. He could stay at home and look after the house, but that meant he would have what the kids called 'an empty' and she would tell him there were to be no parties. She went on at length, but I was only half listening. Next summer seemed an impossibly long way off. Anything might happen before then. I feared and hoped in equal measure.

She had a bottle of Pinot Grigio in the fridge, and had put dishes of crisps and peanuts on the table. Tim was out at a school board meeting. The kids were upstairs in their rooms, and the sounds of their various choices of music mingled in a terrible cacophony. I expect Annie was so used to it that she hardly heard it by now. She had trimmed up for Christmas a couple of weeks ago. She always did it very early and spent a lot of time and energy on it. I was usually late.

'Aye at the coo's tail as usual,' Sandy would say but he seldom bothered to help.

'We haven't done this for ages, have we?' she asked.

'No. We haven't. My fault. I'm sorry.'

'What have you been up to, Helen?' She gazed at me over the rim of her wineglass, more in sorrow than in anger.

'What do you mean?'

'You look quite ill. It's been creeping up on you for the past month or so. Are you all right? I mean losing weight suits you, but I have to say that you don't look very fit on it.'

'I'm fine.'

'Helen. Is there something you're not telling me?'

'What do you mean? I tell you just about everything.'

'I don't think you do,' she prompted, gently.

'Why? Have you been listening to gossip?'

'Is that what it is? Just gossip?'

'What are they saying?'

'Don't you know?'

I shook my head. 'Tell me.'

'Oh you know what they're saying! You must do. They're saying ...' she hesitated. 'Well, they're saying that you're getting much too fond of that sexy neighbour of yours.'

'Don't be daft!'

'I'm not implying it's *true*. I'm just telling you what people are saying.'

That threw me a bit. 'But they would say that, wouldn't they?'

Exaggeration was the norm round here, a kind of game. I had once bought a sympathy card for the supposedly bereaved husband of one of my egg customers, only to discover, just in time, that she was in hospital, recovering from appendicitis.

'Of course they would. He's so charismatic. I fancy him myself. And he could charm the birds out of the trees, if he didn't have this reputation as a bad lad. But maybe that's part of the attraction.'

'Maybe it is.'

'The problem is, Helen ...'

'What?'

She hesitated.

'You don't believe them, do you?' I asked her. 'About me I mean?'

I had been trying to decide what to do: confess and confide in her or deny everything. That was when she took the wind out of my sails.

'Of course I don't believe them,' she said, airily. 'Actually, they don't really believe it themselves. I mean look at him.'

And look at you, she might have added, to complete the put-down. But she didn't. She hesitated, reddening a little. After all, she was my friend, wasn't she? Suddenly everything fell into place. They hadn't been gossiping about me, so much as pitying me for my infatuation.

'You've got a crush on him. Well, we all have, I suppose. But you more than most of us. And it's getting beyond a joke. It must be kind of embarrassing for him.'

'Do you think so?'

'I think, deep down, everyone knows how silly it all is, even the ones who are gossiping. They know that it's all one sided, so they can laugh at you with impunity. Mary's one of the worst, you know.'

'Mary? Good God! Is she?'

I didn't know what to say. I couldn't argue, could I? But it struck me then that nobody in this place would ever see me as anything other than Sandy's wife, Fiona's mum, the egg lady. These were my roles. And I played them very well indeed. I was comfortable with them. Not happy, but comfortable. They would never see me as I saw myself. Inside, I was still that girl who had been so full of hope and ambition. But somewhere along the way, she had got lost, and even I wasn't sure how to find her again. Now, wasn't I just adding adulterer to that list of roles? And wasn't it only exciting because it was so different from all the others?

'That figures,' I said eventually, because I couldn't think of anything better to say.

'But nobody believes it, really. They just think ...' She hesitated.

'Go on. Say it. That I'm making a fool of myself.'

'Can't you see that you've got to stop, Helen?'

'Stop what?'

'Well, stop making eyes at him over the baked beans. Folk notice these things and they're beginning to laugh at you. Stop talking about him all the time. God, you even tagged along to Edinburgh with him. That set a few tongues wagging, I can tell you.'

'I didn't tag. He asked me to go. Via Sandy.'

'I expect you wangled the invitation. Go on, admit it, Helen. The poor guy must have been so embarrassed.'

There was no point in explaining. Suddenly I just didn't have the energy. 'Is that what everyone's saying as well?' I asked.

'No. Of course not. But Mary did. She'd gone over to Drumbrethan with some soup for Sandy or something. She said how embarrassing it must have been for Joe to have to take his aunty to Edinburgh with him. And I know that's Mary all over, and I know you're nowhere near old enough to be his aunty, but there was a germ of truth in it all the same, and that made it even worse somehow.'

'I suppose so.'

'It's kind of pathetic. Oh Helen!' she hugged me. 'I couldn't say this if I didn't know you so well. But I'm so fond of you that I can't stand it. You are making such a numty of yourself over him. Everybody can see it. Everybody's laughing up their sleeves at you. You're my best mate and I can't bear it.'

I took a long drink of my wine, buying time.

'Do you think he's noticed it?' I said, after a while. 'I mean, has he said anything to anybody?'

'Not as far as I know. He doesn't have many real friends here, does he?'

'He keeps himself to himself, that's true.'

'Maybe he confides in his team-mates or something.'

'Maybe.'

'He hasn't had a girlfriend at all while he's been here, has he? Or at least I've never seen him with anyone. Still stuck on his ex, I suppose. Men often are.'

'Well that's a relief. At least he doesn't seem to be too bothered by my unwelcome attentions.'

'Now I've upset you. And I didn't mean to.'

'No, you haven't.'

'But Helen, how could he not notice it? I'm only surprised Sandy hasn't noticed it. You've been making it so bloody obvious to everyone else. Joe's probably used to it. I bet he's a real big cheese at home in Canada. Must have girls falling over themselves to screw him. Groupies. Puck Bunnies, that's what Dean says they call them.'

'Have you talked to Dean about this?'

'No. Of course not. I wouldn't. But we've talked about Joe. Dean saw that article your Fiona was flashing around. He said all these ice hockey players, even the minor league ones, have a big opinion of themselves. They're full of themselves. And they treat women like dirt. He said when they're all washed up back home they just come here for the money. Imports they call them.'

'And he'd know all about it, would he?'

'Well, maybe not.' She relented, hearing the anger in my voice. 'Maybe Joe isn't quite like that.'

I liked Annie, I really did. She meant well. She was calling it as she saw it. And who's to say that in her position, I might not have thought exactly the same thing?

Afterwards, it struck me that even if I had confessed everything there and then, she wouldn't have believed me. She would probably have thought that I had made it all up. She would have assumed I was going mad, obsessed, a potential stalker. One more unwelcome role to add to the list.

'You're not offended, are you?' she asked, anxiously.

'No. No, I'm not offended. It won't matter in the spring anyway.'

'Why not?'

'Well, I expect he'll go back to Canada in April. That's when the season ends over here, you know. He'll probably be joining another hockey team.'

'Will he?'

'So he says. I think he's had offers. So maybe he isn't quite washed up yet.'

'So he talks to you, does he? He tells you things. Aunty Helen?'

Patronizing cow, I thought. The phrase just popped into my head and almost out of my mouth, but I held it in. I was so angry. I can't remember ever being so angry as I felt at that moment. It was as though rage had ignited a small conflagration inside me. I thought if I opened my mouth to speak, flames would shoot out at her. But I managed to reply coolly enough.

'Oh yes. He talks to me about all kinds of things. He treats me just like his aunty. Sad, isn't it? But I don't mind.'

'Well, the sooner he goes back home to Canada the better. That's my opinion for what it's worth.'

I sighed. 'I'm sure you're absolutely right, Annie. For what your opinion is worth. Then we can all get back to normal. Shall we open another bottle? What have you been up to, anyway? I feel as if I haven't seen you for ages.'

I think if I had walked home that night, I might have gone in and seen Joe there and then. I might have told him I would go back to Canada with him and everyone else could go to hell. But the weather was awful and Tim ran me home. So instead, I fretted and fumed all night long and got up in the early hours of the morning to drink tea by myself in the kitchen, trying to calm down, wondering what to do. Siggy ignored me and slept on, but Jess came and rested her head on my knee, her brown eyes glistening with sympathy. I stroked her silky head. Conflicting emotions made war inside my head: love for Joe, concern for Sandy, worry about Fiona. What to do, what to do, I kept thinking.

It was the next night that Fiona threw the real spanner in the works. She had gone out with Lee, along with some of the other players and their girlfriends, for a pre-Christmas celebration. Joe hadn't been there. Afterwards I didn't know whether to be relieved that he couldn't be blamed, or sorry that he hadn't been there to supervise them in some way. I think if he had been with them it would never have happened. The hospital phoned us at around midnight. We had only just begun to worry about her. Road accidents, car crashes, drug overdoses flashed across my mind, but they were as reassuring as they could be in the circumstances and surprisingly kind. Once more, alcohol was the problem. Fiona had got so drunk that even her companions had become worried. Thank God they hadn't just abandoned her. They had done the right thing, however late in the day. She had been carted off to hospital to have her stomach pumped.

When we got to the waiting room, Lee was there with another young player – I barely gave him a second glance – accompanied by a dishevelled girlfriend wearing a short black dress, too flimsy for the time of year, and heels so high that she teetered like a stiltwalker. Her legs seemed naked and purple with the cold and she kept tugging the inadequate skirt down in a vain attempt to cover her thighs, whenever the door of the A and E department swung open to let in a blast of cold air. Lee had the good grace to look ashamed of himself.

'I don't know what happened,' he said. 'I didn't realise she was drinking as much as she was. Honest to God, Mr Breckenridge.' He appealed to Sandy. 'I had no idea until she passed out on me.'

I thought of all that Joe had told me about some of the players and what they did with and to the girls who followed them around and I flinched. My mouth was dry. I didn't really believe him, but there was no point in making a fuss here in the hospital. Fiona was what mattered now.

Sandy was looking at Lee as though he didn't recognise him, punching one big fist into the other hand. But Lee was younger and more agile. I stepped in between them. 'For God's sake, Lee, will you just go. Take your pals and go, now. Please don't make things any worse than they already are.'

'All right,' he said. He looked slightly indignant, willing to argue with Sandy, but he had obviously been drinking too, and the dishevelled girl pulled at his arm.

'Come on, Lee, baby. She's right. Let's go. There's a cab outside. Let's go now.'

Sandy and I spent a miserable and sleepless hour or so pacing up and down the waiting room and castigating ourselves for neglecting our daughter, but it occurred to me that I had been neglecting her in ways that Sandy knew nothing about. And I hadn't exactly been avoiding alcohol myself over the past few weeks, had I?

At last the doctor came through to tell us that she was better and that we could go in and see her. He looked very tired.

'It happens,' he said. 'Don't go blaming yourselves. It's a difficult age.' He didn't look much older himself, but old enough to know better. 'She's probably learned her lesson. I'll get somebody to come in and talk to her before she's discharged. But it does happen to the best kids from the best homes you know.'

I pulled him to one side, trying not to let Sandy hear. 'She's OK, isn't she? She hadn't been assaulted had she? Nothing like that.'

He looked startled. 'No. No I don't think so.' He frowned. 'No. She's not distressed. Well, only with the alcohol. There were no signs of any kind of assault. Believe me.'

'Thank God.'

Fiona looked like a little girl lying there in the white bed in the too small hospital gown. She looked like she had looked when she was eight and had been seriously ill with chickenpox, except that this time she had no spots. Instead, her skin was greenish grey in the artificial light.

She could remember very little of the past few hours, except that she knew she had made a fool of herself all over again. Her head was aching and her dignity was at an all time low. She clutched at our hands and sobbed, tears streaming down her face. 'I won't do it again, mum, dad. I promise I won't ever do it again.'

'You know you could have killed yourself?'

I had warned Sandy not to harass her, but he couldn't resist saying it. Besides, the doctor had told us what an unholy mixture she had drunk: vodka and lemonade, white wine, rum and coca cola and heaven knows what else.

'I'm so sorry,' she kept sobbing, over and over again.

I sat down beside her and took her hand. It felt clammy beneath my fingers.

'Why did you do it? How did it happen?'

'We went to a club and nobody checked my age or anything because they knew all the rest of them. Hockey players. It was great.'

'But the drink?' I asked. 'Where did all the drink come from?'

'People kept buying me things. They just kept appearing on the table in front of me and I kept drinking them. I couldn't seem to stop. Sweet drinks. It felt good and then not so good.'

There had been no kindly Joe to pick her up and bring her home, either. To give the kids their due, they hadn't just left her, but who knows what else they might have had in mind. Some of the other players and their wives had gone home, leaving Lee and Fiona and the second couple. They had all got into a taxi, but then they had been alarmed to find her unconscious, and the taxi driver had brought them straight to the hospital.

'It was just a celebration,' she said. 'The team won last night. It was a celebration.'

'Some celebration,' said Sandy, dryly. He squeezed her hand, and then leaned over and stroked her forehead. 'Ah hen, hen, don't do that to your old dad again,' he said. 'I can't bear it when you're ill.'

– Chapter Nineteen –

SOMEHOW OR OTHER I got through the Christmas preparations. I did a lot of shopping in a hurry, had a wrapping marathon, made and iced a cake and trimmed up the house with holly and ivy from the hedgerows. Sandy brought in a tree and Fiona and her friends got the tattered cardboard boxes of decorations down from the attic. Some of them dated from Sandy's granny's time and were very precious: old hand-blown baubles, a fat glass Santa, a delicate silver budgie, an angel in a lacy dress. I bought new lights – I couldn't be bothered wrestling with the old set – and then the girls trimmed the tree.

It was reassuring to see our daughter indulging in such a normal pastime. She had been unusually subdued ever since her hospital experience. Lee phoned her once or twice, but she wouldn't speak to him. On both occasions I answered the phone, and he seemed very taken aback. I didn't shout at him or argue with him. I just told him that she was out. I think Joe had a word with him because he didn't call again, and then over the Christmas holidays, when we were alone together, Fiona confided in me that the evening had already been a disaster anyway, much more of a disaster than she had cared to admit. She had been too embarrassed to tell me before, but eventually she couldn't keep it to herself any longer. The dishevelled girl in the six inch heels had been all over Lee like a cheap sweater, as Sandy would have put it, and he had seemed to like it. In the taxi, just before she passed out, Fiona remembered hearing the two young men talking about a foursome and she didn't think they meant a trip to the cinema.

'It was awful, mum,' she told me, pathetically. 'I didn't even fancy the other guy; he was sweaty and horrible and he had spots all round his neck. How could they even think I'd want to do that?'

Quite easily, I thought, remembering some of the things Joe had told me. They may even have had the idea that she would consider it a privilege.

'Better not tell your father.' I kissed her. 'You've had a narrow escape. Chalk it up to experience.'

Just as well she had passed out, I thought with a shudder. Just as well the boys had had some remnants of conscience about her.

Christmas Day was extremely bizarre. I suppose Christmas Days often are. We find ourselves in strange and unnatural situations. But this was worse than most. It was always very much a family occasion for Sandy, and the various branches of the Breckenridges took turns at cooking Christmas dinner. This year it was my turn to entertain Morris and Mary and their two little girls, as well as two elderly and unattached female cousins of the family, Senga and Maggie. There was also Sandy's Uncle Jock and Morris's mother, Isa. My sole surviving uncle had decided to stay in Glasgow where he usually celebrated Christmas with a few old army pals.

I knew that Joe had a game in Cardiff a few days before Christmas. The next game was to be played at home, between Christmas and New Year. I knew that he might be at a loose end unless he had been invited out by one of the other players or the coach, but I didn't think I could do anything about it. Just before Christmas, however, Sandy and Morris got talking to Joe down in the pub and invited him to have Christmas Dinner with us. They came up and told me what they had done, congratulating themselves on their Christian charity, and also with giving Joe a narrow escape.

'We rescued him from Maisie's clutches,' they told me, gleefully. 'Apparently she'd told Mary she was going to ask him to come and share her turkey crown with her. He'll have a much better time of it up here with us, won't he?'

I had bought Sandy a sweater in soft Italian wool and he gave me a new vacuum cleaner with all kinds of fiddly attachments. I know we needed one, but it almost reduced me to tears. It struck me that Mary might have suggested it.

'Why don't you hit him with it, mum?' said Fiona, shocked.

Joe came up from the cottage at around eleven on Christmas morning.

He was wearing narrow black pants, a white shirt, a blue silk tie and a soft leather jacket, in honour of the occasion. Even his shoes were well polished. He looked handsome and as elegant as a young businessman. It unnerved me. It wasn't the casual way I was used to seeing him.

I was crimson from the kitchen and I smelled of roast meat. I had spent the previous evening wrestling with an obscenely large and muscular turkey, a few feathers still clinging gruesomely to its breast and its strapping legs. Sandy liked his turkeys to be free range individuals. I set the alarm and got up early, just to shoehorn it into the oven. Now, everything seemed to be under control but myself. Mary had descended on me with her usual domestic efficiency and got everything organised around me, including the sprouts which she always cooked beautifully with crispy bacon bits. She really was a fine cook, which bugged me even more than usual. I was grateful to her and irrationally cross with her, all at the same time. My mind couldn't be said to be on the job in hand.

I had bought a tin of chocolate biscuits and a bottle of good whisky for Mary and Morris and they had reciprocated with a bottle of port and a supermarket 'gift pack' of cheese. I had concentrated my real gift buying efforts on the children, but Sandy, with the air of a conjuror, handed Mary a slender, nicely wrapped package. It proved to contain a blue silk scarf, nothing like the horsy effort he had brought back from the show for me. I had to pretend not to be surprised but in fact I was astonished. So was Mary, apparently, because she flushed pink and showed the dimple in her chin. It struck me that she looked quite pretty, but Morris only grunted when she showed him the gift.

'Oh nice,' he said and then grinned at me. 'Maybe I should have got you something special as well, Helen.'

'Don't be daft.'

Joe was carrying a small kit bag, from which he produced a bottle of real French champagne, not the sparkling wine that Sandy had thought would 'do fine', and a big box of chocolates which he handed to Fiona.

'Don't eat them all at once. And you can share them with your mum and dad.'

'I'm supposed to be on a diet,' she said, but she didn't refuse them. Instead she shyly planted a kiss on his cheek.

He had brought a basket of flowers for me: red and white roses with winter greenery: a dangerous and extravagant gesture, but one permitted by the season, I suppose. When he handed them over, our fingertips touched and we looked briefly into each other's eyes. Joe smiled a rueful smile and shrugged his shoulders, minutely. What could I do, he seemed to be saying. What the hell else could I do but come?

'Blood and bandages,' said Mary, glancing at them. 'Red and white flowers.'

It was an old superstition. Red and white flowers were believed to be unlucky; they meant sickness.

Sandy poured sherry for everyone as they arrived, and I went upstairs to get changed.

In spite of everything Joe was relaxed and happy. He seemed to enjoy his turkey, and even managed to charm Mary by complimenting her on the Christmas pudding that she had made several months earlier and fed with brandy every week. As we were filling the dishwasher, she admitted that she might have been wrong about him.

'He seems quite nice,' she said, grudgingly. 'Sandy seems to like him well enough anyway.'

It sounded as though my husband was the arbiter of taste in such matters.

'Yes. I think Sandy's got used to him. They're quite good friends.'

After the meal, Uncle Jock, Morris, his mother, and the elderly cousins all went into the sitting room. They took a bottle of whisky and a big dish of chocolates with them, but they were soon fast asleep and snoring in horrible chorus. Siggy yowled at the kitchen door and Jess joined him in a Christmas truce. They were trying to get at the repulsive remains of the turkey, but when I wouldn't let them in, the cat stalked upstairs, tail held high, and made himself comfortable on our bed instead. Jess went and stood hopefully by the back door. Fiona tried to chat up Joe for a while, realised that he was friendly but preoccupied and, with a final disgusted look at her slumbering relatives, took the two little girls up to her bedroom to play with her new make-up and her old dolls and teddies. It was, in short, a typical Breckenridge family Christmas.

'Do you fancy a walk?' said Sandy to those of us still standing.

'Why not?' said Mary. 'My husband seems to be out for the count. What about you, Helen?'

I glanced at Joe. 'Do you want a walk, Joe?'

'OK. I wouldn't mind.'

We took an ecstatic Jess and went up the hill in the general direction of Poldarrach, like that first day when I had met Joe leaning on a gate. It was a dry afternoon, though very cold. At first Sandy and Joe strode out together, but after a while – and I don't know how, because we certainly didn't engineer it – Mary and Sandy fell behind us, deep in conversation, and Joe and I pulled ahead, not saying very much, partly because we were concentrating on the desperate struggle to avoid touching one another. It still amazes me sometimes, that physical imperative. The way it can override everything: commonsense, propriety, necessity. I stuck my hands firmly in my pockets and I could see that he had done the same thing.

'How have you been?'

'I've been all right. Not bad. Why? Have you been worrying about me?'

'All the time,' I said, truthfully.

'Really?'

'Really. I think about you so much. Did it help? Telling me?'

'I think it did. A bit. I still get very angry. But I've been sleeping better. In fact I've been sleeping a lot. More than I've slept in years. But I miss seeing you, Helen. I miss you like hell.'

'You do see me.'

'I see you like a neighbour. It isn't enough. Not for me anyway. If I didn't have my hockey I don't know what I'd do.'

'If I didn't have the farm I don't know what I'd do. Mind you, Christmas kept me busy.'

'It was good of your husband to invite me.'

'It was good of you to accept.'

We turned round and looked back. Sandy and Mary had fallen far behind and were standing looking over a fence. Sandy was waving his arms about, obviously giving her a lecture on some aspect of husbandry. Jess was panicking about the separation between us, running in long loops to encompass both couples. She preferred people to stick together, but at last she gave up and sat down beside Sandy, panting.

'Has Lee said anything to you?' I asked Joe. 'About that night with Fiona.'

'No, but I had quite a lot to say to Lee. Most of it unrepeatable. Jeez, he should have known better. She's just a kid. What's worse, she's *your* kid. Mind you, who the hell am I to talk?'

'I think she's lost interest anyway.'

'Just as well. We're not much of a catch, when all's said and done.'

'Who aren't much of a catch?'

'Male athletes, Helen. You know what? We spend too much time in locker rooms. Too much time in an atmosphere of undiluted testosterone. It gives us a skewed view of the world. Days, weeks, Christ, years of our lives are spent telling bad jokes about the size of our pricks and worse stories about women. Half of us are screwed up from the start.'

'That's a bit cynical.'

'Maybe so.'

'And not really true, is it?'

'There's some truth in it.'

He wasn't looking at me. He was looking at the wintry landscape, as bleak as his thoughts.

'We divide our lives you know. We divide ourselves in two. There's the guy you see, the public face, and there's the other, the locker room guy, but when we hit the real world we can't get the two halves together. Some of us, it's like we're fractured. The lines show as surely as these scars on my face. Do you understand what I'm saying?'

'Maybe. But you have more reason than most for behaving badly.'

'Sometimes I don't know what I'm doing to you, Helen, or whether I should hate myself for it. Am I just using you? Is that locker room guy just using you? That's what I ask myself all the time.'

'And is he? Just using me?'

'I guess not. I guess against all the odds, the real guy underneath just loves you to death.'

We drew steadily ahead until the slope of the hill hid our companions. Then Joe pulled me behind a big tree beside a field gate and kissed me greedily.

'They'll see us.'

'I don't think so. Oh Helen I need ...' he looked down at me and started to laugh. My back was against the tree and his knee was between my legs. 'You see? What kind of a friend am I to you? I need to get you into bed, Helen. I need to make love to you. For Christ's sake, Helen, if I don't fuck you soon, I'll go crazy.'

His hand slid under my skirt. I felt my body's immediate, almost painful response to him, to his words.

'Let's walk on,' I said. 'Before I lose the plot completely, Joe!'

So we walked on and before too long Jess came running up and then Sandy and Mary plodded over the brow of the hill. They were arm in arm, still talking with animation.

'Do you think we should head for home?' asked Sandy. 'The natives will be getting restless.'

'Yes. They'll be prowling about looking for tea and turkey sandwiches and mince pies.'

Much later on, just before he left to go back down to the cottage for the night, Joe handed me an envelope. 'Hockey tickets. For the New Year game. Only two of them, I'm afraid. It's going to be a sell-out and they were all I could get. But you'd better come!'

Annie and I went together. Sandy said he would rather stay at home and watch football on the telly. He wasn't mad about the game, and Fiona had lost all interest in watching Lee skate about the ice.

'I wouldn't care if I never saw another hockey game again in my life,' were her precise words.

Once again the seats were good ones. The arena was almost full, and the crowd was in New Year mood, good natured, determined to enjoy themselves whatever happened.

'Did you have a good Christmas?' Annie asked, slyly.

'Not guilty this time, Annie. It was definitely Morris and Sandy who asked him. I had nothing to do with it.'

'I know. Tim told me. Poor Helen. Can't seem to get away from him, can you? Still, it was nice of him to give you these tickets. He must have enjoyed his dinner.'

'I think he did.'

It happened in the third period and it was an accident. The Kestrels were going through an extraordinarily good patch; they had won six games on the trot and tonight it seemed as though they would win a seventh, in front of an enthusiastic home crowd. They were four up by the end of the second period, and we thought our acrobatic netminder was going to get his shutout as well, with no goals scored against him. I was just enjoying watching my gorgeous gladiator, Joe, like a bird in the air, curving and turning, skating like an angel. I was trying to pretend for Annie's benefit that I was more interested in the game, but it wasn't very easy. And I was worrying about what would happen afterwards, because Joe had said why didn't we meet him in the bar for a drink, and Annie had agreed with alacrity.

It was a deflection off a stick.

The way I think it happened, the way it was described afterwards, because at the time it was too fast to tell, was that one of the opposing team connected with the puck. From there, it flew straight into another stick, a home team stick, not a pass. It was a swift but accidental deflection. The puck rose into the air at a crazy angle. You have to understand how fast and hard these things are. The frozen vulcanised rubber disk hit Joe in the face at extreme speed. A few inches higher, a slightly different angle, and it would have come off his helmet. But it didn't. It collided with his face. You could hear the crack from where we sat. I felt a searing pain in my own head, saw blue flashes in front of my eyes. Briefly the rink swung around me. As I put my hand out to steady myself, Joe crumpled onto the ice like a downed bird.

'Oh my God,' said Annie. 'Poor Joe.'

But I don't think she realised the gravity of the accident.

'Helen? Are you all right, Helen.' Annie had her arm round me.

'Yes. Yes I'm fine.' I wasn't though. And neither was Joe. The world see-sawed and then righted itself. Afterwards I knew that I had felt it for and with him, an uncanny sensation.

There was a puddle of blood on the ice, crimson on white. Red and white roses. Blood and bandages.

They carried him off on a stretcher. It looked as though he was unconscious. I wondered fleetingly if he might be dead. I stood up and fought my way along the row with Annie behind me, remonstrating with me.'

'Helen, there's nothing you can do!' she kept saying.

Behind us, there were a few minutes left to play, but neither team had their minds or hearts on the game, although the Kestrels won, as predicted.

As we came out of the arena door, we saw an ambulance parked outside, lights flashing. I rushed over to it as they were lifting him in, and it all seemed like a scene from a movie. Annie was still running along behind me.

'For heaven's sake! They won't let you ... Helen ...'

I ignored her and instead caught at the arm of the paramedic who was just closing the ambulance doors.

'Please. I'd like to go with him.'

He turned around and looked at me suspiciously. 'And you are ...?'

'His cousin. And his next door neighbour. He hasn't got anybody else here, nobody at all. They're all in Canada. Oh God, it looked so bad! I've got a key to his house. I can fetch things for him. Please.'

'She is his cousin,' said Annie, loyally. 'She's telling the truth!'

The paramedic relented. I suppose he figured that I couldn't be some crazed puck bunny. I was too respectable-looking for that. Also, desperation lent me conviction.

'You can't ride in the ambulance, hen. They're working on him. But why don't you follow on to the hospital? They might be glad to have you there. You can give them all his details. It's pretty serious.'

I looked around at Annie.

'OK,' she said with a sigh. 'I'll give Tim a call and get him to tell Sandy. We'll go to the hospital.'

She didn't say much on the way to the hospital, except, 'His *cousin*?'

'Well. You know what they're like. What else could I say?'

'I don't know.'

By the time we had parked the car and found our way back to A & E, they had whisked Joe away somewhere. But the clerk on the desk was an old school mate of Annie's and friendly enough. She said she would find out exactly what was happening and get back to us. We sat among the Sunday night drunks and junkies and waited. I had to bite my lip to stop myself from bursting into tears.

'I've seen more of this place than I really want to in the last few weeks,' I said, shakily.

'My God, Helen!' Annie looked at me with narrowed eyes. 'You have got it bad, haven't you? Really.'

I nodded, but said nothing.

After a bit she took my hand. 'Have I got hold of the wrong end of the stick here?'

'What do you mean?'

'Well, you don't get this upset over a crush, do you?'

'He's my good friend, Annie. He could be dying. He could be dead. Isn't that reason enough?'

'It couldn't be that bad, could it? Not just from a puck!'

'It *could* be that bad. He took it full in the face. And he's already got a metal plate in there. It's like being shot, Annie. Don't you understand? A puck to the head. It's like being shot! God knows what damage it's done.'

She went over to the machine and brought us a couple of cups of sweet black coffee.

After a little while, the same casualty doctor who had attended to Fiona came through and spoke to the woman on the desk. She nodded in our direction and he walked over to us. 'Mrs Breckenridge?' He looked and sounded surprised to see me. 'How's your daughter?'

'Fine. Much better thank-you.'

'Are you a relative of Mr Napier,' he asked, puzzled.

'A cousin,' I lied, again. 'But he doesn't have any closer relatives over here. His family are all back home in Canada. We're near neighbours as well. His cottage is right next door to our farm. That's why I came. That's why we were at the game. He gave us tickets. How is he?'

'We've got a surgeon coming in to have a look at him as a matter of urgency. There's a lot of damage, just as you'd expect. We've stabilised things as best we can but he'll need surgery.'

'But he'll be all right?'

'We'll know more when the surgeon gets here.'

'Can I see him?'

'He's under sedation right now. He was in a lot of pain when he came round. Maybe tomorrow. Do you have phone numbers for his relatives in Canada?'

'Yes, I have. Or at least I can get them tomorrow.'

I was lying again, but I knew I could get them easily enough. I had the key to his house. He had given me a key, ostensibly so that I could keep an eye on things when he was away with the team.

'Then maybe you could give them a ring for us, and let them know what's happened. He's in no immediate danger, so far as we know, but it's going to be a long job. No denying that. And maybe you could come in tomorrow. He might be up to having a visitor by then.'

'Tell him I was here. Tell him Helen was here, will you?'

'I'll do that. Yes.'

Later, I rang Joe's sister, Frankie, introducing myself as Joe's neighbour. I had found the number beside the phone in the cottage. I told her what had happened.

'Oh my dear Lord,' she said. 'Not again!'

She sounded warm and friendly but panic stricken. I managed to reassure her that he wasn't at death's door, that he was being well looked after and that I would keep them informed. Should I phone Joe's ex-wife, I asked, diffidently.

'Oh no,' she said. 'I'll do that.'

'Will she want to come over and see him?'

There was a short pause. 'I doubt it,' she said, eventually. 'I doubt very much if she'll be on the first plane over there for a hockey injury. They don't have that kind of relationship. Not now.'

I gave her my phone number and told her to call at any time. Later on that day, I went in to the hospital to see Joe.

He looked as though he had gone several rounds with a heavyweight and lost. He was hooked up to a drip and a monitor of some sort, but I was relieved to see that he was propped up in bed and conscious, if a little dazed. Apparently they had to wait until the swelling subsided before they could even begin to repair any of the damage. The puck had hit him on one side of his face, the opposite side to the side with the plate in it, just below his eye, bending his nose in the process. One of his cheekbones had shattered under the blow, 'like cornflakes' the surgeon remarked with a certain grim relish, and would have to be reassembled, piece by piece, pinned and plated, teeth reimplanted.

He was in a side room all by himself. I wanted to kiss him, embrace him, make it better, but he was much too bruised, and he could hardly speak, his mouth was so swollen. I sat beside him, held his hand and told him what his mother and his sister had said. When he tried to speak, the words were so garbled, both from the concussion and the injuries, that it was very hard to understand him, but eventually I realised what he was saying.

'At least now one side of my face will match the other.'

A puck to the head, I thought. With all the accompanying pain and damage. Just like love itself.

– Chapter Twenty –

JOE WAS IN hospital for some weeks, during which he had to endure several long and tricky operations. Fortunately, plastic surgery is a Scottish speciality. Or so I'm told. By the time the surgeons had finished with him, his face was neatly rebuilt, although it was hard to see beneath the bruising and swelling, the repairs protected by a metal cage. He was fuzzy with anaesthesia, painkillers and the remains of concussion. His short-term memory was still lousy but improving. In fact he was only allowed to come back to the cottage because I volunteered to keep an eye on him, do some cooking for him and generally make sure he didn't over-exert himself. He looked like something out of a horror movie and I still fancied him.

He was so fragile that lovemaking would have exhausted him, so he had a very restrained convalescence.

'Like a monk,' he complained.

I was happy just to be looking after him, but Annie made fun of me all the time. Still, from the way she sometimes looked at me, with a half smile on her face, I thought that she had begun to question her earlier assessment of the situation. Now, she just couldn't be sure what was going on, and I certainly wasn't going to enlighten her.

Joe's sister flew over to see him in early February. She was a pretty young woman, with the same dark hair and brown eyes as her brother, and I liked her a lot. She tried to persuade him to come back home with her right away, but he said he was happy with his plastic surgeon, the team insurance was paying for it, and he would be staying in Scotland at least until spring, when he would be free to go back to Canada if his doctors gave the go-ahead. There would be no hockey for Joe until the following season at the earliest. Even then they didn't really recommend it, but everyone knew that Joe wouldn't take a blind bit of notice of them if he wanted to play. Which he did. He was already making plans to train during the summer.

One icy February afternoon when Joe was sleeping, just before she was due to fly home to Toronto, Frankie came up to the farmhouse and we drank tea together, huddled round the range in the kitchen, the warmest place in the house.

'What a wonderful place this is!' she said, gazing around. 'How old is it?'

'Very old. The house is about three hundred years old, but some of the outbuildings are probably a lot older. You can see a house up here on maps from the 1600s and it's a little drawing of a building with two chimneys. That means it must have been quite a substantial place, even then.'

'Aren't you lucky to live here! I have friends with an old house, back home, but it's only about a hundred years.'

'It's interesting, yes. But it could do with a lot of work, and we don't have enough disposable income to do it. Everything we own is tied up in the farm.'

'I suppose so.'

'With an old building like this, everything costs more. It needs re-wiring and that's a big job. Huge. You'd have to make channels through the stones and some of them are granite. We've had a bit of it done and it takes forever. We lose slates every winter. The chimneys leak. It's a constant worry. And it's cold. We can't afford to replace the windows and we can't afford to heat it properly, so it's always cold.'

'It's warm enough in here.'

'It is. But we rush from room to room in winter.'

'I never thought about it like that.'

'People never do.' I poured her some more tea, cut another slice of cake. Unlike her brother, she seemed to be very fond of what she called 'English tea.'

'Old houses don't like being disturbed you know. Whenever you try to do anything major to them, they seem to exact a terrible revenge somewhere else. Things fall down. It's a precarious business.' I had become convinced of this over the years. One job always spawned several more.

'You sound as though you wouldn't mind moving.'

'I wouldn't mind much. The garden's nice, but even in summer, the house is quite dark. The windows are so small. It was practical before double glazing. I sometimes think I'd prefer somewhere a bit smaller and more manageable.'

'Like Joe's cottage?'

'That kind of place would suit me just fine. It's a lovely wee house. But I don't think my husband would want to move. His family are built in with the stones here.'

'But isn't Joe's cottage old as well?'

'It is, but Louise had a lot of good work done over the years. Easier with a smaller place. And from what I hear, Joe isn't likely to sell it just yet, is he?'

'Probably not.'

'Well we're glad to hear it. He's a good neighbour.'

'He's had a hard time. My lovely brother.'

I nodded. He had had a harder time than she knew. Occasionally, over the past few weeks, I had tried to broach the subject with him again. 'You ought to tell your family what happened to you,' I would say. 'You ought to tell your sister at least.'

But he would only sigh. 'I don't know.'

'Why not? You've told me. You've made a start. It would explain so much for them.'

'It's not the same.'

'Why isn't it?'

'Because my mom and my sister would blame themselves, wouldn't they?'

'Oh Joe,' I had replied, thinking of the way I felt about my daughter. 'I expect they're blaming themselves already.'

'Has he told you?' Frankie asked now, staring at me with candid brown eyes, just like her brother's. 'Has he told you about his problems over the years?'

'A bit. He could hardly keep them a secret could he? There's too much online. The kids round here ferreted it out.'

'You can never live your past down now, can you? It's online forever. Poor Joey. He's been such a mess and we can never quite figure out why.

Mom reckons it's because we lost our dad so young. You can get over divorce, but you'll never forgive a parent for dying on you. But he's his own worst enemy. He started out with so much promise.'

'He still plays a great game.'

'He does, doesn't he? So why should he go off the rails with so much determination, Helen? Too much success too soon, maybe?'

'Maybe.'

I ached to tell her but there was nothing I could do. The revelation, if it came at all, had to come from Joe himself.

'I love him dearly but I could never really help him. We hated to see it. All that anger. There seemed to be so much rage in him. But, you know, it seems to suit him over here. He's calmer than I've seen him in a long time.'

'He's been severely concussed,' I said. 'His head is probably all over the place.'

'Oh I know that. But there's more to it than that.'

'Is there?'

'Oh sure. He's more in control. Happier, I suppose. I haven't seen Joey really happy like this for a long, long time. Maybe not since our dad died. Even with a face like a piece of raw meat, he's happy. Well, happier. I don't know why that should be. He says it's all down to the place and the people here. But I think he means it's all down to you, Helen.'

I didn't know how to respond. I'm sure I blushed. Hoped she wouldn't notice.

'I don't know,' I said, cautiously. 'He's been very popular in the village. He's made a place for himself here. We all hope he comes back. We hope he doesn't sell the house.'

'Oh no. I don't think he's going to do that in a hurry. He tells me he wants to hang on to his little piece of Scotland, even if he doesn't play hockey here next year.'

He planned to go home, see his family and spend as much time with Alicia as Carrie would allow. He had bought himself a laptop. Well, I'd ordered it for him online. Now, with Carrie's blessing, he spoke to his daughter every day or so. At least his accident had prompted that much of a reconciliation and I was glad of it.

Most of the time, even after Frankie went home, I tried to avoid talking about the future, his future, because it filled me with dread. 'I know you'll look after him for us, Helen,' she had said just before she left. I wanted to drag my feet to slow time down as I had that day at Poldarrach, and yet I was desperate for him to be well. He seemed equally reluctant to talk about the future, said he needed to explore a few job opportunities that had presented themselves in Canada, but he might decide to come back to the Kestrels next year. The offer was there if he was fit enough. He still couldn't make up his mind what to do for the best.

'Hell,' he told me despairingly.' If I can't have you, I don't know what I want.'

But I think we both knew that he ought to stay in Canada. It would be safer for both of us if he stayed there, even if he allowed himself the luxury of an occasional holiday in Scotland. And maybe by the time he came back, we would both have come to our senses. That was the unspoken agreement between us, or so I thought. For the time being, though, we just lived in the present. I had plenty of excuses to visit him and the cottage was our refuge, but we had the satisfaction, or frustration, of behaving impeccably most of the time too. For several weeks, Joe's health would hardly permit anything else.

Time passed inexorably and soon there were signs of spring everywhere: daffodils on the grass verges around the village and the dense white embroidery of blackthorn blossom on all the hedges. Usually, I was glad to see these things, but this year they filled me with dread. Fiona was at home on study leave, working hard. She was due to sit her sixth year exams when she went back to school. I love spring, love the steadily lengthening days. Every year I find myself full of a sort of unfocused and unspecified hope for the future. But the last week of Joe's stay was one of the worst times of my life. It was right up there with Louise's death and the heartbreak of my dad's stroke and my mother's final illness. I had this constant pain in my chest, a physical hurt.

Sometimes I felt like marching straight down to the cottage and telling him that yes, I would go back to Canada with him now, right away. Just let me get the ticket. But then the misgivings would start. He was still a young man. The years between us meant very little now, but what about when I was sixty or seventy or eighty and he was ten years younger? What if he wanted more children? It wasn't out of the question for me, but I was full of uncertainty. What if he could never really come to terms with his past? What if the drinking started again? And above all, how could I betray Sandy, when he had done nothing wrong?

Instead I bickered with Sandy and Fiona all the time. I began to understand those people who leave home to buy a loaf of bread or a packet of cigarettes and never come back again. Sometimes I would lie on the bed and literally bite the pillow. There was no sense in me at that time, only desire. And so, now that Joe was feeling fitter and stronger, I had begun to ration our encounters. I had no doubt of his love for me, or mine for him. But damaged as he was, mentally much more than physically, I thought that maybe he loved me as a patient will become fixated on their doctor or therapist. How could I risk my entire life on that possibility?

At last, towards the end of windy March, which had come in like a rampant Scottish lion, but looked set to go out in lamblike docility, he phoned me. It was a few days before he was due to travel home to Canada. I had been ticking them off in increasing despair.

'Could you do me a favour, Helen?'

'Yes of course. What's the problem?'

I wondered why he was using the mobile. The signal kept breaking up, making his voice sound strange and choppy.

There was a pause. Then he said, 'It's a real nice day here.'

'Here? What do you mean?'

'I'm at Poldarrach.'

That must have been why the signal kept breaking up, having to find its way through all the hills between us. He had gone there on purpose and found an excuse to phone me, knowing I wouldn't be able to resist him.

'You mean right now? You're there now?'

'I had to come and look at the place again. I'm alone here. Listen, listen to me, Helen. Don't hang up.'

Of course I wouldn't hang up. My fingers were clutching the phone so hard that they were tingling.

'I don't suppose ...' He stopped. The line crackled. 'I don't suppose you could ...'

'You want me to come there? Now?'

'It will have to be now. It's the last time, Helen. The last time. Please come.'

I looked at my watch. I said, 'Give me twenty minutes or so.' I slammed down the phone and ran out of the house. I didn't stop to think or to rationalise. My fingers were shaking so much that I could hardly get the key into the ignition. I had to sit there for a few moments and try to calm down. Then I couldn't get the damn pick-up into gear and bunny-hopped it all the way down the road. I could see Sandy on a tractor three fields away but I was fairly sure he hadn't seen me.

'Oh God,' I kept saying, as I drove off. 'Oh God, oh God. What am I doing?'

Poldarrach was a basket of golden afternoon light, like the first day I had taken him there. His vehicle was parked under a tree but there was no sign of anyone else in the car park. I left the pick-up beside it and ran over the bridge and up towards the old pilgrim road. I knew exactly where he would be. Sure enough, he was sitting there, looking down at the village, waiting for me. He stood up when he saw me coming and then he stepped forward and wrapped his arms around me so fiercely that he made breathing difficult. He blotted out my sun. More than that, he was the sun in my sky, my bright bird, and when he had flown away, my days would be cold and dark. I looked up at his face, running my fingers over the scars. A puck to the head. His hurt plain for all to see. The swelling had gone down, though the red lines were still there, crazy paving. Two plates now. He would probably set off all the metal detectors at the airport when he flew home.

We kissed fiercely, and one thing lead to another on the springy turf beside the ancient track. As usual, it was unseasonably warm in Poldarrach. They had known a bit about climate, those early settlers who had built the first houses here. The ancient village enfolded us in its silence and we made love for the last time, tenderly, carefully and very gently, because he was still fragile. Afterwards, I thought ruefully how it was like the last scene in ET. Come with me. Stay with me.

Now I knew what it meant to love someone to distraction.

'I love you.'

Sometimes it isn't enough to say those words. Sometimes they seem inadequate, but those simple words are all we have.

'I love you too,' he said. 'I still want you to come with me, you know.'

'I can't. It would be so complicated And it wouldn't be fair on anybody.'

'Life's not fair.'

'I know. But we don't have to make it any worse, do we? Fiona needs me this year at least.'

'But then she'll be off to university, won't she?'

'I can't leave Sandy. He's a good man. He's done nothing wrong. And besides, it wouldn't be fair to you either. You've got a whole other life to lead, haven't you Joe?'

'Oh honey!' He just shook his head. 'I don't know about that. I really don't know about that. I don't want a whole other life. I just want this one, but with you in it.'

We were lying there on the lumpy turf, our heads pillowed on his jacket. We were lying in each other's arms, as close as we could possibly be. God knows what we would have done if tourists had arrived, hillwalkers or cyclists. But nobody came. I could feel his heart beating against my own, could feel his warm breath on my cheek.

He was still beautiful in spite of his injuries, or perhaps because of them, like some precious vessel, smashed and rebuilt, beautiful and passionate, and I believed now that he wanted me for myself. I wouldn't forget any of it. Not one kiss. Not one touch. Nothing.

Before we went away, we walked around the village again on that circular path that lead back to the place where we started. We went past the inn and down the row of houses and over a threshold, among the heaped stones. I closed my eyes and held his hand.

'I wish this was our house and we could live here, just the two of us. I wish there was some magic we could do to make it all come true.'

We stood together, imagining the house as it had once been, warm and smoky instead of a sad old heap of stones.

Then we walked on. And it was all a kind of goodbye: the mill, the stream, the kilns, the shell of a village that had once been home to people who couldn't have been all that different from the folk in our village. Poldarrach would have had its Maisie Murtagh and its Charlie McGowan and its innkeeper, like Fergus with the beautiful daughters. It would have had couples like Sandy and me. There would have been lovers and thieves, heroes and villains, interlopers and damaged people as well.

We crossed the burn and kissed on the high bridge. When he finally let me go, Joe told me to drive away first so that he could watch me leave. But he couldn't let go of my hand and then he leaned into the pick-up to kiss me one last time, and I thought my heart would break. It was a good thing I knew the road so well, because my eyes were misted with tears. It was a good thing I was going back to an empty house too. Sandy was still out in the fields. Fiona was down in the village. I splashed my face with cold water, changed into clean clothes and resumed my normal life as soon as possible. When there is only one thing to do, that is what you do, no matter how much you think you won't manage it. You just get on with it.

Joe flew home to Canada a few days later. Sandy had offered to drive him to the airport, but he took a taxi to the station and got the train to Paisley instead. He had sold the four wheel drive to one of the young farmers. He left the keys of the cottage with me and that same day I went down there on my own, ostensibly to check that everything was switched off. What I actually did was sit on the bed for a long time. He hadn't changed the sheets, and I buried my face in the pillow. It smelled of his shampoo and cologne. It smelled of him. I pulled back the covers, got in and just lay there for a while until the heat of my body intensified the scent of Joe. I closed my eyes and, crazily, willed him to be there. Maybe that's why he had left the bed as it was. Or maybe I was reading too much into it. Men don't usually go for such extravagant gestures, do they?

– Chapter Twenty One –

S O THAT WAS that. I had done the right thing, and should have
been rewarded by peace of mind and a growing contentment with
my marriage. That was what was supposed to happen, wasn't it?
That was the kind of ending the stories predicted. And they lived happily
ever after. Except that all I had were regrets and an aching heart. After
a while the edge went off the misery, but it wasn't replaced by anything
approaching happiness. Instead a profound gloom descended on me. I
knew that I needed to find something to wake up my vegetating mind,
something to give me a space in the day when I wasn't thinking about
Joe. Some question to which Joe wasn't the answer. But I woke up each
morning feeling exhausted, and it was all I could do to get through the
day. Nothing helped, not the line dancing, nor the farm work, whether
it was seeing to the hens or delivering the eggs, or soldiering through a
mountain of year end paperwork. The steadily lengthening days and the
beautiful scents of the may blossom and bluebells that had replaced the
blackthorn only served to highlight my misery. I didn't know what to do
with myself. I waited for it to get better, but it only got worse.

'Why don't you see the doctor?' asked Annie. 'You seem so very
down. He might be able to give you something. There's no shame in
asking.'

But I knew pills weren't the answer. I was sad for a reason, and anything
the doctor could prescribe would be masking my symptoms, not tackling
the deep, underlying malaise. For all my high-minded decision to focus
on my marriage, it seemed to be falling apart, gradually but relentlessly,
like a house whose foundations have been undermined. Sandy and I just
stopped communicating. We had nothing to say to each other. Perhaps
unwisely, I spent a lot of time in the cottage. I bought fabric, dug out

Louise's old sewing machine and made new curtains and cushion covers, an act of faith in Joe's eventual return, although everyone else in the village seemed to think he had gone for good. It was demanding and difficult, because I was no great shakes as a seamstress, but it felt reassuring to be concentrating on something. I did a lot of reading as well. More history of all kinds, but especially Scottish history. It was nice and peaceful down there with no routine jobs demanding to be done. Well, the jobs were still there, but it was easier to ignore them. I felt faintly guilty about reading at home. Sandy wasn't a great reader and couldn't understand why anyone would want to waste too much time on books. Fiona's obsession with reading had always phased him slightly but he would say, 'I suppose she must get it from you.'

I started thinking about university courses again. Wondering what it would be like to go back as a mature student. Not to Edinburgh, but Glasgow was close enough for me to be able to commute. That was as far as I had got. Thinking about it.

'Maybe you'll be able to buy the cottage for the farm, when he sells it,' said Annie. 'You could do holiday lets. Make a bit of extra income. It would be a nice wee project for you.'

I pulled a face. A nice wee project. Dear God. Taking bookings. Changing beds. Wrestling with duvets. Cleaning loos.

'Maybe he won't sell it. Maybe he'll come back.'

'Don't kid yourself, Helen. He'll be moving on. He's that kind of guy. I know he was well paid in the past, but sooner or later, he'll need the money. Got a whole other life to lead, that one.'

Was that what I was afraid of? A whole other life, one that couldn't possibly involve me?

'I've been thinking about going back to university.'

'Have you? What would Sandy say to that?'

'I have no idea.'

I know what he said about the cottage though.

He said, 'You use that place as though you owned it.'

'Well, maybe we will some day.'

The fact was, I could phone Joe from the cottage or he could phone me. We could talk at length and nobody would know about it. And in spite of all our good resolutions, that was exactly what we began to do.

He started it a couple of weeks after he got back to Canada, emailing me first at the farm, then timing his call to an hour when he knew I would be there, in spite of the time difference. I don't think I would have been brave enough to phone him, but I remember the thrill of hearing the shrill ringing in the empty house.

'It's so good to hear your voice.'

'I needed to speak to you, Helen. I really needed to speak to you.'

'Are you well?'

'I'm fine. Getting better every day. I got headaches for a while. I still get the odd dizzy spell, but nothing major. And my face is healing nicely. Mom says she thinks I'm better looking but she's biased. Or maybe the surgeon tidied me up a bit while he was at it. And I'm back on the ice now. Slow and steady.'

'I'm so glad you're well again.'

'And what about you, Helen?'

'Me? Oh I'm fine. Same old same old. You know?'

'Yes. I do know.'

He had left some money behind for me to pay his bills for him, although he generally phoned me. We emailed too, of course. I had my own account on the farm's computer and nobody else ever looked at my emails, though we were very circumspect and reserved any words of love for our private phonecalls, just in case Fiona took it into her head to pry. We even talked about getting another laptop or tablet for the cottage. I needed to see him, but I was reluctant. It would have been too painful. I think he felt the same. As it was, the intimacy of our two voices whispering words of desire was enough. Almost. It surprised me how easily I had come to terms with deceiving Sandy. Maybe I rationalised it to myself because Joe and I were no longer together. Not physically, anyway. Illicit lovers deceive themselves almost as much as they deceive other people.

Later that summer, Joe said, 'I've been coaching a few hockey schools to pay my way. But I've started training for real now. I'm sure I'll be able to play again next season.'

'Are you sure that's what you want to do?' I couldn't help but imagine more accidents, more shattered bones.

'I think I do, Helen. There's a few years left in me yet. Trouble is, I don't know which will give out first now: the knees or the head!'

'Don't joke about it.'

'What else can I do?'

I didn't want to ask him, had refrained from asking him for weeks, but I couldn't help myself.

'Will you be coming back here?'

There was a silence. I was suddenly aware of all the miles between us. Miles, air, oceans. He sighed. 'I just don't know. I have that option for sure. They say they definitely want me back for another year. And if I come, I'll get the chance to do a bit of coaching over there. Maybe juniors as well. I'd like that. It would suit me. Help train up some Scottish kids. It would be good experience for me.'

'But?' The thought crossed my mind, as it always did, that maybe he had come to his senses in other ways. Maybe he didn't want to see me again and that was why he was hesitating.

'It isn't that I don't want to see you again, Helen.'

'But?' I repeated.

'But it's hard, you know? Seeing you, and knowing that I can't have you? So sometimes I think that maybe you're right and maybe I should stay away. For both our sakes.'

'Then maybe you should.'

There was another long pause.

'Do you really mean that?' he asked, very quietly.

'No. Sadly, I don't mean it at all.'

'Thank God for that. I was just going out to shoot myself.'

'Don't do that.'

'I don't know what to do for the best and that's the truth. I've had the offer of a position as assistant coach over here as well. That may be the way to go eventually. That's what my head tells me. But my heart says not yet. I want to carry on playing. I just wish you'd tell me what to do.'

'How on earth can I, Joe?'

'I guess what I mean is, I wish you'd tell me to come back.'

'Let me know as soon as you decide.'

'You'll be the first person I call. Honest.'

So we left it and time passed, and we made no decisions. It was as though we were waiting for someone else to decide things for us.

The summer wore on. Fiona got a job in the kitchen at the pub, which was alarming, but she seemed to have learned her lesson at last, or maybe she was just growing up, and she had no more problems with alcohol, or none that we ever saw, none so acute. We never got round to taking the family holiday we had planned. Sandy kept saying he couldn't leave the farm, and inertia gripped me. To our relief, Fiona passed all her exams. She had got a place at Edinburgh University to read English and History, which gave me a pang of remembered grief, as well as joy for my daughter. We were both very proud of her. I think Fiona herself was too full of the adventure of leaving to notice any of the strain in her parents' relationship. She would be gone with the swallows in September.

That would leave just the two of us rattling about the draughty old farmhouse on our own. Would Sandy and I 'find each other again', as women's magazines and romantic fiction said we should? I couldn't see it. There seemed nothing left to find. We had lost something and it wasn't just that first all-consuming passion that I was feeling for Joe and realised would be transitory. No. We had even lost the contentment in each other's company, the companionship that should have been our reward for all our years together. I saw it all the time and envied it in Tim and Annie. They still liked each other a lot. Laughed together. I think I had stopped enjoying Sandy's company so long ago, that I had forgotten what it felt like. Working at a relationship was one thing, but this was more like hard labour. We never laughed together. Affection had been replaced by a mild but persistent irritation. Or maybe I never had loved him enough. In which case it was all my fault for being so feeble as to marry him in the first place. That was the uncomfortable truth I clung to. None of this was Sandy's fault. He was blameless and that made it much worse. Our marriage was like a shell after the egg has hatched. It was already in pieces. All the king's horses and all the king's men wouldn't be able to put this one together again.

Late in the summer, Fiona, who had been working in the mini market to earn a bit of pre-university cash, was invited to spend a couple of weeks in Ireland with Lizzie's family, in a holiday cottage in Donegal.

'Would you mind?' she asked.

'No. I think you should go. You could do with a break before term starts. Away you go and enjoy yourself.'

The house was empty without her, like a rehearsal for her absence. When I thought of the future all I could see was a miserable descent into middle age, cooking conventional meals for Sandy and Bruce, feeding chickens, wading through mud, wrestling with the accounts and line dancing with Annie, or whatever stunt we happened upon for next year and the year after and the year after that. Time would pass quickly. Another twenty years and retirement would loom. The thought of it didn't fill me with excitement or hope. Only fear and revulsion. You don't need anybody for line dancing. You don't need a partner. You can do it and keep your mind and body occupied and you don't need anybody else at all.

Bruce was very disappointed at not getting the cottage to live in and so was Charlie McGowan.

'A perfectly good house, lying empty there,' he said to Sandy and Sandy agreed with him.

'Why don't you write to Joe?' said Sandy. 'Ask him if he wants to sell?'

'Why should I do that? He told us he's not ready to sell yet. He doesn't need the money. He may even come back to the Kestrels. Besides, it's my bolt hole. I'm quite happy about it being empty. I get to use it without paying for it. It's great.'

Actually, it was a blessing for Charlie, because he finally moved to town and found himself a new job and that summer he found a new wife too, what Annie called a Wedding Cake: a glossy young woman with big blonde hair and blue varnished fingernails. Then Betty, who had had a slight stroke and got rather frail all of a sudden, moved in with them, but I wondered how she would get on with the Wedding Cake and whether they would live happily together and who would win out in the end: Betty or the Wedding Cake? My money was on Betty. Maisie Murtagh missed Betty terribly, but eventually she took up with one of the elderly men who was a leading light in the bowling club and has a stall at the monthly antique market in the town. She baked cakes and shortbread biscuits for him, and he gave her a new hat – well, not exactly new, because it came from his stall – a toque in green felt with a diamante brooch on the side. She started helping him with his stall and they seemed very happy together.

Annie and I didn't exactly fall out over Joe, although for a while the irritation remained, like a sore place in our friendship that never quite healed over. But I was still reluctant to confide in her, reluctant to tell her what had really happened. The bombshell, when it came, was from a wholly unexpected quarter.

In early August, much to everyone's astonishment, Mary and Morris split up. There was a tremendous quarrel and Morris, quiet, kindly Morris, smashed a whole twenty four piece dinner service on the kitchen floor. Soon afterwards, Mary went off to live in a rented flat in town, leaving the two little girls behind her, with Morris struggling to cope on his own. The village was loud in its disapproval of Mary's behaviour but Sandy, much to my surprise, refused to do anything about it. He even seemed reluctant to talk about it.

'Leave well alone,' he said. 'It's none of our business.'

'How can we leave well alone? We have to do something about the kids, at least, Sandy.'

I couldn't believe that Mary wouldn't have confided in Sandy. Had Morris been having an affair? What on earth could have caused such an earthquake in their lives? But Sandy didn't seem any wiser than I was.

'You never know what goes on in a marriage. Morris says he doesn't want any help. He says he'll manage. And anyway, Aunty Isa is going to lend a hand.'

Soon after that, Isa moved into the farmhouse, and Morris began to look a little less harassed.

'How could Mary do it?' I asked Sandy. 'What on earth possessed her to go off and leave her girls like that? I can hardly believe it.'

That part amazed me. How could she leave her kids? I could imagine myself leaving Sandy, but I don't think I could have left Fiona behind, not when she was so young. Mary's daughters were only eight and eleven years old. But it seemed she could, and after all, men do that kind of thing all the time. It was what Joe had done, when I thought about it. Albeit reluctantly.

Sandy shrugged. 'You never know what goes on behind closed doors, do you?' he said. 'Maybe she thinks they'll be better off with Morris and their granny.'

'But she was always so maternal. So settled. She seemed so settled and contented.'

As I never had been, I thought, guiltily.

'Was she really?' asked Sandy.

'Well it seemed that way to me.'

Nobody knows anything, I thought. Nobody knows what another person may be feeling. Nothing is ever as simple as it seems on the surface.

'The girls seem to be coping well enough anyway,' observed Sandy.

This was true. I had been up to the farm and had to admit that the atmosphere there was calm and cheerful, better than it had ever been when Mary was in residence.

'But I'll go and speak to her if you like,' said Sandy. 'See if she needs any help.'

That night, as he had promised, he drove into town to see Mary, and I took advantage of his absence by going down to the village to visit Annie.

Right from the start, I sensed that she was feeling uncomfortable with me. There were long gaps in our conversation. It had almost never happened to us before and it puzzled me. I thought we had put our differences, such as they were, behind us.

'Where did you say Sandy was?'

'He's gone into town to see Mary.'

'Has he?'

'We thought he should try to sort something out with her. Get them at least to talk about the kids and make some kind of arrangement for her to see them or for them to visit her. Morris doesn't want Sandy to interfere. But she does want to see them, seemingly.'

'So they're managing all right up at the farm?'

'Yes. In fact Morris looks ten years younger.'

'That figures.' Annie pulled a face. 'Mary can't be the easiest of people to live with.'

'But isn't it incredible how quickly everything can just crumble like that?'

'It's alarming, isn't it?'

'Sandy's right, you never know what's going on behind closed doors, do you?'

'No. You never do.'

She was looking at me strangely again, frowning, holding her wine glass in both hands. We were sitting beside an open window. You could hear the roars and yells from the kids playing football in the park. Somewhere in the garden, a thrush sang a long and complicated theme with variations. The heron cruised over, long pterodactyl legs trailing as he eyed up the garden ponds for fish and frogs. I found myself thinking bizarrely that the heron wouldn't eat the whole frog. Just the head. You would find revoltingly headless froggy corpses in your garden from time to time.

Annie fell silent again.

I had phoned Joe that afternoon. He had still not made up his mind whether he was coming back to Scotland, but he couldn't leave it much longer. Crunch time was coming. It had been good of the Kestrels' coach to keep the option open for him as long as this. Joe was using the accident as an excuse, but I think he was fit enough now.

'I'll do whatever you want,' he said. 'If you don't want me to come, just say the word. I'll sell you and Sandy the cottage and you can do what you like with it.'

But I couldn't say it. I couldn't say come and I couldn't tell him to stay away either. I was caught in the net of my own principles. There was no solution.

'For God's sake, Joe, just decide, one way or another. Just decide and let me know!'

I had slammed the phone down on our last conversation and now I felt forlorn. With Annie sitting opposite and staring at me in that peculiar, quizzical way, I found the tears running down my cheeks. There was nothing at all I could do about them. They just poured quietly out of my eyes. I wasn't sobbing or anything like that. I was just shedding tears, copious quantities of tears. I felt as though they had been building up for months and now the dam had burst. Much like Joe, earlier in the year.

She was beside me instantly, her arms around me. 'Oh God, Helen, you know, don't you? I thought you must!'

'Know what?' I asked, but she ignored the question.

'Don't cry You'll set me off. It's not as bad as all that. It'll get better. Honestly. It will get better. You just have to decide what you're going to do.'

'But that's the problem. I don't know what to do, Annie!' Had she guessed then? Had she finally realised exactly what had been going on?

'How can I upset everyone? How can I turn everything upside down and ruin things for everyone? When it might not work out after all.'

She sat back and looked at me. 'No. There's that of course. It might not work out. And that's very tolerant of you. But surely, that's not your problem.'

'Of course it's my problem. If I ask him to come back and it doesn't work out ...'

'Come back?' She stared at me in open amazement. 'Has he gone already then? When did this happen? My God, I didn't know he'd actually gone. Did he go today? Did he tell you?'

There was a long pause while we looked at each other, realising that neither of us knew what on earth the other was talking about.

'Wait a minute,' said Annie, who was marginally less confused than I was. 'Who exactly are we talking about here, Helen?'

'Joe. I'm talking about Joe. I thought you'd guessed.'

'Guessed what, for heaven's sake?'

'In the hospital that night. I thought you must have guessed.'

'Guessed what?' she repeated.

'That we've been having an affair.' The relief of saying it aloud. The blessed relief of confession. But I saw the shock on her face.

'Jesus. Are you sure?' Annie said.

I started to laugh in the middle of my tears.'

'It's not something you can be mistaken about, is it? I may be a bit daft, but I'm not deluded. I know it seems unlikely but we did have an affair. I'm telling you the God's honest truth. I know there's almost ten years between us and you don't know what he sees in me, but he must have seen something because we've been ...'

'You are, aren't you? Well fuck me.' She stopped, her hand over her mouth. 'Oh no,' she said, outrageously. 'I suppose he was fucking you.'

We began to laugh. We laughed until we cried. She poured out more wine.

'Tell me about it,' she said. 'Christ, I must have been blind. Either that, or you're a bloody good liar!'

'It's a long story but we just ...' I was going to say, 'we just get on' but I changed my mind. 'We love each other, Annie. We still speak all the time. I phone him. He phones me. He's even asked me to go to Canada with him.'

'Has he really?'

'I know it seems incredible and I know I'm years older than he is, but he has.'

'I wish you'd stop saying that. You're not exactly old. If it was the other way round, nobody would even comment.'

I knew it was true. And I knew Annie had changed her tune. But it made me feel a bit better to hear somebody else finally saying it, somebody other than Joe, who said it all the time.

'He's got the chance to come back here for a year. Maybe more than a year. He doesn't know what to do. I thought we were being very sensible. I thought I could give him up for Sandy's sake and for his own sake too. I told him that if he went home he could get some perspective on things.'

'And?'

'It doesn't seem to have worked.'

'Then tell him to come back.'

'How can I? Besides, there are other things too, Annie. Oh there's more to it than you know. He's had his problems.'

'So it seems.'

'And I can't tell you all of it. He had some bad experiences when he was younger. It explains a lot. But it made me wonder if he wasn't just fixated on me in some way. I wondered if he might come to his senses if he wasn't seeing so much of me.'

'Which might take a little time after that puck to the head.'

'I feel so guilty about it all.'

'Do you?' She looked at me shrewdly. 'Why do you feel guilty, Helen?'

'Well, about Sandy of course. He hasn't done anything to deserve this. And I've betrayed him. I've betrayed him in every possible way. It's unforgivable.'

There was a long pause. And then she said, 'So he's done nothing to deserve it?'

'We've had a good marriage. He's been a good husband and a good provider. Just what my mother wanted for me. I don't know what to do.'

She stared out of the window. The days were beginning to draw in a little, though the kids – back at school after the summer holidays – would play evening football until darkness fell. I suddenly remembered what she had said a few minutes ago.

'Annie?'

'What?'

'If you didn't know about me and Joe ... what did you mean when you said things would get better? That was what you said, wasn't it?'

She looked into her wine glass, her face scarlet.

'So what were you talking about? What did you think was going on that would get better?'

'Oh for fuck's sake,' she said, vehemently. 'What am I supposed to say? It's Sandy, you silly cow. I'm talking about your husband.'

'What about Sandy?'

And then she really took the wind out of my sails.

'I mean Sandy and this thing he's been having with Mary.'

I stared at her. I think my mouth actually fell open.

'With *Mary*?'

'Yes, Helen. With Mary. He finally admitted it to Tim last week. And Tim told me. I've been wondering what to do about it ever since. You're my best friend and I felt as though I was betraying you by not telling you. How could I not tell you? But how could I tell you either?'

'Sandy and Mary?' I echoed foolishly.

'Sandy and Mary. Oh, Helen, open your eyes! Are you telling me you never saw it?'

'I can't believe it.'

'If you ask me, I think it's been going on for years. I remember, ages ago, when we first moved here, somebody said to me that Sandy and Mary had once been an item. When they were both very young. I can't remember who it was, one of the oldies obviously. Then you came along and he fell for you, hook, line and sinker. But maybe he always carried a wee torch for her.'

'No. He wouldn't. They wouldn't ...'

'Helen, it's the truth. I wouldn't lie about a thing like this, would I?'

It was a bit like Joe's puck to the head. The room swayed and righted itself. All sorts of emotions collided in my head: anger, incredulity, guilt, irritation at my own gullibility, above all a large measure of relief.

'Have another drink,' said Annie, anxiously.

My teeth were chattering with the shock.

'Listen to me,' said Annie. 'Listen.'

'What?'

'Do you care? Do you really care about Sandy and Mary?'

'I don't know. I don't know what to think any more.'

'Do you know what I'd do if I were in your shoes?'

'What?'

'If I were you, I'd go for it, girl. You asked me what I thought, and now I'm telling you. Think about yourself for once. Do what you want. Move away. Stay here. Study. Get a job. Whatever. That's up to you. But do what you want for once in your life. If you want your Joe to be part of all that, go for it. You phone him and tell him to get back over here as soon as he can. You have the whole other half of your life to live. Everyone else will cope.

– Chapter Twenty Two –

I DIDN'T GO HOME that night but I didn't phone Joe immediately either. I think I had too much residual guilt to do it. You could say that I had got into the habit of it. I stayed with Annie and Tim, and Annie spoke to Sandy on the phone. The following morning we met at the farmhouse. Annie wanted to come with me, but I wouldn't let her. Thank God Fiona was away. In retrospect it was quite funny as well as sad. There were a number of 'pot and kettle' conversations of the 'you did this' and 'you said that' variety, but the truth was, we were both absolutely and completely in the wrong, which turned out to be something of a relief.

Eventually, we calmed down and stopped hurling gratuitous insults at each other and began the long and messy process of dismantling our marriage. We were a nine days' wonder in the village and some people blamed me and Joe, making various wild assumptions, even before the truth came out, and some blamed Sandy and Mary. Maisie still finds it hard to speak to me when I meet her down in the shop. I can see her choking on the words. All kinds of things happen in the village but she hasn't quite come to terms with this one yet, perhaps because it was so totally unexpected. Maisie, the fount of all village knowledge, never saw it coming. I think she's furious with herself as much as with me, mostly because she didn't get the whole picture before everyone else.

Poor Morris was the only one who escaped censure. Actually, he's not poor at all. He's still living and working on his farm with his girls and Isa, and he manages very well, so far as I can see. I visit them often and do what I can to help. Morris always makes me welcome. The girls see Mary on alternate weekends, although Morris speaks to her as little as possible. I think that he would like to confide in me, would like to talk to me about his wife and my husband and their treachery, but I steer clear of such conversations. After all, I'm not exactly innocent, am I? Who am I to discuss adultery with anyone?

As for Sandy and myself, after the arguments abated he moved into Mary's rented flat in town and I went back up to the farm. For a week or two, Sandy would come in to work and Bruce would keep things going while he wasn't there, but it was plain that nothing could ever be the same again and drastic measures would have to be taken. Fiona came back from Ireland and, when I told her as gently as I could what had happened, she blamed me. But once she had spoken to her father, she blamed both of us.

We had a blazing row.

'You're both as bad as each other!' she said. She was furiously angry and who could blame her? 'You should be ashamed of yourselves. It's disgusting. That's what it is. Disgusting!'

In retrospect, I think she found it especially disgusting that her parents might be involved in physical relationships with other people. After all, we were much too old for that kind of thing. She didn't say it out loud, but she was thinking it.

She left me her dirty washing, packed up some clean clothes and went back to stay with Lizzie's family again.

The following day, however, she phoned me from Lizzie's house and we talked for a while in a careful, civilised fashion.

I said, 'We still love you. We both still love you.'

She burst into tears at that. 'What will I do? It's all so scary! You've turned my whole world upside down.'

'I know. And I'm sorry. I'm so sorry. But you're on the verge of leaving anyway, Fiona.'

'I still need a home to come back to.'

'Of course you do. Why wouldn't you? And you'll always have that. Always. In fact you'll probably have two of them.'

'But are you and Joe really going to get together? Like my dad and Mary?' The thought of it clearly revolted her.

'I don't know. Nothing's decided yet. He's still in Canada. He may not come back at all. And I'm not at all sure that I'd be able to go over there to be with him, even if he wanted me to.'

I would be able to go over on holiday, but it would be very difficult for me to live and work there. I had checked. Unless we married, eventually, and he forked out a very large sum of money, and even then it might not happen.

It struck me that Fiona and Lizzie must have been discussing it. I know that Annie had spoken to her, trying to sort fact from rumour for her.

The following day, we met in a cafe in town and drank lattes and pussyfooted around each other. But at least she didn't shout at me, and she hugged me before she left. The day after that, she came home to the farm, although I don't think she has forgiven me or her father yet. She was planning to move into university accommodation as soon as term began, but she said we could take her and her stuff through to Edinburgh, so long as Sandy and I did it together, and I thought we might be able to manage that without killing each other on the way. We would just have to try, for Fiona's sake.

Maybe after a while, she won't feel quite so betrayed and perhaps, as she gets older, she'll begin to understand. Not yet, but in due course. Who knows? I'm not even sure that I understand it properly myself yet. But the channels are open and it helps that she has friends with divorced parents. God alone knows what we'll do at Christmas. I can't think that far ahead.

With the help of a couple of solicitors, we began divorce proceedings. Morris told Mary he would burn the farm down rather than sell it, and I think she believed him. Or perhaps, like the rest of us, she had finally found her conscience. At any rate, she sent for her clothes, her sewing machine and her Lladro ornaments, but told him he was welcome to keep the rest. Including her daughters. That's what they said down in the village, although it wasn't quite like that. It never is black and white like that, is it? And if Morris had been the one to leave, there would have been disapproving comments, but nobody would have censured him in quite the same way as they censured Mary for running off and leaving her kids in a comfortable home with a loving father. Maybe Mary had felt trapped too, had just gone along with other people's expectations of her. Which was an uncomfortable thought.

I'm still not sure exactly how Sandy felt about her unexpected altruism but the solution soon became obvious. It was the only solution really. Our farm would have to be sold instead. Sandy's poor dad would have been birling in his grave. They said that down in the village as well. There had been Breckenridges at Drumbrethan for a hundred years and more. A bit like Cold Comfort Farm and the Starkadders, I thought, but there was nobody to say it to, except Annie, and even she didn't understand the reference.

'What?' she said. 'Cold what?'

In a way, I think Sandy might have been relieved. It had all become a burden to him and he was sick of trying to make ends meet. So perhaps, like me, he was ready for a change and maybe he had even had the same thought as me: 'I hate my life.' That idea disturbed me for a while. I was allowed to be discontented, but the thought of Sandy searching for a way out upset me. It hurt my vanity, I suppose. Our whole relationship had become habitual. We had lived uncomfortably in our marriage as we had lived in that cold old farmhouse, because it was what we had done for so many years that change seemed impossible. We were part of the landscape. And when we upset our personal applecarts so comprehensively, the whole community seemed to be disturbed. Our upheaval sent shock waves through the village. People are made profoundly uncomfortable by change, even when it involves mere acquaintances. Resentful even. This isn't a stable community by any means. No community ever is. It's full of changes, people moving in and out, and it's full of small factions too. But it's held steady by all kinds of unseen checks and balances, and even a small upheaval in one part can cause chaos elsewhere.

Most of the land was to be sold off to a big neighbouring farm owned by Jim and Margaret Elliot. Just as Sandy had been waiting hopefully for Joe's cottage, the Elliots had been waiting hopefully for Drumbrethan to come on the market. They had kids who were interested in farming, so Drumbrethan would solve the problem of who would inherit their farmhouse. It was the way of the future, even here in this traditional corner of the West of Scotland: bigger farms with economies of scale. In the meantime, though, they planned to rent it out. The thought of dismantling and dividing up the contents of the house appalled us both. It wasn't just our own things, but the heavy furniture, the ornaments and pictures that had belonged to Sandy's family for generations, as well as the possessions I had brought from my parents' house. It seemed like a sacrilege to destroy the entity that the house had become. In fact there was a sense in which we felt worse about breaking up the house than we did about breaking up the marriage.

We've come to an agreement with the Elliots that quite a lot of the furniture can be left for the new tenants. Fortunately, Fiona left for Edinburgh and Freshers' Week before anything too drastic got under way. I helped her to pack up her own possessions, and we drove her through to her hall of residence, promising that the rest of her things would be safe. I don't know about Sandy, but I still felt horribly guilty. How would she cope with being away for the first time from a home that she knew was being dismantled in her absence? I vowed that whatever happened, there would be somewhere comfortable and homely for her to return to at Christmas.

'You can come and stay with us for a while,' said Annie, while all this was going on. 'Just till you get yourself sorted out.'

But I didn't go to Annie's house. Instead, I went to Joe's cottage, not just because it reminded me of Joe all the time, but because of the memories it held of my dear, lovely Louise.

Sandy and I are treating the clearing of the farmhouse like a laborious project, an unpleasant task that has to be got through, somehow or other. It's a little like the aftermath of a bereavement. We've arranged to sell what we can't leave or accommodate between us. We'll send the beasts to market and have a farm sale to dispose of any machinery the Elliots don't want or need. Then we'll split the proceeds. Sandy will be able to buy somewhere small for himself and Mary, there will be money for Fiona to finish her education debt free, and I'll have just about enough to get myself started on ... what? What will I do with the second half of my life? And where will I go to live it?

'You have to phone Joe,' said Annie, a little while ago. 'Phone him or email him. He needs to know what's been happening. You need to talk to him about all this, at least.'

But I think I just had so much to cope with that I didn't want to add one more complication: that of learning how he would react to the news. So I kept putting it off.

For a week or so I found myself going online without opening his emails. I would reach for the telephone twenty times a day, but it seemed too easy. Like Joe himself, I didn't think I deserved a happy ending.

I put the cottage telephone on call monitoring and for a while I didn't even answer Canadian calls, although Joe phoned me several times. The only person I would speak to was Fiona, in Edinburgh, who seemed relieved to be away from it all. It was Annie who kept me from sliding towards depression. She walked up the hill and fed me cups of tea and toast in the morning, soup and glasses of wine in the evening. She took me out shopping. She practically forced me to go for walks. She even managed to coax me into the pub with Verena and Mandy. The autumn line dancing would be starting soon but I told them I didn't want to go.

Predictably, it was an exasperated Annie who dialled the number at last, said, 'Joe, Helen has something important to tell you,' and put the phone into my reluctant hand.

I had no idea how he was going to take the news. What would he do, now that my situation had changed, now that I was essentially a free woman or would be when the divorce came through? Would he be relieved or alarmed? I could feel my heart pounding as I told him about Sandy and Mary. The silence at the other end only compounded my anxiety.

'I don't believe it,' he said at last.

'It's true though. All this time, while we've been worrying about the two of us, Sandy and Mary ...'

'Honey, I don't care about them. But I thought ...'

'What?'

His voice shook a little. 'Ah God, Helen, I thought you didn't want me any more. You didn't answer my calls or my emails. I thought you didn't love me any more. I thought you'd stopped even going to the cottage.'

Why was he saying this? Had he decided to sell up as well? Would I be completely homeless? My first thought was for Fiona. She needed somewhere to come during vacations and would for a few years yet. She still wasn't very comfortable with her father and Mary. Maybe I could get a job, rent somewhere and then buy a flat as soon as the money was sorted out. My mind galloped on in this way, so that I hardly heard what he was saying.

I said, 'But I do love you. I love you very much. And actually, Joe, I hope you don't mind, but I've been living here in the cottage. Just while I get myself sorted out. Just while I make some plans. But I can leave. I'll understand. I can leave if you need to sell the place.'

'What plans? What will you do now?' he asked.

'I don't know. My mind keeps going round and round in circles, but I don't know. I realise just how feeble I've been all my life. I haven't the faintest idea what to do next. Or what I really want to do.'

Annie was right, even though she was prone to exaggeration and fiercely loyal to me. For my whole life so far, I had accommodated myself to everyone else, and now I had lost all sense of ambition or even hope. It was years since I had done anything just for me. Even the line dancing had been Annie's idea, not mine. Maybe that was why I had been so reluctant to phone Joe. Maybe I had been thinking about frying pans and fires.

'You just need a little time, honey,' said Joe, thoughtfully. 'Time to recover your nerve. It's like getting back on the ice again after an injury. You haven't lost the knack, you're just kind of rusty. And afraid of falling.'

'I suppose so.'

'Did you mind leaving the farm?'

'No. No, I don't think so. That hurt Sandy more than me. Clearing it all out is terrible. It's still going on. You can't do it overnight. There are things I miss. Christ, I actually miss the hens a bit. But no. Not much else.'

'You could do anything you want, you know. You could go back to college. You could make a whole new start.'

'I know. But I'm so scared.'

'Yeah. Well it is frightening. Starting over. But if I can do it, you can.'

I felt myself spiralling downwards into misery. It wasn't enough any more just to hear Joe's voice. It wasn't that I wanted or expected him to solve all my problems at a stroke. I knew that I had to stand on my own two feet for once. If I had learned anything from the years of my marriage, it was that one person can't ever provide you with the ultimate happy ending. But for all these months, Joe had been relying on me. Now, I needed his support, his sympathy, his love. How would he respond? I was aware of the miles between us. Of the years between us. Of all the differences of background and culture between us.

We had so little in common. I saw him in my mind's eye, fire dancing on ice, skating like an angel, using the edges of the blades, moving swiftly over the alien medium like a big bright warrior. I saw him weeping in an Edinburgh hotel room. I saw this warm, clever, talented man buried beneath the damage of years. I saw the desire for trust beneath the betrayal, the hope beneath his despair. I saw him lying on the white ice, with the red blood crystallising beneath him. Red roses and white. Blood and bandages. Love came like a puck to the head and there wasn't a thing we could do to stop it or shield ourselves in time. It was part of the mysterious dance, part of the game. Neither of us was indispensable to the other, and I think we both knew that we could survive alone, if need be, but our mutual affection, our friendship, linked us as surely as the telephone lines carrying all the words between us.

'Listen,' he said. 'Why don't you just stay put for the moment. Where you are. In the cottage.'

'Would you mind?'

'Would I mind? Helen, just do whatever you like with the place. You love it as much as I do.'

'That's true.'

'Fiona too. She's welcome any time. You know that. There's the spare room. Fix that up for her.'

'I suppose I could do that. Yes.'

'But you know what? You wait there.' He said it as though he were just down the road, as though he could jump in a car and be at the cottage in a few minutes.

'Wait for what?'

'For me, you *doofus.*'

'Are you coming back then?'

'Sure I'm coming back. Wild horses wouldn't stop me now. What did you think?'

'You don't have to do this, you know. You don't have to come back for me. Not if you don't want to.'

'I'm coming back for all kinds of reasons, Helen, and not only for you. I wouldn't want to lay that on you. But I decided for myself.'

'What about your daughter?'

'I've seen quite a lot of her. We've been building bridges. I think Carrie will let her come over with Frankie. You know. For a visit. Maybe a couple of times. It's more than I hoped for.'

'When are you coming?'

'I've got a flight booked for later this month. I spoke to the coach yesterday. It's a bit late, but I'm coming back to the Kestrels for another season at least. You're just part of the plan. A very big part of the plan now. But I want you to make some plans as well. For yourself. Maybe we can fix something between us. Make things right for both of us.'

I had to sit down. The legs just went from under me.

'Are you all right, Helen?' he asked, across the miles. He sounded so close and warm.

'I think so.'

There was a pause.

'I told my mom,' he said, into the silence. 'I told my mom about the coach. I told Frankie first and then mom.'

'What happened?'

'She cried. They both cried. '

'But they believed you.'

'Oh sure. They believed me. I don't know why I thought they wouldn't. Mom blames herself. But you were right. She was blaming herself anyway. And this way it's different. Worse in some ways. But better in others.'

'They love you very much.'

'Honey, you lose all perspective.'

'I know.'

Frankie said it was a good job he'd killed himself, because she'd have done it for him. Slowly and painfully.'

'Are you glad you told them?'

'I think so. I still feel like somebody flattened me. But ... I don't know. I got some counselling. Finally. I probably need some more. I *do* need some more. But maybe I'm ready to move on. The bastard ruined half my life so far. Why should I let him ruin the other half? Why should I give him that power? After all, he's dead. I'm still here.'

'You're right.'

'You did it you know. You broke the ice for me.'

'I just listened to you, that's all. You were ready.'

'And what about you?'

'You've made more decisions than I have, Joe. You're doing better than me.'

'Listen. Fiona's going to need you to be around at least for the next few years. Even if she doesn't know it now. But you have to think about yourself. About what you want to do, once she's really flown the nest.'

'I do. I know.'

'No you don't. It's something you've never really thought about properly. I don't mean I won't be there for you. I will. But I've got hockey for now. Doesn't matter where I play. Hockey's hockey. And afterwards I might have coaching. If I behave myself. If I can be a good boy. And I think I can maybe behave myself, with a little help from you.'

'What are you saying, Joe?'

'I'm saying that you need something for you as well. Something for you and nobody else. As well as me. How does that sound? It might be college again. It might be something different. Only you know that. Only you can decide. But you have to give yourself some options. Then we can work it out together. Decide what's best for both of us. Decide how we can fit in with each other. How we can manage. How we can live in two countries at once, and make the best of things. Jeez, Helen, you might even have to marry me!'

As proposals go, it wasn't the most romantic in the world, and I wasn't even divorced yet. I didn't know whether to laugh or cry, but it felt good.

'What will the village make of it all?'

'The village will cope. They may not like it. But it seems to me they always cope. Even Maisie. But you? Will you cope? With me? With one big bad hockey player. With yourself?'

'I think so.'

'I have a long way to go as well. You see, when push comes to shove, we're all pretty selfish. But I don't think I can do it without you, Helen. I don't think I can do it on my own.'

Which is why I'm sitting here, in Louise's cottage, which is our cottage now, thinking about the future. It seems to me to be full of possibilities and not all of them involve Joe. But I can't foresee that I'll ever stop loving him, even though there are so many aspects of his life that are foreign to me. Even though we both have daughters, and they certainly have first claim on our affections. Fiona and I will be all right. She'll be here for Christmas. It will be tricky, but we'll cope. Three of us. And then she'll spend some time with her father and Mary. Joe has been seeing Alicia. He tells me that Carrie sometimes brings her to his mother's house and there's a kind of peace between them, although no reconciliation. There's a new man in Carrie's life. Alicia loves him too, and that hurts Joe, but he's making the best of it. Love isn't finite. The more you give the more you get. One and one makes ... oh an infinity of problems and possibilities for both of us. For all of us. Balancing on ice, using all the edges. Dancing the dance.

It's late autumn, almost winter. They say it will be a cold winter. They are predicting snow and ice. The house martins and swallows are long gone, flying south in search of the sun. The rows of nests are empty and forlorn. The hockey season is here. I've lit the fire because it gets very cold now at nights, even though the days are quite fine. It has been a sunny autumn, for once. Siggy is sitting on my knee. There will be plenty of smelly kitbags for him to monopolise. I tell him so, burying my face in his fur that is both musky and sweet. He purrs his agreement. Jess, who has, it seems, come to terms with him, is asleep on the hearthrug. Sometimes they even curl up comfortably together. She twitches and yelps, chasing rats in her dreams. Sandy wanted to take her with him but she wouldn't have been happy in town and Mary never liked muddy footprints, even when she was a farmer's wife.

Sandy has got a job selling agricultural machinery and Mary is cooking in a small restaurant in town. She's a very good cook and seems to be making quite a name for herself. I wonder whether Sandy has any chance of being happy away from the farm. Or with Mary for that matter. But perhaps they have as much chance of happiness as me and Joe. As any of us, really. It's all a bit of a gamble, isn't it? I'm sitting here, with Siggy on my knee, and I'm looking at Louise's old photograph album. There's the picture of handsome Freddy. And there's poor Mario with his beautiful face, his wide set brown eyes, his high cheekbones. Like Joe. If I turn around suddenly, I think I might see Louise standing behind me.

'Never settle for second best, Helen,' she says, with a little sigh.

I'm waiting for Joe. Whenever I think about him my heart gives a lurch of ... desire ... anticipation ... anxiety? I don't know. The Gallopers are in the shed. Maybe this winter he'll finish them. I should have known when he left them behind, carefully covered by tarpaulins to protect them from the damp, that he always intended to come back for them and for me.

I offered to pick him up from the airport but he said no.

'I want you to be in the cottage when I get there. I want to come through the door and see you there.'

He said he would hire a car instead. This is a quiet lane. For the moment, the farmhouse stands empty, waiting for its new tenants, and I sit down here in Louise's cottage, balanced, dancing on ice, for which a partner is not essential but certainly helpful, dancing on the fine line between one life and the next. For these moments, I am completely happy. Few people travel this road except on foot. When I hear the car turn up from the village, I will finally be sure that he is coming.

– THE END –

Author's Note

THIS IS A love story, a book about village life, but also a book about the sheer joy of ice hockey. A few years ago, the UK saw a big renaissance of interest in professional ice hockey with the setting up of the so called Superleague, involving several high calibre teams. This was somewhat controversial in that these teams mostly employed 'imported', particularly Canadian, players, but it undeniably raised the standards of play for the spectators who had the privilege of watching some world class hockey on home ice. The standard of coaching for young, aspiring British players, my own son included, was excellent and inspirational.

Although there are still teams throughout the UK playing good, enthusiastic and entertaining hockey, the Superleague lasted only from 1995 to 2003, after which it was disbanded and replaced with the Elite Hockey League. It is remembered by many spectators as a mini Golden Age of British ice hockey. Now there seems to be a similar renaissance under way. My own seasons spent as a 'UK hockey mom' inspired at least some of the background to this novel, a time I remember with a great deal of affection, not least because of the off-ice chat and laughter. Hockey was and remains a very inclusive sport.

Although Ice Dancing is entirely fictional, there have been real life problems of abuse in this as perhaps in every sport and in many other areas of life besides, and it is hardly possible to exaggerate the dreadful consequences. The challenge must surely be for all of us to exercise vigilance, while maintaining a sense of proportion that allows our children to participate in various desirable activities in safety. There are no easy solutions. On another topic, the wartime internment and deportation of

Italians who had made their homes in Scotland for many years, and the subsequent loss of the Arandora Star, are matters of shameful fact and, given the more recent experiences of the Windrush generation, have by no means been consigned to history.

Catherine Czerkawska

Printed in Great Britain
by Amazon

60483999R00152